LIPS HIPS TITS POWER
THE FILMS OF RUSS MEYER

CREDITS

LIPS HIPS TITS POWER
The Films Of Russ Meyer
Doyle Greene
PERSISTENCE OF VISION VOLUME 4
ISBN 1 84068 095 4
Copyright © Creation Books 2004
All world rights reserved
Published 2004 by Creation Books
www.creationbooks.com
Design: The Tears Corporation
Front cover image: *Beyond The Valley Of The Dolls*
Inside cover image: *Supervixens*
Illustrations by courtesy of The BFI; The Graveyard Tramp; and the Jack Hunter Collection

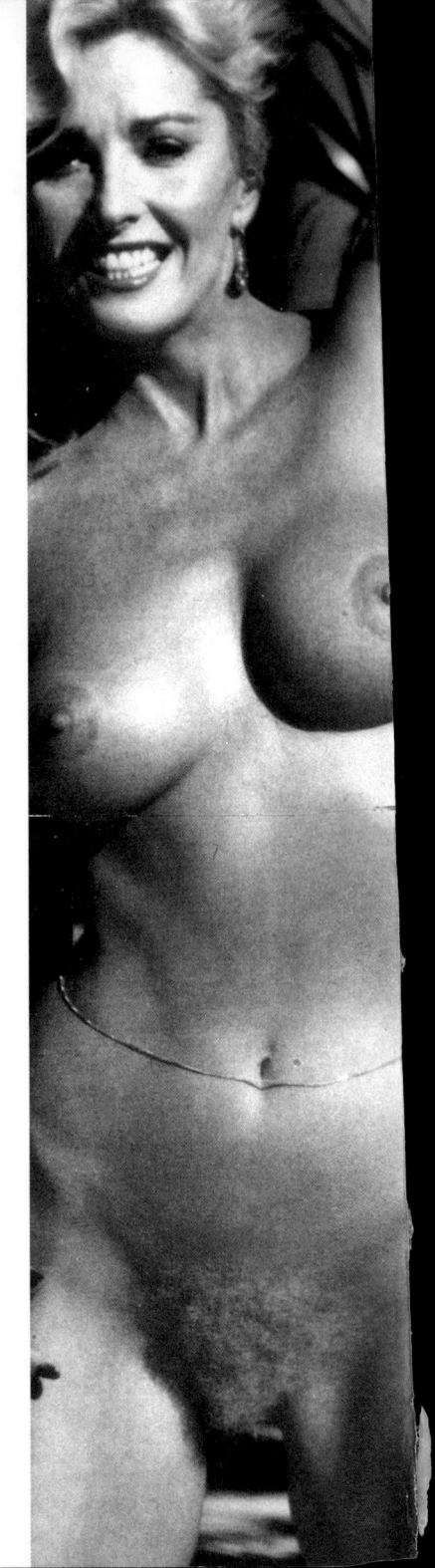

CONTENTS

005	Introduction: **Why Russ Meyer?**
007	Chapter One: **Reading Russ Meyer**
019	Chapter Two: **Nudie-Cuties**
039	Chapter Three: **"Welcome To Violence"**
107	Chapter Four: **Swinging Sixties**
157	Chapter Five: **"Beyond The Valley Of The Dolls"**
189	Chapter Six: **"The Death Of Sexploitation"**
195	Chapter Seven: **Surreal Seventies**
229	Filmography
231	Index of Films

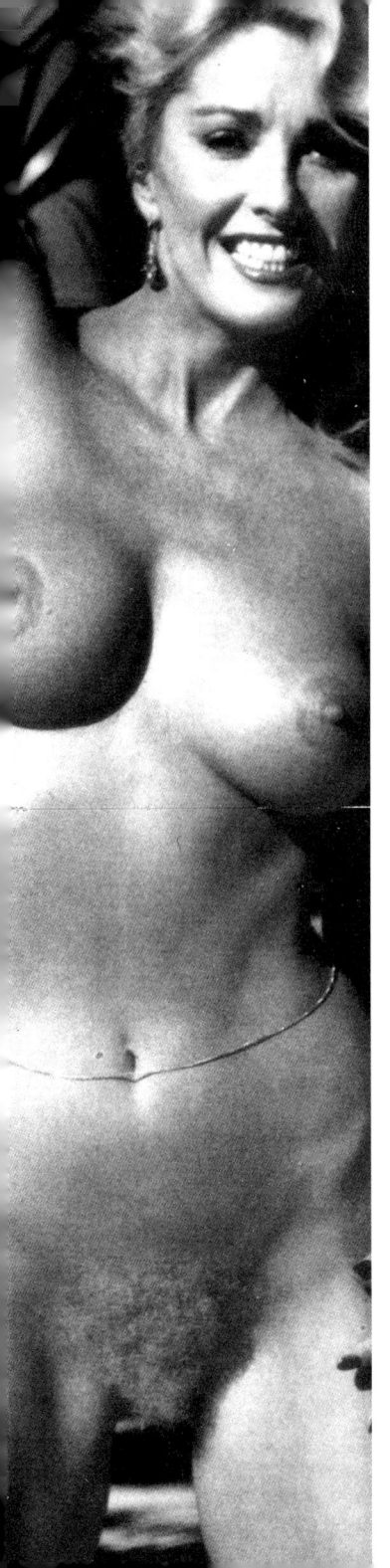

> "Sexuality must not be described as a stubborn drive.. it appears rather as an especially dense transfer point for relations of power."
> –Michel Foucault, *The History of Sexuality, Volume 1*

> "My point is of no return – and you just reached it!"
> –Varla, *Faster, Pussycat! Kill! Kill!*

Russ Meyer, publicity shot

INTRODUCTION
WHY RUSS MEYER?

*The more pretensions a film has to art
the more bogus it becomes.*[1]
— Theodor W. Adorno

[1. *Minima Moralia: Reflections of Damaged Life*, trans. E.F.N. Jeffcott (New York: Verso, 1997), 203.]

The Russ Meyer Debate

Perhaps no film director has bridged, if not altogether eliminated, the distinctions between "art film" and "B-Movie" more so than sexploitation-film legend Russ Meyer. His films, originally seen in grindhouse theaters and drive-ins, are now more likely to be seen in museum and film society retrospectives. Whether Meyer's films constitute "art" or "trash" has made him one of contemporary cinema's most controversial figures. Some have hailed Meyer as an innovative, satirical, surrealist, avant-garde sexploitation *auteur*. Long-time supporter and occasional screenplay collaborator Roger Ebert suggested "serious film historians ... will discuss him with such other radical structuralists as Mark Rappaport, Chantel Ackerman, Sergei Eisenstein, and Jean-Luc Godard... if they can get past the heaving bosoms."[2] John Waters proclaimed Meyer, not entirely facetiously, "the Eisenstein of sex movies."[3] David Frasier, among others, argued Meyer is as deserving of *auteur* status as Alfred Hitchcock or John Ford in that "his style is his signature, as recognizable and as outrageous as his themes, techniques, [and] his humor."[4]

Others, to put it mildly, have been far less enthusiastic about his work: it has been suggested on more than one occasion that his unorthodox shot composition and jarring, rapid-fire editing reflects artistic desperation and

[2. As quoted in David Frasier, *Russ Meyer – The Life and Films* (Jefferson, NC: McFarland Classics, 1990), 25.]

[3. *Shock Value* (New York: Thunder's Mouth Press, 1995), 192.]

[4. *Russ Meyer – The Life and Films*, 25.]

incompetence rather than any creative vision, and that his films reflect not only the vulgarity of burlesque humor but kitsch aesthetics.[5] Moreover, any arguments made in favor of Meyer's artistic legitimacy will not be aided by Meyer's own assessment of his work, since he has proudly proclaimed his experiences as a World War II combat photographer and industrial filmmaker, as well as Al Capp's *Li'l Abner*, to be his primary influences. Often referring to his own work as "cartoons," Meyer has often dismissed any serious analysis or interpretation of his work, claiming the only measure of a film's success is by "the number of butts in the theater."[6]

Nonetheless, there is a far more important issue at stake rather than whether or not Russ Meyer is a filmmaker with any artistic validity or technical ability. The most frequently enduring and serious criticisms of Meyer's work revolves around the almost cavalier, misogynistic violence and overt breast fetishism in his work. At worst, his films can be read as textbook examples of what film theorist Laura Mulvey argued is the dual-nature of (male) cinematic spectatorship: seeing the woman both "de-valued" through the narrative punishment of the female characters (the sexual assaults and domestic violence that routinely appear in Meyer's films) and "over-valued" by the camera's fetishistic depiction of the female body (Meyer's well-known obsession with large breasts).[7]

However, for a director considered to be highly sexist in a film genre notorious for its misogyny, Russ Meyer's films reflect a profound tension and ambivalence regarding issues of sexuality, gender, and power. Indeed, Russ Meyer's work can be read as far more than mere sadistic and fetishistic exercises of male cinematic spectatorship and affirmations of phallocentric, patriarchal order. His films provide a formidable, satirical, brutal and inherently problematic discourse of sexuality and gender in their most intimately political sense.

5. See, for instance, Gordon Burn, "Rising Below Vulgarity," *Sight and Sound* (December 1996): 14-16.

6. As quoted in Frasier, 156; see also 180.

7. See "Visual Pleasure and Narrative Cinema," reprinted in *Film Theory and Criticism: Introductory Readings*, 4th ed., ed. Gerald Mast, Marshall Cohen, and Leo Braudy (New York: Oxford University Press, 1992), 753.

CHAPTER ONE
READING RUSS MEYER; OR, THE 120 DAYS OF DOGPATCH

The unconscious is not a theater, but a factory.[8]
— Gilles Deleuze

[8. *Negotiations*, trans. Martin Joughlin (New York: Columbia University Press, 1995), 114.]

Sex and Violence

In an interview with Russ Meyer, Jim Goad suggested to Meyer that "plenty of sexploitation films have sex and violence... your movies are the only ones to feature *simultaneous* sex and violence." Meyer responded, "both of 'em, the sex and violence are jokey. And they're outrageous and overdone."[9] This brief exchange succinctly epitomizes two major tendencies and tensions that occur throughout Russ Meyer's films: one, the interaction of both sex and violence; second, the interaction of comedy and horror, or what Meyer called "*the thin edge of humor and evil.*"[10] It is this unsettling assemblage of sexuality, cruelty, and comedy that makes Meyer's work so problematic: he infuses the depiction of sex and violence with farce and slapstick comedy, with scenes of sexual intercourse, rape and murder infused with the same kinetic, comic brutality as the Three Stooges or the ribald energy of cartoon animators such as Tex Avery and Chuck Jones.

Meyer depicts "sex and violence" as pure, immanent *libidinal flows* which are not binary oppositions but interchangeable variants, one capable of operating independently from the other and frequently *at the same time*. Sex is often violent and confrontational, such as in the controversial shower scene in *Vixen*, where the predatory title character violates the most essential of sexual taboos, incest, by having sex with her brother. Regarding the shower scene,

[9. *Answer Me!: The First Three* (San Francisco: AK Publications, 1994), 6.]

[10. As quoted in *Re/Search #10: Incredibly Strange Films*, ed. V. Vale and Andrea Juno (San Francisco: Re/Search Publications, 1986), 79. Emphasis mine.]

Meyer noted, "strangely enough, what I achieved on film with her and her brother really represents the way I like to screw – I mean like a football scrimmage."[11] Conversely, violence is charged with sexual excitement, exemplified by Varla and Tommy's erotic, *mano a mano* duel to the death in *Faster, Pussycat! Kill! Kill!*. Such a primal depiction and intersection of "sex and violence" in Russ Meyer's work echoes the work of French philosopher Georges Bataille, who wrote, "Violence, *the core of eroticism*, leaves the weightiest problems unanswered."[12] Furthermore, "eroticism" in Russ Meyer's films is markedly similar to Bataille's definition of "eroticism":

"Eroticism only includes a domain marked of by *the violation of rules*. It is a matter of going beyond the limits allowed: there is nothing erotic in a sexual game like that of animals... *eroticism... only consists in the fact that accepted forms of sexual agitation occur in such a way that they are no longer allowable*. So it is a matter of passing from the licit to the forbidden. Man's sexual life developed out of the accursed, *prohibited* domain, not the licit domain."[13]

In Russ Meyer's work, the "erotic" has nothing to do with the romantic or the sensual; "eroticism" is rooted in *transgression*: a moving beyond the civil and the civilized in an attempt to return to animal libidinal drives and behaviors (a theme I will return to in regard to Russ Meyer's "naturalism"). Sex itself is not an invariable, stubborn drive which is monolithically repressed or even repressible, but a variable, immanent, undefined and indefinable *libidinal potentiality* that springs forth with the same suddenness and ferocity as Meyer's rapid-fire editing. It is manifest in and through the complex relationships between the fighting and fornicating caricatures that make up Meyer's film universe: the crude, cruel, and comic depictions of rape, sadism, and sexual intercourse itself; the role of homoeroticism and homeosocial order; the satire of social constraints that regulate sexual behavior such as marriage and prostitution; even the politics inherent in voyeurism and burlesque humor. These are all various zones where "power" and "sex" collide. Unlike some who argue that Meyer presents a strong code of sexual morality in his films, I would suggest there is no pre-defined "transcendental ethic" of sexuality in Meyer's films. Rather, the sexual ethic is generated out of the primal conditions it exists under: an ethic of pure immanence. It is the work of the Marquis de Sade that prefigures the analysis of sex consequently found in Russ Meyer's work. Giorgio Agamben noted, "Sade's modernity does not consist in having foreseen the unpolitical primacy of sexuality in our age. On the contrary, Sade is as contemporary as he is because of his incomparable presentation of the absolutely political (that is 'biopolitical') meaning of sexuality."[14] Indeed, in page after page of Sade's work from *Justine, Philosophy in the Bedroom,* and *The 120 Days of*

11. As quoted in Vale and Juno, eds., 85.

12. *Erotism: Death and Sensuality,* trans. Mary Dalwood (San Francisco: City Lights, 1986), 192. Emphasis mine.

13. *The Accursed Share, Vol. II: The History of Eroticism,* trans. Robert Hurley (New York: Zone Books, 1991), 124. First emphasis mine.

14. *Homo Sacer: Sovereign Power and Bare Life,* trans. Daniel Heller-Roazen (Stanford: Stanford University Press, 1998), 135.

Sodom, verbose discussions alternate with repetitive, graphic sexual acts and arraignments, rendering the sex act itself as a point of pure political immanence. While Russ Meyer's film world is slapstick and kinetic as opposed to Sade's relentless demonstrations, I would contend both Sade and Meyer essay the relationship and even elimination of any difference between sex and violence in the utterly political realm of sexuality.

"The Thin Edge of Humor and Evil"

In her book *Irony's Edge*, Linda Hutcheon noted that "satire" and "irony" have lost a certain sense of power in the wake of deconstruction, poststructuralism, and especially postmodernism which emphasize the "slipperiness" of meaning and entail that every text can be treated "ironically." Hutcheon's work suggests a return to a more traditional analysis of irony and satire and the dialectical function that entails. Irony's *advantages* include its ambiguity and textual complexity, its humor and irreverence, and its controversial, subversive qualities. In contrast, irony's respective *disadvantages* include having an ambiguity that misinforms the reader rather than complicating the text, being irresponsible rather than being irreverent, and being insulting and offensive rather than provocative and subversive.[15] I believe the binary relationship that Hutcheon expresses, the "dual-nature" of satire (the *apparent* verses *actual* meaning), as well as satire's "double-audience" (those who read the text *literally* versus those who read it *ironically*) is essential in understanding Russ Meyer.

Much of Russ Meyer's satire is not only a satire of American social, sexual, political, and cultural institutions (especially marriage and sexual "Puritanism"), but a vicious parody of narrative genre forms and stereotypes: the handsome, leading man; the damsel in distress; the romantic triangle; the happy ending. All these generic devices are treated with not only irony, but a certain amount of contempt. His films are full of implausibilities; melodramatics; laughable film clichés; kitsch vulgarity and obviousness; histrionic and, at times, laughable acting. But rather than being kitsch or simply inept movie making, Meyer freely incorporates bad taste in all its cinematic, theatrical, and literary forms; they are depicted, presented, and satirized in all their turgid glory. As Roger Ebert noted about *Beyond the Valley of the Dolls*, "One of the New York critics... found it full of stereotypes and clichés. The critic apparently was unwilling to believe that each stereotype and cliché had been put into the film lovingly, by hand."[16]

Furthermore, what separates Meyer from kitsch is his absolute rejection of any *sentimentality*. His characters absurdly plow through one episodic event after another. Rape and murder are played for laughs as much as for their tragic outcomes, while tragedy is as likely to tickle the funny bone as touch the heart. Like any good comedy or farce, a Meyer film contains a fair

---

15. See *Irony's Edge: The Theory and Politics of Irony* (New York: Routledge, 1996), 48-56.

16. "Russ Meyer: King of the Nudies," originally published in *Film Comment* Jan/Feb 1973. Copy courtesy of www.fmcinema.com/russmeyer/ebert.html, page 9 of 14.

number of pratfalls and (unintentionally?) hilarious one-liners; like any good tragedy, many of his films conclude with some sort of cathartic battle, more often than not killing off several cast members. Fred Chappell compared *Faster, Pussycat! Kill! Kill!* to Kyd's *The Spanish Tragedy* and described Meyer's work as "very odd, serious attempts, full of big, gloomy archetypes and Gothic puzzlements."[17] Conversely, John Waters pointed out that Meyer's films are impossible to take seriously, with "plotlines... so hilarious all [the viewer] can do is laugh right along with the director."[18] In this context, cult-film historian Danny Peary has acerbically criticized Meyer for his unwillingness (or inability) to do any film that is *not* farce.[19]

At this nexus of satire, comedy, and tragedy I would like the situate Al Capp's *Li'l Abner*, a pivotal influence in Meyer's work, on two levels: one, the depiction of husky morons and buxom women living in a bizarre cartoon vision of America as a rural, backwater hell; second, as a satirical, sinister critique of American culture, and even the modern condition. Marshall McLuhan wrote:

"The sophisticated formula used with [Capp's] characters was the reverse of that used by the French novelist Stendahl, who said, 'I simply involve my people in the consequences of their stupidity and then give them brains so they can suffer.' Al Capp, in effect, said, 'I simply involve my characters in the consequences of their stupidity and then *take away* their brains so they can do nothing about it.' Their inability to help themselves created a sort of parody of all the suspense comics. Al Capp pushed suspense into absurdity. But readers have long enjoyed the fact that the Dogpatch predicament was a paradigm for the human situation in general."[20]

The vision of America as "Dogpatch U.S.A." is central to Meyer's films. His characters and not only recall and resemble the comics and various characters of *Li'l Abner*, but his films depict the almost Beckettesque predicaments of stupid, inept caricatures who can do nothing except suffer their own stupidity, absurd situations, and doomed existence. Adorno wrote, "Kafka and Beckett arouse the fear which existentialism merely talks about."[21] Meyer, like Kafka and Beckett, also depicts a universe both utterly absurd and yet infinitely horrific.

The question of satire also invokes what might be considered an affinity between Russ Meyer and Bertolt Brecht. As Brecht argued about his "epic theater," there is a fundamental shift *from representation to commentary*... The epic theater's choruses and documentary projections, the direct addressing of the audience by the actors, are at the bottom of all this."[22] In Meyer's films, the viewer is placed in a situation where the on-screen world is indeed *both* a representation and a commentary on that representation. Rather than "characters," Meyer's films are populated by "caricatures," exaggerated

17. As quoted in Kenneth Turan and Stephen F. Zito, *Sinema: American Pornographic Films and the People Who Make Them* (New York: Praeger, 1974), 23.

18. *Shock Value*, 192.

19. See Frasier, 89-90.

20. *Understanding Media* (Cambridge: The MIT Press, 1994), 165-6. In counterpoint, McLuhan positioned Chick Young's *Blondie*, which proposed "a pastoral world of primal innocence from which America had clearly graduated." (167).

21. "Commitment," in *The Essential Frankfurt School Reader*, ed. Andrew Arato and Elke Gebhardt (New York: Continuum, 1994), 314.

22. *Brecht on Theater: The Development of an Aesthetic*, ed. and trans. John Willet (New York: Hill and Wang, 1992), 126. Emphasis mine.

CHAPTER ONE ◊ READING RUSS MEYER

archetypal and comical figures, and perhaps the most important figure in a Russ Meyer film is the *narrator*, who functions as an outside, "authoritative" voice in the film, an *intermediary* between the film and the viewer. Often times the narrator is an off-screen voice providing prologues that introduce the film in a documentary-style setting while also providing convoluted commentary on the characters and what will happen in the film. Similarly, the narrator provides epilogues which summarize the film, describing the successes and failures of the characters, their character flaws, and the "moral" message of the film. In some films, the narrator actually becomes an on-screen presence who speaks directly to the viewer rather than interacting with the characters (*The Wild Gals of the Naked West, Lorna, Up!, Beneath the Valley of the Ultravixens*). What is especially important about these narrations, be they on or off-screen, is that they are both verbose and absurd, and often satirize what has occurred or what will occur in the course of the film. Ebert recounted:

"One of the chief delights... were the spoken narration he used for prologues, epilogues, and the underlying of morals of stories... they are designed to sound portentous and universally significant while, in fact, having little meaning at all ... I was awaked at six one morning by a telephone call. Meyer wanted to read the epilogue he has just written [for *Cherry, Harry, and Raquel*], and found it so amusing that he could hardly get it out between gasps of laughter... Audiences reacted in the same way, and yet (of course)... it is part of the film's socially redeeming content."[23]

23. "Russ Meyer: King of the Nudies," page 1-2 of 14.

These "messages" often satirize the "socially-redeeming" content that was necessary to include in sexploitation fare. While nudity and simulated sex could be shown, the films also had to provide a "moral" message or ending which denounced the "vice" that had been shown on-screen in order to avoid legal and censorship problems. With Russ Meyer, the moral is itself satirized, along with the generic strategy needed to make the film "socially-redeeming." Another aspect of satire and parody is the use of modernist and "high-culture" influences in the context of sexploitation cinema. Many of Russ Meyer's films incorporate a compendium of film and cultural sources, ranging from the "canonical" to the "disreputable" in an altogether surreal assemblage. Kenneth Turan and Stephen F. Zito suggested the most interesting sexploitation films of the era, especially those by Russ Meyer and producer David Friedman, shared a "parodistic use of high and popular culture."[24] *The Defilers* (1964), a "roughie" written and produced by Friedman and directed by cult-film legend R. L. Frost, was based on John Fowles' novel *The Collector*. The H. G. Lewis-Friedman production of the "ghoulie" *2000 Maniacs* (1964) borrows from an unlikely source in *Brigadoon* by depicting a town of ghosts that reappears after 100 years, in this case to violently

24. *Sinema*, 21.

11

avenge the deaths of their forefathers in the American Civil War. Perhaps the most bizarre example is the Michael and Roberta Findlay's "roughie-kinkie" *Take Me Naked* (1966), which dispensed with the standard, lurid "roughie" narration in favor of the poetry of French eroticist Pierre Louys. In fact, it was not uncommon for serious art-house European films and American sexploitation films to be seen at the same theaters. Friedman said, "nobody was buying Ingmar Bergman because he was a great director. They were buying him because he was showing some tits and ass."[25] Similarly, one can see Russ Meyer as a juncture between high and low cinema, a sexploitation filmmaker who bears uncanny similarities to Eisenstein and Brecht (although it is safe to say Meyer certainly does not share their Marxist politics). *The Immoral Mr. Teas* (1959) was "inspired" by Jacques Tati's 1953 Chaplinesque comedy *Les Vacences de M. Hulot (M. Hulot's Holiday),* and light touches of comic surrealism can be seen in all of Meyer's "nudie-cuties." Neo-Realism was a key influence on Meyer's roughies: if Tati's film "inspired" *Mr. Teas*, then *Bitter Rice*, a 1948 Neo-Realist film, similarly "inspired" *Lorna* (1964); both films are stark, gritty tales of young, voluptuous women and their struggles in rural isolation and poverty.[26] Meyer himself sites Erskine Caldwell's Depression-era novels such as *God's Little Acre* (1933) for influencing *Lorna* and *Mudhoney*. In turn, the black and white style, sexually-charged violence, and tough-talk dialogue of the roughies recalls *film noir* and the "hard-boiled" fiction of writers such as James M. Cain, Jim Thompson, or even Mickey Spillane. *Faster, Pussycat!* could be described as a drive-in movie done by Luis Buñuel. The late 1960s films, especially *Cherry, Harry, and Raquel*, recall Godard and Pier Paolo Pasolini in their fragmentary editing and disjointed narrative as much as their sex and violence recalls the Hollywood action cinema of Don Siegel or Sam Peckinpah. Finally, Meyer's mid-1970s surrealist sex films appear as equal parts Warner Brothers cartoons and the art-films of Federico Fellini.

However, to consider Russ Meyer's film career as simply based on satire does not fully address the intense problematics with his work. One basic issue is Russ Meyer's very status as a "satirist." As a satirist, Russ Meyer has been compared to Voltaire, and such films as *Vixen, Supervixens,* and *Ultravixens* chronicle and satirize the main character's encounters with various bourgeois hypocrites in the vein of Voltaire's *Candide*.[27] However, it might be said that the burden of proof is to prove Voltaire is *not* a satirist, whereas with Russ Meyer the burden of proof is to prove he *is* a satirist, rather than a no-talent, breast-obsessed misogynist. It is my contention that a close textual analysis of Meyer's work consistently indeed reveals a satirical and parodic tendency of not only other films and a vast array of other cultural products (literature, theater), but also contemporary political relationships, especially issues of American sexual politics in the 1960s.

---

25. As quoted in Vale and Juno, eds, 102.

26. See Riccardo Morrocchi, Stefano Piselli, and James Elliot Singer, eds., *Bizarre Sinema! Wildest Sexiest Weirdest Sleaziest Film; Sexploitation Filmmakers. Masters of the Nudie-Cutie, Ghoulie, Roughie, and Kinkie* (Florence: Glittering Images, edizioni d'essai, 1995), 26.

27. See Frasier, 19.

CHAPTER ONE ◊ READING RUSS MEYER

Nevertheless, some very real concerns do appear in Russ Meyer's work. If one can consider irony as the act of saying one thing and meaning another, on ehas to consider the fundamental problem of satire is "getting the joke." One has to ask if it is even possible that a rape can be presented in a "jokey" manner, and if some images have in intrinsic power that makes any irony impossible. To argue from an "intentional" aspect, one could (wrongly) suggest that since he meant his sexual assaults as "comic," they *have* to be read that fashion. One has to consider if certain images can be seen ironically, if a rape scene can say one thing and mean another, if images and representations of rape and sexual assault are permeated with a "potency" that cannot be ironic, yet alone "joked about." The very use of irony maintains "a thin edge" (to paraphrase both Hutcheon and Meyer) between an act of subversion and an act of complicity due to the ambiguity of how, or even *if*, the image and the message can be separated. Given Russ Meyer's work, one needs to consider the degree that irony is used to create and reinforce the textual problematics: on one hand, offering a transgressive commentary on sexuality and morality, yet also questioning the degree that the very impact of his images, despite the joke, subverts the film's satirical, and even political, effectiveness. In this way, rather than Voltaire, I would again evoke a far more insidious figure in French literature in comparison to Meyer: Sade. It is the pervasive Sadean depiction of the inherent politics of human sexuality, the "making visible" of the relationship between sexuality and power, which makes Meyer's work so controversial, and, at times, quite difficult.

Russ Meyer and "Naturalism"

In the previous discussion of the interplay between sex and violence, it was suggested that the "erotic" in Russ Meyer's films is rooted in the collision between animal drives and civilized conduct. In his book *Cinema 1: The Movement Image*, Gilles Deleuze discusses a cinema of "naturalism" based on "the impulse-image." "Naturalism is not opposed to realism, but on the contrary, accentuates its features by extending them in an idiosyncratic surrealism."[28] Naturalism, as Deleuze defines it, posits the clash of "originary worlds" (the world of animal instinct) and "derived milieus" (the world of civilization) and the clashes of "impulses"(animal drives) and "modes of behavior" (civilized conduct).[29] Tom Conley describes this interaction as the nexus between a world of "instinct" (the originary world) and a world of "language and history" (the derived milieu) where humans are "beasts," devoid of ethical or moral constraint.[30] In many of his films, Meyer presents unreal, isolated worlds where human instincts of lust and violence are uncontainable: "the town so bad we wuz ashamed to name it" (*The Wild Gals of the Naked West*); the backwater hell of *Lorna*; Spooner, Missouri, a poverty-stricken rural town headed towards mass psychosis (*Mudhoney*); forbidding *chiaroscuro* deserts (*Motorspsycho!, Pussycat!*); the

28. *Cinema 1: The Movement Image*, trans. Hugh Tomlinson and Barbera Habberjam (Minneapolis: University of Minnesota Press, 1986), 124.

29. See *Cinema 1*, 123-30.

30. See "From Image to Event: Reading Deleuze through Genet," *Yale French Studies* 91 (1997): 49-63. I am highly indebted to Conley's work on "the originary world."

LIPS HIPS TITS POWER ◊ THE FILMS OF RUSS MEYER

banks of the Colorado River (*Common-Law Cabin*); the Canadian forests (*Vixen*); barren deserts with phallic rock formations (*Cherry, Harry, and Raquel*; *Supervixens*); a garish, kitsch version of Hollywood (*Beyond the Valley of the Dolls*); the sex-mad cartoon come to life of Small Town, USA (*Ultravixens*). At the same time, there exists an often isolated point in the "originary world" where "civilization" or a "derived milieu" exists, a place in which the characters's actions revolve: Lorna and Jim's home (*Lorna*), The Wade farm (*Mudhoney*), the Old Man's dilapidated farm *(Pussycat!)*, Hoople's Haven (*Common-Law Cabin*), the Boland mansion (*Good Morning... and Goodbye!*), the fishing lodge (*Vixen*). These are the sites and spaces where civilization and civilized conduct attempt to reign in the originary world, a battlefield between instinctual impulse and modes of behavior, and the derived milieu is continually besieged by the instinctual forces of the originary world. Thus, the bedroom becomes a primary battleground for sexual and political domination; social prohibitions of sexuality such as marriage and the incest taboo are washed away in the tide of libidinal impulses. Thus, in this Deleuzian sense of the term, Meyer can indeed be considered "naturalist." In Meyer's film world, realism is distilled into primitive drives (lust, violence) and fetishistic obsessions (breasts, phallic symbols), which emerge as an "idiosyncratic surrealism," equal parts cartoonish sex-romp and existential, violent horror.

These primal "originary worlds" serve as an important part of Meyer's symbolism as well. In all of Russ Meyer's films, there is an emphasis on *nature*; most of the films are set in isolated desert, forest, or backwoods rural areas. Yet there is little hippie idealism or small-town nostalgia in Meyer's work. Rather, "nature" is used in the sense that it appears in Bataille's work: the attempt to return to *animal* nature, the transgression which constitutes eroticism. It is in Meyer's vast landscapes where sexual energy can unfold; however, these backgrounds also serve a very specific symbolic function. Within these untamed regions where libidinal flows are expressed, certain landscapes are specifically coded as "masculine" and "feminine." It is *not* the characters who determine gender, but the *landscapes* around them which distinguish "male" and "female."

The desert is the site of *male* libido. Deserts, badlands, and mountains are connected with male libidinal flows. This appears in the apocalyptic man-to-man struggles in the deserts in films such as *Motorpsycho!*, *Supervixens*, *CHR*, and *Pussycat!* (given that Varla is not only the most beautiful woman but the toughest guy in the film). One (sadly!) unfilmed scene Meyer described to John Waters was of "Two, big nude guys with big dicks wrestling out in the desert. Then a woman runs in and tries to give them head, but they just ignore her."[31] Conversely, forests, meadows, and water (rivers, streams, etc.) are connected to *female* libidinal drives. Water is a consistent symbol of female sexual libido: the outdoor, nude swimming scenes in *Lorna* and *Good Morning... and Goodbye!*; the

31. *Shock Value*, 200. The scene was meant as a parody of a scene from D.H. Lawrence's *Woman in Love*.

shower scene in *Vixen*; or the inserts of two naked women underwater intercut into a montage with a lesbian encounter in *Cherry, Harry, and Raquel*. The outdoors of the forests are also designated areas of female sexuality, especially in *Vixen* and *Good Morning... and Goodbye!*, which features Haji as a mystical character "the Catalyst," equal parts female libido and living flora.

The Battle of the Sexes

Needless to say, Russ Meyer is often criticized for the sexism in his work. However, the relationship of nature to gender rather than characters to gender allows "gender" itself to be treated as a perverse construct that is often problematized and satirized. Meyer's women are both well-endowed exaggerations of the female ideal, and also Amazonian superwomen who are frequently more "masculine" than their male counterparts, many of whom are physically, mentally, or above all, sexually inferior to the women in his films. Ebert noted:

"If there are sex objects in a [Russ Meyer] film, they are probably the male leads, who are tantalized, tempted, dominated, thrown around, tortured, abused, cast aside or simply dominated by powerful women... Meyer is almost unique in the world of popular eroticism in seeing women not as passive victims but as aggressive sexual beings who demand that their needs be met."[32]

Similarly, Eddie Muller and Daniel Faris, observed, "Critics who lambast Meyer as a sexist missed a vital aspect in all of his films: he esteemed women who had, as he simply put it, 'guts.' In the sexual battlefield he depicted, women didn't lie back and take it; they dished it out – but good."[33] Even feminist critic B. Ruby Rich pointed out in her positive reevaluation of *Faster, Pussycat!* that while the film undeniably objectified women, it also presented a refreshing and radical deconstruction of feminine stereotypes: not only traditional stereotypes of females embodied by the screaming, fainting hysterical Linda, but feminist film stereotypes which insist on "positive role models," satirized by the man-bashing, go-go dancing, hot-rodding lesbian Varla.[34] My own view is neither to champion Russ Meyer as a unlikely feminist director nor dismiss him has a male-chauvinist pig. One has to keep in mind that Meyer's work is not a criticism of masculinity or in any way "anti-phallocentric": he is an admirer of both tough, powerful males and (especially) females. His work is infused with a strong masculine ethos, and he is not at all a critic of masculinity *per se*. The men who are objects of scorn are his tough-guy, "he-man woman haters" (many of whom are latent homosexuals); his sadistic cripples; his bookworms; his milquetoasts; his "cluckoids"; his husbands who are unwilling or unable to do their duty in bed. Less satisfactory is that male homosexuals also tend to be objects of a certain

32. "The Immortal Mr. Meyer," *Playboy* (June 1995): 90-2.

33. *Grindhouse: The Forbidden World of "Adults Only" Cinema* (New York: St. Martin's Griffin, 1996), 100.

34. "What's New, *Pussycat?*," *The Village Voice*, 17 January 1995: 56.

amount of stereotypical derision as flaming or mincing figures in Meyer's films, and another "thin edge" that Meyer often treads is between homoeroticism and homophobia. Likewise, Meyer has a certain contempt for "femininity": shrinking-violets; passive victims (both male and female); and women who take the punishment that men give out. Whereas Meyer said he admired women with "guts," I would suggest it might be more accurate to say Meyer admired women with "balls": both in the sense of male testicles and a cocksure attitude. Ideally, Meyer presents a world where gender is dismantled and even eliminated, a film world dominated by "men with big tits."

"The Eisenstein of Sex Films"

If Russ Meyer is known for one thing besides big breasts, it is his rapid-fire editing style. Critics contend Meyer's jolting editing is yet another indication of his filmmaking incompetence. In fact, much of Meyer's editing technique was born out of technical and budgetary concerns: limited finances; Meyer's experience as an industrial filmamker editing and utilizing stock footage; and the problems of dealing with less-skilled actors. Meyer primarily used exotic dancers and pin-up models for his female leads, and Frasier noted "Meyer vowed never to let acting ability take precedence over anatomical considerations, relying instead on his skill as an editor to compensate for any acting deficiencies."[35] There was also a need to defuse the erotic content of the films. While Meyer films feature sex and nudity, they do so in jarring, unerotic ways. As Frasier observed, "Meyer's rapid-fire editing with its heavy use of crosscutting and intercutting took the edge off sex scenes by refusing to let them develop sexual tension."[36] While done as a strategy to avoid obscenity problems for his films, the pace and flow of the fragmentary images of sexual encounters and the female body rarely lend themselves to being erotic; rather, any eroticism self-destructs. At the risk of being crude, there is nothing for the (male) viewer to 'grab onto'."[37]

John Waters was quite correct in referring to Meyer as "the Eisenstein of sex films." Eisenstein's theory of montage is a sequence of shots designed to produce an "intellectual shock" which jolts the viewer into making metaphorical associations between the shots:

"Montage is an idea that arises from the collision of independent shots – shots even opposite to one another: the 'dramatic' principle ('dramatic'...used here in regard to the methodology of form – not to *content* or *plot*!)... this popularized description of what happens as a blending has its share of responsibility for the popular miscomprehesion of the nature of montage... for, in fact each sequential element is perceived not *next* to each other, but *on top* of each other."[38]

35. *Russ Meyer – The Life and Films*, 150.

36. *Russ Meyer – The Life and Films*, 14.

37. See Frasier, 12. See also Craig Fischer, "Beyond the Valley of the Dolls and the Exploitation Genre," *The Velvet Light Trap*, Number 30 (Fall 1992): 22.

38. *Film Form: Essays in Film Theory*, ed. and trans. Jay Leyda (San Diego: Harcourt Brace and Company, 1949), 49.

This is not to say that Eisenstein's films lack narrative. While they have plots and characters, the dramatic "meanings" of the film are generated by shot juxtapositions and intellectual association between the shots. Russ Meyer's films operate in this same way: the meanings are often generated by the intellectual collision of individual shots rather than the narrative structure of the film, such as in *Lorna* and *Beyond the Valley of the Dolls*, which I will argue have narratives whose apparent "meanings" are completely subverted by their editing and "intellectual montages." To this degree, Meyer also freely uses *nondiagetic* footage, or footage that is not part of the film's narrative. Craig Fisher noted, "the inserts are an example of what Christian Metz calls the *nondiagetic insert*, defined as an 'image that has a purely comparative function, showing an object which is external to the film.'"[39] In some cases this is stock footage to symbolize the sex act (*Eve and the Handyman*) or to comment on it (the stock footage of a demolition derby that is intercut into a sex scene in *Finders Keepers, Lovers Weepers*). Other times these non-diagetic shots are filmed by Meyer for the film but have a metaphorical rather than a narrative role in the film, such as the bizarre inserts of Uschi Digard in *Cherry, Harry, and Raquel*. This shots are not part of the narrative, and often actually *disrupt* narrative continuity and even baffle the viewer. However, the inserts serve important functions in generating the symbolic meanings of the film through associative montage. In this sense, Meyer's use of intellectual montage and nondiagetic inserts are almost a throwback to silent cinema. As Ebert noted, "His cuts to subjective substitutes for the same action are so literal, so direct, so basic, that they recall a kind of filmmaking not seen in commercial cinema since the Twenties. Some of his effects are so old-fashioned that in his hands they seem positively experimental."[40]

Russ Meyer: A Cinema of Excess

In short, with Russ Meyer one is presented with a cinematic world of exaggerations: exaggerated breasts, exaggerated fucking, exaggerated violence, exaggerated caricatures, exaggerated narration, exaggerated landscapes, exaggerated editing. It is a film world of excess where a Sadean power struggle is wielded in a cruel and absurd theater of a surreal, "white-trash" America. It is also a film world that destroys dichotomies and paradigms: between sex and violence, comedy and tragedy, "humor and evil," high and low culture, avant-garde modernism and kitsch bad taste. In this overall context, the films of Russ Meyer might next be examined.

39. "*Beyond the Valley of the Dolls* and the Exploitation Genre," 21.

40. "Russ Meyer: King of the Nudies," page 9 of 14.

EVE PRODUCTIONS, INC. PRESENTS
EUROPE IN THE RAW

CHAPTER TWO
NUDIE-CUTIES

> *It is only the time taken in the shedding of clothes that makes the public voyeurs... Woman is desexualized at the very moment she is stripped naked.*[41]
> –Roland Barthes

[41. *Mythologies*, trans. Annette Lavers (New York: Hill and Wang, 1997), 84.]

The Birth of a Genre

By 1959, Russ Meyer was an established industrial filmmaker, writing and directing documentaries for such companies as Southern Pacific and Standard Oil; he was also a well-known pin-up photographer whose work appeared in such magazines and *Playboy* and *Adam*. Both careers figure prominently in his first major foray into sexploitation filmmaking, *The Immoral Mr. Teas* (1959). The industrial film techniques can be seen in *Mr. Teas'* mock-documentary style and the narration that compensates for what is otherwise a silent comedy. As noted, *Mr. Teas* was also "inspired" by Jacques Tati's comedy, *M. Hulot's Holiday* (1953). Sexploitation producer David Friedman referred to *Mr. Teas*, not necessarily disparagingly, as "a cheap American version of *Mr.* [sic] *Hulot's Holiday*."[42] In regard to the pin-up influence, Meyer stated, "[*Mr. Teas*] was based on my experience doing stills for *Playboy*... the girl-next-door, the common man, the voyeur, little nude photo essays."[43] *Mr. Teas* was not only an unprecedented financial success, but it virtually created the "nudie-cutie" genre that dominated sexploitation filmmaking in the early 1960s. Prior to *Mr. Teas*, the dominant strategies of exploitation nudity ranged between the "exposé" film, in which lurid subject matter was both depicted and decried on-screen, and the "healthy lifestyles" film, a pseudo-documentary approach in which interminable

[42. As quoted in Vale and Juno, eds., 102.]

[43. As quoted in Vale and Juno, eds., 82.]

scenes of nudist-camp activities were shown (volleyball and sunbathing the most common). The "transition from exploitation to sexploitation began with the nudie cycle of films designed to thrill (primarily male) viewers at the sight of the (primarily female) body."[44] *Mr. Teas* is often considered the film that heralded the shift of "exploitation" to "sexploitation," and more importantly, was the first "nudie" film to consciously deal with themes of male voyeurism. However, to suggest that *Mr. Teas* and the subsequent nudie-cuties simply were only "*about* naked women... and about *looking* at naked women,"[45] and that these films were "the most innocent and gentle of all sex-exploitation genres,"[46] ignores an important ideological aspect of these films: the politics of looking at naked bodies.

Paintings and Pin-ups

In the nudie-cutie, one sees a historical tradition of the ideology of the bourgeois nude characterized by Western painting. Indeed, the "canonical" nude and the "disreputable" pin-up are only different to the degree that one undergoes what John Berger called "mystification... the process of explaining away what might be otherwise evident."[47] In short, the issue is not so much if a piece of "pornography" is "great art," but to what degree the history of "great art" has been a history of "pornography." To merely discuss the nudie-cutie as a type of innocuous "looking" at naked women ignores a fundamental cultural issue epitomized by the nude in recent art criticism: who is the bearer of sight (usually male) and the object of sight (usually female). In his famous maxim on Western painting, Berger observed, "*Men act and women appear*. Men look at women. Women watch themselves being looked at."[48] The nudie-cuties are precisely about this relationship of men seeing nude women and women being seen nude, yet the vast majority of these films fail to problematize, yet alone question, this arraignment. While the nudie-cuties abandoned the exploitation strategies of the "exposé" and "healthy lifestyles" to present the naked (female) body as unabashedly natural and beautiful, such an ideological project also heavily relied on what Michel Foucault termed "The Repressive Hypothesis," the belief in Western culture that "sex" is a monolithic drive repressed by equally monolithic "repressive" forces.[49] One of the primary architects for the "Repressive Hypothesis" in America was Hugh Hefner's *Playboy* magazine, which not only promoted (male) sexual health and freedom against "Puritanical" morality of the 1950s, but equated sexual adventure with *laissez-faire* economic liberty. As Gay Talese noted, "Hefner associated romantic adventure with upward mobility and economic prosperity, believing that men who were successful in bed were also successful in the boardroom."[50] In this context, one might consider the degree that cultural discourses of sexuality such as *Playboy* and the nudie-cutie were not reactions against "repressive" American attitudes

44. Morrocchi, Piselli, and Singer, eds., 13.

45. Muller and Faris, 82.

46. Turan and Zito, 18.

47. *Ways of Seeing* (New York: Penguin Books, 1977), 15-6.

48. *Ways of Seeing*, 47.

49. See *The History of Sexuality, Volume I: An Introduction*, trans. by Robert Hurley (New York: Vintage Books, 1990).

50. *Thy Neighbor's Wife* (New York: Dell, 1980), 90.

CHAPTER TWO ◊ **NUDIE-CUTIES**

The "nudie" phase of Meyer's career started with the now-lost short *The French Peep Show* (1950) – a film of the burlesque dancer Tempest Storm – and also included *This Is My Body* (1959), *Naked Camera* (1960), *Erotica* (1961), *Europe In The Raw* (1963), and *Heavenly Bodies* (1963).

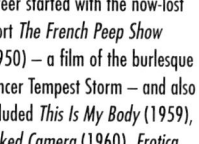

Stills from *The French Peep Show*

Europe In The Raw

Heavenly Bodies

towards sex, but to what extent these discourses were merely examples of a nebulous variety of strategies of discussing "sexuality" that benefitted some (men) and excluded others (women).

Returning to Laura Mulvey's work, in the nudie-cuties one can often see both the "de-valuation" of the female character in the leering and often demeaning humor as well as the "over-valuation" of the female body as a fetish-object. The woman becomes both object of adolescent derision and adult desire. Yet, in rare cases (notably, Russ Meyer and Doris Wishman), nudie-cuties also offer more problematic relationships of voyeurism and bourgeois sexual ideology. In this context, Meyer's three most well-known nudie-cuties will be considered.

THE IMMORAL MR. TEAS (1959)

The Politics of Voyeurism

The Immoral Mr. Teas starred Meyer's WWII-buddy Bill Teas as the title character. As in several subsequent Meyer films, the character shares the same name with the actor, creating a blurred distinction between character and performer for the audience. It also bears mention that the humor of Meyer's nudie-cuties is not simply the standard burlesque fare, but often recalls the more surreal sight-gags of television-comedy pioneer Ernie Kovacs. While narrator Franklin Lasko asks the audience to consider the condition of "the common-man," Teas is shown in various mundane activities, the narrator's description matching the on-screen activities. "What is he thinking?" asks Lasko while Teas is shown not only parodying Rodin's *The Thinker*, but suggesting that the model for Rodin's masterpiece is a fellow seated on the toilet. The shot cuts to a shot of Teas from the chest up, wearing a suit and his ever present straw-hat. "And where is he going?" wonders Lasko. The next shot answers the question: Teas is on a treadmill in a crowded street, pedestrians walking past him. He is, in effect, "going nowhere," a condition that will mirror the rest of Teas's actions, or more correctly, *inactions*.

The remaining hour of *Mr. Teas* revolves around the title character's misadventures with the opposite sex. Teas, a bike-courier, spends the day delivering packages to various offices, admiring the cleavages of a nurse, waitress, and secretary in close-ups – these three characters figure prominently in the later film. The next scene chronicles his day off at the beach, and shows most clearly the influence of Tati's film. A blonde model doing a photo shot throws Teas's day out of control. Teas spies on her during the model's topless photo shoot, and she in turn interrupts his fishing by sunbathing next to him, with Teas's "fishing rod" twitching uncontrollably between his legs. As with most of Meyer's males, Teas is only a ladies' man from a distance. He goes to great,

LIPS HIPS TITS POWER ◊ THE FILMS OF RUSS MEYER

comic inconvience to sneak his own photos of her topless photo session. However, when she joins him on his fishing perch, a tree branch over a pond, and begins to undo her bra, Teas panics and throws himself into the lake.

Mr. Teas is often incorrectly described as a film in which the main character gains a sort of supernatural power to see through women's clothing after a trip to the dentist. Teas, as Meyer, pointed out, simply begins to "hallucinate."[51] Indeed, much of the nudity played out in *Mr. Teas* is based around hallucinations, bizarre scenes and visions that almost resemble the

51. As quoted in Charles Schnieder, ed., *Cad: A Handbook for Heels* (Los Angeles: Feral House, 1992), 40.

CHAPTER TWO ◊ **NUDIE-CUTIES**

surrealist paintings of René Magritte. In the first hallucination, Teas sits in a dentist's chair, wearing a blue jumpsuit against an orange-red background. The naked nurse is shown from behind, next to Teas, and the dentist operates a pedal-powered drill with which he removes a grotesquely and comically large molar. In the second hallucination, the blue-clad Teas sits in front of a solid yellow background, nonchalantly eating a watermelon while the previously-seen waitress walks around him, clad only in an apron. She helpfully dabs Teas's chin, who appears either ignorant or indifferent of her presence. This also suggests a theme seen in a number of future Meyer films: men are frequently more

23

attracted to women as mother figures or domestic servants rather than sexual partners. The third hallucination depicts Teas obliviously dictating to the aforementioned secretary, who sits naked behind a desk. Following this set of hallucinations, Teas goes to the woods in an attempt to relax and has an erotic dream (or, perhaps, another hallucination) about the nurse, waitress, and secretary as they frolic in the woods in the nude and strike typical pin-up poses. In the dream, Teas watches them, peeping from behind foliage and tress: again, only interacting with them as a detached voyeur. Finally, overwhelmed by these visions, Teas vainly visits a female psychiatrist, the hilariously named Mrs. Floodback, but spends the session hallucinating that she is naked behind her desk. "Some men just enjoy being sick," Lasko concludes.

Most of *The Immoral Mr. Teas* is spent *watching* Mr. Teas *watch* undressed women. One of the film's most overt essays on voyeurism is a scene at a strip club that intercuts the dancer, a grotesque close-up of Teas's eye behind a peephole, and the sparse audience of horny men, one of them being Russ Meyer himself in a cameo. Setting a pattern for much of Russ Meyer's film career, the male who has opportunities to have actual sexual contact with a women usually ignores her or consciously refrains from the act. Even when Mr. Teas hires a French prostitute, the shot cuts to her ironing his jumpsuit: a domestic, rather than a sexual act. Any opportunity to move beyond acts of voyeurism are either missed or purposely avoided. Also, the vast amount of nudity occurs only within the realm of fantasy: Teas's "hallucinations" or dreams. The on-screen nude is rarely depicted as anything except a fantasy image, a product of Mr. Teas's sexual fantasies, and in these fantasies Mr. Teas is not even engaged in sexual activities, but only as a passive participant, a detached observer, an individual almost oblivious to the nude woman standing next to him.

Despite the film's box-office success and its notoriety, *Mr. Teas* is in my opinion the least interesting of Meyer's three major nudie-cuties, lacking the richness and complexity of subsequent films. However, *Mr. Teas* does remain interesting to the degree it neither overcomes its voyeurism, given the very presence of the nude woman on-screen, nor prevents itself from wallowing in voyeurism due to the internal critique that is offered. It is a film about *both* the female anatomy and the male voyeur. In this way, David Frasier has quite perceptively summed up the problematic of *The Immoral Mr. Teas*:

Mr. Teas, the perpetually put-upon Everyman, acts as a stand-in for the audience.

"His look-but-don't-touch voyeurism parallels the experience of his audience which can never hope to meet, yet alone attain, the fantasy women who excite the senses. The women... are all pin-ups come to life. They lack the emotional substance to make them real and are thereby immune to any form of relationship other than visual."[52]

52. Russ Meyer – The Life and Films, 18.

CHAPTER TWO ◊ **NUDIE-CUTIES**

EVE AND THE HANDYMAN (1961)

All About Eve(s)

Meyer's follow-up to *The Immoral Mr. Teas* was *Eve and the Handyman*, another essentially silent, burlesque comedy made up of narration, music, and sound effects. *Eve* stars famous pin-up model and Meyer's then-wife Eve Meyer (again, the character and performer share the first name), who appears in a variety of roles, and Anthony James-Ryan, who portrays the Handyman (James-Ryan collaborated with Meyer extensively throughout his career as a co-writer, associate producer, and cameo actor in a number of Meyer films). Throughout the film, Eve Meyer appears in a tan trench coat and black beret; this "Eve-Spy" character also provides the voice-over narration as well as following and observing the Handyman over the course of his daily comic misadventures with a variety of women, who are all also played by Eve Meyer: a secretary, a nurse, a waitress, a hitchhiker, and a braless bar patron who plays pinball with heavy emphasis on the body English. The use of the same actress in multiple roles establishes Eve as a fetish-figure incarnate: an image-ideal that becomes the female obsession of the Handyman. Certainly, while the use of Eve Meyer in these multiple roles was primary a budgetary concern, her recurring appearances result in her various permutations creating a fetish-image that is the inescapable fantasy-female of the Handyman.

Eve begins with the Eve-Spy character as she arrives at the Handyman's home and begins to observe him sleeping. Throughout the film, Eve-Spy shadows the Handyman, a reversal of the usual cinematic-voyeuristic relationship of the active male watching the passive female. Unlike *Mr. Teas*, where Bill Teas is a *male* stand-in for the male spectator, Eve-Spy, the female, is the possessor of the (cinematic) gaze, a *female* stand-in for the male audience. As the Handyman sleeps, two art-objects hang over his bed: one, a modern art sketch of a frowning woman with a fig leaf covering her vagina (a sexually-dissatisfied "Eve," the first woman); the other is a kitsch embroidery that reads "mother." These images over the Handyman's bed mark it as a site of both Oedipal guilt and sexual repression. When the alarm-clock goes off, the Handyman is unable to shut if off. Exasperated, he throws it out the window where it lands in a street cleaner's trash barrel (the trash collector is nearby urinating). The still-ringing alarm clock proceeds to arouse the neighbors. The camera executes low-angle zooms upward to individual apartment windows and a sight-gag follows each zoom. The humor is again highly reminiscent of Ernie Kovacs. In one, an overweight woman in a black wig and floral print dress opens a closet door and a dead hunter falls out (?!); in another shot, a confused Franklin Bolger pulls off the bed covers to reveal himself dressed in boxing gloves and trunks, ready to spar. In a later, surreal vignette also recalling Kovacs, the Handyman answers an

25

Eve Meyer

CHAPTER TWO ◊ **NUDIE-CUTIES**

emergency phone call and rushes off into the woods, where he meets Eve Meyer dressed as a nurse. He dons surgical garb, and "Eve-Nurse" prepares tools and assists him as he performs a delicate (off-screen) operation.[53] After several tense moments of close-ups of the Handyman's furrowed brow under his surgical mask, Eve-Nurse's concerned stare, and various tools being passed between their hands, the viewer sees the end results. The Handyman holds a tree branch upside-down and slaps it twice, and the sound of a crying new-born is heard. As Eve-Nurse looks on admiringly, The Handyman departs with humble modesty. Meanwhile, Eve-Spy has been intercut into the scene as well, watching the drama unfold from behind a tree. The last shot depicts the now-planted branch next to the mother tree, the anthematic music satirizing the mock-heroism of the scene, as well as satirizing the strong Oedipal issues that underscore the film.

For the most part, *Eve* revolves around the Handyman's encounters with the various "Eves" as Eve-Spy observes from a voyeuristic distance. In one such encounter, the Handyman is washing windows atop a high-rise while Eve-Spy watches with pocket binoculars from below. She shows more concern for the Handyman's safety than he himself does, as he is preoccupied with Eve Meyer playing a secretary. As the Handyman watches "Eve-Secretary," her breasts jiggling as she types, he absent-mindedly fondles his safety latch as a kind of masturbatory gesture, unaware that releasing the latch will result in him plummeting to the pavement below. Fortunately, he emerges unscathed, much to Eve-Spy's relief. Another encounter takes place at a diner where he again desires Eve, this time playing a waitress. As the camera shoots a close-up of Eve-Waitresses's cleavage, Eve-Spy's narration speaks of the need for the Handyman to "satisfy his sweet tooth." He orders two scoops of vanilla ice cream with a cherry atop each one. The sexual metaphor is clear, and to make the obvious even more obvious, Eve-Waitresses's breasts hang over the ice cream as she serves it to the Handyman. The montage juxtaposes close-ups of Eve's breasts straining against her waitress outfit, the Handyman's terror-filled eyes, and the two scoops of ice cream. The montage creates a metaphor not only of sex (breasts) but of sight (eyes), the ice cream signifying the Handyman's aghast, bulging eyes as much as Eve's breasts, serving to once again comment on male voyeurism as well as female anatomy. Frustrated, the Handyman slams his silverware on the counter and bolts from the diner, unable to eat the ice cream or even "bear the sight of it." The omnipresent Eve-Spy, watching the scene from the sidewalk through the diner window, bursts into laughter. In another Eve/Handyman encounter, Eve Meyer appears as a hitchhiker who sheds an article of clothing each time a vehicle fails to stop for her. Finally down to her panties and high heels, the Handyman's dilapidated pick-up truck arrives on the scene and stops. As Eve-Hitchhiker gives him a seductive look, the Handyman handles his dilemma with white-knuckle, wide-eyed panic (recalling the scene in the diner).

53. Kovacs once did an operating room scene that parodied the popular hospital TV dramas of the era. The camera shows the point of view of the patient has surgeons and nurses hover overhead. In the last shot, the whole operating room is shown: the surgical team has been slicing a turkey.

LIPS HIPS TITS POWER ◊ **THE FILMS OF RUSS MEYER**

CHAPTER TWO ◊ NUDIE-CUTIES

Finally, he acts: the shot cuts to the driver's side of the vehicle as it speeds away, Eve-Hitchhiker hold a set of overalls over her body. This situation is again observed by Eve-Spy, who is intercut watching the display through a cartoonish, oversize telescope.

In between these "Eve" encounters and the final meeting with Eve-Spy herself, the Handyman stops at an art studio, where modern art and beatnik types create paintings and sculptures and engage in various sight gags (such as the consumed artist who processes his thoughts by chewing on the paint-soaked tip of his brush). With the arrival of nightfall and the departure of all the artists, the Handyman is left alone in the studio and he reaches out to touch a sculpture of a woman. It is his first, tentative attempt to make contact with a woman, although it is not a woman *per se*, but only the representation of a woman. Using a long shot and somber shadowing, it is a rare moment of poignancy for a Meyer film. The next scene also takes place in the studio but out of narrative continuity — it is back in the daytime and the artists have reappeared. The Handyman observes a painter applying various shades of "grassy color," "tree green," and "shadow" onto a canvas with a roller, finishing a detailed landscape in a matter of seconds (a technique actually done by applying white paint onto a completed painting and then showing the film backwards). Intrigued, the Handyman tries the same technique, only to paint the word "MOTHER" in big, red letters, suggesting his Oedipal complex is so powerful he lacks the imagination for anything else.

On returning home, the Handyman sits on his bed, lonely, dejected, and weary. Eve-Spy enters his room and finally makes contact with the Handyman; she begins a strip-tease and opens her trench coat, revealing herself – as a Fuller brush salesman. A neon sign hangs from around her neck, and the coat's interior is lined with dangling hair brushes. As she begins to comb the Handyman's hair, a close-up of Eve's eyes cuts to a nondiagetic close-up of a cat's eyes, signifying Eve as a feline predator. This begins a furious montage of images, including stock footage: a woman's hands playing violin; a close-up of the eyes of the "Eve" in the sketch of the woman over the bed, referencing both Eve Meyer's eyes and the cat's eyes; a woman's hands playing harp; a boiling teapot; male hands playing a saxophone; mallets pounding on a kettledrum intercut with two trains cars linking that ends with two cymbals crashing; oil pumps; more musical instruments; a rocket launching; and finally, a close-up of a candle flame being extinguished. The metaphor of sexual intercourse generated by the montage is both blatant and comical, substituting for the then-unallowable scenes of actual sexual contact. The next morning, the Handyman rises out of bed: he is now a secure, self-confident "playboy" (pun on the magazine intended). He uses Eve's scarf for an ascot, and her hands emerge from the bottom of the frame to produce a set of keys: his rusty pick-up truck is now a sleek convertible, and he drives away, presumably to a new string of successes.

Eve and the Handyman manifests a theme common in Russ Meyer's films: women as both the objects of male sexual fantasies and women as sexual superiors of men. In the cartoon-surreal world of *Eve*, both themes are established by the multiple roles assigned to Eve Meyer. The Eve-Spy is the omnipresent watcher, amused by the comic problems of the Handyman in his encounters with the other "Eves," the objects of male lust (as in *Mr. Teas*, a waitress, nurse, secretary). Throughout the film, Eve Meyer has a dual-role: that of predator and prey, master and object of male lust. What is also especially interesting about *Eve* is the problemization of the female image and the *Playboy* ethos of masculinity and femininity. By casting Eve Meyer in multiple roles, she becomes an uncanny fetish-object, a obsessive female-ideal which continually haunts the Handyman. In Eve's finale, it is the woman, Eve-Spy, who is the sexual aggressor. She has to take the initiative and seduce the hapless Handyman. While the film seems to end in a sort of lame perpetuation of the *Playboy* myth that a sexually successful man is an economically successful man, it is also in the ending that the contradictions of the myth become apparent. It is only through the woman's sexual power that the man finds his own sexual potency (a theme that reappears in *Good Morning... and Goodbye!*). On his own, the Handyman personifies the dark and unspoken side of the *Playboy* myth: the man who has *failed* in both the bedroom and the boardroom. "There's many a strange fish," Eve concludes in the narration, "but the biggest catch is a happy ending." Her closing statement reflects the irony of the film.

WILD GALS OF THE NAKED WEST (1962)

"How the West was Fun!"

Meyer's last nudie-cutie, *The Wild Gals of the Naked West* is one of his more visually stunning films, with surreal settings and some of Meyer's most frenetic editing this side of *Mondo Topless*. *The Naked West* also features a screenplay by Jack Moran, who later wrote the screenplays for some of Meyer's best work: *Faster, Pussycat! Kill! Kill!*; *Common-Law Cabin*; and *Good Morning... and Goodbye!*. *The Naked West* continues in the pattern of *Eve and the Handyman*, emphasizing surrealist and absurdist humor as much as leering, eye-rolling sex jokes. Indeed, "naked west," is an apt description of the film, not only for its abundant nudity, but a "stripping" of the Western to its barest generic forms. It is not merely a burlesque parody of the Western, but, as Jim Morton observed, "an oddly stark abstraction... almost like a Beckett play."[54]

Virtually plotless, *The Naked West* starts out as an avant-garde version of a high school educational film, where the staples of the Western are reduced

54. Vale and Juno, eds, 80.

CHAPTER TWO ◊ **NUDIE-CUTIES**

to fragmentary shots, symbols, and descriptions. The film begins with a narrator describing "the men and women who lived and died," as picturesque Western landscapes and skies are shown, suggesting the heavens and eternal life, and their "pungent earthiness," which cuts to a shot of the ground suggesting not only the scent of cattle and manure, but the "earthiness" of their rambunctious sexual behavior which is later featured throughout the film. An almost hallucinatory montage follows chronicling the battles between the U.S. Cavalry and Native Americans, somewhere between Eisenstein on acid and a minimalist rendition of John Ford's "U.S. Cavalry" films. This montage begins with a close-up of a bugle, a cavalry flag, and the handle of a saber in quick succession. A shot of a rushing stream is match by the narrator's somber intonation of "the rescue... too late, or the charge towards disaster." When the narrator says the word 'ambush', there is a cut to a shot of a wave smashing against a rock. The furious montage continues as the narrator describes the "the painted Redman," showing a shot of running pools of paint, who used his surroundings "as no human could" which cuts to a shot of badlands plateaux. The montage concludes with a symbolic eulogy to the U.S. Calvary: the image of a blood-soaked saber embedded in the beach being pummeled by the tide; a burning cavalry flag on the beach at sunset, and a half-submerged bugle in a stream.

    This sequence cuts to "The OK Corral," and describes in wonderfully strained hyperbole the legendary gunfighters who roamed the land "with steel in their hands, and finally their bellies." The camera shot is a point-of-view, long take of a gunslinger cautiously maneuvering through a stable. When the gunshot rings out, the camera veers skyward and falls to the ground. Given that the assailant is never seen in the frame, one could assume the gunslinger satirically met his fate by the most cowardly of Western deeds: being shot in the back. The mock-documentary then draws to a close with the narrator reflecting on Westward Expansion with a brief montage of "Denver (a stock shot of downtown Denver), Las Vegas (a shot of neon lights),... and San Francisco!" (a shot of the Golden Gate Bridge). He eulogizes the many towns that fell by the wayside, where western legends "once moved and killed" (equating them to hunting predators rather than men who "lived and died"). Bemoaning the fact that these places now only exist as tourist curiosities, the narrator waxes nostalgic that their ghosts might live on.

    This romantic sentiment is quickly subverted by a double-barreled shotgun that points out of the window of an abandoned shack, directly at the viewer. The transition from satire to all-out farce begins at this point, with the film taking an abrupt and absurd turn with the introduction of Jack Moran as a cowboy ghost whose ancient appearance is achieved with white cotton eyebrows and moustache. Moran takes over for the mock-documentary, voice-over narration, functioning as both an on-screen and off-screen narrator for the

CHAPTER TWO ◊ NUDIE-CUTIES

remainder of the film. Fueled by liquor and cigarettes, he proceeds tell the story of a town "so bad... we wuz ashamed to name it." While the myths of the West are told in terms of generic military symbols and landscapes in the narrated prologue, the story of the town abruptly introduces the viewer to cartoonish cowboys, Indians, and, of course, saloon girls in a barrage of unsettling, strange images and surreal sight gags. Again, Ernie Kovacs is the best comparison. The viewer sees montages of booze-swilling, slovenly cowboys (one being Russ Meyer), grotesque rubber masks, close-ups of revolvers being fired against solid color backdrops, and swinging breasts. The sets are simply painted rooms with scenery sketched on the walls: the town saloon is a wall with shelves of bottles drawn on it, the town hotel a room with a dresser similarly drawn on the wall. Such backdrops give the film a pop-art surrealism highly reminiscent of the 1950s Warner Brothers cartoons of Chuck Jones.

There are also several running gag that are intercut, repeated, and appear intermittently throughout *The Naked West*. Pasty-clad dance hall girls play strip poker with oversize cards and lasso cowboys from the balcony of the saloon. A cowboy parodying Harpo Marx continually chases a topless saloon girl through the streets of the town. An off-frame suitor pours champagne for a women, only to have the glass continually shot by a drunken cowboy. Indians armed with mortars, bazookas, and tommy-guns wait in the hills – all are played by Anthony James-Ryan, satirizing the notion that "they all look the same." A cowboy who attempts to use an outhouse has it repeatedly tipped over by two pranksters (when the viewer sees the interior of the outhouse, it is a modern, immaculate, tiled bathroom). One hilarious running gag consists of two cowboys who blast away at each other in the street with a seemingly endless supply of bullets, parodying the Western cliché of never having to reload. When they do finally exhaust their ammunition, the continue their battle with fisticuffs, each delivering one well-measured blow at a time. This lasts through much of the film, and the male bystanders are much more interested in the fight than the sight of a naked woman bathing nearby in a watering trough.

Any semblance of plot revolves around the arrival of a decidedly unstatuesque stranger, undoubtedly from the East Coast, who is humiliated in the town saloon by the locals. He returns to clean up the town, dressed in a garish red cowboy outfit with a pale blue bandana and matching oversize ten-gallon hat, brandishing twin six-guns with two-foot long barrels. He doesn't just bring law and order to the town, but "civility": marriage licenses for the saloon girls, a Victorian bathing suit for the woman publicly bathing, and a peace pipe for the Indians. He is hailed by the townspeople, who Meyer hilariously depicts by inserting a stock shot of a stadium filled with cheering people. With the town cleaned up, Moran bitterly complains "the town plum died of goodness... no fightin'... no funnin' (an obvious euphemism for "no fuckin'")... no drinkin'." The

FILMS PACIFICA Inc. present
WILD GALS of the NAKED WEST
EASTMANCOLOR

bawdy saloon girls are now students in "Mrs. Floodback's School for Girls" ("Floodback" also the name of the psychiatrist in *Mr. Teas*), and the fist-fighting cowboys now entertain themselves with knitting and playing jacks, activities commonly reserved for "little girls." Moran laments, "I ain't sayin' evil is good...

CHAPTER TWO ◊ NUDIE-CUTIES

.but people need a twinge a' meanness in 'em. Somethin' for the good to work against... keep the blood a-movin'."

In *The Naked West*, one sees the beginnings of two tendencies that are essential in Russ Meyer's work. One is the use of a generic formula and conventions which are transformed into a satirical, absurdist universe. The other is the conflict between animal impulse and civilized conduct, a struggle Meyer views at best as a necessary evil and at worst a castrating surrender. This tension between "animality" verses "civility" will form the basis of all of Russ Meyer's later work.

EROTICA
PAD-RAM Enterprises, Inc.

EROTICA

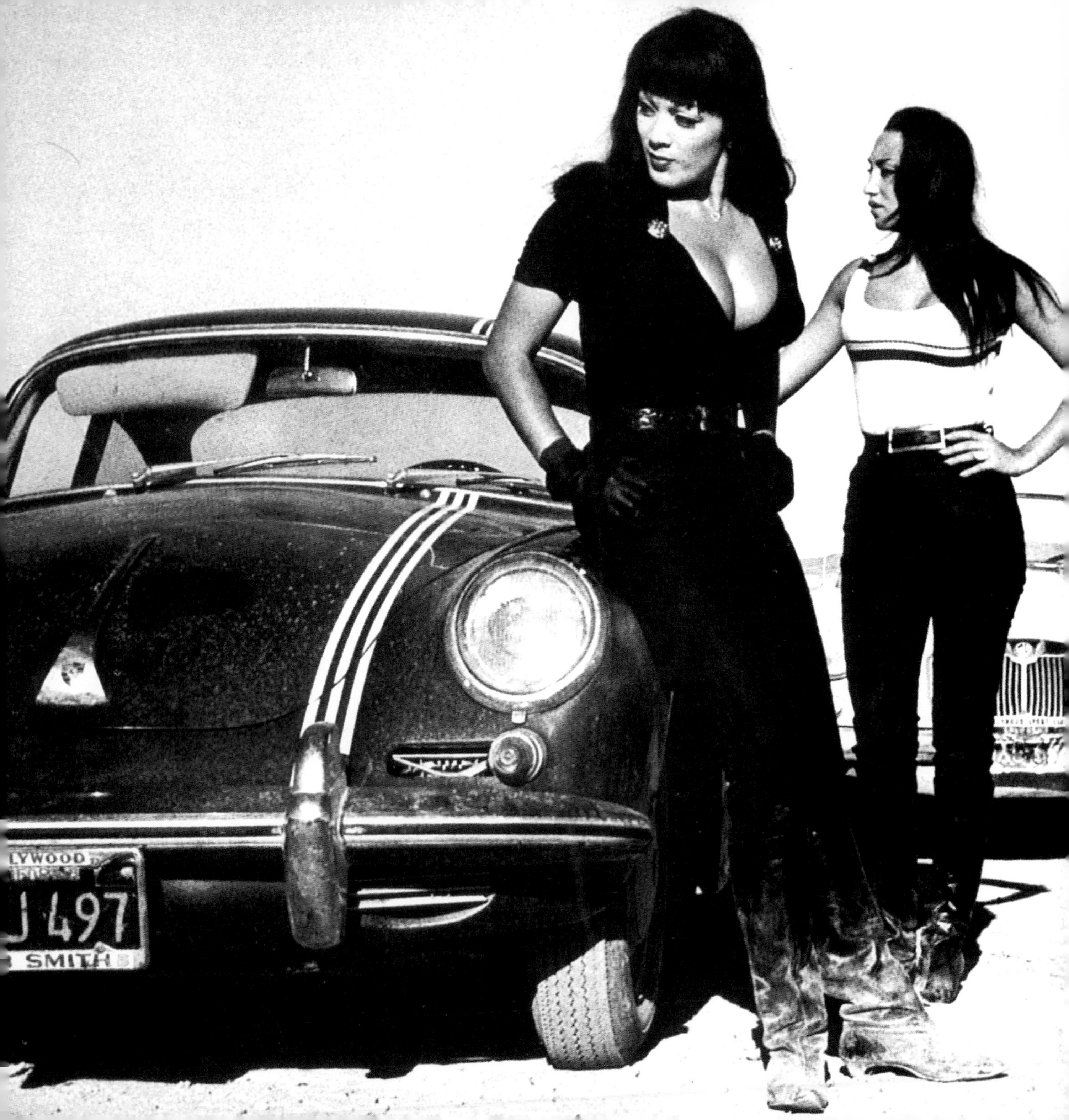

LYWOOD
J 497
SMITH

CHAPTER THREE
"LADIES AND GENTLEMEN, WELCOME TO VIOLENCE"

55. *The Portable Nietzsche*, trans. Walter Kaufmann (New York: The Viking Press, 1968), 192.

Are you going to woman? Do not forget the whip![55]
—Friedrich Nietzsche

56. See Muller and Faris, 85.

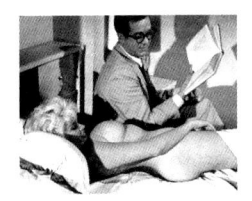

Promises! Promises!

57. See Turan and Zito, 17-8.

58. See *Grindhouse*, 93.

Roughies, Kinkies, Ghoulies

By 1964 the nudie-cuties became both predictable in their conventions and irrelevant in their discourse. Between 1959 and 1963, literally hundreds of nudie-cutie films followed in the wake of *The Immoral Mr. Teas'* success. Most were a endless collection of corny, burlesque jokes punctuated by females in various "tits and ass" shots (full frontal nudity was still expressly forbidden). While controversial for their time, mostly for legal reasons, today the nudie-cuties seem almost insufferably anachronistic and innocuous. By the 1970s, the last vestige of this style and humor, Benny Hill, was inoffensive enough for the BBC.[56]

In addition to genre exhaustion, one major factor in the decline of the nudie-cutie was competition with mainstream Hollywood nudity: Jayne Mansfield broke the taboo on nude scenes in 1963 with *Promises! Promises!*, which was little more than a star-studded nudie-cutie.[57] Eddie Muller and Daniel Faris also suggested that the nudie-cuties also lost their relevance in the wake of growing cultural unrest and pessimism in America during the early 1960s, specifically the national trauma of JFK's assassination, Vietnam, and racial strife.[58] However, given the centrality of misogyny in 1960s sexploitation films, one element conspicuously overlooked by Muller and Faris is the rise of feminism in the 1960s and the subsequent backlash. Betty Friedan's seminal denunciation of female myths in America, *The Feminine Mystique*, was published in 1963, and compared the domestic position of the women to "a comfortable concentration camp."[59] Of course, this is precisely how marriage and female domesticity is depicted in *Lorna* and other Meyer films: a stupefying and suffocating existence of social and sexual boredom. Patriarchal response to the feminist critique was equally acrimonious. Historian William O'Neill noted that in the 1960s, "anti-feminism seemed the only remaining respectable prejudice... Men commonly denied being sexual bigots on the grounds that they didn't hate women as such, only those that didn't know their place."[60] And here one could add the words of feminist Robin Morgan, who noted, "knowing our place is the message of rape."[61] Indeed, by 1964, sexploitation films underwent a profound change, one in which "putting women in their place" was often graphically and disturbingly theorized and acted out.

Some have suggested that Meyer, who invented the nudie-cutie with *The Immoral Mr. Teas*, also began the roughie cycle with *Lorna*. Muller and Faris noted, "whether he was the first or not [is] irrelevant. Slinging his camera like an old-west gunfighter, Meyer swaggered into tough-ass territory and showed everyone how it was done. Abandoning his pop-art color, bouncy scores, and buffoonish humor, Meyer created *Lorna*."[62] Indeed, more important than who created the roughie is considering the ideological implications of the roughie and its related forms, the "kinkie" and the "ghoulie." I hasten to point out these stylistic differences are more superficial than substantial, and while I will be briefly defining each of these forms, even sexploitation film aficionados vary greatly in their placement of specific films in specific categories.[63] My purpose is to look at these films as a cultural discourse of sexuality and gender and how these films may (or may not) depict and represent a patriarchal and even sadistic vision of male and female relationships in the turbulence of the 1960s.

Given this, the stylistic differences between *Mr. Teas* and *Lorna* are striking. If the nudie-cutie emphasized a burlesque and pin-up view of American sexuality, the roughie offered lurid, sensational stories of moral decay and psychological studies of sex and violence. If the nudie-cutie was Pop Art and *Playboy*, the roughie was *film noir* and exploitation tabloid. In some respects, the roughies marked a return to traditional exploitation films topics such as adultery, drug abuse, and prostitution and infused them with a more provocative sexual content including nudity, simulated sex, and most ominously, rape. Overall, the roughies were melodramatic, dark, seedy, and often unpleasant film experiences, with the characters inevitably punished for the descent into "vice" with dire narrative consequences. Perhaps the most notorious "roughies" are Michael and Roberta Findlay's *Flesh* trilogy: *The Touch of her Flesh* (1967), *The Curse of her Flesh* (1968), and *The Kiss of her Flesh* (1968), which chronicle the torture-murders of women by main character Richard Jennings (played by

59. As quoted in Sara Evans, *Personal Politics: The Roots of Women's Liberation in the Civil Rights Movement and the New Left* (New York: Vintage, 1980), 18.

60. *Coming Apart: An Informal History of America* in the 1960s (New York: Times Books, 1971), 198.

61. As quoted in Peter N. Carroll, *It Seemed Like Nothing Happened: The Tragedy and Promise of America in the 1970s* (New York: Holt, Reinhart, and Winston, 1982), 114.

62. *Grindhouse*, 100.

63. For instance, Muller and Faris refer to the Olga films as "kinkies" and the Findlay's *Flesh* trilogy as "ghoulies." Morrocchi, Piselli, and Singer, eds, classify the Olga films as "roughies" and the *Flesh* films "kinkies."

CHAPTER THREE ◊ "WELCOME TO VIOLENCE"

Michael Findlay), and are set to some of the most misogynistic narration ever recorded.

The *kinkie* took the roughie formula to the extreme. Like the roughie, the kinkie explored the dark side of human sexuality, both in their stark, black and white *noir* style and their frequent themes of rape, sado-masochism, and lesbianism, which eroticized sexual relations between women but equated lesbianism with envy and hatred of men.[64] Two seminal kinkies are Joesph P. Marwa's *Olga's Girls* and *Olga's House of Shame* (both 1964), starring Audrey Campbell as the lesbian sadist Olga. Unlike the roughies's melodramatic, exploitation plotlines, kinkies were virtually plotless sexual encounters with little or no dialogue, save an off-camera narrator who recapitulated the on-screen action with lurid adjectives and monotonal intonation. The roughie and kinkie can also be seen as a precursor to the "transgression cinema" of the New York underground in the 1980s, such as the films of Richard Kern: his legendary collaboration with Lydia Lunch, *Fingered* (1986), represents the roughie taken to the *n*th degree. The *ghoulie* was by far the most graphically violent and explicit of the sexploitation films, a sort of film version of the macabre E.C. comics of the1950s featuring visceral scenes of dismemberment and mutilation. Not coincidentally, most ghoulies were done in color. The undisputed master of the ghoulie was Herschell Gordon Lewis, who directed the legendary *Blood* trilogy: *Blood Feast* (1963), *2000 Maniacs* (1964), and *Color Me Blood Red* (1964). These are the obvious ancestors to the "splatter" or "slasher" films that generated much controversy in 1980s for their alleged misogyny, such as the *Friday the 13th* series.

Regarding the depiction and representation of women, it is virtually impossible to defend the blatant misogyny in many of these films, and there is certainly both a "over-valuation" of the female nude and an explicit "de-valuation" of women, ranging from the lesbian, man-hating sadist (the *Olga* films), the manipulative "cocktease" who (deservedly?) descends into prostitution (Friedman's 1966 *A Taste of Honey, A Swallow of Brine!*), objects of abduction and sexual enslavement (the *Olga* films, *The Defilers*), objects of misogynistic rage (the *Flesh* trilogy), or woman who are literally no more than dismembered parts (*Blood Feast*): in Mulvey's terms, objects of both voyeuristic desire and narrative punishment. Turan and Zito noted:

"The image of woman is... that of the classic, castrating bitch-goddess... women in the roughies are [also] victims of male lust and domination, they are to be used and abused, trained in their duties and hard pleasures the same way as a dog is trained by a cruel master... women are to be feared and therefore subdued... *blood rather than semen becomes the symbolic fluid of erotic expression.*"[65]

64. See Vale and Juno, eds., 86.

Olga's Girls

Blood Feast

65. *Sinema,* 24-5. Emphasis mine.

41

LIPS HIPS TITS POWER ◊ THE FILMS OF RUSS MEYER

Some argued that the nudie-cutie was far less offensive and disturbing than the roughie, echoing the observation by Lenny Bruce that most Americans would rather have their children watch a man killing a woman rather than making love to her.[66] Certainly the very thought of the "raincoat crowd" masturbating to a typical roughie in a run-down theater puts an ominous slant on the Sexual Revolution. Yet while the nudie-cutie perpetuated the sexual and cultural ideology of the bourgeois nude, the roughie reflected a far darker and problematic study of sexuality and power where domination and aggression are as integral to "sex" as intimacy and romance, again comparable to the Marquis de Sade. Keeping in mind Turan and Zito's observation that "*blood rather than semen* [was] *the symbolic fluid of erotic expression*," Michel Foucault noted:

"The new procedures of power... were what caused our societies to go from *a symbolics of blood* to *an analytics of sexuality*. Sade... [was] contemporary with the transition from 'sanguinity' to 'sexuality'... Sade carried the exhaustive analysis of sex over into the mechanisms of the old power of sovereignty and endowed it with the ancient but fully maintained prestige of blood, the latter flowed through the whole dimension of pleasure... while it is true that the analytics of sexuality and the symbolics of blood were grounded in to very distinct regimes of power, in actual fact the transition from one to another did not come about (any more than these powers themselves)... without overlappings, interactions, and echoes."[67]

Peter Levenda noted, "Power shifted – according to Foucault – from the *symbol* or sign of the blood towards the *object* of sex; Machiavelli moving down the talk show couch to make room for Freud, who will take it with him when he leaves."[68] However, what Levenda omits is the brief but crucial appearance of Sade on said talk show between Machiavelli and Freud. Sade is the intermediary where these two regimes of power "overlap, interact, and echo," where the "symbolics of blood" and the "analytics of sexuality" converge. Rather than a binary between "blood" and "semen," the roughies continue the Sadean project where blood and semen are *both* "fluids of erotic expression." While the nudie-cuties spawned popular and sexist teen sex-comedies such as *Porky's* (1982), the roughie was predecessor to such problematic (and frequently misunderstood) films such as *Last House on the Left*, *Ms. .45*, *Slumber Party Massacre*, and the notorious *I Spit on Your Grave*, where the sexual relationships of men and women are depicted and determined though acts of rape, murder, dismemberment, and castration.[69] The roughies of the 1960s can be certainly be read as texts that reflect a sadistically patriarchal and phallocentric order in an era where women were "forgetting their place"and were brutally reminded of "knowing their place." However, especially in the case of Russ Meyer, they also provide intense texts

66. See Muller and Faris, 80.

67. *The History of Sexuality, V. I*, 148-9.

68. *Unholy Alliance: A History of Nazi Involvement with the Occult*, 2nd ed. (New York: Continuum, 2002), 37.

69. My treatment of the roughies is highly indebted to Carol J. Clover, *Men, Women, and Chainsaws: Gender in the Modern Horror Film* (Princeton: Princeton University Press, 1992). Clover read the modern "slasher" and "rape-revenge" films as not simply being reductively read as uniformly misogynistic texts, but films that challenge and radically reconfigure cultural and political notions of "sex" and "gender." Interestingly, one of the critics who lead the charge against these films was Meyer compatriot Roger Ebert, who vilified the "slasher" film as sadistic and misogynistic, and in particular vilified *I Spit on Your Grave* as a disgusting rape-fantasy (however, Ebert expressed a fondness for *Last House on the Left*). One can only assume what similar-minded critics would make of the rape scenes in Russ Meyer's films, some co-scripted by Ebert.

CHAPTER THREE ◊ "WELCOME TO VIOLENCE"

which theorize the inherent relationship of sex and power. In this context, a textual analysis of each of Russ Meyer's four roughies will follow.

LORNA (1964)

Deconstructing "Lorna"

Faced with the declining interest in the nudie-cutie, Meyer conceived *Lorna*: "I said, I must do something like foreign films, only it will be Erskine Caldwell, and it will be a morality play, and we'll borrow heavily from the Bible, and I'll find a girl with giant breasts."[70] Given the influence of *Bitter Rice*, *God's Little Acre*, and *Li'l Abner*, one is tempted to point to *Lorna* as a rather malicious critique of "the idiocy of rural life." In *Lorna* and the subsequent *Mudhoney*, Meyer presents caricatures of ignorant, libidinous, and licentious Southern sexpots and hillbillies living, raping, and killing each other in isolated squalor. However, regarding the specific influence of *Li'l Abner*, Meyer explained his interest in Al Capp as a discussion of sexual politics. "If you study his cartoons, the women are all bright, voluptuous, and/or ugly, but they're the ones who really control the men."[71] Likewise, Frasier observed, "In *Lorna*... as in *Li'l Abner*, one is immediately stuck by the incongruity of a stunningly beautiful and physically awesome woman living in primitive, squalid conditions and relentlessly pursued by men neither her physical or intellectual equal."[72]

If female passivity is treated problematically in *Eve and the Handyman*, it is treated with absolute contempt in *Lorna*, and turned on its head by *Faster, Pussycat! Kill! Kill!* and subsequent Meyer films. As a point of comparison, I would briefly like to offer another discourse of sexuality in the same medium as Capp and contemporary to Meyer: the underground comics of Robert Crumb. Like Meyer, Crumb's work frequently deals with the relationship between sexuality and politics, and does so in such a satirical manner that it is difficult to tell who the target of satire is: masculinity, feminists, or the artist himself. Also like Meyer, Crumb was frequently attacked by critics for male chauvinism, and perhaps in response to this criticism wrote *Motor City Comics* in the late 1960s, both featuring Lenore Goldberg, his depiction of a feminist, counter-culture female. Yet by the second issue Lenore has already given up on revolution and retired to a rural commune to roam naked, make love and babies, and generally fit into the traditional female role of domesticity. As Mark James Estern observed, "What is upsetting about Crumb's attitude towards women is that he seems unable to escape chauvinism... the lead stories in *Motor City Comics* Nos. 1 and 2, in which 'Lenore Goldberg and her Girl Commandos' are featured, both end in cop-outs: in [No. 1] Lenore talks revolution while blowing her boyfriend, and in [No. 2] she has a child and decided that 'life goes on an'

---

70. As quoted in Turan and Zito, 22.

71. As quoted in Goad, 5.

72. *Russ Meyer — The Life and Films*, 7-8.

43

LIPS HIPS TITS POWER ◊ THE FILMS OF RUSS MEYER

things change'."[73]

    Indeed, in Crumb one sees an utterly reactionary critique of the social and sexual position of women. Crumb's "Lenore" finds satisfaction in both rural isolation and female domesticity; for Meyer's "Lorna," these are the very conditions of her alienation. Unlike Crumb, who attempts to be feminist and fails, *Lorna* reads like a misogynist fantasy: a sexually-frustrated housewife yearns for excitement, falls in love with the escaped convict after he rapes her, and is eventually killed for her sin of adultery. However, rather than simply catering to misogynistic fantasies, *Lorna* can be read as a darkly satirical and even profoundly political critique of the role of women in American culture. The

73. *A History of the Underground Comics* (Berkeley: Ronin Press), 130.

CHAPTER THREE ◊ "WELCOME TO VIOLENCE"

problematic, and political, depiction of femininity occurs not at the level of *content*, but of *form*. As noted previously, Meyer's methods recall the "radical aesthetics" of Eisenstein and Brecht. This is not to say any implementation of "montage" or "estrangement" necessitates a politically radical work of art. Rather, Meyer's use of intellectual montage and estrangement between film and spectator in *Lorna* serves to complicate the seeming ideological coherence in what appears to be a highly sexist film. In *Lorna*, montages set up parallel, metaphorical and overt (read: heavy-handed) relationships between characters. Following her sexually-unsatisfying encounter with her husband, Lorna (Lorna Maitland) wanders outside, contemplating the possibility of leaving "this god-forsaken hole." A hallucinatory dream sequence follows, with Lorna living it up in a superimposed world of glitz and neon lights. A close-up of the ecstatic Lorna freezes: the scene abruptly cuts to a loudspeaker, the sound of wailing saxophones merging into the sound of a blaring siren, then to a shot of a prison. Just as Lorna has contemplated "freedom," the film depicts a prison break, suggesting Lorna's own status as a prisoner attempting to escape from her social and sexual situation. From the shot of the prison, the camera lurches through weeds, swamps, and streams. The series of shots retroactively becomes point-of-view shots when a close-up of the escaped convict (Mark Bradley) lurches into the frame. This convict, who has been thematically linked to Lorna's situation of confinement through both the montages of escape and the presence of nature signs which become associated with the woman, is next shown in a close-up washing his face in a stream. The shot cuts to a shot of Jim (James Rucker), Lorna's husband, washing his face in the sink: their positions and the camera angle are nearly identical. The convict and Jim now become cinematically connected, and indeed, their "positions" are metaphorically identical in the course of the film: *both* become important figures in enforcing Lorna's servitude. Soon after, Jim prepares his lunch: a close-up of his knife slicing food cuts to a close-up of a switchblade compulsively chopping at the rail of a boat; the next shot reveals the knife-holder to be Jonah (Doc Scortt), the cretinous, vile sidekick of the alcoholic woman-hater Luther (Hal Hooper). Here the All-American, handsome Jim is connected to a far more repulsive and disturbing depiction of American masculinity; also, this foreshadows the connection between (phallic) "blades" and a homeosocial, masculine order attained in the film's violent and tragic conclusion. Throughout this brief cycle of cinematic metaphors and comparisons, meaning is produced by the dramatic form (the collision of shots) rather than dramatic content (narrative).

The Brechtian character of *Lorna* is evident from the opening scene. Meyer violates continuity rules by not offering a stable shot but instead a tracking shot of a road. After the camera speeds down the road for several seconds, including dissolves to exaggerate the amount of time passed, it comes to a halt as the viewer confronts an archetypal Southern preacher (James Griffith) standing in the middle of the road. He directly addresses the audience, spouting Biblical dogma about sin and retribution. While a character in *Lorna*, throughout the film the Preacher interacts with the viewer, and not the other characters except to comment on their actions to the audience with apocalyptic doom and fury. The narrator in *Lorna* also becomes an object of satire, a parody of Southern evangelicalism, whose sermons amount to little more than a pastiche of fragmented and occasionally misquoted excepts from the Bible. As noted earlier, Meyer's narrations and narrators often qualify and satirize the very messages the film is "required" to promote, the social and moral message of sexual fidelity as well as the ideological project of many of the roughies, establishing the place and position of women.

After delivering his sermon, the Preacher dramatically steps aside and lets the camera pass, and it continues to speed down the winding road, with an ensuring montage of the camera speeding pass nameless rural towns, close-ups of asphalt, and long desolate stretches of road. The camera pulls to a stop as two males burst out of the bar: Luther and Jonah. Unable or unwilling to score at the bar, they soon encounter Ruthie (Althea Currier), who is drunkenly trying to make her way home. Ruthie seems thoroughly out-of-place in the rural poverty of the town. Unlike the slovenly men, who wear the same clothes during Lorna's two-day narrative span, Ruthie is dressed in a cosmopolitan outfit, as if returning from work in the city instead of a rural bar. She rebuffs Luther's attempts to pick her up, and as she walks away, Luther and Jonah pursue her home. Luther knocks on the door, and after being told in no uncertain terms by Ruthie to leave her alone, he forces his way through the door and proceeds to sexually assault her in the bedroom while Jonah watches from the porch, observing through a window.

It is important that *Lorna* begins with a rape, and the depiction of rape becomes a necessary parameter in *Lorna*'s discussion of sexuality and power, especially given the pivotal rape of Lorna by the Convict later in the film. Ruthie, in one sense, is introduced to the film only to be raped, and once her "purpose" is served, she is not seen for the remainder of the film. She is introduced, pursued and literally "put in her place" by being raped in the bedroom. Yet Ruthie's rape not only demonstrates "the woman's place", it designates who "the woman" is. Carol J. Clover wrote, "If [a woman] is raped because she is a woman, then the logic of popular culture also dictates she is a woman because she is raped."[74] In this regard, rape is not only an act of demonstrating male power over women, but a signifying practice of designating who is male and female. In the narrative of *Lorna*, the title character first expresses dissatisfaction with her role as "a woman," accepts through rape the status of being a "woman," and is ultimately eliminated for being "a woman." Also critical to this scene is the role of Jonah,

74. *Men, Women, and Chainsaws*, 160.

CHAPTER THREE ◊ "WELCOME TO VIOLENCE"

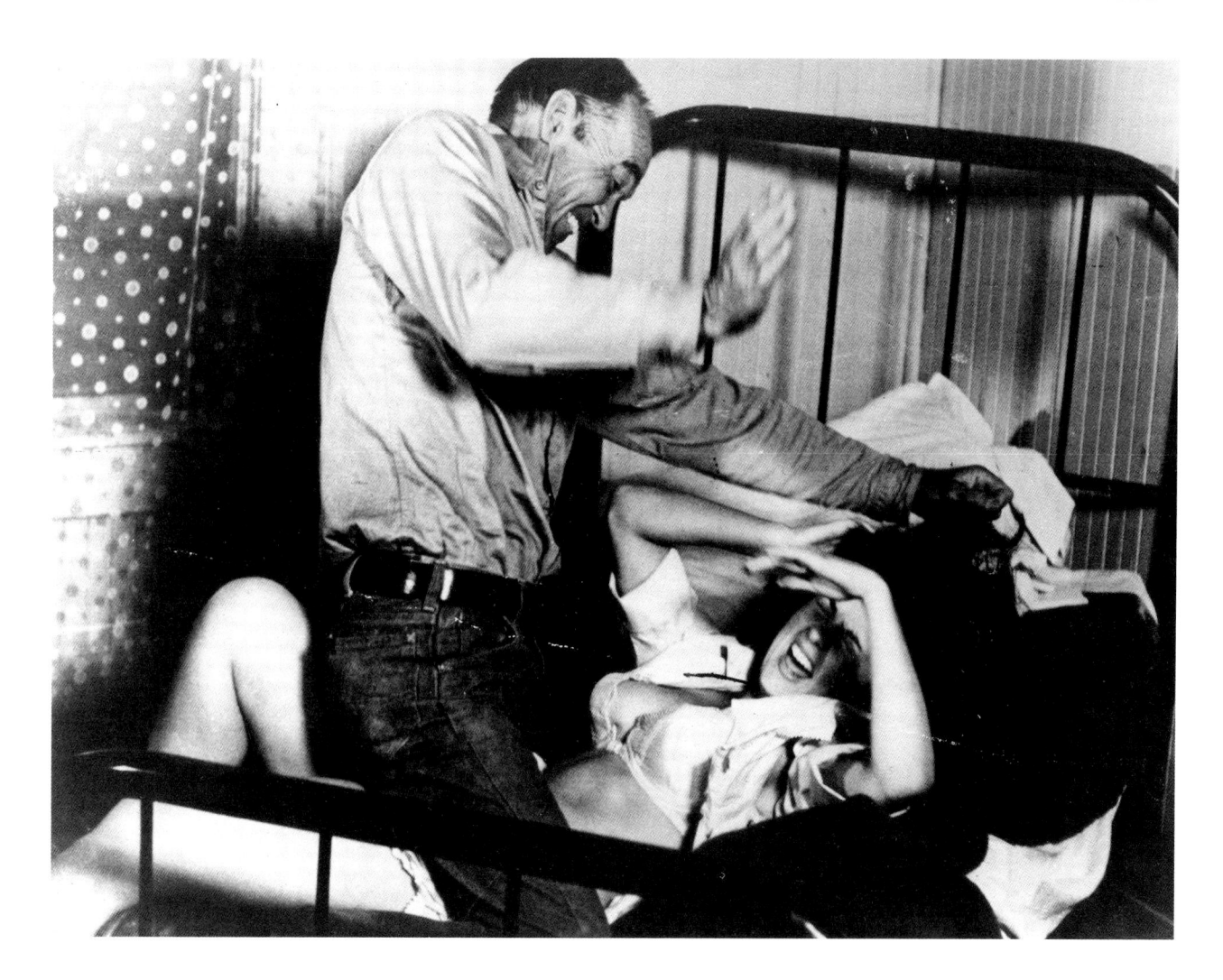

who is intercut into the rape sequence growing visibly excited as the rape becomes more violent. As the rape nears its conclusion, he closes his eyes and shudders, seemingly reaching a climax in his pants while watching the scene. Jonah represents the male spectator and the "sadistic-voyeuristic" drive; he is a parody of the male viewer, both a "mirror" of the male spectator watching the scene and a satirical critique of Meyer's own perceived audience, the adult-theater "raincoat crowd" who patronized the roughies for sadistic and sexual pleasure and satisfaction. It also finally bears mention that Ruthie is an

48

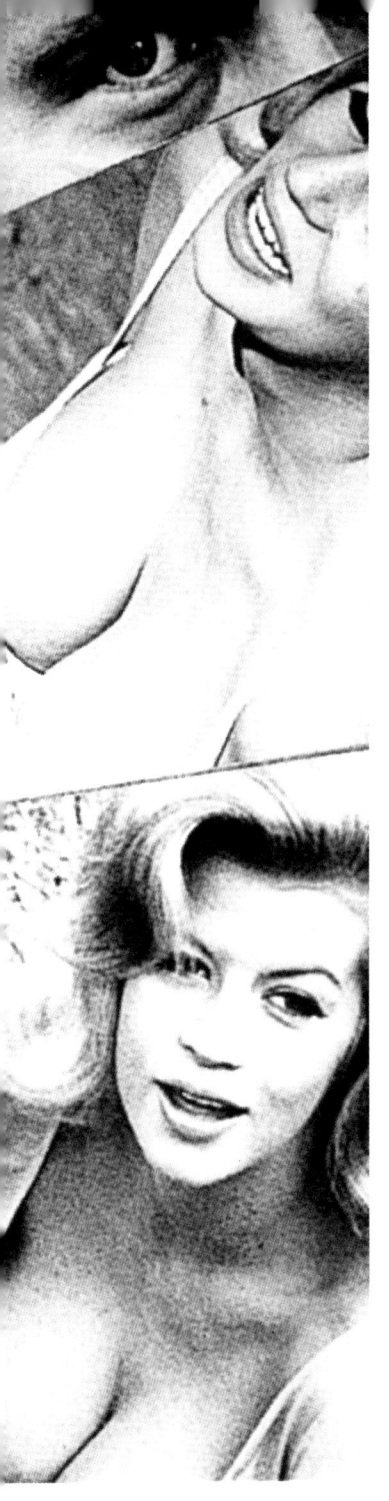

CHAPTER THREE ◊ "WELCOME TO VIOLENCE"

unwilling participant in the proceedings: bloodied and sobbing, she denounces Luther as "a dirty bastard" as he exits.

Following the rape, Luther proudly swaggers out and is met by Jonah, who rushes to his side. "Did she hurt you, Luther?," he absurdly asks, homoerotically examining Luther's body for injuries. Luther's rape of Ruthie also becomes important in establishing the pecking order of a homeosocial, misogynistic social order, with Luther designated the "man" because he committed a rape, now dominant over the doting, submissive Jonah. Nonetheless, Luther is still dissatisfied, and barks, "You know the broad I really want!" Luther's ominous threat cuts to the opening credits. The word LORNA appears over a swampy, rural river, connecting the female name to water and nature images. As the credits continue, the camera moves downstream, not unlike the opening shots down the highway. *Lorna* stars Lorna Maitland in the title role, again obscuring the relationship between actor and character (Lorna Maitland plays Lorna, James Rucker plays Jim), and when referring to "Lorna" one is simultaneously referring to the actress and the character. Moreover, the cocktail-jazz title song, composed by Hal Hooper, the actor who plays Luther, is repeatedly heard as an instrumental theme alongside Lorna's on-screen presence: an irony is established between Lorna and her musical theme, which was composed by the actor portraying a rapist.

As the credits end, the scene shifts to a small house on the banks of the river late at night. The shot cuts to a lantern and the pans to Jim working on correspondence school homework while he overhears Lorna having an erotic dream. The shot cuts to Lorna lying in bed as he enters from the background, undresses, and joins her (of course, he leaves his underwear on). The shot of Lorna and her husband in bed pans across the bedroom and to an open window as the wind blows through the curtains. For an interminable length of time, about 20 seconds, the camera stays on the curtain as Lorna implores her husband to have sex with her (one hesitates using the term "making love" in a Russ Meyer film).

This long take on the curtains is important in two respects. One is that it continues to manifest a relationship between Lorna's sexual desires and the *outdoors*, the window opening to the outside from the restrictions of the bedroom, which has previously been coded as the site of male domination over the female (Luther's rape of Ruthie). The bedroom becomes a site of both rape and male-dominated intercourse, a blurred distinction of vital importance in Lorna's subsequent rape by with the Convict. The other function is far more subtle and ironic. I would argue here that Meyer is also satirizing the cinematic depiction of "eroticism" common to both "art" and "sex" films at the time. Meyer stated about his films, "The public was waiting for something new... I think they were becoming disenchanted with some of the so-called European sex-films, like some

49

of the early [Gina] Lolbrigida films, in which there's *a lot of promise but never any kind of real fulfillment... they would always cut to the curtain blowing* and things of that nature."[75]

Meyer's use of the blowing curtain here can also be read in reference to a specific cinematic cliché that is referenced to sexual arousal and disappointment for both the female character and the male spectator. Indeed, the shot of the blowing curtain abruptly cuts to a shot of a visibly displeased Lorna lying next to her spent husband: the building eroticism of the scene is comically and sardonically negated. The male spectator's sexual disappointment, not seeing anything happen on-screen, and Lorna's sexual frustration are connected to the cliché of the blowing curtain, "promise without fulfillment." For both the male spectator and Lorna, "nothing happens."

Naked, Lorna gets out of bed and walks to the open window; she stares out, and then dons a robe and walks outside. A flashback begins. In a breathy, echoed, at times nearly inaudible voice, Lorna describes her formative relationship with her husband. Her narration is matched by a montage of shots, all of which are slightly out of focus and waver. As she talks about Jim being shy, a gentleman, wanting to improve himself, and "putting her on a pedestal," the viewer sees shots of clothes strewn across the grass. This cuts to a shot of sunlight streaming through the tree branches as Lorna describes how much she began to care about Jim. This shot, in turn, cuts to a montage of shots of water: a ripple in a pond cuts to a running stream which cuts to river currents and finally cuts to an out of focus shot that resembles both flowing water and sunlight flowing through tree branches. To state, or thoroughly overstate, the relationship between water and female libido, Lorna's narration becomes more erotic and breathless during this quick succession of water images. She describes how she asked him to, wanted him to, and *"even gave him my permission,"* but instead Jim put her "back on the pedestal" and told her his intentions were honorable.

These nature scenes cut to another montage: imposing, low-angle, canted shots of a church exterior and cathedral spires that tilt at unnerving Expressionist angles, the images still wavering. Over these intimidating architectural images of religious morality, the wedding vows are remembered and recited in Lorna's voice-over, until she reaches "I now pronounce you – ," at which point the shot cuts to a close-up of Lorna back outside her home as she contemptuously spits "– man and wife." This sequence of shots offers a critique of marriage as something used to rein in or restrain sexuality, a theme common to all of Meyer's films. As Bataille wrote, "Sexuality appeared to contain something so foul and dangerous, so equivocal, that one could not approach it without taking multiple detours. This is what the rules of marriage were designed for."[76]

75. As quoted in Turan and Zito, 11. Emphasis mine.

76. *The Accursed Share, Vol. II*, 126.

CHAPTER THREE ◊ "WELCOME TO VIOLENCE"

As Lorna looks into the river, a point-of-view shot shows Lorna's own distorted reflection in the water. It is this distorted reflection that helps to define the dream-sequence that follows. In this "dream," Lorna imagines a life outside her rural captivity, a life of cosmopolitan adventure set to swinging jazz and night clubs (parodying the vision of American consumer modernity celebrated by *Playboy*). The sequence becomes a barrage of clichés and kitsch visions of neon lights, advertisements, and saxophones superimposed over Lorna, who guzzles champagne and joyously dances topless save for a string of pearls. The subjective view (Lorna's vision of a happy life), and the objective view (the camera's translation of that dream via montage and kitsch images) becomes blurred, and in later films Meyer will often insert subjective, non-diagetic inserts into the story to express inner thoughts of characters or make metaphorical statements about the narrative. Lorna's reflection in the water can also be read in the context of Jacques Lacan's famous "mirror-stage," the moment in which the subject recognizes oneself in the mirror as both a distinct entity and yet not the whole of the world, a moment of both narcissism and alienation. Yet Lorna appears as only a distorted, unrecognizable form in "the mirror," a shapeless unformed being. It is with the dream sequence that she enters "the symbolic order," the realm of language and signification, by which Lorna becomes (over)determined by the world of signs (literally). Indeed, she not only enters the realm of language, but Louis Althusser's realm of "ideology... [as a] system of representations... in ideology, the real relation is invariably invested in the imaginary relation, a relation that *expresses a will*... a hope or nostalgia, rather than describing a reality."[77] Not only is Lorna's dreary existence confining, but her dream of freedom from her rural and sexual confinement is only an *image* of freedom: a pathetic dream of cosmopolitan leisure. This sequence concludes with the aforementioned cut to the prison break, where Lorna's dream of freedom is matched by the Convict's flight from prison. However, Lorna's "escape," her relationship with the Convict is one that eventually offers no freedom or escape, but rather, seals her doom.

77. *For Marx*, trans. Ben Brewster (New York: Verso, 1991), 231, 233-4.

"Strange Bedfellows": The Rape of Lorna

After Jim goes of to work at the salt-flats with Luther and Jonah, Lorna walks to a nearby stream and swims in the nude. In many of Meyer's films there are scenes of nude women in the water: bathing, showering, swimming. While the cynic could rightly argue that these are obvious ways for Meyer to incorporate female nudity, it is also a constant thematic device to equate female libido with water. There are various shots of Lorna posing in the water: in one, she is waist deep in the stream with arms stretched upward picking leaves off trees; in another, she is laconically resting in the water with her breasts barely submerged out of view. Again the question of the bourgeois nude is raised, and

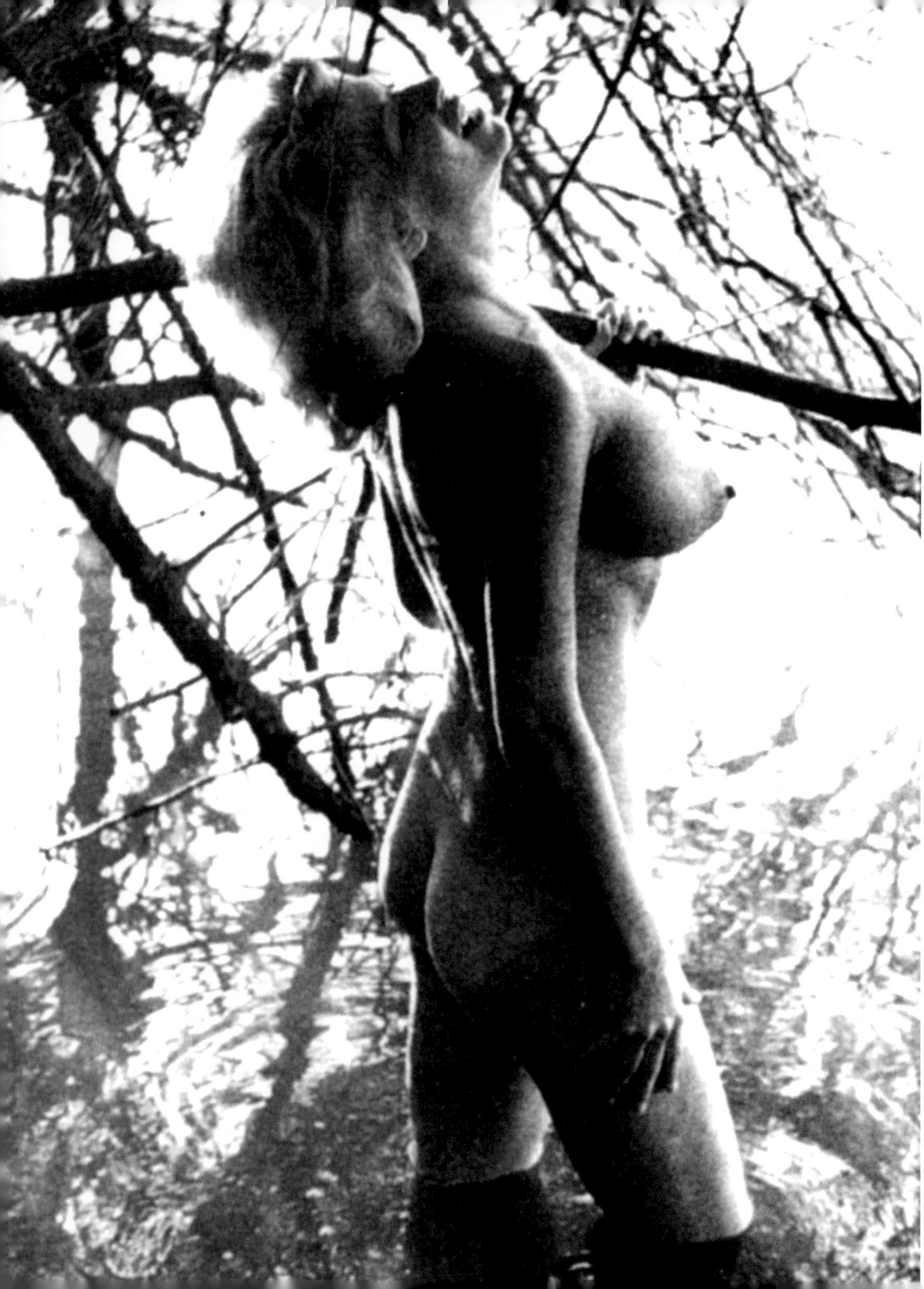

CHAPTER THREE ◊ "WELCOME TO VIOLENCE"

the relationship to the pin-up nude and the painted nude. It is not a stretch of the imagination to imagine Lorna's poses in canonical nude paintings, as well as obviously pin-up photography (two mediums not at all distinct from each other, as Berger observed).

Lorna's bathing is accompanied by an easy-listening version of the title theme (as noted, given Hal Hooper's authorship, a musical motif inscribed with the threat of rape). This is a contrast to when the theme his heard when she dresses while Jim prepares to leave for work: this version is a percussive, electronically-treated piano that resembles the prepared piano pieces of John Cage rather than the cocktail-jazz version that accompanies her bathing. Lorna's bathing music is pleasant, harmonious, and even innocuous, suggesting a placid, kitsch sense of enjoyment; obviously the music heard earlier suggests martial and musical "discord." Moreover, like the rape scene that is intercut with Jonah as he watches the assault on Ruthie, the bathing scenes are intercut with shots of the Convict. The crosscutting both defuses the eroticism of watching Lorna bathing and heightens the tension of their inevitable encounter. Musically, the shots of the Convict are accompanied by a jazz drum solo, both arrhythmic and atonal, which also interrupts the flow of the bathing music. There is a sense of intrusion and impending conflict; both the intercut shots and scores overlap and "collide" against each other as the Convict nears his inexorable approach towards Lorna.

When the Convict finally encounters Lorna, he simply attacks and rapes her. Lorna, who initially resists, succumbs, and then begins to enjoy the attack. However, the rape scene is far more problematic than it appears. As the actual rape unfolds, the music is harsh, furious, and discordant, matching the convict's violent domination over Lorna. When she succumbs and begins to enjoy the rape (or, as I would suggest, the moment when rape and intercourse become equated), the cocktail-jazz version of the "Lorna" theme swells into the foreground, a dark, satirical statement of the theme's inherent relationship to rape and domination as well as an utterly perverse mockery of romance film clichés. Moreover, if spectatorship, as Laura Mulvey argued, is necessarily established between the male spectator and the male character, the viewer is placed in the position of identifying with *both* the rapist and Lorna. The male spectator has previously been attached to both Lorna (the shot of the blowing curtain that connects Lorna and the male spectator's sexual frustration), as well as the Convict (the point-of-view shots during the prison escape). In the rape scene, there is a critical moment where an orgasmic Lorna is shown from the point-of-view of the Convict, where the male spectator is linked to the rapist, and the fantasy of a (female) victim enjoying being raped. This shot is followed by, or more correctly, *collides* with point-of-view shot from Lorna's perspective, putting the (male) spectator in the position of being raped as a close-up of the lurching, leering

Convict is shown. The (male) viewer is forced to "identify" with both the male attacker and the female victim.

Defenders of Meyer have mistakenly defended the rape scene itself; Morton wrote Lorna "doesn't mind – at least it takes him more than two minutes to come."[78] Even Bataille subscribed to the myth that sexual assault arouses women: "many women can not reach their climax without pretending to themselves they are being raped."[79] Others such as frequent Meyer critic Danny Peary have expressed understandable reservations that Lorna finds sexual enjoyment in being raped.[80] However, to either dismiss the rape scene or dismiss the entire film because of the rape scene neglects an essential theme in Meyer's work: that sex is charged with violent aggression and violence is charged with erotic release (to recall Bataille: "violence, the core of eroticism, leaves the weightiest problems unanswered"). Rape and seduction, intercourse and assault, violence and eroticism all become indistinct and interchangeable variants of libidinal drives, where human sexuality has an extraordinary political dimension. It is here that Meyer's depiction of rape has a highly unlikely "political bedfellow": feminist and anti-pornography activist Andrea Dworkin, who made a similar, inseparable connection between rape and intercourse: "Intercourse occurs in a context of a power relationship... intercourse as an act expresses the power men have over women. Without being what... society recognizes as rape, it is what society... recognizes as domination."[81] *Lorna* also theorizes this very equation of rape and intercourse as the means of domination by which Lorna is "put in her place" for the remainder of the film. As noted, Lorna's captivity is both as a sexual prisoner to her husband, who can not fulfill her sexually (the bedroom scene) or socially (the dream sequence). When the Convict rapes Lorna, he does so in a meadow by the stream: a male intrusion and victory in the female site (or zone) of sexual energy. Thus, nature images, closely linked to sexual desire by the woman, are tied to nature itself ("Mother Nature") and the depiction of male domination of nature. Lorna's rape in the meadow is consistent with a cultural metaphor where domination is equated to both woman and nature, as noted by Max Horkheimer and Theodor W. Adorno: "As a representative of nature, woman in bourgeois society has become an enigmatic image of irresistibility and powerlessness. In this way she reflects for domination the pure lie that posits the subjection instead of the redemption of nature."[82]

The grotesque absurdity of Lorna falling in love with her rapist is played out through the rest of the film. Having been "conquered," Lorna brings the Convict back to the site of social convention and morality, the home, and away from her now-conquered domain, the outdoors. The convict has not only become her "lover" but her "conqueror," her act of transgression against the construct of matrimony also an act of surrender and compliance to the Convict. While she bitterly complains about being "cooped up like an animal" and being told when

78. Vale and Juno, eds., 86.

79. *Erotism*, 107.

80. See Frasier, 81.

81. *Intercourse* (New York: The Free Press, 1997), 125-6.

82. *Dialectic of Enlightenment*, trans. John Cumming (New York: Continuum, 1997), 71-2.

CHAPTER THREE ◊ **"WELCOME TO VIOLENCE"**

to "sit up and when to lie down," she is utterly submissive to the Convict (she can, at least, manage to refuse to make lunch for Jim earlier in the film). First, she goes and buys groceries, and learning of his identity, returns home to confront him. However, she quickly suggests that she join him rather than turn him in, to which he angrily responds by telling her to make him something to eat. She obeys. He then decides to rest, and Lorna follows him, diligently unmaking the bed for him, and they again engage in sexual intercourse, unaware that Jim and the others have left work early. Again the intercourse is depicted problematically: there is a point-of-view, extreme close-up of an open mouth in the act of a kiss, and it is impossible to tell whose mouth it is. Identification is ambiguous, and there is no clear delineation between the point-of-view of Lorna, the Convict, and the (male) spectator; there is even the possibility, given the homoerotic subtext of the film, that the male spectator is briefly "making it" with the Convict. The music now becomes a hard-bop version of the "Lorna" theme, as if a middle ground had been negotiated between the free jazz signifying the Convict and the schmaltzy jazz signifying Lorna. Moreover, the sex scene is intercut with reoccurring shots of Jim and the others headed down the river in a boat, returning to Jim and Lorna's home. Not only does this foreshadow the impending disaster, but it serves as a crude metaphor for sexual intercourse as the boat full of men plows through the water. When she hears the arrival of her husband, Lorna bolts out of bed, looks outside, and hurriedly begins to dress. As she turns to face the Convict, a medium shot shows Lorna again next to the bedroom window: it is now closed and the curtain motionless. Whereas Lorna imagined "a way out," the freedom of the open window and the outdoors, she has actually found herself more trapped than before (the entrapment of the closed window and the indoors). By submitting to the Convict, Lorna ironically, in the cruellest sense of the term, becomes an obedient servant relegated to kitchen and bedroom duties.

Adding Insult to Injury: The Death of Lorna

By the conclusion of *Lorna*, she has been raped into compliance and submission, but Lorna also has to be punished for her infidelity, in that sexploitation films of the era had to provide socially-redeeming messages (read: consequences) in order to avoid legal obstacles such as censorship or obscenity charges.[83] During the events with Lorna and the Convict, there is an important subplot running parallel to them: the narrative involving Jim, Luther, and Jonah at work in the salt-fields. The Preacher also appears, just as the men arrive for work and after the assault on Lorna. He offers more profoundly ominous (and absurd) commentary on adultery, lechery, and gossip, all directed at the audience, spouting verbose Biblical analogies about Jim and Luther as they walk past him. He also interjects the story of Sodom, foreshadowing the impending death of

83. Despite *Lorna*'s contrived moral ending, the film was banned in Florida, Maryland, and Pennsylvania.

LIPS HIPS TITS POWER ◊ THE FILMS OF RUSS MEYER

Lorna for her "sins." Again, the "representation" becomes "commentary," a moment of Brechtian theater where the actions of the characters and reactions of the audience are mediated by the Preacher's evangelical *non-sequiturs*.

Much of the subplot concerns Jim enduring, if not always comprehending, Luther's drunken but unknowingly accurate insults about Jim's inability to satisfy his wife and Jim's preference for "making it" with his correspondence school books. Yet it is only when Luther composes an obscene song attacking Lorna's virtue (again recalling the intertextual irony of the "Lorna" theme that was composed by Hal Hooper, the actor playing Luther), and finally calling her "a slut" that Jim is pushed towards physical violence. In the

CHAPTER THREE ◊ "WELCOME TO VIOLENCE"

midst of the barren salt-fields, Jim and Luther slug it out with both their shovels and then their fists. Finally, Jim emerges the victor, pummeling Luther into submission. The point-of-view shot of Luther being beaten is tied to masculine violence, recalling Lorna's point-of-view shot of her rapist. Jim's fists flail at the camera trapped below him: here the cinematic barrier between character and audience is not only broken, but the spectator is "attacked" by a character in the film. Jim also quickly disarms Jonah of his phallic switchblade when he tries to intervene, and Jonah responds with frustrated crying, a "feminine" response to his quickly-lost masculinity. One of the most absurd moments in the film becomes Luther's transformation for woman-hating rapist to "sensitive guy" after his beating by Jim. Of course, Luther's new-found tenderness, contriteness, and sympathy for Lorna all reek of satire. His new-found "feminine" side is the product of a masculine beating. Thus, when Adorno wrote, "without a single exception, feminine natures are conformist,"[84] it is not to say that women are naturally submissive or conformist, but rather the conformity of "femininity" is a production of masculine domination and violence (although it should be stated that Meyer is probably far less a critic of "masculinity" than Adorno).

In *Lorna*, the final battle for Lorna's fate is between the Convict and Jim, with Lorna a powerless bystander and spectator to her own destiny. The final battle takes place in the front yard, an "outdoors" that is constrained within the private property of the home, signifying the status of the female as sexual property being fought for by two men. It is the politics of this "erotic triangle" that Eve Sedgwick noted:

"The power relationships between men and women appear to be dependent on the power relationships between men and men, [which] suggests that the large-scale social structures are congruent with the male-male-female triangle... We can go further than that, to say that in any male-dominated society, there is a special relationship between male homeosocial (including homosexual) desire and the structures for maintaining and transmitting that power."[85]

Jim has already spent himself defending Lorna in the salt-fields, and quickly proves to be no match for the Convict. Whether motivated by shame, a retreat to social and sexual convention, and/or the need to construct a moral ending for the film, Lorna rushes into the fray to save her husband, who is about to be impaled by the Convict with a pair of tongs. Luther snaps his fingers and Jonah hands over his switchblade; as the "man" is the homoerotic couple, Luther can appropriate Jonah's phallic weapon at will. As Lorna and the Convict struggle, Luther hurdles the switchblade into the convict's back (a method of murder seen in a number of future Meyer films). Lorna is trapped under the convict as he falls on top of her mortally wounded, and she is fatally impaled by the tongs, once

---

84. *Minima Moralia*, 96.

85. *Between Men: Male Homeosocial Desire and English Literature* (New York: Columbia University Press, 1985), 25.

again "penetrated" by the Convict. As the couple fall out of the bottom of the frame, the shot cuts to a stunning reverse zoom that reveals the Grim Reaper standing on a rocky hill, a moment that juxtaposes both kitsch melodrama with the beauty of Expressionism, silent cinema, or Ingmar Bergman. The sobbing Jim crawls over and separates the dead couple, "too late" in preventing their tragic union.

    The Preacher again appears on-screen and stares directly into the camera. He piously (and laughably) asks "Do you do unto others as they do unto you?" He then pauses, and bellows, "Woe to the libertine who preys on the weak, for the hour will come when he shall be the weak," which is matched by a close-up of the switchblade that zooms backward, recalling the shot of the Grim Reaper, revealing the corpse of the convict. "A victim of greater libertines," he continues, which cuts to a shot of Luther and Jonah, the "victors" in an apocalyptic moment that establishes a perverse homeosocial order that eliminates "otherness" of the female body (Lorna) and assigns "femininity" to the male characters (Jonah's submissiveness, Luther's contriteness, Jim's hysterical sobs). While heterosexual order is marked by the domination of the one (the man) over the other (the woman), the male homeosocial order is achieved by erasing the other (the woman) entirely. Indeed, death itself is associated with penetrating phallic signifiers: the switchblade, the pair of tongs, the Grim Reaper's scythe (again, one can recall the early montage of Jim's knife and Jonah's switchblade that connects the two men). The Preacher then reprises the tale of Lot's wife, "who looked back and was turned into a pillar of salt." This cuts to a non-diagetic insert of the idyllic nude: the dead Lorna laying in the salt-fields, her genitalia strategically covered by dunes of salt. In another cruel irony, Luther escapes narrative punishment for raping Ruthie by becoming a nice guy, but Lorna is required to pay for her infidelity, a product of rape, with death. Yet, in the film's internal logic, Lorna has not been turned into salt for her sins and transgression, but is rather a casualty of masculine violence and domination: her naked, lifeless form laying in a barren zone of masculine libido; in the black and white film, the salt-fields appear much like desert sand, and the desert becomes central to Russ Meyer's later films as a site of masculine libidinal energy. "As ye sow, SO SHALL YE REAP!" the Preacher warns the audience. The reference to "reaping" also again references the Grim Reaper, connected to patriarchy by the phallus in the form of phallic weapons and the death and elimination of the woman. The warning is not only trite, but sinister and sardonic. As the screen fades-out, the establishment of a sadistic, patriarchal order, the ideological project of the roughies, is achieved, but only in a problematized, deconstructed and satirized form. In this context, *Lorna* is a film that both constructs and implodes the roughie. The inherent and intimate relations between power and sexuality are essayed through the double-edged sword of "humor and evil."

CHAPTER THREE ◊ "WELCOME TO VIOLENCE"

MUDHONEY (1965)

"Too Much Freud and Not Enough Flesh"

Following *Lorna*, *Mudhoney* is another tale of rural claustrophobia, sexual frustration, and smoldering violence, this time set in Depression-era Missouri; it incorporates many of the same stylistic influences that made up *Lorna*: Erskine Caldwell, Neo-Realism, *film noir*, and *Li'l Abner*. Meyer has also wryly referred to these films as his "John Steinbeck period."[86] However, *Mudhoney* was not an overwhelming financial success. Frasier noted the film's "lukewarm reception Meyer attribute[d] to an unsophisticated sexploitation audience more interested in flesh than Freud."[87] Indeed, as my analysis of *Mudhoney* will suggest, there is a real truth to his statement: *Mudhoney* is a film that teems with as much Freudian theory as it does stale swamp water and powder-keg passions. However, unlike the Oedipal model of sexuality that *Eve and the Handyman* relied on, it is Freud's later theoretical work that figures prominently in *Mudhoney*. Horrified by the carnage of World War I, Freud questioned why humanity seemed determined to destroy itself. His work from *Beyond the Pleasure Principle* (1920) to his death in 1939 was devoted to the discussion of two conflicting drives which shaped the course of civilization: Eros and Death. Freud wrote:

"Civilization is a process in the service of Eros, whose purpose is to combine single human individuals, and after that families, then races, peoples and nations, into one great unity... libidinally bound to one another... Man's natural aggressive instinct... opposes this programme of civilization. The aggressive instinct is the derivative of and the main representative of the death instinct which we have found alongside of Eros... the struggle [is] then between Eros and Death, between the instinct for life and the instinct for destruction."[88]

The "instinct for destruction" is depicted in *Mudhoney*'s rural isolation with Sidney Brenshaw, played by Hal Hooper, who reprises his role as an alcoholic, woman-hating rapist from *Lorna*. The first shot of the film is of the town whorehouse, and the sound of a loud party can be heard as the shot cuts to a pair of boots stumbling out the front door (the boots are those of Brenshaw). The camera tracks the pair of boots as they drunkenly make their way to a pick-up truck, and cuts to a close-up of the boots stepping on the gas pedal. *Mudhoney*'s credits then begin over a point-of-view shot from the backseat; the back of the driver's head is visible on the left side of the screen as the car races forward. The point-of-view belongs to the viewer, who is in the position of helplessly being "along for the ride" with the drunken driver. This shot alternates with a close-up of a tire spinning against the road. Both motion and stasis are implied: *motion*

86. As quoted in Ebert, "Russ Meyer: King of the Nudies," page 5 of 14.

87. *Russ Meyer – The Life and Films*, 9.

88. *Civilization and Its Discontents*, ed. and trans. James Strachly (New York: W.W. Norton and Company, 1969), 77.

in the point-of-view shot of the car's forward path, *stasis* through the spinning tire and the desolation of the unchanging scenery. The montages articulate the tension of "going nowhere fast," and serves as a visual metaphor of Brenshaw's "death drive" (pun intended). While Meyer points to Steinbeck, it is also quite possible to compare *Mudhoney* to the great French naturalist writer Émile Zola, whose characters often undergo similar descents into hell: alcoholism, madness, murder, and ultimately self-annihilation.

Herbert Marcuse wrote, "man leans to give up momentary, uncertain, and destructive pleasure for delayed, restrained but 'assured' pleasure."[89] Sidney Brenshaw represents the figure who does *not* relinquish monetary and destructive pleasure for the restrained pleasure offered by civilization. However, he does not simply represent the Freudian *pleasure principle*, the want-of and striving-for immediate gratification, prior to entry into the *reality principle*, the regime of civilization. Brenshaw's anti-social and licentious behavior and actions are equal parts pure self-will and pure self-destruction: he embodies what Marcuse calls *the nirvana principle*, "the terrifying convergence of pleasure and death."[90] And while Sidney Brenshaw certainly can not be considered a sympathetic character, he does serve as sort of a tragic character, in that his actions are the result of his fatal flaw, the drive of the death instinct. Sidney's alcohol-fueled spiral of violence and destruction is, in this sense, both his downfall and his release from the maddening economic, social, and sexual constraints of the town. Marcuse argued, "the death instinct is destructiveness not for its own sake, but for the relief of tension. The descent towards death is an unconscious flight from pain and want. It is the expression of the eternal struggle against suffering and repression."[91]

Arriving at a farm house, the viewer still only sees boots as the figure climbs out of the truck. Wavering unsteadily, an empty pint of booze falls from between his legs, as if he had just evacuated a bowel in the form of a bottle of alcohol. He attempts to break down the front door, shown by shots of flailing boots and pounding fists; he even employs the truck to try to ram down the door. This cuts to a shot of a woman's bare feet walking across the floor to unlock the door. He barges in, and the viewer finally sees Sidney Brenshaw's sadistically leering face in a tight close-up. The shot cuts to Brenshaw's beleaguered wife, Hannah (Antoinette Christiani), cowering in bed, holding a sheet over her as a shield. Sidney, as if by pure instinct, enters the house and proceeds to rape her (one can easily assume this is not the first time this has happened). As in *Lorna*, the rape serves to designate male domination over women, and the attack occurs in the bedroom, a common site of sexual struggle in all of Meyer's films. Not surprisingly, Hannah is raped by Sidney a second time in *Mudhoney*, and this attack occurs in the other site of female domesticity: the kitchen.

The violence of the rape cuts to a pair of men's shoes kicking a can; the

89. *Eros and Civilization: A Philosophical Inquiry into Freud* (Boston: Beacon Press, 1966), 13.

90. *Eros and Civilization*, 25. The nirvana principle is radically difference to the convergence of pleasure and death that Bataille views as the pinnacle of eroticism. For Marcuse, the nirvana principle is a horrific phenomenon when destruction becomes the ultimate pleasure, such as war, concentration camps, and nuclear arms.

91. *Eros and Civilization*, 29.

CHAPTER THREE ◊ "WELCOME TO VIOLENCE"

camera follows the can as it stops at the bare feet of a woman. Recalling the previous scene which focused on Sidney's boots and Hannah's bare feet, it is a unsettling, darkly comic transition. Given the previous scene, the viewer almost expects another rape to take place, but the figures are revealed to be the honorable stranger to town Calif McKinney (Meyer veteran John Furlong) and the innocent, deaf-mute prostitute Eula (Rena Horton). One key reason Eula is a deaf-mute was due to Horton's limited English and heavy German accent, which would have thoroughly been out of place in a Midwestern whorehouse. Nonetheless, Eula's role as a deaf-mute also serves as a profound thematic element at the film's conclusion. As in *Lorna*, the transitional montage also serves to establish important links between the characters. First, it foreshadows the relationship and rivalry between Calif and Sidney for both the Wade farm and Hannah, with Calif eventually assuming the role in the Wade household that Sidney presently occupies. Secondly, it foreshadows the relationship and similarities between Eula and Hannah. However, unlike the relationship between Calif and Sidney, which is the *narrative* focal point of the film, Hannah and Eula barely interact throughout the film; rather, their relationship is a *metaphorical* one, with Eula assuming the tragic role Hannah presently occupies in the film's conclusion.

Calif soon meets the rest of the whorehouse occupants: Eula's mother/whorehouse madam Maggie Marie (Princess Livingston), Eula's sister Clara Belle (Lorna Maitland from *Lorna*), and Injoys (Sam Hanna), the "hired hand" ("the hired *what*?" says Clara Belle, nudging him with a burlesque wink). These characters could be directly out of the pages of *Li'l Abner*: Maggie Marie's resemblance to Mammy Yokum borders on the uncanny, Lorna Matiland as Clara Belle is a lewd antithesis from *Lorna*, and Injoys is pure rural caricature, dressed in overalls and wearing a bushy beard. Calif is informed that there is a job available on the Wade farm, where he meets Hannah and her father Lute Wade (played by another Meyer mainstay, Stuart Lancaster). Hannah is severe and hardened by both Sidney's assaults and the demands of maintaining the farm. Because Lute is dying and Sidney shirks his responsibilities, Hannah is forced to do much of the work on the farm; as will be discussed, she is a "productive" object rather than an "erotic" object. Nonetheless, there is an immediate sexual attraction between Calif and Hannah, and this growing interest exacerbates the tensions between Sidney and Calif, who, as noted, become rivals for both Hannah as well as "man of the house" on the Wade farm. Ironically, there is also another similarity between Calif and Sidney: both are "outsiders" in the isolated, insular small town, and are objects of scorn and hatred. Calif is distrusted by his very status as a stranger in town and his rumored "illicit" love affair with Hannah. Sidney himself fuels the rumors, and their relationship is the subject of town gossip and disapproval long before it is ultimately consummated.

The "Secret Alliance": Id and Super-Ego

Sidney is similarly despised by Spooner's residents, simply for his continual pattern of anti-social behavior. His only ally in town is the insufferably pious

CHAPTER THREE ◊ **"WELCOME TO VIOLENCE"**

Brother Hanson (played by yet another Meyer veteran, Franklin Bolger). Like the Preacher in *Lorna*, Brother Hanson is a satirical example of religious fundamentalism. Moreover, in Freudian terms, Hanson is the embodiment of the repressive *superego* to Sidney's *id*. Yet this relationship is far from mutually exclusive; Marcuse observed, "in many cases, the superego seems to be in secret alliance with the id, defending the claims of the id against the ego and the external world."[92] At one point, Hanson takes Sidney aside and warns him to shape up because he is on the verge of "being run out of town." Later, he defends Sidney to the townspeople as someone in need of their prayers and support rather than being the target of their anger. In this unlikely alliance, the repressing Brother Hanson and the licentious Sidney are quite similar. When Hanson accompanies Sidney to the whorehouse, his failed efforts to resist Eula's seductions prompt him to literally run from the whorehouse in anger and shame. His repressed sexual urges are ultimately sublimated into social aggression in his rage as the lynch mob leader, his thirst for violence due as much to his constricted libido as Biblical invective. Similar to Brother Hanson, Sidney's visits to the whorehouse result in sexual frustration rather than sexual release. He never has sex at the whorehouse, and his libidinal energy is released only through destructive, anti-social acts, ranging from routinely raping his wife to juvenile pranks, such as shoving Eula in the lake when he becomes aroused by her. This apparently innocuous act actually foreshadows far greater violence when Sidney drowns Sister Hanson (Lee Ballard) in a river. The relationship between Sidney and Sister Hanson is one of thinly-disguised sexual lust and innuendo, and the viewer expects that Sidney is leading Sister Hanson to the river to seduce her. However, when Sidney "consummates" the relationship, it is through brutal violence. The killing becomes Brenshaw's "convergence of pleasure and death," where, as in the work of de Sade, "murder becomes the pinnacle of erotic excitement."[93]

It is Sidney's final acts of violence, the arson of the Wade farm and the murder of Sister Hanson, which lead to the formation of a lynching party under the leadership of Brother Hanson, the sadistic and self-destructive super-ego who becomes the voice and leader of an enraged and vengeful community. Freud wrote, "It can be asserted that the community, too, evolves a super-ego under whose influence cultural development proceeds."[94] Sidney and Brother Hanson, id and super-ego, become the twin catalysts of the town's self-destruction. The death instinct propels not only Sidney, but Brother Hanson as well, who leads the lynch mob that claims Sidney's life, costs him his own life, and destroys the community as a whole. As Franz Alexander observed, "in the construction of the personality the destruction instinct manifests itself most clearly in the formation of the super-ego."[95]

92. *Eros and Civilization*, 228.

93. Bataille, *Erotism*, 18.

94. *Civilization and Its Discontents*, 99.

95. As quoted in Marcuse, 53.

Sex Objects: Nudes and Prostitutes

In the scene where Sidney and Brother Hanson first arrive at the whorehouse, they see Eula standing naked in a small bathtub, unashamedly washing herself outdoors. They both stare at her: Sidney with prurient glee, Hanson with self-righteous disgust. "Gettin' a good eyeful?," interrupts Maggie Marie in her distinctive, abrasive voice. All of the nudity in *Mudhoney* takes place in an explicitly voyeuristic context, where the naked women is always in the act of *being looked at* naked. Maggie Marie's pointed comments can even be directed at the two chief members of Meyer's audience: the "Sidneys," or the sexploitation "raincoat crowd," who watched these films for sadistic-voyeuristic pleasure, and the "Hansons," the moralistic and hypocritical critics of Meyer and other "pornographers." Even more so than *The Immoral Mr. Teas*, the nudity in *Mudhoney* takes place in a context of women being seen naked; there is a tension constructed between a clothed male and a naked female created through shot composition or montage. When Calif visits the whorehouse, Eula takes him to her bedroom and strips in front of him, his shoulder strategically positioned to conceal her vagina from the audience. As in *Lorna*, any eroticism that is built is negated by dark comedy, in the case of *Mudhoney* by a sudden close-up of the leering, malicious Sidney as he interrupts the "romantic" mood by peering into the room with puerile delight, again serving as an unappealing "stand-in" for the male spectator.

The role and status of the prostitute is an important facet of *Mudhoney*. The whorehouse functions as a point where illicit sexual practices can occur in legitimized, marginalized, segregated, socially-controlled places.[96] In a town where restlessness and repression are staples of rural life, the whorehouse is the only outlet: paradoxically, both taboo and necessity. Furthermore, the whorehouse is a site of *female* domination; it is owned and operated by a mother and the daughters. Injoys, the sole "male" ("the hired *what?*"), is a mere employee and servant. It is a *matriarchal* order, in contrast to a town dominated and even terrorized by male figures (Sidney, Brother Hanson).

Another aspect of prostitution in *Mudhoney* concerns "production." Bataille wrote:

"In the perfection of femininity, idleness has a part, the most significant part perhaps, for the intensity of work *reduces the contrast of the sexes*. The prostitute is the only human who logically should be idle... by living in idleness, the prostitute preserves the completely feminine qualities that work diminishes... a wife is mainly the woman who bears the children and works at home... she is objectified in the same manner of a brick or a piece of furniture... The prostitute is, just as much as the married woman, an object whose value is assessable. But this object is erotic, from one end to the other and in every sense of the word."[97]

96. See Foucault, *The History of Sexuality, Vol. 1*, 4.

97. *The Accursed Share, Vol. II*, 140, 146-7. Emphasis mine.

CHAPTER THREE ◊ "WELCOME TO VIOLENCE"

Thus, one can contrast Hannah to the denizens of the whorehouse, Eula and Clara Belle. Hannah functions as the primary "producer" on the Wade farm before Calif's arrival, doing the work that Lute is unable to do and Sidney unwilling to perform. For Sidney, Hannah is merely a piece of property: she is hardly an "erotic" object, and is raped and abused with the same frequency that Sidney would angrily break down the door or otherwise mistreat farm "property." In this respect, she can not be the object of erotic attention to the lazy, carousing

Sidney: Hannah's "production" is antithetical to "eroticism." In contrast, Clara Belle and Eula, the "idle" prostitutes, are erotic objects *par excellence*, so erotic and forbidden that Sidney can only gaze lustfully at them, never to sexually touch them. In turn, Hannah can be nothing but an erotic object to the diligent, hard-working Calif, who divests her from her productive duties in the household. By reducing her "productive" role, Hannah becomes all the more "erotic" to him. Nonetheless, idleness should not be confused with *passivity*. While Eula embodies the stereotypical Marilyn Monroe sexpot image (a child from the neck up, a woman from the neck down), Clara Belle is a vastly different character. In one scene, she brazenly swims naked in front of Calif, unsuccessfully attempting to get him to join her (a scene perhaps included also a parody of her famous swimming scene in *Lorna*): In the female domain of water, Clara Belle is the sexual aggressor. In another scene at the whorehouse, Clara Belle treats Sidney with sarcastic and sadistic contempt. She dances lewdly in front of him, wiggling her breasts and buttocks, taunting him while Eula sits on his lap and Injoys looks on in vicarious, voyeuristic enjoyment. When Sidney tries to grope her, she spitefully responds by searching his pockets for cash. Finding only twenty-five cents, a very small "wad" of cash which equates his poverty and economic unproductiveness to a small penis and sexual unproductiveness, she allows him a humiliating flash of her breasts and further ridicules him.

Mob Justice

At one point in *Mudhoney*, the dying Lute Wade warns Calif, "the whole town's been cheated by the times… this town *has* to hate." Trapped by the pressures of the Great Depression, Prohibition, and a climate of Puritanical sexual repression embodied and enforced by Brother Hanson, the citizens of Spooner are stagnating economically, socially, and sexually. Until his death, Lute Wade serves as the voice of reason in the film and in the community. With Lute's death and the burning down of his farm by Sidney, who is incensed the farm has been left to Calif in Lute's will, one can argue that "civilization" itself has been eliminated; in Deleuze's terms, the "derived milieu" is obliterated, leaving only the "originary world" of impulses. Thus, Spooner relentlessly moves towards irrational mob violence, and it is Calif and Hannah who emerge as the last remaining voices of reason. Not surprisingly, they are the only two in the film to establish a "healthy" sexual relationship, and unlike the assaults she endures from Sidney within the confines of the home, the consummation of her relationship with Calif takes place in a lush meadow. As the only couple who have a "productive" sexual relationship, abeit one that exists outside of marriage which makes them town pariahs, they are seemingly immune to the town's explosion of violence. Also absent from the orgy of mob violence are the women of the whorehouse, who regulate sexuality through capitalism, and are thus

CHAPTER THREE ◊ "WELCOME TO VIOLENCE"

98. *Eros and Civilization*, 86.

"productive" both sexually and economically in a town otherwise stunted by the Great Depression and sexual repression (Injoys, however, can clearly be seen as a member of the lynch mob).

In the conclusion of *Mudhoney*, the "libidinal bind" that brings people together is not achieved through Eros, but Death; Marcuse observed, "destructiveness, in extent and intent, seems more directly satisfied in civilization than the libido."[98] *Mudhoney* ends in a flurry of violence: Sidney swinging from a noose, dead at the hands of Brother Hansen, who has in turn

67

been shot by Calif. However, "reason" does not triumph: Calif and Hannah have planned to leave the town even prior to the lynching, and the final events only further serve to convince them that there is no place for them in Spooner. Amid this violence, Eula has inexplicably sensed the trouble in the town and wandered away from the whorehouse. As if somehow "hearing" the commotion, she races to the scene and sees the dead Sidney dangling from a noose. Suddenly, she screams, and embraces Sidney's lifeless legs. The final scene suggests not only Freud but Lacan, with Eula's sudden entry into the "symbolic order," the regime of language and "The Law," heralded by a blood-curling shriek. The transition of Eula into Hannah is completed: the sensuous and innocent girl transformed into the hardened and severe woman. One can not believe that Eula will ever be the same: she is traumatized and psychically "raped" by the lynching in the same way Hannah has been by Sidney's constant abuse. The lynch mob reacts with shock and shame, with Russ Meyer appearing in a cameo as a now-distressed member of the lynching party. A long, high-angle shot is shown of the mob as it begins to aimlessly drift apart, and the shot is inscribed with an on-screen warning: ONE MAN"S EVIL CAN BECOME THE CURSE OF ALL. This shot of the mob freeze-frames, trapping the aftermath of the lynching as a point of History where the moment of trauma can never be erased. Even as the film fades to black, the ominous music and the wail of police sirens continue until they fade out as well. The town has done nothing less than commit collective suicide, the logical result of the death instinct in its aggregate form. In this way, *Mudhoney* can only echo the pessimism of the final pages of Freud's *Civilization and Its Discontents*: "the fateful question for the human species seems... to be whether and to what extent their cultural development will succeed in mastering the disturbance of their communal life by the human instinct of aggression and self-destruction."[99]

99. *Civilization and Its Discontents*, 104.

MOTORPSYCHO! (1965)

The Biker-Film

Motorpsycho! is probably the least considered, or as I would contend most overlooked of Meyer's four black and white roughie films, perhaps simply because it is in the unenviable position of following *Lorna* and *Mudhoney* and proceeding the legendary *Faster, Pussycat! Kill! Kill!*. When mentioned, it is usually in connection with the "biker-film" genre of the 1960s, a genre some claim Meyer even invented with *Motorpsycho!*. Certainly, the film is inspired by, and even parodies, the original biker-film, *The Wild One* (1954), itself based on events in Hollister, California in 1947, when a motorcycle rally turned into a two-

CHAPTER THREE ◊ "WELCOME TO VIOLENCE"

day siege of the town. However, I would argue that the biker-film genre, which helped launch Hell's Angels as a national phenomenon, actually began with another 1966 biker film, *The Wild Angels*, which featured Peter Fonda and Nancy Sinatra, offspring of American cultural icons, as unlikely biker outlaws. *The Wild Angels* did not portray the "biker" as anarchistic, free-wheeling "fuck the world" outlaws but as an extension of the Beat Generation: disillusioned, alienated, existential, literate, articulate, and proudly non-conformist, an image that reached its cultural apex in another Peter Fonda biker film, *Easy Rider* (1969). And while many of the Angels allegedly admired *The Wild One*, they were incensed about *The Wild Angels* to the point of not only creating their own "documentary," *Hell's Angels on Wheels* (1968), but suing and threatening the life of *The Wild Angels* producer Roger Corman. Nonetheless, the Hollywood biker-film continued towards depicting the biker experience as a soul-searching quest to fully live the American experience: *On the Road* on Harleys. Very few biker-films attempted to make the biker a true outlaw anti-hero, an antithesis of the peace and love experience: Al Adamson's "*Citizen Kane* of biker-films," *Satan's Sadists* (1969) is a notable exception. At the other extreme, several biker-films dispensed with the nobility altogether and simply presented bikers as sociopathic animals rather than heroic rebels verses repressive and oppressive "squares." *Born Losers* (1969), which marked the debut of American counter-culture icon "Billy Jack," is one such film. And while *Motorpsycho!* has more in common with this brand of biker-film, it ultimately has more in common with other films, and other genres altogether.

Motorpsycho! borrows and parodies the basic elements of *The Wild One* in its story of a biker invasion of a small town, yet the film's villains are far from the prototypical biker images of the tattooed, bearded colossus; the young, idealistic wanderer; or even the images of Marlon Brando and Lee Marvin from *The Wild One*. *Motorpsycho!*'s "biker gang" number three scooter-driving miscreants – the actors were allegedly kept away from actual motorcycles for fear they would injure themselves. They are more absurd parody than imposing presence: the opening shots of the film, the gang driving down the highway, is bound to produce laughter rather than fear. All three are also pure caricature. Brahmin (Stephen Oliver), the leader, has a Mod haircut and a hippie vest. He is later revealed to be recently discharged from Vietnam, and he suffers from flashbacks and battle-related mental illness (possibly the first example of the "crazy 'Nam vet" that became a staple villain in 1970s film and television). Dante (Joesph Collins), a 1950s style greaser with an Italian accent, could be straight out of a "JD film." The last of the three, Slick (Thomas Scott), is a lanky "drop-out" loner with a transistor radio constantly blaring in his ear. One is tempted to compare them to a Charles Starkweather rather than a Hell's Angel; they are indistinct, amoral sociopaths. In this context, a brief but fruitful comparison to

69

Motorpsycho! would be Arch Hall, Sr.'s exploitation epic *The Sadist* (1963). Like *Motorpsycho!*, *The Sadist* is a stark, black and white film set in a barren desert where a sociopathic killer (played by Arch Hall, Jr.) and his girlfriend menace three stranded teachers (two male, one female). The killer and his girlfriend physically and psychologically torture their victims and murder the two male teachers before they themselves are killed in a tense, life or death confrontation. The allusions to Starkweather in *The Sadist* are overt, and Arch Hall, Jr. even bears an uncanny resemblance to Starkweather (excepting, of course, Hall's surfer blonde hair). In this regard, it is perhaps better to begin to consider *Motorpsycho!* by placing less emphasis on the "motor" and more emphasis on the "psycho."

The Sadist

The Territorial Imperative

Ultimately, *Motorpsycho!* might best be considered as a precursor to such "rape and vigilante films" as Sam Peckinpah's *Straw Dogs* (both 1971) and Michael Winner's *Death Wish* (1974), which is little more than a Hollywood "roughie." All three films center around a husband, who, through varying circumstances, takes the law into his own hands following the rape of his wife. However, *Motorpsycho!* not only prefigures these films but addresses its themes of rape and revenge just as complexly, if not more so, as these other films. As in the case of *Lorna* and *Mudhoney*, *Motorpsycho!* sets the stage with a sexual assault of a woman. The first shot of the film shows a beautiful, buxom woman sunbathing, the stripes on her bikini accentuating her already formidable figure. Her husband, in full fishing gear, fishes in a nearby pond. Not only does he proceed to ignore her amorous advances, but he becomes infuriated when she dives in the water and "screws up the fishing." "You got the best on your line right now!" she retorts. As in the case of many Meyer films, one is presented with a voluptuous, overtly sexual young wife and a sexually disinterested older husband who, as in *Mr. Teas*, is more interested in fishing than fornication. The scene cuts to the credits, and a close-up of Slick's radio hanging from the handlebars. The credits roll over shots of the bikers as they careen down the highway on their scooters, and the cast is introduced under the headings "the men" and "the women" making explicit the divisions, and even battle lines, drawn between the sexes.

    The three hoods and the couple meet. Seeing the woman, Brahmin stealthily approaches, bends, and kisses her. Her eyes are closed, and she initially responds warmly, but recoils in horror when she realizes that she has just kissed a stranger. Her response, in effect, may not only be in the horror of being violated but in the horror of also having briefly failed "the blindfold test" between her husband and a total stranger. This articulates favorite Meyer themes regarding marriage: one, that marriage does not promote passion, but deadens it; and two, that sexual excitement is frequently found outside the bonds

CHAPTER THREE ◊ "WELCOME TO VIOLENCE"

of matrimony. Nonetheless, the husband reacts with complete outrage, expressing another male characteristic in Meyer's film: husbands are often indifferent or ignorant of their wives' sexual needs, but react with anger if another man (or woman) expresses any sexual attention in their spouse. Brahmin responds by beating the man, then raping his wife. The shot of Brahmin attacking the woman is replaced by a wipe, in which one shot pushes the other shot off the screen. A wipe usually takes place from one side of the frame to the other; however, in *Motorpsycho!* the wipe begins in the center of the screen and moves to each side. This kind of wipe is a metaphor of the filmic depiction of rape, where one shot is forcibly parted in the center as the next shot enters. The shot of Brahmin atop the woman is parted by a shot of a truck tire rolling to a stop as it approaches the camera. The truck belongs to Cory Maddox (Alex Rocco, who went on to a long and successful career in film and television),

LIPS HIPS TITS POWER ◊ THE FILMS OF RUSS MEYER

and his wife Gail (Hollie K. Winters), although Cory refers to her by a pet-name, "Angel." In the Russ Meyer film canon, they are an anomaly: a happily-married couple. Cory, the town veterinarian, is on the way to see a client and Angel on her way to visit a friend. Of course, Angel is beautiful and curvaceous, and she wears only shorts and a man's shirt tied at the bosom, exposing her midriff. As she walks directly towards the camera, the camera fixates on her crotch until it arrives in medium-close-up. At this point another wipe splits the screen: the shot of Angel's crotch is parted in two and replaced by the shot of the radio dangling from the handlebars used in the opening credits which prefigured the first rape. Here the transition and montage is violent and crude, and literally foreshadows Angel's fate: her vagina being ripped in half by the bikers.

Indeed, the next scene is the initial encounter between Angel and the bikers, which takes place on what the street sign darkly and ironically calls "Blythe Way." The hoods block Angel's path and begin driving around her in circles, a direct parody of the famous scene in *The Wild One* where Kathie is chased and encircled by the bikers that have invaded the town. As in the case of *The Wild One*, it is the romantic male lead who intervenes, but instead of Marlon Brando it is Alex Rocco who steps in and successfully breaks up the scene, dispatching Brahmin to the ground with a contemptuous shove. Unlike the first husband, Maddox manfully and decisively defuses the threat to his wife. Appropriately, the scene shifts to Cory and Angel's bedroom. It recalls and reconfigures the bedroom scene in *Lorna*: a husband working late at his desk, his wife sleeping naked in the other room. However, the scene plays out antithetically to *Lorna*, where Jim, the husband, takes the romantic initiative and promptly (pun intended) fails to satisfy his wife. In *Motorpsycho!*, Angel initiates the proceedings and Cory is more than willing; he even postpones an important client so he can spend the night with his wife (to further exaggerate the intimacy of the scene, Meyer films the bedroom encounter almost entirely in close-ups). Such behavior is unlike married couples in other Meyer films, where the husband is usually unwilling or unable to fulfill his sexual duties with a sexually aggressive and often intimidating wife.

The important client turns out to be buxom Jessica (Sharon Lee), the bored wife of a wealthy rancher who has summoned Cory to check on a pregnant mare. The conversation soon turns to the new horse she has, the one for "breeding purposes." Maddox concurs that the horse "ought to make a fine stud." The sexual innuendo of the conversation speaks for itself. When Maddox wonders about her husband's whereabouts, Jessica lists any number of cities he could be in and adds, "He has his fun... I have mine." The scene shifts with a disorientating transition: the camera seemingly spinning in circles while a slide guitar glissandos. The viewer suddenly sees Dante, smiling and dancing to the rock music from Slick's ever-present radio, and the next shot cuts to him

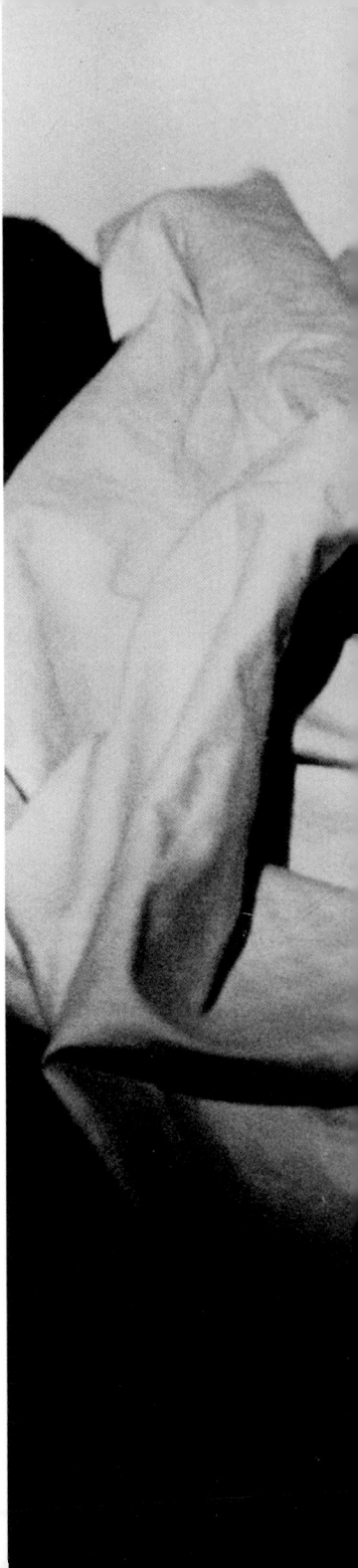

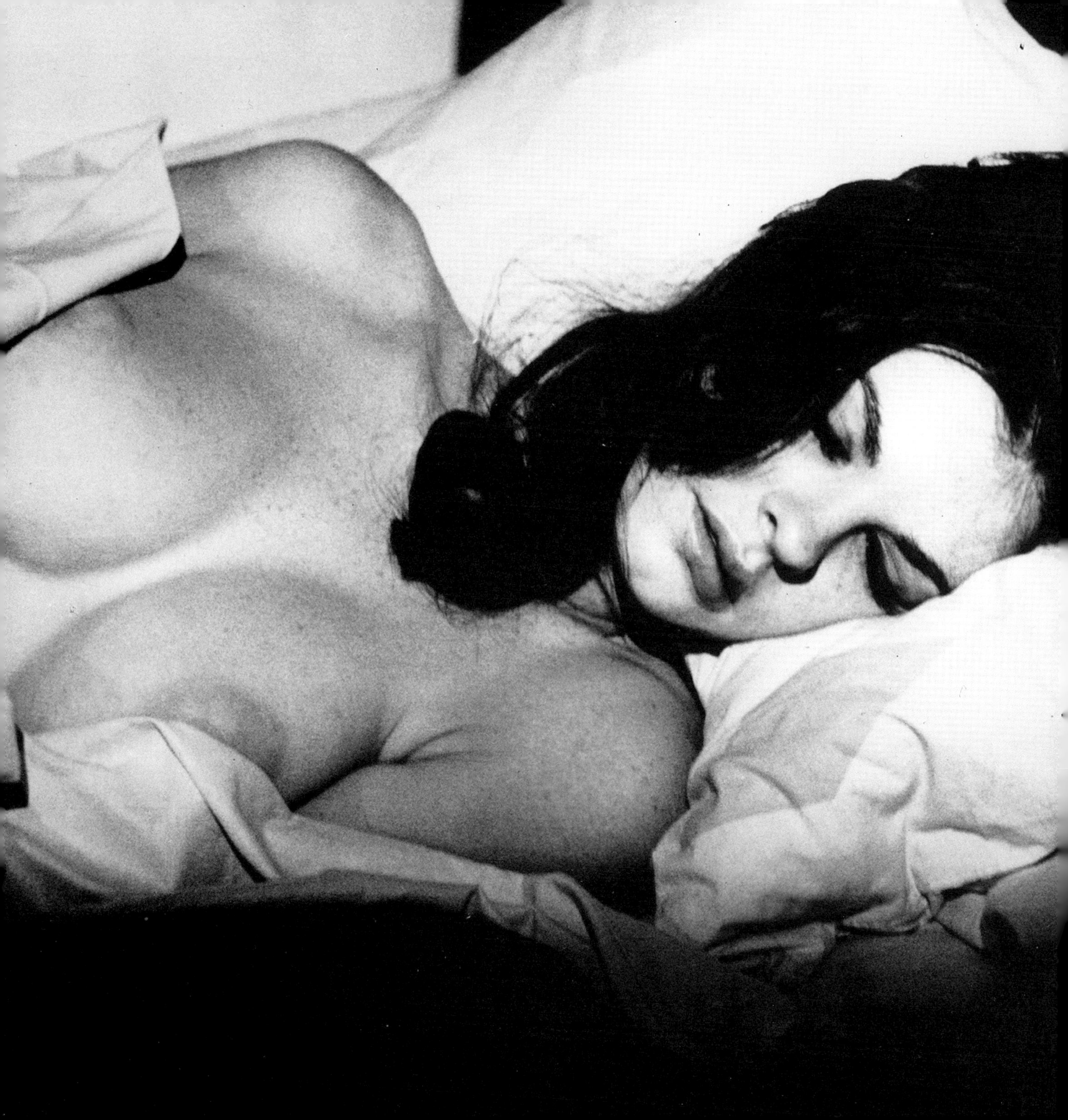

grabbing the crying, frightened Angel, forcing her to dance with him. It is obvious that the bikers are not only assaulting Angel, but are doing so in the Maddox's own home. Jessica's statement about "He has his fun... I have mine" also darkly and ironically refers to the assault, and the implication that a women has "fun" being sexually assaulted, an issue explicitly taken up later in *Motorpsycho!*. Unlike later Meyer films, specifically *Supervixens* and *Up!*, Angel's assault is depicted in disturbing symbolism and dark comedy rather than graphic depictions of rape. As Dante forces Angel to dance with him, Brahmin looks on with sadistic-voyeuristic enjoyment (again, a stand-in for the male spectator watching the rape-scene in the theater for vicarious pleasure). At another point during the assault, Slick uses the Maddox phone to make a long-distance phone call to his mother (!); he hilariously informs her about the gang's travels together: "He's an Army guy teaching us Army stuff like Judo and camping-out... and he thinks of his mother a lot." Another unsettling shot depicts Dante dancing by himself, Slick obliviously listening to his radio, and Angel sobbing, sitting on Brahmin's lap in a macabre parody of the family portrait. As Angel tries to get up, Brahmin viciously pulls her back by the hair and kisses her.

    The "spinning transition" cuts to a montage of Jessica kissing Cory, creating an eerie juxtaposition between the two "couples." Jessica propositions Corey and then walks away: a horse whinnies in the background to comically underscore the seduction effort. However, Cory declines and drives away. Indignant, Jessica muses, "Well, some gal's got it made!" The scene "spins" back to the assault, where again Jessica's comment, "Well, some gal's got it made!" becomes utterly perverse black comedy. Angel is crying and disheveled, bleeding from the nose; she is on her knees, just below Brahmin's crotch, situated between his spread legs. The connotation of forced fellatio is obvious in the shot. Yet rather than submit, she knees Brahmin in the crotch, and the assault viciously escalates. The shot cuts to a gas pump nozzle pushed in to a car, an obvious montage suggesting vaginal penetration. The car belongs to Maddox; as he fills the car with gas the three rapists recklessly roar through the gas station. Maddox speeds away, as if sensing something terrible has happened.

    The scene shifts via an iris effect that begins in the center the screen and expands out in a circle to cover the previous scene: it is a close-up of a police siren. This effect serves to signify the overriding presence and question of "the law" in the next sequence, with Russ Meyer providing a crucial thematic cameo as the sheriff of the town. He lifts the sheet covering Angel and inspects the damage to her genitalia with vicarious enjoyment. "Those three hoods must've had a *ball*!" Meyer exclaims, much to the disgust of the ambulance attendant. The word "ball" is punned to suggest both having a good time (or "fun") and the slang term for sexual intercourse. Accompanying Cory and Angel in the

CHAPTER THREE ◊ **"WELCOME TO VIOLENCE"**

ambulance, the sheriff seems bewildered at Cory's anger. "Nothing happened to her that a woman ain't built for," he sneers, as if the idea of having a vagina necessarily infers a woman is "built for" sexual assault. When the sheriff implies that Angel may have been "askin' for it," Cory explodes, screaming at the sheriff if it looks like she enjoyed what happened to her and if she "asked" for that to happen (critics of Meyer's sexism are suggested to pay close attention to this darkly self-referential scene). Maddox realizes that the law is not simply inefficient, or even indifferent to rape, but that a patriarchal order may in fact *condone* rape.

Of the "rape-vigilante" films, Peckinpah's *Straw Dogs* was deeply influenced by anthropologist Robert Ardrey's book, *The Territorial Imperative*. Ardrey's highly-debatable thesis claimed male competition primarily stems from the primary instinctual drive to secure property, and thereby the reproductive rights that come with the ownership of property (Ardrey even suggested that sexual arousal came during acts of competition for property). In the context of the rape-vigilante films, the violation is inflicted when one male appropriates and infringes on the territory of another male. The raped woman is simply an extension of this battle for property between men: she is sexual property that "comes with the territory." This is characteristic of the classic 1970s rape-vigilante films *Straw Dogs* and *Death Wish*, in which the outrage is not the rape as much as that the rape occurred on the male's property. In *Death Wish*, Paul's (Charles Bronson) wife and daughter are raped in their upscale home, and in *Straw Dogs* Amy (Susan George) is raped in the home by the town bullies who eventually try to break into the home in the film's grisly conclusion. The fact that the assaults take place in the home is vital to both these films. As to whether or not Maddox's rage over his wife's assault falls under "the territorial imperative" can be debated. Certainly, the rape takes place in the Maddox home, or Cory Maddox's "territory," and his failure to prevent the assault stems from his own brief indiscretion into another man's "property." Nonetheless, Maddox's rage seems more to stem from a legal system that has nothing but contempt for what his wife has experienced. However, rather than decrying a liberal justice system that coddles criminals and handcuffs police as so many of the 1970s vigilante films did, Maddox's rage is directed against the legal system run by the "pigs," meaning "male-chauvinist pigs," specifically the film's representative of "the law," sheriff and director Russ Meyer himself. In terms of its sudden shift to a naturalist revenge saga, *Motorpsycho!* also differs greatly from the rape-vigilante films of the 1970s. Unlike *Straw Dogs*, Maddox is not gradually pushed into an explosion of animal violence as is the milquetoast math professor (Dustin Hoffman), nor is Angel shown as an accomplice in her own rape (as some critics of *Straw Dogs* have accused Peckinpah of doing to Amy); *Motorpsycho!* goes to great lengths to point out that Angel was *not* a willing participant in her assault.

75

LIPS HIPS TITS POWER ◊ THE FILMS OF RUSS MEYER

Unlike *Death Wish*, Maddox does not undergo a gradual moral or ethical crisis (Paul becomes physically ill after his first killing). Cory's decision to take vengeance is immediate and intractable.

Deserts and "Just Deserts"

As the ambulance speeds away across the screen and into the background, another vehicle comes from the opposite direction; many of the intersections between the characters takes place in this way, their inexorable proximity to each other established by their appearance in the same shot while the character is still there or has just departed. In the car are Ruby (veteran Meyer actress Haji) and her slovenly husband Harry (Coleman Francis). They are another archetypal Meyer married couple: a young, attractive, well-built woman and an older, much less-attractive man. They are engaged in a heated verbal exchange, him insulting her background and behavior; she, in turn, belittles his sexual performance and personal hygiene. As he raises his hand, about to slap her, the

CHAPTER THREE ◊ "WELCOME TO VIOLENCE"

sound of a tire blowout is heard (at first, one suspects a gunshot), which startles the viewer, underscores the visual violence of the scene, and foreshadows Harry's fate. As Ruby goes off to relieve her bladder and Harry begins to change the tire, the three bikers show up. Quickly, the tensions escalate, particularly when Slick finds a loaded rifle in the rear of the truck. As the couple is physically and psychologically intimidated by the bikers, Harry offers them the services of Ruby, obviously for sexual purposes, in order to save himself. The woman again is treated as sexual property between men who is "built for" male enjoyment. Incensed, Ruby spits at the bikers and attacks Harry after he has tried to sell her out. The confrontation quickly ends when the firearms-incompetent Slick accidentally shots Harry in the stomach, and Brahmin shoots Ruby as she attempts to flee. Brahmin then shoots the engines out of the bikes, tying them all to the crime. This action can also be seen as a symbolic gesture in the context of *genre*, signifying their uselessness in a film freely incorporating elements of the Western, *film noir*, and melodrama into a surreal assemblage of naturalist violence. Any resemblance to a "biker-film" is quite literally eliminated.

LIPS HIPS TITS POWER ◊ THE FILMS OF RUSS MEYER

Cory soon arrives onto the crime scene. Ruby has only been slightly wounded and joins Maddox, and they soon encounter the gang. The subsequent battle further exposes the glaring implausibilities and comedy of the film. Cory, in his quest for revenge, has not even bothered to bring a weapon, Brahmin's military experience apparently did not include marksmanship, and the gang retreats from the fray, knowingly leaving Ruby and Cory alive despite outnumbering them and being armed. However, in the film's most perverse

CHAPTER THREE ◊ "WELCOME TO VIOLENCE"

moment, Cory is bitten by a rattlesnake after the confrontation and he orders Ruby to "suck out the poison." He pulls her by the hair and makes her suck and spit out the poison from his leg. "Look at it! SUCK IT!" Maddox yells. The suggestion that Maddox is forcing Ruby to engage in oral sex on him could not be more overt or unsettling: Maddox becomes "a rapist" himself. The comedy is as utterly black as the blood the half-sick Ruby spits out: the "fluids of erotic expression" are not just semen and blood, but *poison* as well.

The traditional relationship between male hero (Cory) and female damsel-in-distress (Ruby) is turned on its head, with Ruby now forced to protect the incapacitated Maddox. Indeed, Ruby not only saves Maddox's life once by "sucking him off," but saves him a second time when Dante inadvertently wanders into their camp, having abandoned the now-psychotic Brahmin, who has murdered Slick and is now completely delusional and reliving flashbacks of Vietnam. In turn, Cory is completely delusional and reliving flashbacks of a torrid sexual encounter with Angel. In yet another perverse juxtaposition, war and marital/sexual bliss are equated. Aware that the helpless Maddox could easily be killed, Ruby seduces Dante, only to plunge his knife deeply into his back as he lies on top of her. Not only is the distinction between sex and violence erased, with fucking equaling killing, but Ruby uses a phallic instrument to kill Dante, stabbing or "penetrating" him, creating a reversal of gender by making Ruby "the male" who does the stabbing and Dante "the female" who gets stabbed (as Clover suggested, "A woman is not just raped because she is a woman, but a woman because she is raped"). Here it is Ruby who metaphorically "rapes" and kills Dante. The latter half of the film takes place in the desert, the site of masculine libido, and Ruby survives by becoming "a man," including even taking over the traditional "male-hero" role for part of the film.

The steadily diminishing cast of characters inevitably sets the stage for confrontation between Maddox and Brahmin. Brahmin invades the camp, and Ruby is immediately wounded. Maddox suddenly makes a miraculous recovery, righting the dramatic situation so the traditional melodramatic triangle of male hero, male villain, and endangered female is now intact for the film's climax. Much like the classical Western, the final battle is staged through a montage of close-ups and long shots; as Bill Nichols observed, "[it is] a narrative tradition as old as Griffith and highly prevalent in the Westerns of John Ford: long shots to convey the epic sweep of historic events, and close-ups to individualize those characters whose destiny we will follow."[100] In fact, Maddox, the hero the audience identifies with, is shown almost entirely in close-up; Brahmin is shown almost exclusively in long-shots, the black and white cinemaphotography rendering him indistinct in the desert landscape. As he marches down the desert hill towards Maddox, firing his rifle wildly, he begins to shout what appears to be incoherent phrases, but in fact is almost Brechtian commentary about the

100. *Ideology and the Image* (Bloomington: Indiana University Press, 1981), 186.

film's narrative. "It's all over!" Brahmin yells as he descends the desert slope, announcing that the film is indeed almost "all over." "Did you pull the pin on that grenade?" he loudly asks, providing a cue for Maddox to fashion an explosive device out of some nearby dynamite. In a series of close-ups, the dynamite is shown being tied while Maddox holds it tightly between his thighs. His transfixed stare as he watches the fuse burn, the dynamite next to his crotch, tightly clenched in his hand, suggests sexual arousal as well as primal violence. As Brahmin nears Maddox, he yells, "Comrade... I'm giving you a permanent discharge!" The word "comrade" not only refers to the communist forces in Vietnam, but the symbolic "comradery" between Maddox and Brahmin. Both have descended into madness: Brahmin into shell-shocked delirium, Maddox into a psychotic quest for vengeance that has left him literally "snake-bit." The "permanent discharge" not only puns the end of one's military service, but both death and sexual release (the discharge of semen), a point literalized by the proximity of the sexualized dynamite to Maddox's crotch. The film literally ends with an explosive climax (or "discharge"): Maddox hurdles the dynamite at Brahmin, killing him in the ensuing explosion.

With the gang now dispatched, Maddox returns to the same calm, considerate person seen in the beginning of the film, not only because his thirst for revenge has been sated, but perhaps because now the heterosexual couple has been reestablished with the elimination of the bikers, with Ruby substituting for the absent Angel, whose condition is left conspicuously unanswered in the film's conclusion. Ruby even thanks Maddox, to which Maddox replies, "for what, almost getting you killed?" His response serves as a commentary on the thankless role Ruby has throughout the film. When Maddox tells her she'll "be alright," she responds, "in L.A.?" "Anywhere," he answers. Ruby is leaving the brutal originary world of "anywhere" manifest in the barren desert, and returning to civilization, the derived milieu of Los Angeles. The close-up of the couple dissolves into a shot of Maddox's Jeep as it drives away, presumably back to civilization. The out-of-gas pick-up truck that brought Ruby into the film sits abandoned and useless in the lower left of the screen. All three have escaped the originary world: Brahmin through psychotic self-destruction, Maddox through cathartic revenge, and Ruby through asserting "masculinity" in a man's world (the desert).

Motorpsycho! is one of Meyer's most undervalued films. It is a film that analyzes the sexual politics between men and women from its critique of the phallocentric law of sheriff/director Russ Meyer to the perversity of Ruby sucking out Maddox's "poison." It also establishes the formula that Meyer would follow in his subsequent films: mixtures of dark comedy, satire, and genre parody that depict the battles and power relationships between men and women in isolated landscapes where sex and violence is one and the same.

CHAPTER THREE ◊ "WELCOME TO VIOLENCE"

FASTER, PUSSYCAT! KILL! KILL! (1966)

"Booted, Belted, and Buckled!"

Faster, Pussycat! is a film that combines sexploitation trash, naturalist, *noir* violence, and surreal melodrama into a seamless whole. Beyond that, *Faster, Pussycat!* is also a profound and hilarious satire of American sexual politics.

    One factor in *Pussycat*'s success was the presence of Tura Satana in the role of Varla, the sadistic go-go girl/hot-red gang leader. While Erica Gavin's performance in *Vixen* is probably the most famous in any Meyer film, it is Satana's Varla who has become the most iconic character in the Meyer film canon. Part Apache and part Japanese, Satana was gang-raped at the age of ten and subsequently trained extensively in karate and aikido. As a teenager in the 1950s, she was the target of anti-Japanese bigotry. She also lead an all-girl gang (ironically, her gang name was "Kitty"), and eventually did time in reform school as a result of her activities. Satana eventually found her niche in the world of exotic dancing; among the venues she performed at was Jack Ruby's Carousel Club. She also appeared in bit parts in a number of Hollywood films such as *Irma la Duce* and *Our Man Flint*, but her cult-film status rests on her performances in *Astro-Zombies*, *The Doll Squad* (both directed by cult-film legend Ted V. Mikels), and, of course, her electrifying performance in Meyer's film. Meyer himself as described the casting *coup* by saying "that was one of the few times I've really lucked out in casting a role – I couldn't have found another girl that had that configuration, and really knew karate and judo and was as strong as a fucking ox."[101] Given her biography, her intimidating on-screen presence was almost natural.[102] Meyer cast regular Haji, who plays Varla's submissive girlfriend Rosie, recalled working with Satana as exotic dancers before they made *Pussycat!*: "We worked at a club called The Losers... Tura and I got along great, but a lot of girls were afraid of her. She was pretty bad, no one would dare use her makeup or hairbrush, or even borrow anything from her."[103] Not surprisingly, Tura Satana and Haji play go-go dancers, along with Lori Williams, who completes the trio as the irrepressible Billie; Williams's performance itself would have stolen the movie had it not had such a dynamic presence as Satana in the lead. In one respect, they are a vastly superior parody of the trio of bikers in *Motorpsycho!*: an amoral, sadistic leader (Varla/Brahmin); an ethnic caricature sidekick (Rosie/Dante); and an undependable, independent loner looking for fun (Billie/Slick). The women seemingly spend their spare time driving hot-rods and fist-fighting, two all-American masculine activities, not to mention seducing and/or humiliating men (two activities not mutually exclusive in a Meyer film).

    While narration is usually a staple in Russ Meyer's films, it is conspicuously absent from his two previous films, *Mudhoney* and *Motorpsycho!*,

---

101. As quoted in Vale and Juno, eds., 78.

102. Recommended articles and interviews with Tura Satana include: Mark Isted, "Go-Go Tura!!! Satana!!!," *Psychotronic Video* #12 (Fall 1992); Michael Musto, "La Dolce Musto," *The Village Voice*, April 20, 1996: 43; Al Ryan and Dan Cziraky, "Tura Satana," *Femme Fatales*, vol. 4, no. 2 (Fall 1995).

103. As quoted in Matt Maranin, "The Best of the Breast! Russ Meyer's Vixens Speak," *Boing Boing* #14 (1995), 24.

LIPS HIPS TITS POWER ◊ THE FILMS OF RUSS MEYER

and the absence of narration allows these films a certain gritty realism (not that Meyer's films are realistic by any stretch of the imagination). Narration reappears gloriously in *Pussycat!*, which begins with a black screen and the strains of diabolical jazz music (in fact, some of the music is cannibalized from *Motorpsycho!*, creating another connection to that film). As narrator John Furlong begins, two parallel vertical lines appear on-screen. They electronically pulsate and spasm in synchronization to Furlong's voice. As he proceeds with the narration, more lines appear; by the end of the narration segment they fill the screen. Like all of Meyer's narration, *Pussycat!*'s prologue contains more than a hint of satire: on one hand it lends an ominous seriousness to the film, yet its verbosity subverts any seriousness. With the narration to *Pussycat!*, Meyer also lays his thematic cards on the table from the first second, and Furlong's delivery is impeccable: equal parts classroom professor and exploitation huckster.

Ladies and gentlemen, welcome to violence: the word and the act. While violence cloaks itself in a plethora of disguises, its favorite mantle still remains... sex. Violence devours all it touches, its voracious appetite rarely fulfilled. Yet violence doesn't only destroy – it creates and molds as well.

The trademark Meyer intersection of sex and violence is made literal: "the word and the act." Whereas *Mudhoney* depicts its final violence as cathartic self-destruction born out of sexual frustration, *Pussycat!* makes clear that sex and violence are one and the same. Instead of dichotomies of sex (productive) and violence (destructive), sex and violence are *equally* productive and destructive.

Let's examine closely then this dangerously evil creation, this new breed encased in the supple skin of woman. The softness is there, the unmistakable smell of female – the surface shiny and silken, the body yielding yet wanton.

At this point the enemy is defined, the battle lines drawn. Initially the narrator places the woman in the classic role of seductive and malevolent *femme fatale*: a "dangerously evil creation" yet "supple... yielding yet wanton." Given the rise of feminism in the 1960s, as well as the ideological slant of many of the roughies, the "dangerously evil creation" could be read as feminism, embodied in and by powerful females, "this new breed" of woman who are soft and supple on the outside, who have "the unmistakable smell of female" (the scent of perfume or female sexual arousal), yet a "creature" capable of both seduction and destruction of men. As Jim Morton noted, "At first Varla appears as nothing more than a sadistic bitch, but by the end of the film she seems almost supernatural. The plot mechanics are similar to those of a monster movie, with Varla the monster. We know she is evil and will die, but we can't help rooting for

82

CHAPTER THREE ◊ "WELCOME TO VIOLENCE"

[104. Vale and Juno, eds., 86]

her; next to her the 'heroes' are a washed-out and bloodless lot."[104] Varla is correctly termed "a monster," a thing both "female" (buxom, seductive) and male (powerful, aggressive): a sexual aberration in the strictly defined sexual roles of 1960s America. In short, Varla is the "monster" of feminism, and yet, of course, the archetypal Meyer woman, physically and sexually powerful: "a man with big tits." And given Meyer's satirical depiction of sexual politics and the central role Varla plays in the film, the apparent return to sexual normalcy at the end of the film is rendered highly problematic by the time *Pussycat!* reaches its furious climax.

But a word of caution... handle with care and don't drop your guard. This rapacious new breed prowls alone and in packs, operating at any level, anywhere, and with anybody. Who are they? One might be your secretary, your doctor's receptionist, or a dancer at a go-go club!

Here the narration recalls the tone of 1950s science-fiction films which often served as Cold War allegories: seemingly normal human beings who are actually alien invaders (i.e. communists), where "friends" and "enemies" are no longer distinguishable. In *Pussycat!*, this is taken one step further, where "heroes" and "villains" are not only readily identifiable, but even "men" and "women" themselves. As to who these "enemies" could be, they could be "secretaries... receptionists... or go-go dancers." Not coincidentally, these three types of "females" are Meyer's favorite targets of male voyeurism (specifically in *Mr. Teas*). Also parodied is the *Playboy* myth of "the girl-next-door," that the woman met yesterday could be the playmate of tomorrow.[105] This myth is given a cruel and hilarious twist in the *noir*, surreal world of *Pussycat!*, where the "girl-next-door" could actually be the harbinger of doom.

[105. See Burn, 14.]

    The moment that the narrator ends with "go-go dancer," the shot cuts to Tura Satana bent over backwards, dancing in a sequined bikini, arms swinging wildly, as The Bossweeds' classic "Pussycat theme" explodes onto the soundtrack. Soon shots of Varla, Rosie, and Billie are quickly intercut with close-ups of male bar patrons as they ogle the dancers (in this context, Varla is "bent over backwards" trying to please the men in the audience). Meyer maintains a spatial distance between the female dances and the male patrons by cinematically separating the males and females: The women are shown individually or collectively dancing, forming montages with leering, singular male faces in close-up; however, the men and women never occupy the same shot and are never shown in the same film frame. A cinematic barrier is not only set where the men literally "look, but don't touch," but a strict division of the sexes is again manifest: men on one side, women on the other (recalling the division of the sexes in the credits of *Motorpsycho!*). The pace of the editing speeds up as the

83

LIPS HIPS T!TS POWER ◊ THE FILMS OF RUSS MEYER

sequence continues, increasing the momentum of the shots as if nearing an orgasm. The men, grotesque close-ups trapped in the confines of the film frame, grow more hilariously agitated, sexually aroused but unable to vent their sexual energies except by hilariously chomping on cigars and badgering the women to "Go, baby, go! Wail! *Harder! Faster!*" A series of rapid close-ups of the juke box cuts to a shot of a car radio, and the male shouts are replaced by tangibly evil, female laughter. The shot cuts to Varla sitting and laughing maniacally behind the wheel of her sports car. She is now in complete control, "behind the driver's seat," away from the oppressive gaze of males. The shot of Varla driving the car provides the orgasmic "release" from the frenzy of the montage, the "Faster!" command of sexual ecstasy (the accelerated thrusting of sexual intercourse) is connected to the eroticism and the sexual thrill of sports cars and high-speed driving. The pent-up sexual energies of the male voyeurs finds its outlet in speed and the open road, in turn suggesting both the ideological signification of the automobile (personal freedom and mobility), as well as the sexual fetishization of the automobile. Yet the "muscle cars" in this case are driven by women, subverting the domain of the hot-rod as an All-American male activity, and transferring masculine power to the women "behind the wheel."

The credits begin and the title of the film appears; underneath the title each of the women is shown in profile driving a sports car: first Varla, then Rosie, and then Billie, the hierarchy of the gang. Shots of the sports cars winding down the highway are shown as the credits appear, and after the credits are completed, Billie's car suddenly veers off the highway and proceeds to a nearby lake. Disgusted, Varla and Rosie turn around to retrieve her. Jumping out of her car, Billie sprints to the shore and dives into the water, fully clothed. Not only is it typical of her impetuous behavior, but the scene also certainly reinforces the connection to water and female sexual libido. Billie is by far the most sexually-outgoing of the three, and her impromptu swim is fused with an exaggerated sense of sexual release. Varla orders Rosie to go into the lake and fetch her. Billie taunts her, telling Rosie she "has it all warmed up for her," referring to the water, her own wetness (female genital sexual arousal), and Rosie's lesbian desires. Rosie responds by calling he a "sponge – an' I'm-a gonna enjoy squeezin' you out!" A fight ensues in the water, and Billie emerges out of the water first, the apparent victor. "She wears the pants all right, but she always manages to strip her gears!" proclaims Billie; a sarcastic comment on Rosie's failure to attain "masculine" superiority over her. She is closely followed by the seething Rosie, who warns her, "You washed, and now I'm-a gonna spin dry you!" The fight moves to the beach, as if fighting, a "masculine" act, must be moved onto dry land (sand, shore, or the desert) and out of the female domain of water. Furthermore, Rosie's metaphor indeed suggests that she is going to "spin dry" Billie by beating the female "wetness" out of Billie. Meanwhile, Varla watches the cat-fight with

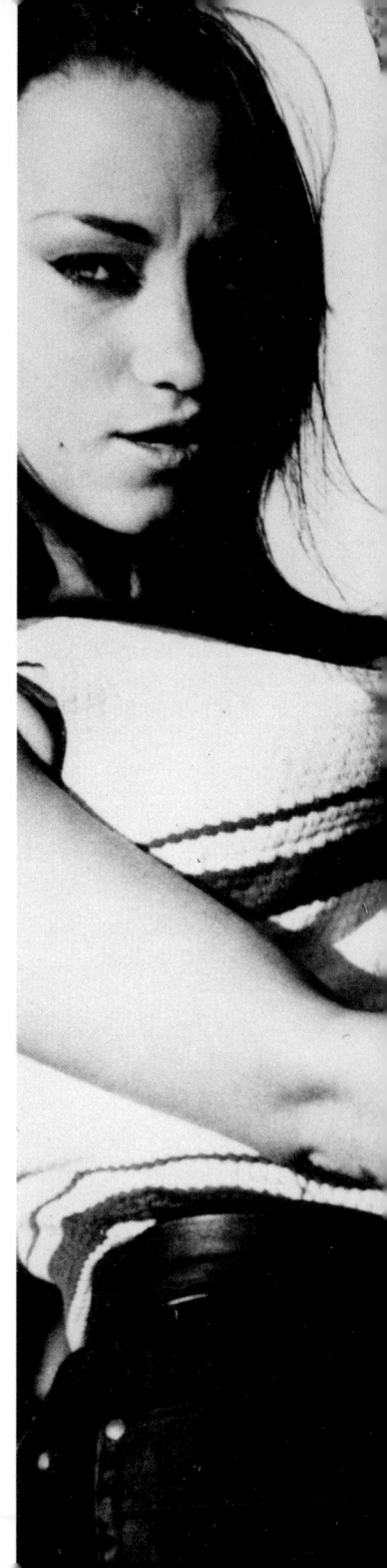

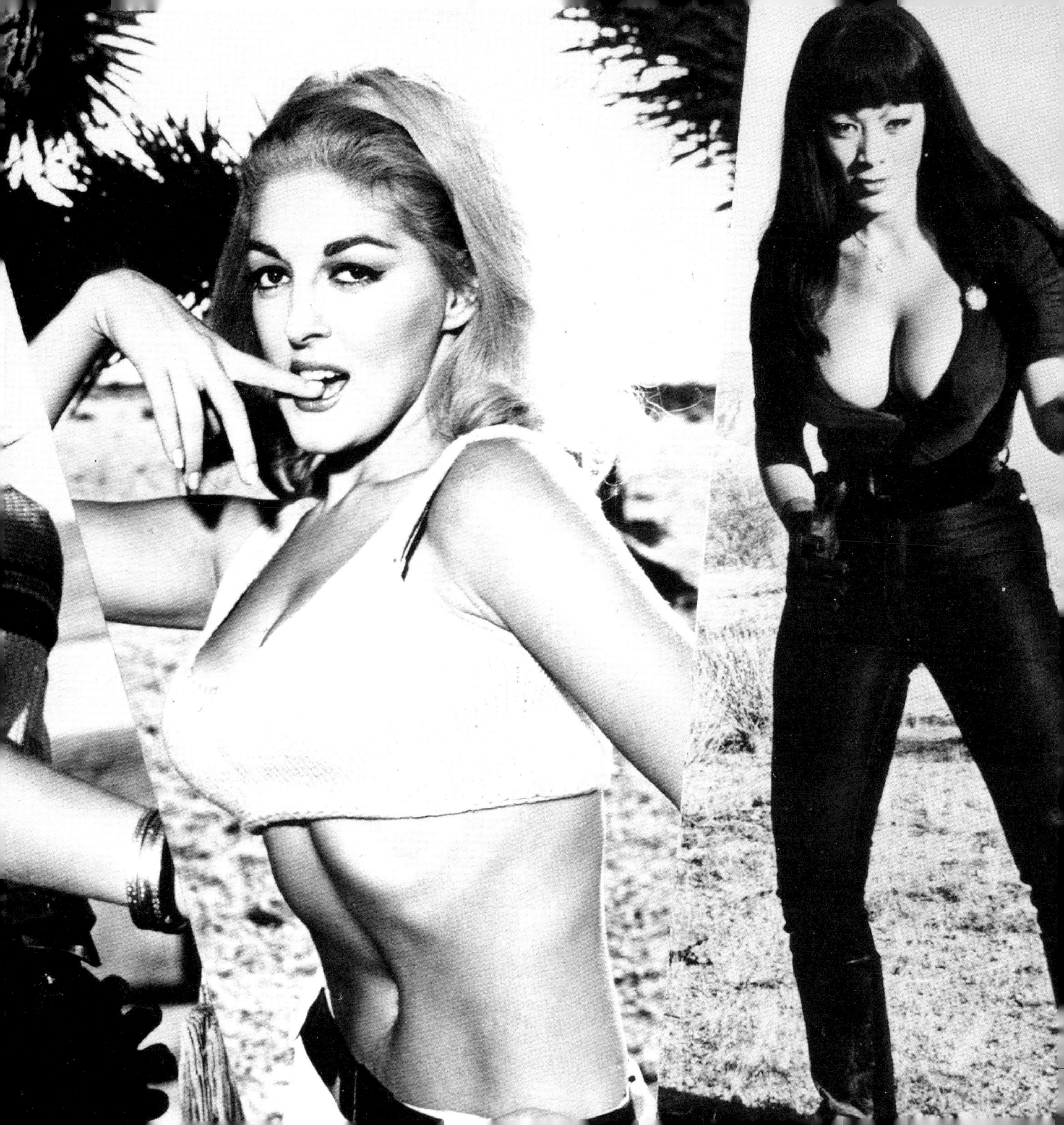

detached pleasure: the sadistic voyeur *par excellence*, turned on by the erotic violence of the cat-fight as a *man* might be. What is equally important is the "androgyny" of Varla. Rather than attempt to eliminate sexual difference, Varla exhibits *both* highly exaggerated male and female characteristics. She is obviously female with her plainly visible cleavage, sultry expression, painted eyebrows, and long, black hair. However, she is equally masculine in her demeanor: her black, leather outfit; her chauvinistic treatment of Rosie; her smoking of dark, filterless cigarettes; even her posture watching the cat-fight with one foot on the bumper, leaning against the car, her forearm on her knee, the other hand on her hip. Stunningly female, she also projects a cold manliness and even a *macho* swagger. As John Waters quite accurately noted, "[Varla] gives new meaning to the word *butch*."[106] However, Varla soon grows disgusted at the melée, but only because of the lack of enthusiasm: "I've seen better fights at our late shows!" Hovering over them, Varla sneers, "You want to prove something, chickies – let's see who the real chicken is!" Again, the dialogue creates puns, with the term "chick" (an attractive girl) and "chicken" (a coward) equated, emphasizing the linkage in Meyer's films of being "female" to being passive and weak, although this "femininity" can be the quality of *either* a (biological) man or woman, as in the case with the ill-fated Tommy and even Kirk.

The shot cuts to a medium close-up of the grille of Varla's sleek black car; the two white convertibles of Rosie and Billie are then shown from behind, next to each other, with Varla's car between them. Close-ups of the smirking Varla are intercut with close-ups of the obviously nervous Rosie and Billie; also intercut into the scene are shots of their respective cars, from varying distances and angles. It becomes a parody of the generic Western showdown scene. A blast of Varla's car horn signals the start of the chicken run, and the cars accelerate towards each other. In the close-ups of Rosie and Billie, the background sky remains motionless (the cars were probably stationary when the shots were filmed), despite the fact that the cars are speeding towards an impending collision with Varla. Inadvertently, a sense of "time standing still" or "going nowhere fast" is created (as in *Mudhoney*), as if time itself has stopped in the already unreal originary world of the desert. It also foreshadows Tommy's arrival in the desert and his own obsession with "time." Varla's almost orgasmic glee during the chicken-run expresses not only sadistic-sexual enjoyment but the Death Instinct itself, the "death-drive" (pun intended) that culminates in cathartic, self-destructive pleasure, or Marcuse's *nirvana principle*, "the terrifying convergence of pleasure and death." This also prefigures the legendary final duel between the Vegetable and Varla, a moment where the automobile is a nexus for both murder and sexual intercourse, death and orgasm.[107] The others veer off as Varla unwaveringly plows towards them, never once deviating from her potentially life-ending path, her victory punctuated by her evil laughter. The

106. *Shock Value*, 193.

107. In this regard, one possible comparison to *Pussycat!* would be J.G. Ballard's amazing novel *Crash*, his clinical, obsessive study of the car as fetish-object and the car crash as a moment of orgasm. While lacking the obsessive power of the book, David Cronenberg's film adaptation of *Crash* also powerfully captures this relationship.

CHAPTER THREE ◊ "WELCOME TO VIOLENCE"

worn stretches of tire tracks indicate that this is not the first time such a run has been acted out; rather, the chicken-run is a sadistic ritual orchestrated by Varla, not to see who wins (which is a given), but an event orchestrated to repeatedly act out her power. As the cars come to a stop, both Rosie and Billie emerge from their cars, sheepishly removing their jackets. Billie attempts to remain defiant: "You have a funny way of getting your kicks... *real funny*." Rosie, on the other hand, is thoroughly submissive, clearly reminded of her role (or "put in her place") in the relationship with Varla. To add further to her humiliation, she tries to light Varla's cigarette for her, but is too shaken by the chicken-run ("easy, baby, you're almost a fire hazard!" Varla tells her). Varla then orders Billie to fetch Rosie a beer out of her car; while doing so, Billie turns on the car radio and begins to impulsively go-go dance. When told to stop by Rosie, Billie retorts, "my

87

motor never stops running, and besides, you're such a wonderful audience!" The connection between sexual libido and car machinery is clearly made, along with the notion of voyeurism, in which Billie is the sex-object dancing for her spectators in the desert: the decidedly "butch" Varla, who "wears the pants" in the gang, and Rosie, who "wears the pants but always strips her gears."

At this point, another hot-rod arrives in the desert. Tommy (Ray Barlow) enters the scene, dressed in a hideous combination of a windbreaker, black golf shirt, Bermuda shorts, dark socks, and loafers. He compliments Varla on her car as Billie brazenly slinks over to him. "Wanna check under *my* hood?" she purrs. Tommy reacts as if she had spoken in an indecipherable language. He asks permission to run some time-trials, and Varla scoffs, "You could time that heap with an hourglass!" As if on cue, the beach-bunny Linda (Susan Bernard) pops out of Tommy's car: "Did somebody mention my figure?" Gender is connected to time, with Linda, the femininity of an hourglass figure, for Tommy, as will soon be discussed, his masculinity is tied to his prized stopwatch. She is clad only in a bikini, the same garments that the women wear dancing at the go-go club; in *Pussycat!*, the bikini becomes a sign of female acquiescence. And not coincidentally, Susan Bernard posed for *Playboy* prior to appearing in *Pussycat!*, further personifying a demure, girl-next-door image. Linda proceeds to set a picnic lunch and other amenities for the women; she asks if they'd like "a soft drink." The incredulous Rosie responds, "Are you kiddin'? We don't like nothin' *soft*." "Hardness" is connected to the women of the gang, specifically the "hardness" of an erection: women with male attributes. Meanwhile, Tommy gives her his stopwatch and carefully explains to Linda how he wants her to time him in his car, then takes off on his run. "He's the fastest one in our car club, and first in safety points, too!" Linda adoringly swoons. However, distracted by chatting and dancing with Billie and the others, she forgets to time Tommy. Thrilled with his run and visibly disappointed when he learns Linda has not timed him, Tommy is nonetheless the forgiving gentleman. The display visibly sickens Varla, who can scarcely hide her contempt for Tommy, who she berates as an "All-American boy... a real safety-first Clyde!" Tommy attempts to explain how he is always striving for a better time: driving is his quest for self-improvement. His various references to "time" become a means by which he expresses his masculinity. Also, in this context, Linda is little more than an attractive assistant in Tommy's program of self-improvement and self-worth, an exaggerated cliché of "the woman behind the man."

"I don't beat clocks – *just people!*" explodes Varla. She challenges Tommy to a race but Tommy initially backs down (assuming the role of a "chick[en]"), but only agrees to "a friendly little race" with Linda's naive urging. Of course, the race does not pan out in that way. As Tommy takes the lead in the final lap, Varla cuts him off and sends him spinning off the track in order to avoid a collision.

CHAPTER THREE ◊ "WELCOME TO VIOLENCE"

While Tommy sits stunned in the car, Linda attempts to rush to his side, shouting inanities about it being her fault, that he needs her, and other such drivel. Varla, who previously and quite sardonically asked Tommy if he got the watch "by beating someone else's time," referring to the act of stealing someone's girlfriend, angrily rips the watch off Linda's neck, now punningly beating Tommy's "time" by stealing his precious symbol of masculinity, his stopwatch. "He's very proud of that watch – he won it!" Linda pleads, crying, establishing a pattern of hysterical behavior that will last for much of the film. Tommy also attempts to get the watch back, finally telling Varla he doesn't "know what the hell her point is." Varla's classic reply: "My point is of no return – and you've just reached it!" Indeed, they *are* at the "point of no return": the originary world of the barren desert, a site of untamed libido where civilized conduct is swept away by animal instinct.

Varla and Tommy begin to fight, and the sight of the black-clad Varla and the suburban teen Tommy's battle is breathtaking. Their almost apocalyptic struggle is both violent and erotic; they appear as if they are engaged in animal intercourse as much as a life or death struggle (as Bataille noted, distinctions not clear in the world of transgression and animal eroticism). Varla subdues him with a series of karate chops, and standing over the battered Tommy in extreme low-angle shots, basking in his humiliation, she tells him he can leave: the territorial imperative is made clear, and the (masculine) desert is established as Varla's domain (here, as Ardrey would contend, the battle for "property" is the source of her sexual arousal). Tommy nods, but suddenly sucker-punches Varla in the stomach and the jaw as he gets up, a vain attempt to assert his masculine authority. Thinking he has defeated Varla, he walks away, only to be leveled by Varla with a vicious aikido throw. Varla then grabs the prone Tommy's arms behind his back and lifts him while she plants her boot in the base of his neck. Tommy is instantly killed, and Linda immediately faints; the shot of her sprawled body on the desert floor dissolves to a close-up of the unconscious girl's face as she sits in the passenger seat next to Varla. She is now literally "stolen" from Tommy; Varla has not only "beaten his time," but "beaten the time out of him." Indeed, Tommy's "time" has run out entirely.

The scene shifts to a gas station. Mickey Foxx, essentially reprising his role as the grotesque rumor-spreading Thurman Pate in *Mudhoney* (a character part *Li'l Abner* and part Tod Browning's *Freaks*), provides a brief cameo as a gas station attendant in which he sets up the remainder of the film, providing necessary information for the women and the audience about the male counterparts they will soon encounter. When first seeing the Vegetable, Billie licks her lips and exclaims, "What a hunk of stuff – *Whooo!*" Foxx responds, "He's got muscles all the way to his ears... he's kind of a nut... and the Old Man is an even bigger one."

89

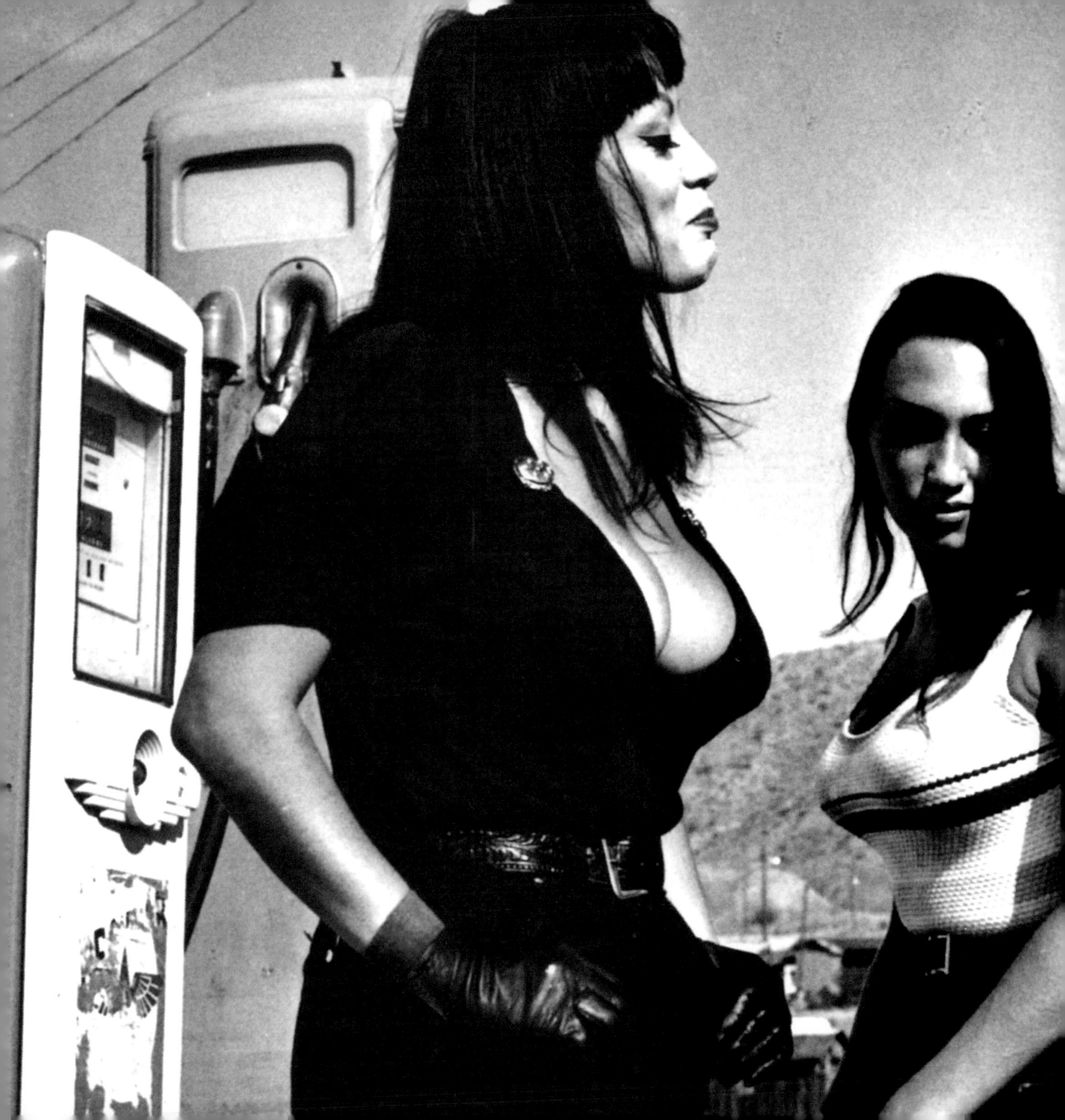

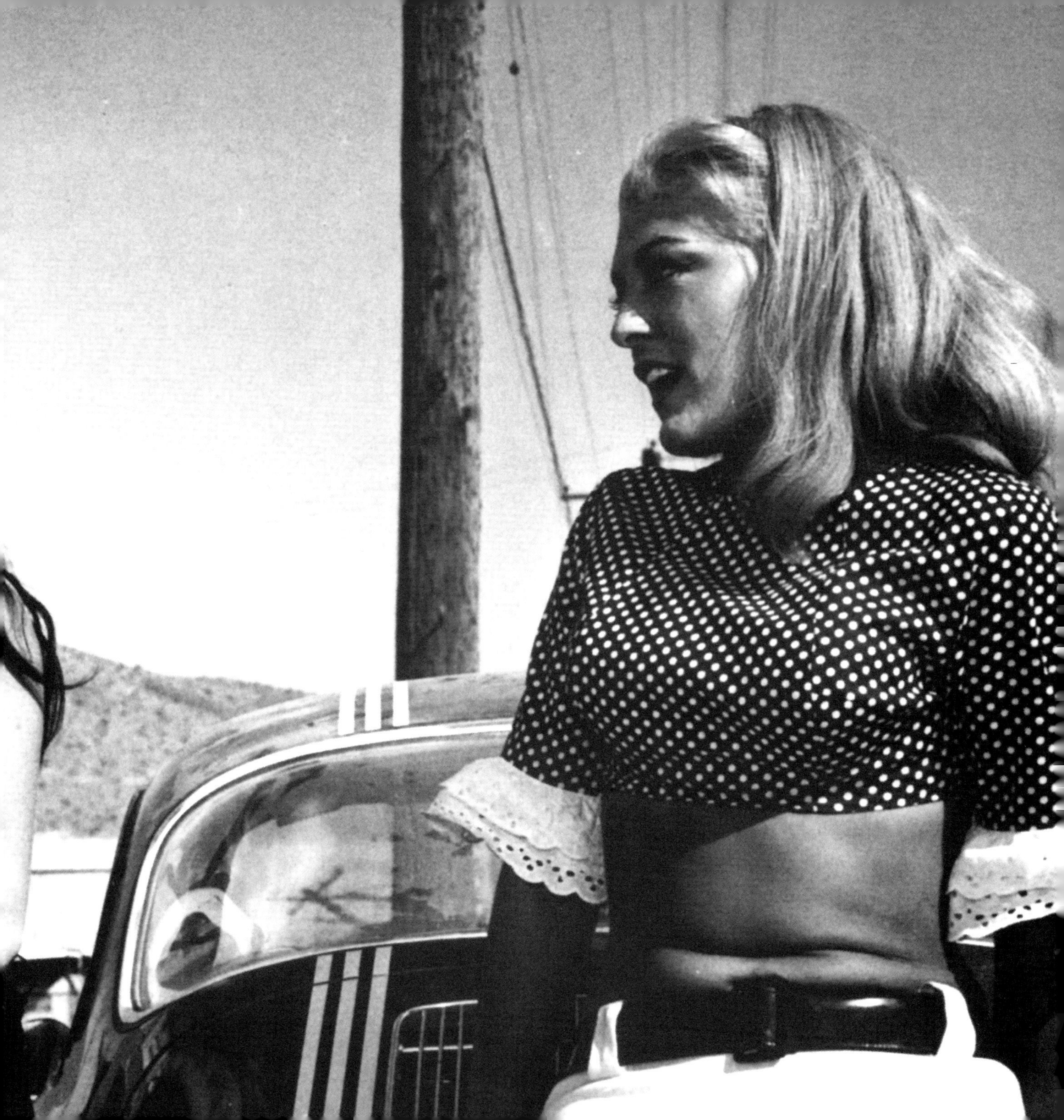

The shot cuts to the Vegetable carrying the paralyzed Old Man like a bride over the threshold; it is a moment of surreal comedy. Informed by Foxx about the Old Man's farm and the fortune in cash he has hidden there, the women decide to investigate.

They Let 'em Vote, Smoke, and Drive – Even Put 'em in Pants!

The arrival at the dilapidated farm in the middle of the desert suggests a rural world of isolation, corruption, and decay: the originary world of instinct has all but conquered this "derived milieu." Stuart Lancaster, who plays the honorable farm patriarch in *Mudhoney*, plays his evil antithesis in *Pussycat!*: a self-hating, misogynistic, psychotic alcoholic. He has two sons. One is the aforementioned Vegetable (Dennis Busch), a muscle-bound, mentally retarded lummox. The other is Kirk (Paul Trinka), the domestic milquetoast who runs the house and covers up what is occurring there: the murders of young women orchestrated by the Old Man and executed by the Vegetable. As in *Lorna*, one sees a psychopathic, homeosocial male order that does not simply exclude "the female", but strives to erase it entirely. With the arrival of the girl trio, the conflicting divisions are based on "gender" lines: "this new breed" of smart. sexy, powerful women verses the decaying male order of a crazed patriarch, retarded muscleman, and henpecked son. Yet the relationships between the adversaries possess a strange synchronicity as well. One is reminded of the parallel relationships between Jim and the Convict in *Lorna*; Calif and Sidney in *Mudhoney*; Maddox and Brahmin in *Motorsycho!*; the male gang and the female gangs in *Motorpsycho!* compared to *Pussycat!*. In *Pussycat!*, there is a sadistic killer who leads the gang (Varla/the Old Man), an obedient servant (Rosie/the Vegetable), and the increasingly belligerent conscience of the group (Billie/Kirk). To hammer the point home, in the hilarious seduction scene between Varla and Kirk, he states, You're a lot like him in a lot of ways," referring to his despotic father.

The opening salvo of the confrontation begins when Kirk catches Varla spying on the Old man and the Vegetable, the latter who perversely holds a kitten (or "pussycat") in his arms. Varla tells Kirk to take it easy, "or can't you tell I'm a woman?" Of course he cannot, Varla is both "man" and "woman," and the Old Man later fittingly describes Varla as being "more stallion than mare." Explaining that she and her girlfriends have innocently stopped to get some water from their water tower after driving all day, the exasperated Old Man unleashes a classic piece of vitriol:

They let 'em vote, smoke, and drive – even put 'em in pants! So what do you get? A Democrat for president! A lot of smoke up your chimney – Russian Roulette on the highway. You can't even tell brother from sister – unless you meet 'em head on.

The Old Man's diatribe covers everything from allowing the women to vote; the Cold War; the cliché of "women drivers" who are stereotypically bad drivers; and the breakdown of traditional sexual roles. He equates sexual politics, the

LIPS HIPS TITS POWER ◊ THE FILMS OF RUSS MEYER

automobile (erotic machines of speed and destruction), and the specter of nuclear war: "Russian Roulette" – a suicidal game in which the loser is killed. The battle of the sexes becomes as apocalyptic as World War III, where men and women can not be told apart, "unless you meet 'em head on" in violent collisions. Nonetheless, it is also quite easy to tell the difference between the men and the women (in the biological sense, at least). The very presence of the sultry Varla is

CHAPTER THREE ◊ "WELCOME TO VIOLENCE"

incongruous against the crusty examples of American manhood. Not surprisingly, the women's vehicles are sleek, modern sports cars, the vehicle on the farm a clunky pick-up truck. The strange, alien otherness of "the female" is exacerbated by the women's "buxoticness" (a neologism coined by Meyer conflating "busty" and "exotic").

An uneasy truce is forged between the men and the women to use some water on the farm, and the sports cars set up camp around the water tower. The connection to women's libido and water is again manifest, it is a spot where they can "recharge their batteries." Billie, the most sexually uninhibited of the three, immediately begins to bathe under the water tower, her bare back to the camera, repeating "Oh yes... Oh God, this feels great!" as if she is on the verge of orgasm. Later, before Varla is about to seduce Kirk in order to find out where the money is, she also takes a shower, again establishing the connection between female libido, sexual arousal, and water. Even at Varla's suggestion, Rosie declines a shower. She is the only member of the group to have no heterosexual leanings, and remains conspicuously "dry" throughout the film, unlike the "sponge" Billie, the most overtly heterosexual member of the group (however, in later Meyer films, water and flora do extend to lesbian desire as well). Varla informs Rosie of the story they will give the Old Man: Linda is a senators's daughter whose boyfriend got killed drag-racing and that they are discreetly trying to return the shaken girl home. Even Rosie has a hard time buying the credibility of the story. "You don't have to believe it – just act it!" Varla admonishes her: a wonderful, self-referential comment at the moment the film itself begins to stretch all credibility. This is made further obvious when the Old Man and the Vegetable approach the water tower: "And now," announces Varla, "this is where our screenplay starts to unfold," a line that comments on the film in Brechtian fashion. Film dialogue (as in *Motorpsycho!*) serves to comment on the representation the viewer sees, as well as tipping off future plots developments (when Varla says the Old Man is "sitting on some bread," she actually reveals the film's ending: the money is hidden under the seat of the Old Man's wheelchair). Their discussion is punctuated by a wonderful shot of the Old Man and the Vegetable in the background center of the frame; in the foreground, Rosie stands on the left side of the frame, Varla on the right. The women's buttocks clearly show "a pair of asses," which is what the Old Man and the Vegetable are as well.

When the Old Man accepts the story, Rosie and Varla decide to do some investigating, leaving Billie and Linda alone. As the Old Man waits on the porch in an agitated state, planning the raping and killing of the women, Billie and Linda make their way into the scene. Billie soon leaves with the Vegetable, while Linda,"the sweet little cottontail," is left with the Old Man, who perversely fondles his shotgun and cryptically says, "The little lady and I'll be safe." The first of two utterly hilarious failed seduction scenes follow. Billie circles the bare-

LIPS HIPS TITS POWER ◊ THE FILMS OF RUSS MEYER

chested Vegetable like a prowling animal as he lifts weights. Her sexual interest is blatant, and she offers to be his manager (presumably replacing the Old Man), and ponders "10% of your action would be enough for anybody" (a thinly-veiled reference to his genital size). The Vegetable is completely oblivious to her advances, concentrating instead on his weights. This reiterates a pervasive theme in Meyer's films: the relationship of beautiful, sex-hungry women and men who seemingly refuse to engage in sex because they are preoccupied with

CHAPTER THREE ◊ "WELCOME TO VIOLENCE"

their own hobbies (fishing) or their personal programs of self-improvement (be it work, school, exercise, or "improving their time"). Billie becomes more and more exasperated as her sexual advances become more overt and remain completely unheeded. Moreover, there is an ominous sense that if the Vegetable did respond, he would not know whether to "kiss or kill" her. Fittingly, the scene is interrupted by a scream; Linda has escaped from the Old Man. In an cruel and ironic plot twist, she makes her way out to the desert, where she "rescued" by Kirk, who is actually returning back to the farm, ensuring that Linda has not escaped from harm, but is placed back in danger.

Death-Machines and Sex-Machines

Varla's return to the farm is heralded by her car speeding towards the camera and stopping just inches away, the left front headlight filling the screen. Her oncoming presence serves to remind the viewer of the imposing sense that both she and car have, an almost tangible evil. It also prefigures the arrival of another equally important machine: the train. After the hysterical Linda is subdued, Kirk anxiously asks his father what is going on, and the Old Man relays the same preposterous story Varla invented. Learning that the Vegetable has gone off alone with Billie, Kirk grows even more upset. The Old Man cynically asks if Kirk thinks the Vegetable needs "Chaperonin'." The mangled word "chaperone" cuts to a montage of the sight and sound of a train as it careens towards the foreground; indeed, in all the shots of the train, it is always moving towards the audience, never away, as if the film viewer was caught in the very path of the train. The shot cuts to the Vegetable, who is on the verge of finally being seduced by Billie. He begins to lurch madly, holding his head in his hands. Another shot of the train speeding towards the spectator cuts to the disturbed Vegetable and Billie, who attempts to console him. With the advent of the train's arrival, the Vegetable is unable to consummate the sex act with Billie: stammering that the train upsets his father, he rushes back to the house. The equally sexually-frustrated Billie berates the Vegetable with a classic *double-entendre*: "You better straighten your tie, Samson, or papa'll be mad!" And when she sheepishly returns to Varla and Rosie, Varla chides her by telling her "You've been a long time coming," "I'll say!" is Billie's almost inevitable response.

In *Pussycat!*, the train becomes a mythic presence, embodying the cataclysmic forces of "Sex" itself. While the automobile is a point where sex and violence, orgasm and death all converge, the train suggests (to excuse the description) something even larger and more powerful: the underlying libidinal force of Death itself made briefly and all-too visible in its inexorable path down the tracks.[108] It is a thundering embodiment of the instinctual forces of the originary world that erupts forth underneath the veneer of "civilization," represented by the Old Man's run-down farm decaying under the onslaught of

108. My analysis here owes greatly to Deleuze's interpretation of Zola's *La Bête Humaine* (*The Human Beast*), in which he argues the novel features the train as an epic symbol of both modernity and the Instinct of Death – the individual characters whose destinies revolve around the train descend into adultery, alcoholism, madness, murder, and self-destruction (indeed, Zola's novel ends with a driverless train careening down the tracks carrying drunken soldiers to the front lines). See "Zola et la fêlure" ("Zola and the Crack"), preface to Emile Zola, *La Bête Humaine* (Paris: Gaumillard, 1976).

97

LIPS HIPS TITS POWER ◊ **THE FILMS OF RUSS MEYER**

CHAPTER THREE ◊ "WELCOME TO VIOLENCE"

animality. Lancaster delivers a wonderfully histrionic monologue as the train roars passed the farm: "Some things never change... (he smashes his fist against his paralyzed legs and grimaces in pain)... sound your warning... send your message... huff and puff and belch your smoke... *kill*!... *maim*!... *and run out unpunished* !... " Kirk interrupts the Old Man's diatribe, asking him who he is talking to. "Ghosts," answers the Old Man, "50-ton, high-ballin' ghosts... runnin' late, as usual." For the Old Man, the train is a constant reliving of the trauma, his paralysis (and presumably his impotence) caused by helping a woman jump the train. The train is a reminder of his lost manhood that fuels his unquenchable thirst for misogynistic revenge: a thirst sated only momentarily by alcohol, rape, and murder. A heated argument between Kirk and the Old Man about the Vegetable ensues. While the Old Man derisively refers to him as "an animal," Kirk describes his brother as something manufactured by the Old Man. Unapologetic, the Old Man refers to the Vegetable as a means for "doin' what humans can't do – ," " – or *won't* do," Kirk angrily interjects. The Vegetable is a creature of pure animal instinct, a surrogate killing animal-machine, the Old Man's "tool" (pun intended) for rape and murder.

The scene shifts to the dinner table for the surreal lunch sequence, perhaps only describable as Norman Rockwell meets Luis Buñuel. Kirk has prepared fried chicken and all the trimmings. "Does he sew, too?" asks Varla sardonically, obviously questioning Kirk's "manhood." Indeed, Kirk tends to the duties traditionally assigned to women: cleaning, cooking, care-taking; in the subsequent seduction sequence with Varla it can be said that Kirk is the passive (female) object of seduction by the male aggressor (Varla). The Old Man is in lecherous, drunken form, his off-color comments punctuated by lewd tongue-wagging. Billie's sexual attention stays on the Vegetable: "Breast or thigh, darlin'?" she purrs; the Old Man interjects. "Take one of each, they're both so tender!" The body parts of the chicken are equated to the body parts of "chicks," or women, and the Vegetable ravenously consumes piece after piece of chicken the same way he rapes and murders "chicks." "Is their any more food?" he asks, oblivious to the mounting tension around the table. Getting drunk with the Old Man, Billie proposes a toast to "trains – they're big, fast, and make a lot of noise." The toast conjures up more "ghosts" of the past and the specter of Death. The Old Man, deteriorating into drunken despair, reveals that the Vegetable "has always been big," and his mother died giving birth to him. The morose Old Man begins to rant about how much he hates the Vegetable, who he blames for his wife's death, and how he came into the world "killing women." The tension around the table explodes into violence when Varla slaps Billie for making a veiled comment about Tommy's murder; this rouses Linda out of her stupor, and she begins rambling about Varla and the murder: 'She kills – with her bare hands!' she screams once again before breaking down into sobbing helplessness.[109]

109. Tura Satana recounted Susan Bernard was a problem both on and off the set. "I could not get her to react. So I had to literally make her *hate* me. I had to make her *and* her mother hate me – because her mother was with her and it was one of those type of things. I haven't spoken to her since the movie" (Ryan and Cziraky, 44); "She was a typical Hollywood brat. I'd get so mad at her I'd turn away and smash a railroad tie with a karate chop" (Waters, 186).

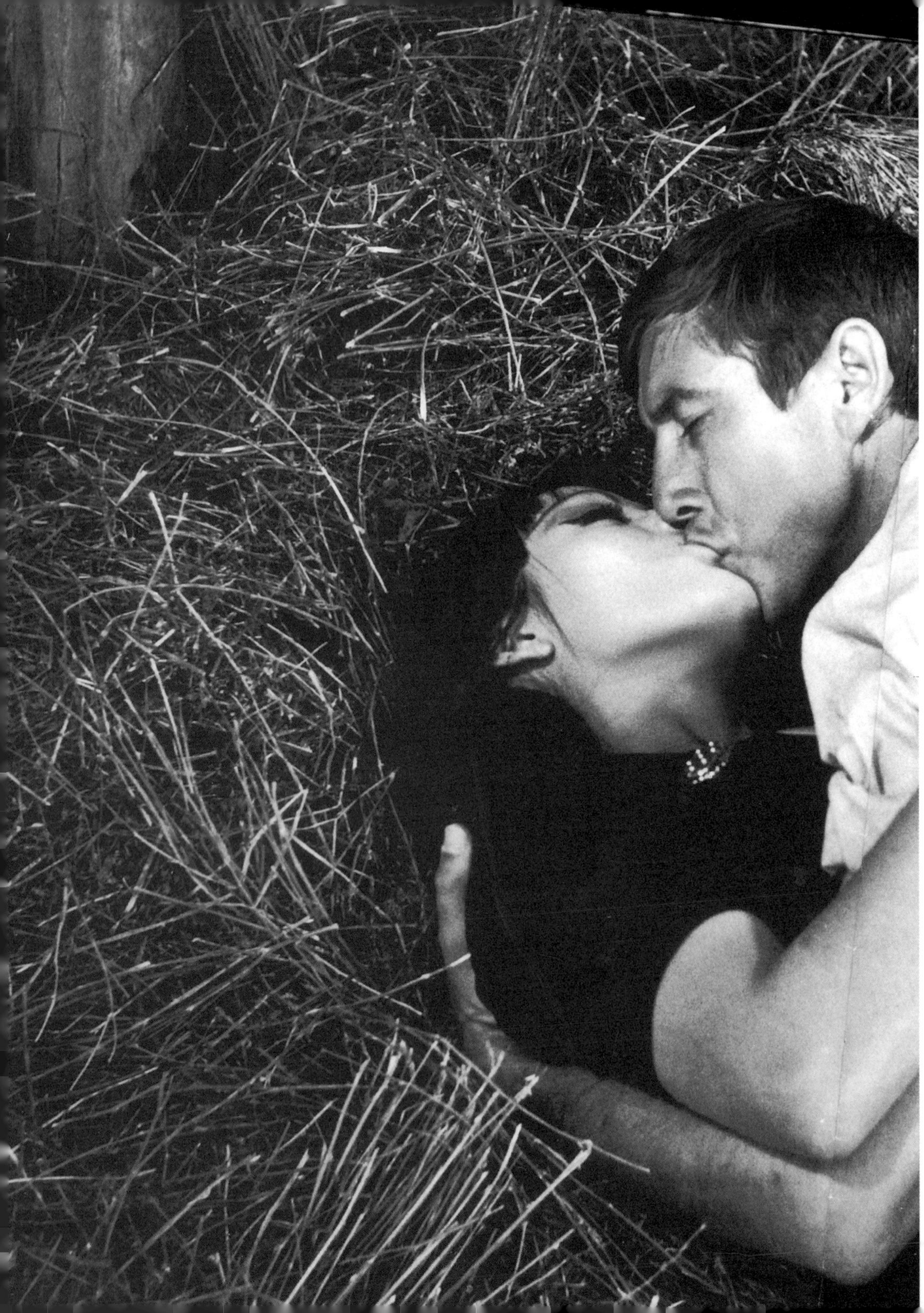

CHAPTER THREE ◊ "WELCOME TO VIOLENCE"

Lunch by now in utter disarray, Varla escorts Kirk from the table to implement her plan. The drunken Billie and Rosie remain with the helpless Linda, and Billie makes some pointed comments about Rosie and Varla's relationship: "You only got one channel, and your channel is tuning in outside – you one-way broads are a drag!" A close-up of Billie slurping on a booze bottle cuts to a close-up of Varla and Kirk kissing, and when Rosie sees Varla and Kirk passionately kissing, she bursts into tears.[110] The montage signifies intoxication, Billie with liquor, Kirk with the seductive power of Varla. "You're a beautiful animal and I'm weak," he pathetically tells Varla, an almost archetypal comment from a man to a woman in a Russ Meyer film. Moreover, she, like the Vegetable, is an "animal," a creature of instinct beyond morality or ethics. As Varla leans back in a hay bale, a wonderful parody of the famous shot of Jane Russell and her bosom in *The Outlaw* (1947), the seduction is about to be consummated, with Varla's ulterior motive, learning the hiding place of the Old Man's money, the next step. However, a seduction is once again interrupted by a Linda escape attempt. The Old Man and the Vegetable pursue her, and Rosie gets Varla's car. "That sounds like my motor running... and that makes twice today," Varla tells Kirk. Again, the linkage between engines to libido is forged, and Varla's "motor" has been "revved up" twice: once by killing Tommy, once by attempting to seduce Kirk. Sex and violence contain the same erotic charge.

Linda's rescue, as was with her first rescue, is ripe with irony. Varla and Kirk are placed in the position of being her rescuers: Varla needs Linda alive to keep her plan intact; Kirk to keep his brother out of further trouble. Linda has once again run into the desert, and the Old Man sends the Vegetable after her, shouting orders at him like an attack dog. In one shot, Linda cowers in the foreground as the hulking, imposing figure of the Vegetable is in the background, a shot that parodies countless generic scenes from monster movies or a panel from an EC comic in the 1950s. Varla and Kirk arrive just in time, and the bulling voice of his father is matched by Kirk's impassioned pleas. The Vegetable struggles with, and finally overcomes, his desire to kill; the shot cuts to the prone Old Man and then a close-up of his hand as he clenches a handful of sand that runs through his fingers, a metaphor for his lost and now-dissipating masculine power that can only be exercised through commanding the Vegetable to kill women for him. With this second assault on Linda, Kirk decides that he has had enough and finally "becomes a man," deciding he can no longer protect his brother or tolerate his father. And, by choosing Linda, Varla's plans are thwarted as well. The stage is set for *Pussycat!*'s conclusion, a violent purge filled with irony and black humor.

Getting the three women together, Varla determines that everyone has to be wiped out. Billie declines, and opts to leave the gang. Her priceless farewell and last words: "See you girls in church." Varla orders Rosie to give up her

---

110. Haji remembered. "When it came to that scene when I was crying because Tura was making out with that man, I didn't understand why I should be crying. But as an actress I just do as I'm directed. Afterwards, I asked Russ about it and he said, 'Well, your jealous because she's your lover and she's with a man...' I said 'Ooooooh! I didn't know we were lesbians!' He should have told me in the beginning, I might have played things a little differently" (Maranain, 24).

switchblade (recalling Luther and Jonah in *Lorna*'s conclusion); a low-angle close-up frames the knife positioned in front of Varla's crotch, suggesting an erect penis. She throws the knife into Billie's back, the scene reenacted from *Lorna* and also recalling Brahmin's shooting Slick in the back in *Motorpsycho!*. The Old Man and the Vegetable also arrive back at the farm, and seeing Billie dead, the Vegetable hovers over her, distraught, unable to comprehend her death. This leaves the Old Man vulnerable, and Rosie and Varla get into her car. There is a slow, tracking shot from the point-of-view of the Old Man in the wheelchair, the malevolent presence of Varla's car again recalling the horror film. His death is clearly foreshadowed when the Old Man is comically unable to get over the porch steps in his wheelchair as the black sports car stalks him, itself a predatory animal-machine. In a hilarious, final act of defiance, the Old Man yells, turns his wheelchair around, and propels it towards Varla's car. Varla accelerates and they meet "head on": sexy, sleek black muscle car verses wheelchair. It is no contest; the Old Man's lifeless body flies off, accompanied by Varla's sadistic laughter. The punch line of the plot is also finally revealed: the money has been hidden under the wheelchair seat all along, and is scattered in the collision.

Rosie is the next person summarily eliminated from the film. While Varla gathers the loot, she sends Rosie to retrieve the (phallic) switchblade. The confused Vegetable remains stationed over Billie's body. Rosie nervously tries to talk him into surrendering the knife. The Vegetable ponders for a moment, than brutally thrusts the knife into Rosie's stomach. The violence is jarring, in that Rosie is a lesbian, and her first "penetration" by a man is not only horrifying, but life-ending. Moreover the possession of the phallic knife, the bestower of masculinity, now passes to the Vegetable.

These sexually-fused acts of violence set the stage for one of the most celebrated scenes in all of Meyer's film: the legendary "car-murder" of the Vegetable. Seeing her lover dead, Varla guns the gas on her car and slams the Vegetable against a wall, pinning him and attempting to crush him. The Vegetable struggles back, shoving against the car. They rock back and forth in the motion of sexual intercourse as the sequence adroitly cuts between the sweating, straining Vegetable and Varla with her face contorted in sadistic pleasure. The "killing-machines" are pitted against each other: Varla's car, the killing-machine of "the new breed... encased in the form of woman," versus the brawn of the Vegetable, the killing-machine of the Old Man. One can argue that this battle represents feminism verses traditional patriarchy, yet the clash also essays the very relationship of power, sex, and violence. The muscles of the Vegetable strain against Varla's eroticized, mechanized instrument of death: her "muscle-car." Violence, sex and death reach a crescendo: driving, fucking, and killing all become forged into one simultaneous act. So dramatic is this scene that many remember the Vegetable being killed; in fact, he defeats Varla's car by

CHAPTER THREE ◊ **"WELCOME TO VIOLENCE"**

stalling it in its tracks. The beaten, perhaps emasculated, Varla gets out of the car and kicks the rear tire. She slowly circles the spent Vegetable and snarls, "That's two out of the falls!" While Meyer does not explain the fate of the Vegetable, one can assume his victory is "short-lived."

Survival of the Unfittest

The film appropriately returns to the vast, barren deserts for the final battle: Varla and Kirk. Kirk and Linda are making their way back to the farm when they spot the pick-up careening towards them. Kirk realizes something is amiss because his brother "can't drive like that!" The pick-up begins to pursue them, and in one shot they are chased down the railroad tracks from a point-of-view shot of Varla, the driver. The shot also suggests what would be the point-of-view of the train on the verge of mowing down the "civilized couple." For an instant, Varla truly does become not only "supernatural," but "mythic," as if the instinctual force of Death itself was embodied by Varla by way of the point-of-view shot. She is a creature of *both* genders, a buxotic woman endowed with not only big breasts but powerful masculinity, a figure of Hegelian proportions (to excuse the pun) – a synthesis of man and woman about to crush the typical, traditional, and outmoded heterosexual couple.

Kirk and Linda get off the tracks and are soon cornered by Varla, and the ensuring fight recalls the Varla-Tommy death match. Like the battle with the Tommy, the violence of hand-to-hand combat is fused with eroticism, with close-ups and point-of-view shots of the sweating Varla atop Kirk. This calls to mind the shot of Jim beating Luther in *Lorna* as well; the point-of-view shot of the victim directs the dominant character's masculine violence towards the film spectator as well. Again, Varla emerges the victor and is about to deliver the *coup de grace* on Kirk when Linda decides to "act like a man": she gets "in the driver's seat" of the pick-up and runs Varla down. Varla's final gestures are as defiant as that of the Old Man. Mortally wounded, she attempts to give Kirk one last karate chop. The close-up of her gloved, gnarled hand and bleeding, contorted face recalls the classic Universal horror films (specifically, *The Wolf Man*). Yet Linda does not emerge from the truck triumphant, but her wailing and sobbing reaches new levels of histrionics, and she runs into the arms of Kirk for comfort. "Calm down," he says, "you saved my life." "I guess I saved my own too," she concurs. They climb into the pick-up and drive away, the camera now lingering on the lifeless desert as the Bostweeds' theme is reprised and the closing credits roll.

While its ending is similar to *Motorpsycho!*, *Faster, Pussycat! Kill! Kill!* offers a fascinating deconstruction of gender through the problematic death of the bitch-goddess Varla. While the voluptuous Varla can simply be read as an "over-valued" fetish-object and a "de-valued" castrating, lesbian sadist, she is perfectly described by the Old Man in the aforementioned line, "more stallion than mare." By the end of the film she is by far the most important character: more man than Kirk and more woman than Susan, the tepid, mediocre couple who ultimately survive the film's bloody conclusion. Indeed, not only is Varla, the male/female "monster," eliminated, but so is the lesbian (Rosie), the perverted cripple (the Old Man), the whore (Billie), and the retarded rapist (the Vegetable), all of whom are sexual aberrations in the sexual climate of 1960s America (it is this expulsion of the sexual "outcasts" and especially the character that is *both* male and female that Meyer also satirizes in his later masterpiece, *Beyond the*

CHAPTER THREE ◊ "WELCOME TO VIOLENCE"

Valley of the Dolls). The triumph is one of the milquetoast male and the hysterical female. The climactic battle in the desert, the site of masculinity, is hilariously perverted when the crying Linda emerges as victor over the powerful Varla: her actions become war crimes in the battle of the sexes. The ending of *Motorpsycho!* establishes the heterosexual order in the form of the happy ending, although this ending is far from unproblematic. In *Pussycat!*, the ending rings utterly false. The victorious Kirk and Linda drive away, leaving a desert landscape literally devoid of vitality and life. In this sense, the film ends on a tone of sinister farce.

Faster, Pussycat! Kill! Kill! is a masterpiece of modern cinema. It is the quintessential Russ Meyer film, an intensely edited film with poetic, trash-talking dialogue which oscillates between *non-sequiturs* and *double-entendres*. It is a razor-sharp mixture of sex and violence, black comedy and *noir* melodrama, dark satire and Gothic tragedy, all set in an isolated, originary world of lust and violence: a "point of no return." It fittingly, and gloriously, marks the close of Russ Meyer's roughie period.

It was during his early "roughie" period that Russ Meyer became involved, incongruously, with the period romp *Fanny Hill* (1964) an Albert Zugsmith production filmed in Germany. Meyer abandoned this project before completion, and has since disowned it.

Fanny Hill

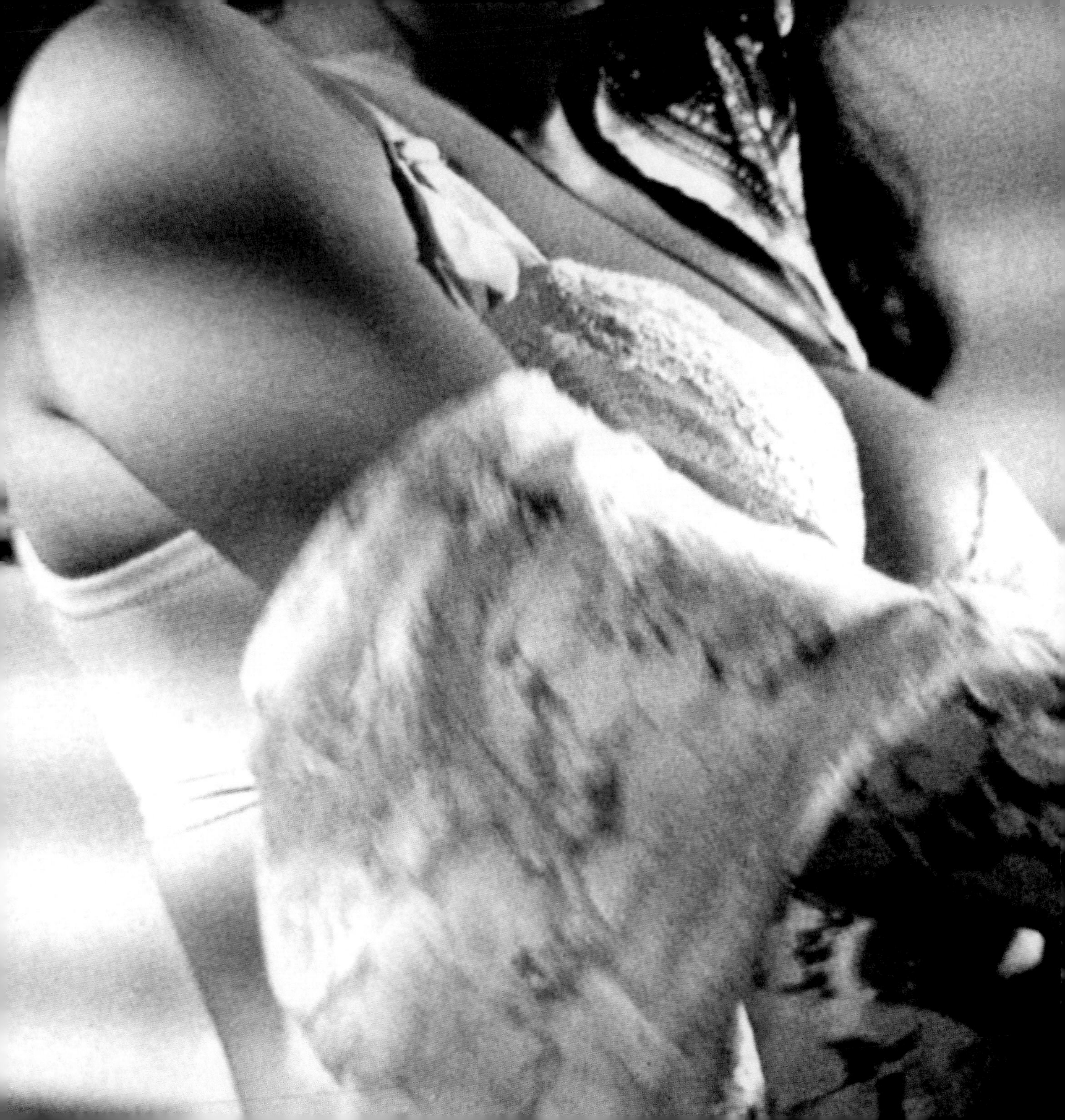

CHAPTER FOUR
SWINGING SIXTIES

*The transgression does not deny the taboo
but embraces it and completes it.*
—Georges Bataille

From Roughie to Revisionism

After *Pussycat!*, Meyer began what is considered his third phase. This incredibly prolific period saw Meyer do six films: *Mondo Topless* (1966), *Common Law Cabin* (1967), *Good Morning... and Goodbye!* (1967), *Finders Keepers, Lovers Weepers* (1968), the box-office bonanza *Vixen* (1968), and the hallucinatory *Cherry, Harry, and Raquel* (1969). While the formula remains the same, parodic sex-satires featuring big-busted women and less-than-manly men, important stylistic changes take place. First, and the most obvious, is the return to *color* in all of its garish beauty. Far from the macabre black and white of the roughies, the films after *Pussycat!* use color as loud and as gaudy as any Pop Art piece or Warner Brothers animation, and the films actually seem to have the actual physical appearance of a cartoon. The second change is the return of *the narrator*: all of these films, with the possible exception of *Finders Keepers, Lovers Weepers*, contain narrated prologues and/or epilogues with a somber narrator describing the backdrop of the film, setting up the themes of the film, and providing summaries of the film which satirize the "moral message" the film supposedly contains. The authoritative voice of the film, the narrations are both portentous and absurd, saying much while saying nothing at all. The third change is the more overt and growing use of *self-reference* in Meyer's film. While there are related themes and moments in the previous films, there is a growing tendency for Meyer to consciously "quote" himself, recycling and refiguring shots, scenes, sequences and plots from his previous films. The fourth, and probably most important change, is the *editing* and *shot composition*. The editing becomes even more rapid-fire than before, with montages becoming a blistering array of images. At times, Meyer uses stock footage (the demolition derby in *Finders Keepers, Lovers Weepers*) as well as shots filmed by Meyer himself that seemingly have no relation to the plot, notably the recurring, jarring inserts of Uschi Digard in *Cherry, Harry, and Raquel*. In effect, these inserts are not narrative, and even serve to interrupt the narrative, forcing the viewer to make associative montages or simply be bewildered by the film. In addition to the stock footage or other inserts, Meyer freely inserts *subjective* shots, shots of character's thoughts or fantasies into the film, as well as objective shots of the camera depicting the narrative. In other words, the camera freely goes between the *first person* and the *third person* perspective. The foremost effect of these editing strategies is that plot becomes increasingly difficult to follow, and to a large degree, makes plot expendable in favor of a freer exchange of images: the pace of the editing becomes more and more frenetic at the expense of narrative, which is reduced to almost surreal soap opera.[111] Finally, the shot composition also grows more extreme: the long shots become longer, the close-ups become closer, and the high-angle and low-angle shots are taken to new extremes, at times creating a sense of vertigo for the viewer. A favored technique of Meyer's is extreme low-angle shots of the women in his films, which exaggerates both their physical attributes as well as their imposing presence. Between the unorthodox shot composition and the radical and disjointed editing, Meyer's films become quite comparable to foreign avant-garde filmmakers such as Jean-Luc Godard and Pier Paolo Pasolini.

111. See Ebert, "Russ Meyer: King of the Nudies," page 7 of 14.

MONDO TOPLESS (1966)

"Busty Buxotic Beauties!"

Mondo Topless serves as important break from the roughie not only in its overpowering color, but its use of a mock-documentary format in place of roughie melodrama. By the end of the film, *Mondo Topless* at once parodies the industrial film format, the often interminable stripping and topless dancing scenes that had come to dominate sexploitation films, and, of course, the *Mondo* genre of shock-documentaries in the 1960s. The *Mondo* genre began in 1963 with the Italian film *Mondo Cane* (1963, dir. Gualtiero Jacopetti): the title roughly translates into "World Gone to the Dogs." The Mondo films were themselves were pseudo-documentaries featuring and contrasting a variety of First World and Third World cultural practices pertaining to food, sex, religion, art, and other

CHAPTER FOUR ◊ **SWINGING SIXTIES**

112. By far the best study of the *mondo* genre is David Kerekes and David Slater, *Killing for Culture: An Illustrated History of the Death Film from Mondo to Snuff* (London: Creation Books, 1993).

curiosities.[112] The *Mondo* films were also notorious for their questionable degrees of authenticity and accusations that some of the events were staged for the camera. Moreover, the *Mondo* films usually featured a narrator who provided highly condescending commentary about the events; when possible, a film personality would be enlisted to provide the narration, such as a very patronizing George Sanders in *Ecco* (1963, dir. Gianni Proia), or Boris Karloff in

109

LIPS HIPS TITS POWER ◊ THE FILMS OF RUSS MEYER

Mondo Balordo (1964, dir. Roberto Blanci Montero). *Mondo Topless* features the narration of Meyer cast veteran John Furlong, whose rapid-fire commentary not only resembles Walter Winchell high on amphetamines, but thoroughly captures the condescending tone of *Mondo Cane* and the other *Mondo* films.

Mondo Topless begins with a shot of the "Twin Peaks" road sign, an obvious aside to not only the San Francisco location but the female anatomy that will dominate the film. It continues as a sort of quasi-travelogue of San Francisco, and could almost play as a straight documentary were it not for the inserts of Babette Bardot wiggling nude in the driver's seat of a stationary car which is intercut with shots of San Francisco streets taken from a moving vehicle. Another, perhaps less obvious, aspect that cues the viewer to the film's satirical nature is the narration: a shot of Alcatraz prison is described by Furlong as "a hotel for visiting tourists" and the tourists on Fisherman's Wharf are ridiculed with as much vitriol as the caustic impersonation the narrator does of American tourists in Hawaii in *Mondo Cane*.

Following this introduction to San Francisco, the viewer is jolted by the sudden turn of the film into a "documentary" on the world-wide "topless" movement, which amounts to an hour-long, rapid-fire montage of topless dancers. Furlong's narration provides both a distraction and a discontinuity between the visuals of interminable topless go-go dancing, and sets up the dancers as objects of ridicule rather than eroticism. In Brechtian fashion, Furlong is both narrator and commentator of the representation of the nude women. On one hand, the seemingly bored and blasé dancers are described with hyperbolic detail by the frenetic Furlong: a scene culled from *Europe in the Raw* shows Greta Thorwald seated, mildly waving her arms, as Furlong calls this a "wildly erotic burst of uninhibited frenzy." On the other hand, *Mondo Topless* also includes interviews with the dancers, recording their thoughts and opinions on issues from the art of topless dancing to the foibles of having large breasts. These comments, hilarious in the context of the film, are introduced by Furlong's own amazed announcement that the audience will hear, for the first time, what these dancers think, only to interrupt them with the rude and uproarious comment, "Enough of this pallaber!" The comments of the dancers offer little in the way of substantive study, but rather reflect an almost intentional banality. The (male) narrator's dismissal of their thoughts and the film's concentration on the women's breasts both echoes and satirizes the male spectator's desire to *see* something happen, rather than to *listen* to it. As Ebert noted, "There seems to be something subtly sadistic going on here; Meyer is simultaneously photographing the women because of their dimensions, and recording them as they complain about their problems... This sets up a kind of psychological Mobius strip."[113]

As a satire on sexploitation, *Mondo Topless* operates through its very monotony to offer a commentary of the often predictable and tiresome pattern sexploitation had fallen into. By the mid-1960s, the remnants of the nudie-cutie had simply become a marginal plot by which a series of striptease numbers could be staged (*Orgy of the Dead*, *Sexy Proibitissimo*, *The Weird World of LSD*). Still, *Mondo Topless* contains its share of sophomoric jokes and puns to keep both the sexploitation audience and the shrewd observer interested, such as the aforementioned first shot of the "twin peaks" sign, or the shot of an underwater photographer's "breathing apparatus" that is a close-up of her bosom. Additionally, *Mondo Topless* includes footage from previous Meyer films: several striptease scenes from *Europe in the Raw* are cannibalized as well as the famous

113. "Russ Meyer: King of the Nudies," page 6 of 14.

Orgy Of The Dead

bathing scene and some test footage from *Lorna*. The mock-documentary format allows these scenes to be thrown in to self-reference Meyer's previous work, be it for shameless self-promotion, narcissistic self-indulgence, or self-referential parody. In regard to the last of the three, there are also more subtle references to previous Meyer films, such as Babette Bardot dancing topless next to a train speeding down the tracks, or Sin Lenee dancing in a shower from a water tower: both are key symbols in *Pussycat!*. In another scene, Darlene Gray, possibly the most well-endowed woman ever to appear in a Russ Meyer film, rolls around naked in mud, perhaps suggesting a "mud honey."

Because *Mondo Topless* is free from narrative constraint, Meyer can indulge in a free-form editing style that juxtaposes images on top of another at blinding speed. Not since Vertov's *Man with a Camera* (1922) have images come and gone with such a relentless flow. Given the film starts with the sound of a telegraph wire and the shots of various dancers are connected by inserts of transistor radios, there is a sense of "electricity" that runs through the work, and the editing itself, free from a narrative basis, is instead derived from a pattern of currents, rymthms, flows, and intensities. Devoid of what Roland Barthes termed "eroticism," in that the *tease* is the erotic component of the *strip tease*, the already-topless women becomes pure objects: tit-wiggling machines caught in the flow of the film. Ultimately, *Mondo Topless* can be seen as an experiment of film form itself, with the barrage of breasts becoming less important and the narrator's cynical commentary and the movement, rhythm and assemblage of shots taking precedence. In this way, *Mondo Topless* could be an example of a minimalist sexploitation film.

COMMON-LAW CABIN (1967)

Into The Originary World

Originally titled *How Much Loving Does the "Normal" Couple Need?*, Meyer retitled the film *Common-Law Cabin* after theater owners complained that the unwieldy title was far too long for theater marquees. Nonetheless, the film reflects Meyer's usual interest in satire and sexual politics on an extraordinarily profound scale; the film introduces the incest taboo to Meyer's films (later central to *Vixen*), and ultimately succeeds in charting the evolution from primitive to capitalist society in its brief 80 minutes of running time. *Common-Law Cabin* not only features a screenplay by Jack Moran, but also features Moran in the starring role as Dewey Hoople, the owner of Hoople's Haven, a run-down tourist trap located in a spot that gives new meaning to the term "the middle of nowhere." Hoople's family consists of his lovely daughter Coral (Adele Rein), who Hoople feels slightly more than fatherly love for, and Babette Bardot as Babette (of course), who plays Hoople's common-law wife and the voice of Hoople's troubled conscience – an external super-ego with a decidedly (and sometimes incomprehensible) French accent: "I only zay what you tink zo you can hear how louzee it zounds." Dewey and Babette are the typical Meyer couple: a lecherous, older man and a voluptuous young woman in a constant state of marital tension. Thrown into this already volatile threesome are the bored vacationers Dr. and Mrs. Ross (John Furlong and Alaina Capri), another older man with a sexually-unfulfilled wife, and the villainous Barney Rickert (Ken Swofford), a sadistic rouge-cop on the run with a fortune in stolen jewels. Later added to the melodramatic fray is the "pleasure-minded" playboy Laurence Talbot III (Andrew Hagara), whose timely arrival provides the solution to the sexual tensions and taboos in the film.

Common-Law Cabin is set on the banks of the Colorado River, and is perhaps an ideal setting for a Meyer film. In the Meyer universe where water is tied to female libido and rugged earth to male libido, the river surrounded by mountains and badlands become a landscape where male and female sexual energy are in constant contact and tension with each other: isolated ponds, muddy streams, sandy beaches. It is in the originary world where libidinal drives are released, often at sites where land and water converge: Rickert and Mrs. Ross have sex in a pond; Rickert attacks Babette in a pond while she swims in the nude; the bizarre jousting match that claims the life of Dr. Ross takes place in the mud; Rickert's attempt to rape Coral, which Talbot prevents, takes place on a beach; Coral and Talbot exchange their first kiss on a muddy beach, which triggers Dewy's cathartic assault on Talbot; and even the quarrelsome Dewey and Babette have time to make out on the beach, away from the constricting confines of the cabin.

As in *Lorna*, the first shot is not a stable establishing shot, but a point-of-view shot of the camera moving down the Colorado River, seemingly caught in the current of the river, which the narrator fittingly describes as "taking and leaving like a woman but with the name of a man." While the river is designated as "male" and has "a man's name," its qualities are explicitly that of "a woman." The narration continues to describe the locale and finally "the desert winds" that carry the "smell of garbage"; at the word "garbage" the shot appropriately cuts to a close-up of Dewey Hoople voyeuristically watching his daughter skinny-dipping through oversize binoculars: the "desert winds" of masculinity are manifested in the odious form of male "garbage": Dewey Hoople, a man who can not escape his sexual desire for his daughter. "Why doesn't she put some clothes on?" the agitated Hoople snarls. "It dozen't zeem to botter her, why should it botter you?" is Babette's short riposte. Infuriated, Hoople threatens to throw Babette "back out to the sailors," who she was presumably entertaining as a prostitute. "At leez day know da difference between a wife an' a daughter!" she

LIPS HIPS TITS POWER ◊ THE FILMS OF RUSS MEYER

fires back. Immediately, the question of incest is already the focal point of the film, and is dealt with blunt and cruel satire.

    Coral, now donning a red bikini, begins to walk back to Hoople's Haven, along a path of signs that reveal the credits of the film in bright, blood-red letters.[114] Indeed, throughout *Common-Law Cabin*, the color schemes of the film are nothing short of blinding. The credits are purposely cartoonish, and when Coral arrive at the cabin, "Hoople's Haven" is written on a sign in blood-red

114. *Common-Law Cabin* is superimposed on the sign that bears the film's original title, *How Much Loving Does the Normal Couple Need?* As is the case of all the credits, the writing is in red except for the word NORMAL, which appears in white, capital letters.

114

CHAPTER FOUR ◊ **SWINGING SIXTIES**

letters identical to the credits. Indeed, "Hoople's Haven" is just as much an artificial and cartoonish "theater" of sexual politics as the credits signify an absurd and cartoonish representation of the world taken by the film. Hoople's Haven is also the only house for miles around and the only remnant of civilization, or "derived milieu," within the originary world of badlands and water, a world of untamed and clashing male and female libido. The originary world both preys on and feeds on Hoople's Haven, its instinctual drives permeating the cabin and its inhabitants. Throughout the film, the cabin is the site of barely controlled impulses and desires, a site that attempts to prohibit the illicit and attempts to constrain sexual urges into socially acceptable forms, and quite hilariously barely maintains its effort to keep sexuality "normal." It is a spot that attempts to tame libidinal forces into manageable behavior into constructs of bourgeois normality as false and artificial as the set of the film. In one marvelous scene, Coral does an impromptu go-go dance to entertain the guests and the sexually aroused/agitated Dewey crushes a glass in his hand while Mrs. Ross roles her eyes in contempt for Coral's "little dance – *how gauche*!" Inside the cabin, there is a constant sexual tension between the parties: Dewey and Babette; Dewey and Coral; Dr. and Mrs. Ross; Rickert and every woman in the cabin. Unlike *Pussycat!*, where there is a strict battle line drawn between male and female homeosocial orders, in *Common-Law Cabin* it is every man and woman for themselves; they *all* interact with competitive, predatory fury. The rivalry between Mrs. Ross and Babette is as fierce and hilarious as any two males in a Meyer film. The two stalk the originary world outside the confines of Hoople's Haven in their dueling red bikinis, and in one scene, Babette is shown chopping wood with a machete while Mrs. Ross contemptuously saunters past – Babette briefly rears up with the machete and the viewer almost expects (and, perhaps, *wishes*) the machete will end up in the back of Mrs. Ross's skull. Another obvious rivalry exists between Dr. Ross and Rickert over Mrs. Ross, but the sickly, passive Dr. Ross lacks the backbone to take on Rickert initially, and instead of fighting for his wife contemplates slicing his throat with a broken bottle, which recalls Dewey smashing the glass in a similar moment of sexual frustration. These respective rivalries reach their most intense and absurd point in a "joust." With Dr. Ross and Rickert serving as the "horses," Babette gets on the shoulders of Dr. Ross, and Mrs Ross gets on Rickert's shoulders. The two men begin to bump into each other as the women try to pull the other off the shoulders of their respective "horses." The pent-up rage of the parties that is barely contained in the confines of the cabin are released in this parody of pre-modernity problem-solving. Fittingly, the "joust" also takes place in ankle-deep mud, the nexus of raw male and female libido. Mrs. Ross and Rickert score the victory when Dr. Ross succumbs to a heart attack as the proceedings grow more heated, his body seemingly unable to endure the descent into the "animality" of the activity. In a stunning close-up, Babette attempts to breath life into Dr. Ross with mouth-to-mouth resuscitation; indeed, she may also be planting the kiss of death on him, as if Dr. Ross has finally achieved erotic pleasure not through sex or violence, but in the release of death.

The "Social-Machine"

In their seminal work *Anti-Oedipus*, Gilles Deleuze and Felix Guattari plot the course of human social evolution through "the coding of desire." First are the "Primitive Territorial Machines" which "codes" desires (such as clans or tribes); second are the "Barbaric Despotic Machines" which "overcode" desires (kings and monarch); third are the "Civilized Capitalist Machines" which continually "decode and recode" desires (modern capitalism).[115] In an almost uncanny sense, it is precisely this evolution of these three social machines that marks the narrative development of *Common-Law Cabin* as the film attempts to solve the most basic problem of the film and society: incest. In the beginning of the film, the triangle of Dewey-Babette-Coral is the basic structure of the film. Unlike the Oedipal triangle, which is marked by the prohibition of incest with the mother by the castrating father, in *Common-Law Cabin* the source of the incest prohibition is denying the relationship between the lustful father and well-developed daughter. Hoople, as the patriarch and proprietor of Hoople's Haven, is unable to manage this most basic of sexual taboos. The milieu of Hoople's Haven corresponds to the Primitive Territorial Machine, where "desire" is in its initial stages of "coding": marriage, adultery, and incest are still issues that need sorting out, where there is a code that has yet to establish "the difference between a wife an' a daughter."

It is with the arrival of the tourists to Hoople's Haven, the Ross couple and Barney Rickert, that "the coding of desire" moves into the Barbaric Despotic Machine of "overcoded" flows. It is the character of Barney Rickert that achieves dominance, the figure by which all flows and coding must be organized. As a crooked cop, a figure where law and crime are manifest into one figure, he becomes sole arbitrator of the licit and illicit, a law which governs, punishes, and takes at will: the law as an overcoding vengeance.[116] Adultery is permitted only through the despotic Rickert, who later vanquishes his rival, Dr. Ross, by defeating him in the "joust," the sport of knights and kings. Rickert also attempts to take control of Hoople's primitive "kingdom" by offering him a lump sum of money, the initial appearance of "capital" in the film. However, money is still irrelevant at this point because it does not resolve the basic problem of incest, in that for Rickert, Coral is not an object of "exchange" ("decoded" desire), but "conquest" ("overcoded" desire). Fittingly, Rickert's attempted sexual assault on Coral, the object of incest and the figure that all coding revolves around, is thwarted by the well-timed arrival of Laurence Talbot III, the young, millionaire

---

115. This is an admittedly highly simplified description of Gilles Deleuze and Felix Guattari, *Anti-Oedipus*, trans. Robert Hurley, Mark Seem, and Helen R. Lane (Minneapolis: University of Minnesota Press, 1983), Chapter 3, "Savages, Barbarians, Civilized Men."

116. See Deleuze and Guattari, 212.

CHAPTER FOUR ◊ SWINGING SIXTIES

pleasure-seeker.

With the arrival of Talbot, the era of civilized man begins (although one might remember Larry Talbot was also the title character in *The Wolf Man* [1941], signifying him as "animal" as well). Dewey fully welcomes Talbot as a potential, wealthy suitor, and actively tries to pair Talbot and Coral. At the same time, he is reluctant to release the object of his sexual obsession, and in a fit of jealous rage, Dewey sprints from Hoople's Haven to the beach after spotting Coral and Talbot kissing (with his oversize binoculars, of course). He savagely attacks Talbot, but the rage proves cathartic when Coral and Babette intervene: he confronts his own incestuous feelings and can now overcome them, especially given Talbot's wealth. Incest can now finally be "decoded and recoded."

The establishment of civility is done in a bloody finale when Mrs. Ross is summarily shot by Rickert, who is in turn eliminated from the film, in true kingly fashion, by being "beheaded." Having commandeered a speedboat for his escape, Rickert instead falls into the river; the runaway speedboat circles around to smash him in the head (in what is perhaps one of the most obvious uses of a manikin stand-in for a human victim in film history). All is back to how it was with the exception of Talbot's addition to the Hoople clan. "It'll be nice to have another man around the house," notes Dewey; certainly, to not only provide heterosexual symmetry between the new couples, but to give Hoople a "son-in-law," or "son-in-*common-law*." Indeed, it is with the advent of the male suitor as well as capital that the transition to civilization can begin by solving the incest problem. Bataille noted:

"The father who would marry his daughter... would be like the owner of champagne who would never invite any friends, who would drink up the stock by himself. The father must bring the wealth that is his daughter... into the circuit of ceremonial exchanges: he must give her as a present, but the circuit presupposes a set of rules accepted in a given milieu as the rules of the game are."[117]

117. *The Accursed Share, Vol. II*, 41.

Thus Coral is put in the circuit of exchange, the object of exchange between Dewey and Talbot that heralds the establishment of the incest prohibition and the entry of capitalism and civilization to Hoople's Haven. The wealth of Dr. Ross and the ill-gotten gains of Barney Rickert are useless in the schema of *Common-Law Cabin* because they do not provide the solution to the incest problem. Dewey is only able to relinquish his daughter with Talbot's arrival, and the arrival of capitalism. Unlike other Meyer films where money is the catalyst for the plunge into the originary world (*Faster, Pussycat!*, *Finders Keepers*), in *Common-Law Cabin* the situation is reversed: capital is the means by which the overpowering drives of the originary world are tamed. The derived milieu of Hoople's Haven,

CHAPTER FOUR ◊ SWINGING SIXTIES

with its new veneer of bourgeois normalcy and affluence, can now withstand the instinctual forces of the originary world. Indeed, as the respective couples return to the cabin, Dewey tells Babette it looks like "everything is turning green," a phenomenon manifest by the lime-green color that saturates the screen (and thus, the originary world). If much of *Common-Law Cabin*'s voyage through the originary world is dominated by the color red and "sanguinity" (blood, bikinis, credits), the end of the film and establishment of civilization and bourgeois "sexuality" is literally defined by a new color: green – the color of money.

GOOD MORNING... AND GOODBYE! (1967)

"Lorna" Revisited

In one interview, Russ Meyer expressed an interest in remaking all of his films. One film specifically mentioned was *Lorna*. Such a remake would not only change the contrived ending, necessitated by censorship pressures that required the characters pay for their illicit behavior, but would reflect the comic spontaneity and parody, as well as a more graphic sexual vulgarity, as seen in his 1970s films.

"[The remake would] show Lorna's flipside. Yea, turn it all around. Sure, the husband's still a cluckoid. Hell, even Lorna cheats on the convict... and the bloke doesn't die... he runs off with Lorna's aunt... she's got great big beautiful tits. And the husband continuing to remain the cluckoid... This time, no one's paying the tab. Including Lorna."[118]

Lorna should not be a considered a tragedy that needs to be answered by a farce; indeed, *Lorna* is *both* tragedy and farce and its cruel ironies make it a highly problematic film. However, the influence of *Lorna* is unmistakable in *Good Morning... and Goodbye!*, and at least three important sequences from *Lorna* are obviously parodied in *Goodbye!*. Jack Moran pulls out the stops in providing his final screenplay for Meyer, delivering yet another superb, absurdist, trash-talking screenplay comparable to his magnificent work on *Pussycat!* and *Common-Law Cabin*.

Goodbye! begins with one of Meyer's most satirical, surreal, and lengthy narrated prologues, rich with both irony and cumbersome, strained metaphors. In archetypal Meyer fashion, it starts as a series of jump-cuts of a well-endowed nude woman (Carol Peters) running through a field, her breasts bouncing, a cocktail-jazz score lilting over the image. With the warmth of a health classroom lecture, the narrator begins the film by posing rhetorical questions to the audience:

118. As quoted in Schneider, ed., 35.

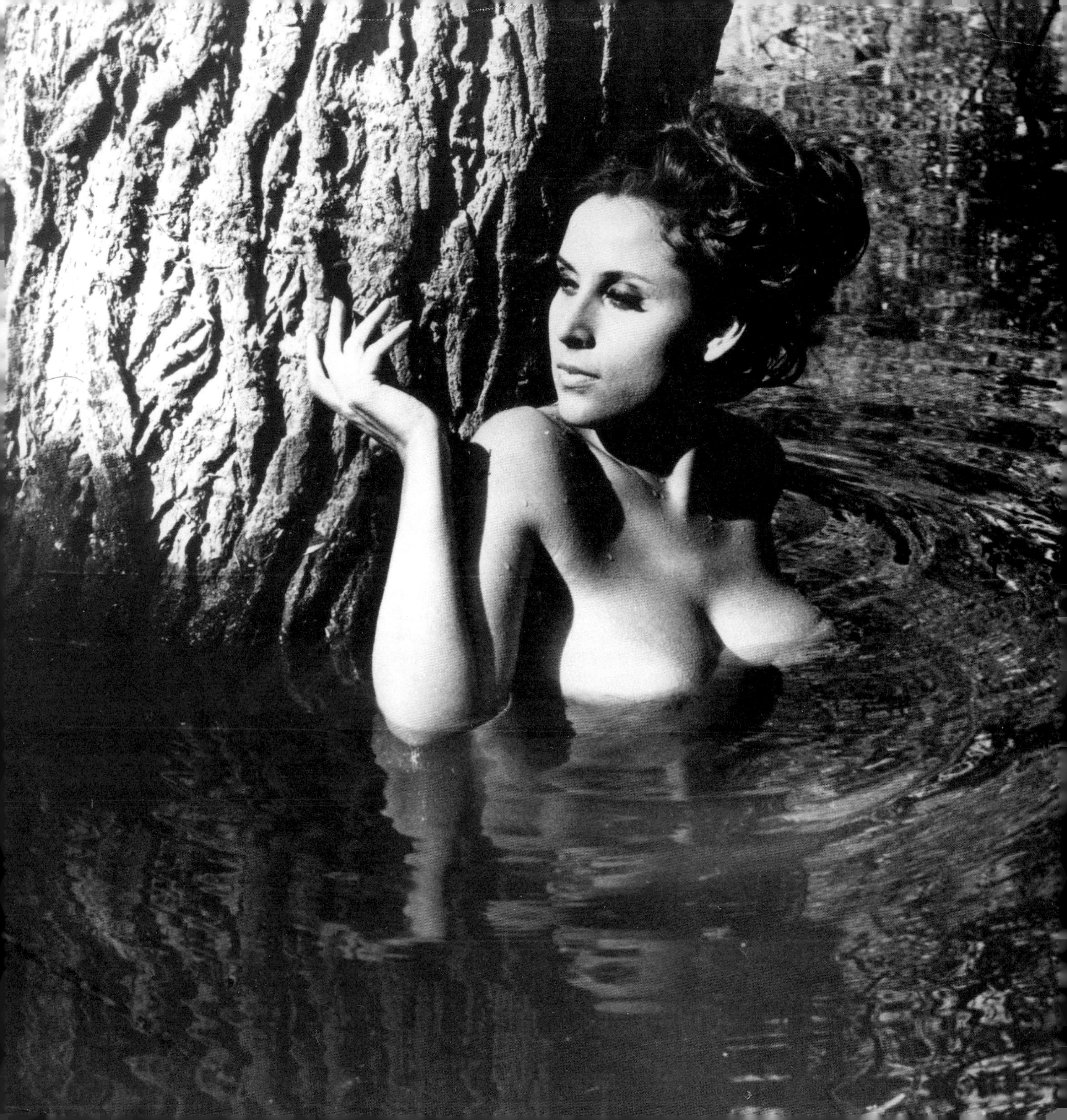

CHAPTER FOUR ◊ SWINGING SIXTIES

How would you define nymphomania? Irregular union? Deflower? Wenching? Voyeurism? Strumpet? Hedonist? Bacchanalia?... Scabrous? Promiscuity? Ribaldry? Paramour? Debauchery? Adulterate? Carnality? You may look to these definitions in what you are about to witness – an adult motion picture that explores the deepest complexities of contemporary life as applied to love and marriage in these United States...

As the narration continues in this ponderous way, the shots of the running nude cut to a rapid-fire montage of shots culled from the film as well as non-diagetic inserts that refer directly to the narration: a shot of a topless women having a deck of playing cards drizzled on her is used to visually enhance the narrator's metaphor of love as a gamble for losers who "crap out, raise on aces and eights, and sucker out on one card bets that bust a pink flush to black."

Over the narration, the camera first follows Angel Boland (Alaina Capri, reprising her role as a bitchy, sex-starved wife from *Common-Law Cabin*) driving a sports car and stopping at a river bed. The narrator muses every story is "like a beef stew... or a casserole" which requires a "body of meat" to give it its flavor. The "body of meat" in *Goodbye!* is obviously the buxom, sexually aggressive Angel, introduced as "a lush cushion of evil perched on the throne of immortality... a monument to unholy carnality, and a cesspool of marital pollution... a shameless, brazen, bulldozing female prepared to humiliate, provoke, and tantalize." Angel Boland satirically references "Angel" Maddox from *Motorpsycho!*, and *Goodbye!* also parodies the storybook marriage between Cory and Angel Maddox; the marriage between Burt and Angel Boland might be best described as "pure hell." During the narration, Angel parks and takes an impromptu nude swim in the stream. While initially recalling Billie's swim in *Pussycat!*, the scene actually bears much closer resemblance to *Lorna*'s bathing sequence; certain shots of the sunlight filtering through the branches and various poses Angel strikes are almost identical to *Lorna*. The scene cuts to Burt Boland (Stuart Lancaster), the next "ingredient" in the story, contentedly driving his car, facing the viewer (the "flipside" of Sidney Brenshaw?). The narrator describes him as having money, success, everything "except manhood... staggering before the summit of sexual communion." Burt is impotent, and unable to satisfy Angel, who responds by taking a plethora of lovers, the current being the construction worker Stone (Patrick Wright). Following Burt, Stone himself is next shown on-screen and introduced as "more than mere flesh and blood – made of steel." As his very name suggests, he is indeed "stone," a man chiseled out of inorganic matter, the archetypal husky, violent he-man that frequently appears in Meyer's film world. The next ingredient added to the film is Lana Boland (Karen Ceral), "the latest version of the farmer's daughter," the obvious reference to the age-old dirty joke about the farmer's daughter set to seduce anyone who passes by. Like Angel, Lana is shown speeding around in a sports car. She quickly encounters Ray (Don Johnson), a local well-to-do boy. The narrator describes at length how the young people of today seem to communicate, but not with words. Indeed, Ray and Lana do everything but "talk": their sports cars circle and follow each other like animals in a mating ritual (which recalls the erotic role of the automobile in *Pussycat!*), the transistor radio becomes a signal that the mating ritual has reached the next level, and they cruise to the beach past a series of garish, Pop Art mailboxes that have the film credits written on them. Quite ingeniously, Meyer has incorporated the theme of "communication" into the opening credits: the film as a bunch of "letter holders" in which "words" are passed back and forth. Indeed, Ray and Lana arrive at the beach, and no words are uttered except for those of the off-screen narrator. In this first instance of courtship, "language" is that of music, motions, and gestures: a pre-verbal, primal form of mating where communication recalls animals rather than humans. Interestingly, Lana is shown arriving on the beach wearing a top and pants, but is suddenly shown dancing in a bikini, a disorientating continuity break matched by the use of an extreme low-angle shot. The display of primal courtship arouses a mysterious figure who rises out of the lake (of course, water being the site of female libido), her bare back to the camera in the foreground while Ray and Lana dance in the background. This cuts to a shot of Haji in the water, appearing as if summoned by the animal ritual; she is, as the narrator states, "a specter of a spectator of a spectacle." She is "the Catalyst," a mystical forest-water nymph, or, perhaps more correctly, a forest-water *nympho* who eventually cures Burt Boland of his impotence.[119] The shot cuts to a series of shots of the Catalyst running nude through the forests as the narrator describes her impending role in the story. With the character of the Catalyst, Meyer has never made the relationship of lush flora and water to female libidinal energy clearer.

119. While called "the Catalyst," in the closing credits Haji is referred to as "the Sorceress".

Talk is Cheap

The scene cuts to a house at night (recalling *Lorna*) as the narration draws to a close, describing a failing relationship in which "you can smell the defeat... the ending of something that never was." The light comes on in the bedroom to reveal Angel and Burt lying in bed. Dialogue between characters is finally heard, and it is a barrage of insults and cutting one-liners. Angel berates Burt for his inability to perform, and he bitterly snarls "I'm not a machine." Indeed, Angel has been described as "a bulldozing female" and Stone as "made of steel." They *are* sexual machines, unlike the all-too-human Burt. "Angel – what a joke!" later spits Burt, as is to purposely emphasize the highly ironic use of the name "Angel." The scene also once again overtly parodies *Lorna*, specifically a shot of

CHAPTER FOUR ◊ SWINGING SIXTIES

Angel disgustedly getting out of bed naked and walking to the bedroom window: the shot is virtually a direct quote from *Lorna*. Yet in this bedroom scene, Angel is scathing and acid-tongued, berating her husband's impotence and proudly proclaiming her infidelities: truly "the flipside of Lorna." Meanwhile, the shot cuts to a collection of kitsch 1960s posters that pans down to Lana crying as she listens to the torrent of insults, her introduction to the sexual language of "words" corrupting her innocent, pre-verbal communication of "sex" with Ray. Her entrance into "the symbolic order" of sex begins, an order where sexual relationships are literally defined by "words" (read: insults) rather than "action" (read: intercourse). And, throughout the film, when Burt and Angel's relationship is not being expressed through sexual insults, it is expressed in metaphors of commerce and capitalism: Angel is continually referred to as "merchandise," and Burt as an "investment."

The next morning, Angel returns home and gives a detailed account of her pervious evening's sexual soirées to Burt. "Do you want a Wasserman, too?" he angrily asks, referring to a test for syphilis; "I'll take him on, too!" Angel retorts. Soon, Lana and Angel have a contentious argument, which prompts Lana to leave the house and go back to the beach. As in *Common-Law Cabin*, female relationships in *Goodbye!* are as bitter and cutthroat as male relationships: Lana is seemingly bent on losing for virginity not for her own sexual pleasure, but as an act of competitive vengeance against Angel. This leads to the distraught Lana's second encounter with Ray, who is in the lake on his surfboard. As she turns up the volume on her car radio louder and louder, Ray draws closer to the shore, again recalling an animal mating ritual. Arriving on the beach, they exchange words for the first time, and the relationship immediately begins to deteriorate. As they dance, Lana announces, "make love to me," to which Ray declines, telling her to stop with "the jive dialogue." While Lana is determined to loose her virginity, her request goes unheeded as Ray casually dances with her, his cool demeanor a way to avoid sexual contact and mask his own sexual fear and inexperience. With the introduction of "words" into their relationship, they have become another typical Meyer couple: a woman who wants sexual satisfaction and a man who is unwilling or unable to provide it for her.

Sexual Healing

In what is the film's most pivotal narrative point, Burt soon begins his cathartic encounters with the Catalyst. Driving through a wooded area, the Catalyst begins to magically appear, striking various pin-up poses in and around his Jeep through a series of jump-cuts. The curious Burt parks and begins to walk around the vicinity. At one point he comes upon a stream and sees his own reflection. Quoting *Lorna*, the camera shows a point-of-view shot of his wavering reflection

123

LIPS HIPS TITS POWER ◊ THE FILMS OF RUSS MEYER

in the water, and suggests that Burt is in mid-transformation, or a being who is not yet completely "formed." This is about to change with his encounter with the Catalyst. Continuing his walk, he steps in a rope snare that leaves him hanging upside-down from a tree branch. It is here that the male prey (Burt) meets the female hunter (the Catalyst). Rather than speaking, she begins a wild dance around him as he hangs in mid-air when the shot cuts to sunlight filtering through the branches (another shot recalling *Lorna*). This shot serves as a bridge to Angel and Stone engaged in an afternoon tryst in a meadow, a tryst completely dominated by Angel (once again, the obvious point of reference and parody is the Lorna/Convict scene in *Lorna*). However, rather than having sex, they are engaged in sarcastic conversation, with Angel denying Stone the satisfaction of completing the sex act with her. To complicate matters further, Stone discovers that his sidekick Herb (Tom Howland) has been watching the scene, another example of how male voyeurism is consistently inscribed into Meyer's narratives. Later, Stone beds Herb's wife Lottie (Megan Timothy), and when they are caught in the act by Herb, Stone beats him to a pulp and then tells Herb to forget about the whole thing. Lottie is incensed and berates the two for attempting to solve the problem like gentlemen ("no lovin', no fightin' – *just talk*!"). In response to her prodding, Stone delivers a series of kicks to the prone Herb and then returns to bed with the obviously-aroused Lottie, the fight a "preliminary for the main event." Violence serves as foreplay to sex once useless "talk" is abandoned.

The film returns to Burt regaining consciousness on the ground. The encounter has left him intrigued, and when he later attempts to explain what happened to Angel, flash forwards of the second encounter between Burt and the Catalyst are inserted as he relates the story. Indeed, Burt and the Catalyst soon have this second encounter, which is again enacted in ritual and exotic dance, the Catalyst dressed only in large daisies that cover her nipples and strategically placed leafy vines which covers her genital area. She is "living nature," a nexus of female libido and the female terrain of flora. Burt is now a willing participant rather than a helpless, hanging spectator as he was in the first sequence. Importantly, no words are uttered throughout the ritual, which again keeps discourse at a level of gestures and movements, save for Burt's guttural, animal groan when he finally ravages the Catalyst.

Master of the House

As Burt regains sexual power and confidence in his two encounters with the Catalyst, he is also able to exert more control over the Boland home and its inhabitants. He arrives home just in time to see the heated feud between Lana and Angel erupt into a jealous fight over Ray in the swimming pool of the house. Burt single-handedly pulls the two out of their own libidinal environment (water), and under his domain (the grounds of the Boland estate). His continuing pattern of growing domination over the females under his roof is made clear when Angel is given a ultimatum: no more lovers or no more marriage ("Why don't I just pack now?" she responds). The confident Burt undresses and begins to bed Angel, there is peaceful silence save for the radio broadcasting stock market reports (once again manifesting the link between their martial relations to commerce). However, their conjugal bliss is short lived when Lana drunkenly bursts into their room, holding a beer can and a cigarette, and proudly announces that she has been deflowered by Stone. Enraged, Burt, using more metaphors equating sex to business dealings, referring to Stone as "a travel agency that's gotten too much of his business" and it will now be "closed down."

In yet another reference to *Lorna*, *Goodbye!* ends with a battle of the male suitors Burt and Stone which quotes and parodies Jim and Luther's fight in *Lorna*. Burt and Stone slug it out at a desolate construction site which recalls the barren salt-mines of *Lorna*, and Herb is on the scene as well, parodying Jonah. However, Herb does not watch the fight with homoerotic adoration for

LIPS HIPS TITS POWER ◊ **THE FILMS OF RUSS MEYER**

Stone, but rather roots for Burt with hilarious enthusiasm, commenting on the action like a Brechtian cheerleader: "Watch it!... Hit him!... Oh no!... Get up!" However, Burt is unable to overcome his rival Stone, who throws Burt in a bulldozer shovel and attempts to put him in a rock grinder; this references the image of Angel as a "bulldozing female," and her symbolic presence is still the metaphorical link between the male characters. However, the battered and put-upon Herb saves the day, climbing aboard the bulldozer and beating Stone senseless with a shovel. The bloodied but victorious Burt intervenes to stop Herb from killing Stone, and then returns home to an awaiting Angel. Nothing is said: the last shot of the couple is a freeze-frame of their kiss. However, Meyer adds a brief but telling coda to the film: a montage of Haji running through rugged grass plains, bringing the film full circle to its original beginning of a nude woman running through the outdoors. Traditional masculinity emerges the victor in this round of sexual politics, with patriarch Burt Boland emerging as champion over Angel. However, one must also remember that Burt's victory is only brought forth by the advent of the Catalyst, the embodiment of pure female libido, a mystical sexual healer. In this sense, *Goodbye!* addresses a problem in sexual relationships in films as early as *Eve and the Handyman*: while both films seemingly depict the triumph of the traditional heterosexual couple, it is *the woman* who is able to produce and channel the necessary power by which American masculinity emerges triumphant.

Finally, *Goodbye!* offers an interesting theoretical examination of the relationship between sexuality and language. At the end, the narrator hilariously recaps the film over the freeze-frame of the kiss, musing that there are "some things worth fighting for, like 'family,' 'love,' and 'sex'... the great three-letter word... .that all the four-letter words befoul." Amid all its strained metaphors, *double-entendres*, and *non-sequiturs*, there is a fundamental issue of the problems of how "sex" is itself communicated. Throughout the film, there is a pattern established where sex is best communicated when it is not corrupted by words, but rather "spoken" by a pre-verbal, animal language of body movements, gestures, and sounds without "all the jive dialogue." With all these problems of signification and meaning, *Goodbye!* remains the first and only post-structuralist nudie-film ever made.

FINDERS KEEPERS, LOVERS WEEPERS (1968)

Meyer noir

Finders marked a change from the previous comic-surreal sex satires, as much as in locale as in tone. Unlike the vast majority of Meyer films which take place in the isolated backwaters of America, *Finders* takes place in the heart of urban Los Angeles. Another distinction between *Finders* and other Meyer films is the relative anonymity of the cast; none of the usual Meyer repertoire of actors and actresses such as Stuart Lancaster, Franklin Bolger, or Haji appear in the film, although John Furlong makes a brief cameo as a bar patron. While highly similar in theme to Meyer's sixties films, *Finders* remains something of a stylistic anomaly. The Los Angeles location and the lack of Meyer's usual cast

LIPS HIPS TITS POWER ◊ THE FILMS OF RUSS MEYER

members create a distinctly "realistic" world, instead of what might be called the "Russ Meyer world," a satirical and surreal cartoon-America populated by various archetypes and caricatures: an "originary world" somewhere between Sade and Al Capp. It is this sense of the absurd that is missing in *Finders*, and rather than a "Russ Meyer" film as such, *Finders*, with its relatively coherent plot, urban locale, and realistic characters, is perhaps the closest Meyer came to Hollywood realism (with certain key exceptions), at times recalling Don Siegel's films such as *The Killers* (1966). In fact, *Finders* was one of his first films to be

CHAPTER FOUR ◊ SWINGING SIXTIES

[sidenote: 120. The film received better than average reviews for a Meyer film, and in Philadelphia was booked into a first-run theater to replace a major MGM release that tanked, *The Shoes of the Fisherman*, a dreary and talky drama about a priest who unexpectedly becomes the Pope. See Frasier, 12.]

treated with some mainstream legitimacy.[120]

Finders is a grim tale of infidelity and crime, revolving around an attempted robbery at a topless bar and the various romantic subplots that come into conflict in the film's violent finale. To a large degree, the robbery itself acts only as a means to bring the romantic tensions and conflicts to a head. Money itself is a manifestation of the underlying drive of sex, and itself is a fetish-object, as alluring and erotic as the topless dancers the men ogle at the nightclub. One clever touch is a close-up of the safe at the club being opened; the combination is approximately 44-24-36, also the ideal "combination" for a Russ Meyer female. If *Goodbye!* takes *Lorna* as its reference point, *Finders* takes its initial inspiration from *Pussycat!*, another film where a robbery scheme serves as a catalyst for the character's entrance into the world of lust and violence. The film begins with cars speeding around a desert flat as a topless woman jumps up and down wearing a red miniskirt and a crash helmet, recalling the drag race that ends in eroticized murder in *Pussycat!* This bizarre introduction establishes a visual metaphor between sex and the automobile that reappears throughout the film. A close-up of the bouncing breasts of the woman in the desert cuts to a close-up of the bouncing breasts of a dancer at the nightclub where much of the film is centered. In this way, the topless nightclub itself also becomes a "racetrack" as well, where romantic trajectories and competitions will be played out. Again recalling *Pussycat!*, the shots of the topless dancer are intercut with shots of male spectators seated around the stage (with one, of course, being Russ Meyer). However, rather than being worked up into fits of agitation, the men watch silently and sip their drinks with indifference, giving the scene a sense of dejection in keeping with *Finders*' grim, *noir* narrative.

The most memorable moments in *Finders* are the sex scenes, not because of their eroticism, but their surrealism. Stock footage and nondiagetic sequences are inserted into these scenes in order to comment on the sexual relationships between characters. In the first sex scene, Paul (Paul Lockwood) and Christina (Jan Sinclair) have a sexual encounter that is intercut with a 19th century scene of a young boy and girl flying a kite (the surrealism of Buñuel comes to mind). This suggests a sort of innocence between Paul and Christina's sexual activity; in one point, Christina shaves portions of Paul's chest with a straight razor: it is not a malicious act, but appears to be the act of two children experimenting with sex, playing "house" or "doctor," or in this case, "barber."[121]

[sidenote: 121. Meyer simply claimed the scene was shot "for the hell of it — can you imagine?" (As quoted in Fischer, 22). In a completely different interpretation, Ebert suggested the scene was one of "symbolic castration" ("Russ Meyer: King of the Nudies," page 7 of 14).]

The second sex scene is between a very intoxicated Paul and Claire (Lavelle Roby), and is intercut with shots of large fountains in the city. Rather than suggesting the obvious interpretation of ejaculation, and keeping in mind water and its symbolic function to female libido, the montage contrasts Claire, who is able and eager to perform (signified by the arching fountains), and Paul, who is *not* able to perform due to his drunken state. Continuing with this motif, Paul

LIPS HIPS TITS POWER ◊ **THE FILMS OF RUSS MEYER**

CHAPTER FOUR ◊ **SWINGING SIXTIES**

returns to his apartment and attempts to rape his girlfriend Kelly (Anne Chapman), a topless dancer at the club. He initiates the attack in the shower, another zone of female sexuality (as will be seen in the immortal shower scene in Meyer's next film, *Vixen*). Fending off Paul, Kelly subsequently initiates a torrid sexual encounter with the club's bartender, Ray (Gordon Westcourt). Fittingly, this encounter takes place in a swimming pool, and in this sequence Meyer intercuts underwater photography of the naked bodies slamming into each other with stock footage of a demolition derby. Frasier has read this montage as a "moral" message about the destructive consequences of infidelity.[122] This reading is supported by the film's final images, in which a distraught Paul kneels over Claire, fatally wounded in the robbery; there is a long, intimate close-up of Kelly punctuated by a montage of images from over the course of the film, a virtual "epilogue" minus the authoritative, voice-over narration. The scene is suddenly rendered comic when the close-up of Kelly is matched by the sound of a car-crash and the whole frame violently shaking, the obscure and inexplicable message "GOODBYE, SAM..." appearing over Kelly's face (the scene also serves as an example of how the poignant and the absurd also "collide" in Meyer's films). The obvious implication is that Paul and Kelly's relationship has been destroyed, or "wrecked" like the cars in the demolition derby. Taking Frasier's analysis a bit further, as in *Pussycat!*, in *Finders* sex, violence, and the automobile are all equated, from the strange introduction of a desert drag-race intersecting around a topless woman to the abrupt inserts of the demolition derby in the midst of an aggressive sex act suggesting the violence and destructiveness inherent in sex itself. In *Pussycat!*, "violence does not only destroy, but creates." In *Finders*, sex does not only create, it destroys.

VIXEN (1968)

"Is She Woman... or Animal?"

Vixen, simply put, was the most important sex film of the 1960s. Shot for a budget of $70,000, *Vixen* grossed between 15 and 16 *million* dollars, and its amazing success was in large part responsible for 20th Century Fox's decision to hire Meyer.[123] Moreover, *Vixen* gained a number of critical accolades in addition to its unprecedented box office. Much discussion about *Vixen* remains centered around its memorable sex scenes, particularly the lesbian encounter and the incestuous shower tryst between Vixen and her brother. The increasingly explicit sex scenes in *Vixen*, along with the incorporation of lesbian and incest themes, was not merely artistic vision, but a response to twin pressures in "mainstream" and "adult" cinema. One was the growing acceptance of nudity in Hollywood films, with name-stars becoming increasingly likely to do nude scenes

122. *Russ Meyer – The Life and Films*, 12, 101.

123. O'Neill called *Vixen* "a socially-unredeeming porn flick ...[by] a genius at titillation... [who was] awarded a big contract by 20th Century Fox" (*Coming Apart*, 220). While I admire O'Neill's work, I certainly do not concur with his cynical and rather uninformed critique of Meyer.

131

(Jayne Mansfield), and new stars whose immediate popularity was generated by their on-screen nudity (Bridgette Bardot). The other factor was the just-emerging trend of "hardcore." The simulated sex in sexploitation films was starting to be supplanted by "beaver films" and full-penetration loops in San Francisco adult venues.[124] Caught in this bind of staying ahead of the mainstream but avoiding hardcore, Meyer created a new kind of sexploitation film: *Vixen*.

124. See Frasier, 13; Turan and Zito, Ch. 7.

Done in 1968, a year of intense, worldwide political and social upheaval, *Vixen* is a political satire that explores the social, sexual, and political issues of the time. Yet the politics extend far beyond the extraneous and even disposable political debate which closes the film. While allowing World War II veteran Meyer to vent some frustration, particularly at draft-dodgers and Marxist radicals, Ebert noted:

"[*Vixen*] ends with a ten-minute sequence in the air, during which the characters discuss Communism, Cuban Marxism, Vietnam, draft evasion, civil rights, and airplane hijacking. This is the socially-redeeming content, of course, and it is just possible that Meyer stuck it all at the end in order to (a) avoid interrupting the main story line of the film, and (b) chase the audience. It's certainly true that the word got around during *Vixen*'s year-long Chicago run: when everybody gets on the airplane... it's OK to go."[125]

125. See "Russ Meyer: King of the Nudies," page 8 of 14.

The Ohio Supreme Court reached the same conclusion about the film; in upholding the state's ban on *Vixen*, the court concluded the so-called political discussions brought up in the film were mere subterfuge designed to give the film a veneer of "social relevance."[126] Still, *Vixen* is one of Meyer's most concretely political films, and explicitly deals with contemporary issues such as race relations, draft evasion, and patriotism in a way that seems fairly reactionary. However, *Vixen* does not so much preach right-wing politics as it does effectively satirize the contradictory politics and positions that would eventually fragment the Left by the early 1970s: the pervasive issues of race, class, and sex. *Vixen* is never apologetic for its sometimes unfashionable politics or its satire, and ideologically is one of Meyer's most confounding films. At the same time, *Vixen* offers some of Meyer's most radical ideas on sexuality to date, ideas that go beyond mere issues of censorship and free love, but rather essays notions of eroticism and transgression quite similar to those of Bataille.

126. See Fischer, 23.

A great deal of *Vixen*'s success has been credited to the fact that it is the first major sexploitation film to feature a dominant female protagonist who is sexually aggressive rather than purely sadistic (the whip-wielding "Olgas" of the roughies). Yet, Vixen is far from the ideal heroine, and is typical of Meyer's female leads of that period. While she is sexually and emotionally dynamic, this

CHAPTER FOUR ◊ SWINGING SIXTIES

does not preclude Vixen from being obnoxious, manipulative, and simply mean. Moreover, Vixen is a racist whose bigotry makes her very unappealing. *Vixen* carries on a tradition of women seen in Meyer's films, strong and sexually aggressive women antithetical to the demure, passive stereotypes associated with "femininity." As Meyer recounted, "Erica Gavin didn't have the best or the biggest tits, but she had an indefinable something that made the picture work. She appealed to women as well as men. I don't mean in a lesbian sense, but I'm talking about her attitude towards being the *user*."[127] Again, one sees that Vixen is an archetypal "Meyer woman": a sexually aggressive woman with a "love'em and leave 'em" attitude commonly associated with men. Indeed, Vixen is very much a "woman" in the biological sense, but a "man" in the cultural sense.

To this degree, I would depart from the dominant criticisms as well as supporters of *Vixen*. Erica Gavin herself later described *Vixen* as "a put-down of women. It says that all women want is sex, that they're never satisfied, and they'll go anywhere to find it. It shows that women have no loyalty, no sensitivity in sexual relationships."[128] Gavin does present a valid criticism of Meyer, in that his female characters are simply one male fantasy, the big-breasted Amazonian nymphomaniac, in place of the standard female stereotype, the submissive sex-kitten. Where I would not agree with Gavin is *everyone* in a Russ Meyer film, men or women, seem to have "no loyalty or sensitivity" in their sexual relationships. Russ Meyer's film world is where the sexual ethic of "find 'em, fuck 'em, forget 'em" is the norm. The other tendency has been to read Vixen as a kind of uninhibited sexual healer, not unlike the Catalyst in *Goodbye!*. Russ Meyer observed, "Everything she touched was improved. She didn't destroy, she helped. If there was a marriage that was kind of dying on the vine, she injected something into it which made it better."[129] Granted, the consequences of Vixen's actions are often positive, but I would tend not to view Vixen as a sort of sexual Good Samaritan. Vixen is not motivated by goodwill, but animal lust. She is the embodiment of a primal, animal sexuality that civilization needs to necessarily negate and constrain. As Bataille wrote, "In the human sphere, sexual activity has broken away from its animal simplicity."[130] It is this "animal simplicity" that defines Vixen's sexual behavior, and the attempt to return to the animal from the civilized which Bataille defined as "eroticism."[131] Vixen is almost predatory in her search for and enjoyment of sex; she is beyond any "ethic" of sexual morality, and taboos against adultery, homosexuality, and incest are all rendered irrelevant by Vixen in the course of the film. Vixen is motivated by pure animal hedonism; what she does sexually is done without any regard to right or wrong. She is another "flipside of Lorna": instead of being the helpless captive in a backwoods sexual prison, she is the queen of a lush, sexual playground. Both the attempts to defend or criticize *Vixen* seem rooted in the need to find a "moral" basis for Vixen's actions: right or wrong, positive or negative, productive or

127. As quoted in Schnieder, 45.

128. As quoted in Danny Peary, *Cult Film Stars* (New York: Fireside Books, 1991), 213.

129. As quoted in Stan Berkowitz, "Sex, Violence, and Drugs – All in Good Fun!" *Film Comment*, Jan/Feb 1973: 49.

130. *Erotism*, 108.

131. *The Accursed Share, V. II*, 76-8. Bataille stresses that the process of rejection and return to animality can never be complete: once humanity enters the realm of civilization, the return to animality can only be incomplete and temporary.

133

destructive. Ultimately, Vixen is, with apologies to Nietzsche, beyond sexual good or evil, beyond any ideas of sexual normalcy and "morality." She is a sexual animal in an fecund originary world where she defines her own *immanent* sexual codes and desires.

Canadian "Bush"

The first screen image of *Vixen* is of a Canadian Flag billowing in the breeze. A seemingly harmless image that gives the film its locale, one must also remember that the film was made in 1968, when the country of Canada was synonymous with draft-dodgers trying to avoid military service in Vietnam; one of *Vixen*'s main characters, Niles (Harrison Page), is a black American expatriate disillusioned by America's racial and foreign policies. A narrator solemnly begins a textbook Meyer prologue, describing "*Bush country*... the Canadian Northwest... where men may still be awed by nature's presence," over footage of majestic forests. "Bush country," can be read as an obvious pun of "bush," the slang term for a woman's vagina. When the narrator says "country," the last syllable is matched by a shot of a pine tree, punningly suggesting "cunt-tree." Thus, the sexual organs of women are equated to flora of the great outdoors, "bush" and "cunt-tree," which is consistent with all of Meyer's films where female sexual libido is signified by the domain of forests, water, or meadows. These are places "where men may be awed": the Canadian Northwest or female genitals.

The film as such begins with a plane landing. The pilot is Tom (Garth Pillsbury), Vixen's husband. He chats with the airport attendant (a cameo by a bearded John Furlong), and the matter soon turns to questions of Vixen's fidelity: the amount of time she has by herself, and how women can get "lonely." Furlong's banter bears some similarity to Luther's insults in *Lorna*, but Furlong lacks Luther's petty maliciousness (he does, however, take his time inserting a gas nozzle into the plane, a often-used symbol by Meyer for sexual intercourse). Much like Jim and his studies, Tom seems more interested in flying, fishing, and running the lodge than in Vixen, but he also remains obstinately trusting of Vixen throughout the film. "Vixen likes to tease... but marriage is a serious responsibility," Tom replies utterly deadpan, explaining to Furlong that Vixen is too busy for infidelity with her duties of taking care of the lodge and "her little brother," a brawny, beer-guzzling biker for whom Vixen clearly has incestuous feelings.

With patented Meyer speed and satire, the scene jump-cuts to the woods where the shapely, bikini-clad Vixen frolics with a male companion. They quickly turn to matters of sex, and not at all quickly enough for Vixen, who rudely tells him to "Hurry up!" Moments later, she uproariously commands her partner to perform cunnilingus on her by telling him to "Go West!": a pun on Horace Greeley's famous adage, "Go West, Young Man!" American frontier expansion

CHAPTER FOUR ◊ **SWINGING SIXTIES**

and Manifest Destiny are tied to sexual conquest; "going west" is also linked to the exploration into "Canadian bush" and going down on a woman (needless to say, a forest and nearby stream are the backdrop for this sexual rendezvous). As in most of the sex scenes in *Vixen*, the faces of the males are also either obscured or facing away from the camera, suggesting they are indistinguishable from one another, and even interchangeable and expendable in fulfilling their function of sexually satisfying Vixen at the moment. Yet there is no sense that infidelity and adultery are treated as "immoral," yet alone a "crime." In *Lorna*, Lorna's lover is

135

an escaped convict, a figure outside the law, an "illicit" figure. Lorna is depicted as a social and sexual convict as well, her adultery "a crime" punished by death. *Vixen* is quite the opposite. In *Vixen*, adultery is depicted as a spontaneous and natural activity: animal sexuality triumphing over the constructs of morality and marriage. Thus, while Lorna's lover is an "outlaw," Vixen's lover is revealed to be a Mountie, the figure of law and order, which seems to legitimatize and give social approval to what might be otherwise called an "illicit" act.

Returning to the lodge, Vixen encounters her burly brother Judd (Jon Evans) and the previously-mentioned Niles. Typical of Meyer, the conversation is equal parts insult and innuendo. Perhaps the most striking aspect of the dialogue is the immediate foregrounding of the incest taboo (much like *Common-Law Cabin*). There is strong sexual tension and interplay between Vixen and her brother, and she makes it clear that if could do better than her current batch of lovers, he is more than welcome to try. Conversely, her comments to Niles are usually racist slurs, calling him "boy" and "Rufus." Niles, in turn, plays up to her racist perception of blacks by satirically over-acting the stereotype of the horny black man whose single goal in life is to have sex with a white woman. Niles only becomes angered when Vixen makes a derogatory comment linking his manhood, or lack thereof, to his *draft-dodging* rather than his race (perhaps a personal commentary by Meyer, a proud World War II veteran who spoke very fondly of his military tenure in a number of interviews). The trash-talking exchange ends with Judd commenting about what Tom would say if he knew what was going on with her extra-marital activities. "If he did, he'd apologize for prying," Vixen replies to herself; it is difficult to assess whether her statement expresses guilt over her activities, resentment over Tom's indifference, or defiance over the constraints and constructs of matrimony.

Titillation and Taboo

Throughout the remainder of the film, Vixen proceeds to break virtually every sexual taboo: adultery, homosexuality, incest, and even a hint of bestiality in the legendary fish-dance. An unhappily married couple, Dave and Janet King (Robert Aikens and Vincene Wallace), have come to the lodge for a vacation, which begins with a dinner party with Vixen and Tom. After dancing with Dave, a trout (?) replaces him as Vixen's dance partner. The extreme low-angle shots of Vixen swaying to the music with the fish cradled in her hands like a penis and finally secured between her breasts are intercut with tilted close-ups of the almost hypnotized Dave, a visibly upset Janet, and an oblivious Tom as he happily grills fish on the barbeque. "Animal eroticism" becomes literalized by the film with Vixen's sexually-orientated dance with the fish. The montage also displays the marital problems between the Kings, and of course, Tom still being the "cluckoid," completely unaware that many of Vixen's sexual adventures take

CHAPTER FOUR ◊ **SWINGING SIXTIES**

place outside of their marriage.
    The couples retire for the night, and the scene shifts between the two. Tom calls for Vixen in the bathroom, and the shot cuts to an incongruous insert of Vixen bathing naked in an outdoor pond, rather than where one would expect, the bathtub. It is left to the imagination whether the shot is a subjective shot from Tom's perspective, or if it is a nondiagetic insert meant to literalize Vixen's animal sexuality and relationship to nature. She then enters the bedroom in a red negligee, and dives into bed with Tom for a vigorous round of sexual action.

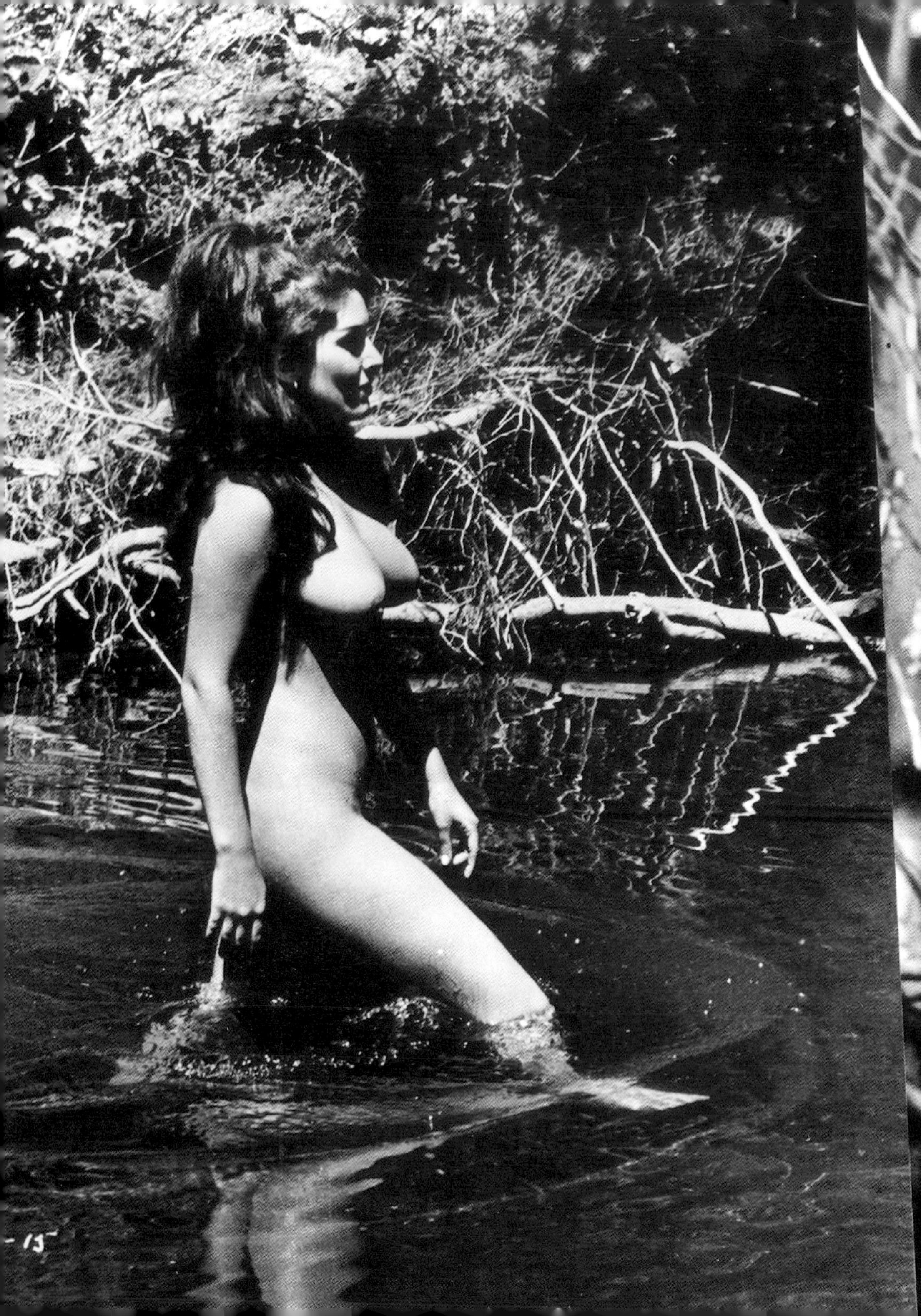

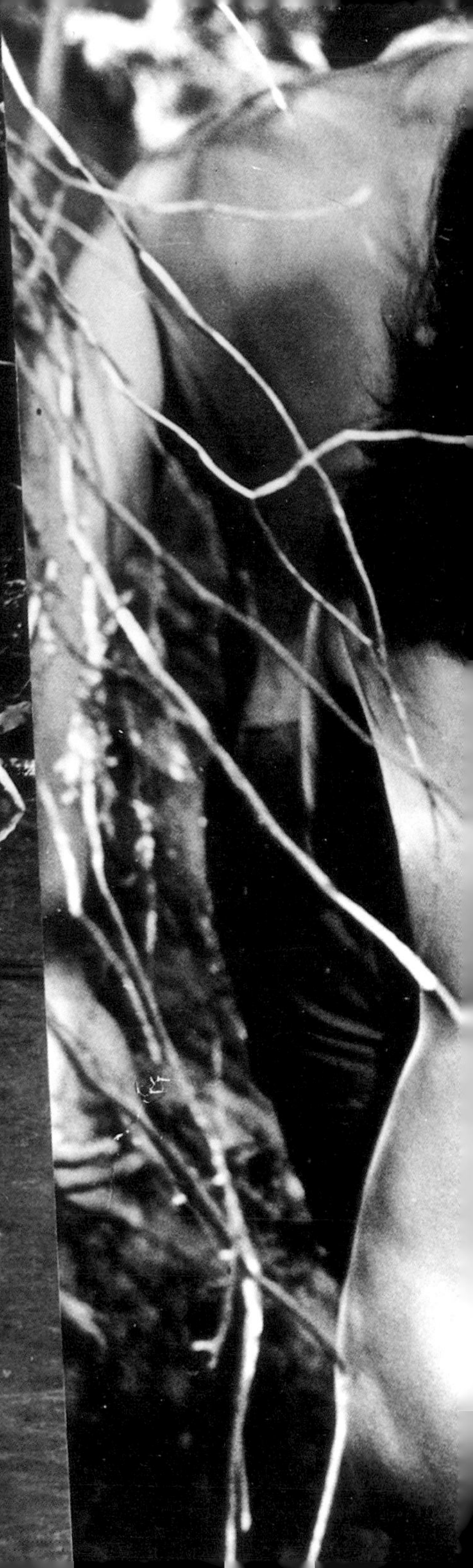

CHAPTER FOUR ◊ **SWINGING SIXTIES**

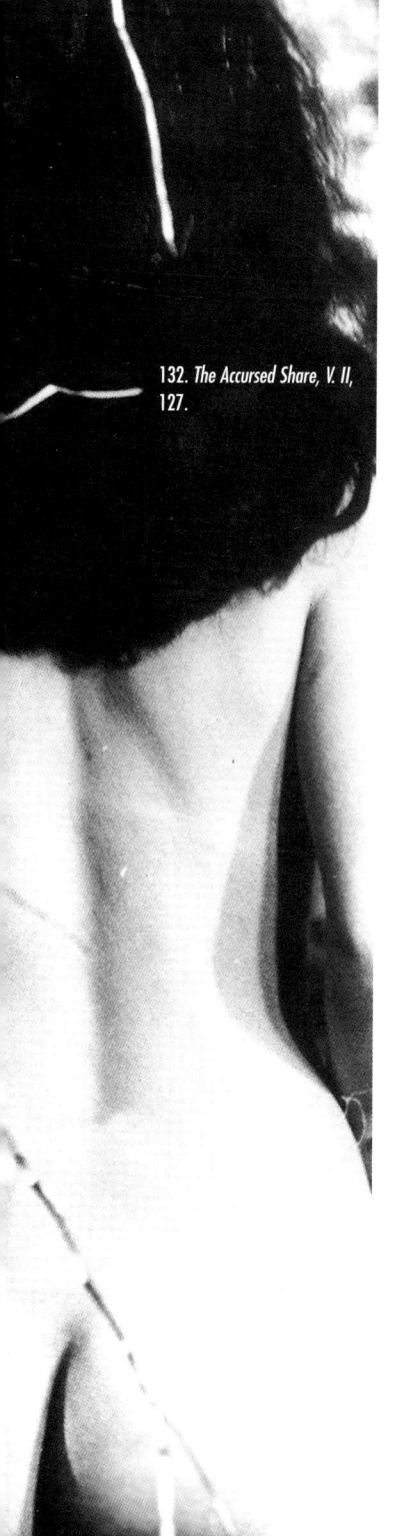

Despite Vixen's regular infidelity, Tom and Vixen are nonetheless a happily married couple, which in the Meyer film universe means they have a successful sexual relationship. As Bataille noted, marriage at its best instills intimacy, "the secret understanding of each other," but it is different from "eroticism ... [which is] developed out of illicit sexuality."[132] For Vixen, she has "the best of both worlds," able to find "intimacy" in marriage and "eroticism" outside of marriage.

The scene with Vixen and Tom cuts to the other side of the wall, where the Kings are residing. Janet asks Dave, "What's on your mind?" and the shot cuts back to Vixen and Tom, suggesting that having sex with Vixen is what is on his mind. Of course, Dave is uninterested in Janet, and her growing sexual frustration is depicted by a nondiagetic insert of her masturbating naked on a rock outside the lodge. The juxtaposition of the two couples is set up: Vixen and Tom having passionate sex while Dave is unable or uninterested in sex with his own wife, leaving Janet even more upset, frustrated, and jealous of Vixen. This developing tension sets the stage for the next morning, when the two couples go on a fishing excursion. Soon Dave and Vixen wander off on their own, and Tom tells Janet in his unflappable straight-face, "She knows all the good spots – and she'll make sure he has a good time." The relationship between Tom and Janet is typical of Meyer: a man who is interested in fishing and completely uninterested in a woman's amorous advances towards him (*Mr. Teas, Motorpsycho!*). Janet's attempt to seduce Tom backfires miserably, ending with her being even more frustrated and berating Tom for being so stupid he can't see that Dave and Vixen "are off making it." Indeed, Janet is quite correct; Dave and Vixen have soon forgotten fishing in favor of running naked through the forest streams and having sex in the shallow water. Again, the florid outdoors becomes a site for female sexual conquest.

Following the fishing adventure, the men go off to hunt. Janet opts to stay home, sullen and frustrated, and Vixen decides to keep her company. When Vixen walks into Janet's bedroom, Vixen's buttocks fills the screen, with Janet's head barely visible below Vixen's crotch; her head is literally between Vixen's legs, foreshadowing the upcoming lesbian encounter between the two women. Like other Meyer sex scenes of the era, the sexual encounter is marked by the use of subjective and non-diagetic inserts. In one sequence a shot of Janet lying in bed in her negligee cuts to close-up of Vixen which cuts to a shot of Janet lying naked in bed. The shot of Vixen's subjective point-of-view is freely intertwined with the camera's objective point-of-view: both Vixen and the camera (and by extension, the male spectator), are "undressing her with their eyes." At a later point, the previous nondiagetic insert of Janet laying naked on a rock is thrown into the encounter almost at random.

Throughout the scene, there is a sense that Vincene Wallace and especially Erica Gavin are not comfortable with the on-screen action, which runs

132. *The Accursed Share, V. II,* 127.

LIPS HIPS TITS POWER ◊ THE FILMS OF RUSS MEYER

counter to Vixen's carefree "sexual healer" persona. The scene itself is as much awkward as it is sensual, and subsequent accounts of the filming of the scene and its effect on Gavin have been described as "traumatic."[133] Again one is reminded of Bataille's work on "eroticism." Eroticism a not only a product of the illicit and the prohibited, but even the *distasteful*:

133. Frasier, 102.

"There is a horror in being: this horror is repugnant animality, whose presence I discover at the very point where the totality of being takes form. But the horror of the experience does not repel me. The disgust I feel does not nauseate me. Were I more naive I might even imagine, and moreover I might even claim that

CHAPTER FOUR ◊ SWINGING SIXTIES

I did not experience this horror and this disgust. But I may, on the contrary, *thirst for it*, far from escaping, I may resolutely quench my thirst with this horror that makes me press closer, with the disgust that has become my delight."[134]

In the lesbian encounter, there is a sense of Vixen taking her own sexuality to new, forbidden levels, a move from heterosexuality to homosexuality that challenges even her sensibilities and thus heightens her sexual excitement (it is important to note that lesbian encounters also become key scenes in Meyer's next two films, *Cherry, Harry, and Raquel* and *Beyond the Valley of the Dolls*). However, the men return home before the encounter proceeds any further, and the disheveled Vixen makes a narrow escape. When Dave engages in small-talk with Vixen and asks her how her day was, her vague responses are satirically matched by a montage of shots from the lesbian encounter that just occurred. When Dave comes on to Vixen, she instead sends him to finish what she started with Janet. Indeed, the next morning finds the King's vacation over but having new-found marital bliss, thanks to the sexual powers of Vixen, and they gleefully make a point of telling Tom to say goodbye to Vixen for them.

Vixen's sexploits with the Kings pave the way for further sexual transgressions: her sexual encounter with her brother. Judd and Niles are sitting around the lodge drinking beer, and Niles nonchalantly wonders aloud where Vixen is. "She's usually out gettin' laid this time of day," Judd retorts, unaware that he is about to be Vixen's next conquest. Conversely, the situation between Niles and Vixen grows more tense. "Go rape a white chick!" she yells at him, and Niles complains that it's the white chicks who are trying to get into his pants. While the dialogue could simply be dismissed as offensive trash-talk designed to denigrate woman and blacks to a primarily white, working class, male audience, Meyer also quite deftly and perceptively points to, and effectively satirizes, the political rifts occurring within the Left at the time: feminists who were rejecting the sexism rampant in the New Left, Civil Rights, and Counter-Culture movements; black militant writers who suggested that racism was due to sexual jealously on the part of whites towards blacks; and white males who were attempting to maintain leadership of "the revolution" under the guise of Marxist rhetoric (a figure embodied by the communist O'Bannion, who appears later in *Vixen*).

While Niles decides to wait outside, Judd takes a quick shower. Vixen follows him into the bathroom, drops her bathrobe, and determinedly flings the shower curtain open. Judd reacts with a mixture of shock and attraction, experiencing the "eroticism" manifest in both attraction and repulsion for his sister. Vixen joins him in the shower and orders him to wash her back, "like when we were kids." "We quit doing this when you turned twelve," is Judd's hilarious response, "we're not kids anymore." "No, we're *not*," Vixen replies stubbornly and

[134]. *The Accursed Share, Vol. II*, 118.

LIPS HIPS TITS POWER ◊ THE FILMS OF RUSS MEYER

even predictably, stating that while they may have gotten older and "civilized," their sexual feelings for each other have not changed. Vixen even proceeds to spur Judd into sexual action with the most basic of children's taunts: "*I dare you!*" The act commences, infusing both animal lust and competitive fury (as mentioned earlier, Meyer described this scene as his archetypal sex scene, where sex becomes "a football scrimmage"). They quickly move into the bedroom, where they complete their sexual transgression. In one patented shot, Meyer films the scene from under the bed with the mattress removed, showing only the bedsprings and Vixen's backside. While the mattress is on the bed in other shots, and is obviously removed to provide a better view of the action, it serves as a disorientating continuity break in the sex sequence, interrupting rather than promoting any voyeuristic pleasure.

However, besides the obvious "post-transgression" consequences, Vixen and Niles are caught in *post-coitus* by the impatient Niles. The embarrassed, even ashamed Judd first tries to play off the encounter ("I've had better"), and then blames Vixen for the whole situation. Vixen sardonically responds if she is now "the bad girl" and chides Judd for suddenly "developing a sense of morality." While Judd desperately seeks to return to the realm of civilization and out of animality, Vixen seeks to remain in the animal world that the bedroom has become: not denying the taboo, but transcending it. She even begs Judd not to leave at one point. For Vixen, nothing "unnatural," yet alone "immoral," has happened between them, but for Judd the violation of the incest taboo has had a deeply-troubling effect. Indeed, Judd's character takes a rather sinister turn, and in order to get revenge on Vixen for "seducing" him, he convinces Niles to go back into the lodge and rape Vixen. Again, the satirical nature of racial and sexual politics in *Vixen* is raised by playing on contemporary myths of race and sexuality. Judd, ashamed of his own animal transgression, instead sends in the 1960s embodiment of raw, "animal" male sexuality, the black man (Niles), to put Vixen "back in her place." Niles storms in, the simmering feud between Vixen and him exploding into violence and attempted rape, and inadvertently Niles has become what he left the U.S. for Canada to avoid: a pawn in the white man's war, except now the battleground has become the bedroom rather than Vietnam. However, the rape is prevented by Tom's unexpected arrival home with his new client, the bearded Irishman O'Bannion (Michael Donovan O'Daniel). Aware of the possible consequences, Judd breaks up the confrontation he has just instigated, ordering Niles to go outside and telling Vixen to keep quiet. Their parting comments are succinct: she calls him "a bastard," he calls her "a bitch." Now ready to carouse, Judd joins Niles, who cannot get his motorcycle started (or rather, his "motor won't run"). Judd sarcastically tells Niles that he "always craps out with the chicks," and he roars off to perform the ultimate of "outlaw-biker" activities: picking up girls at the local school dance.

Personal Politics

O'Bannion, who is paying Tom a handsome fee to fly him to the States, actually plans to hijack the plane to Cuba. Vixen and Tom go in to pack and, of course, have a quick one (here one is amazed how Vixen can recover from the trauma of an attempted sexual assault to exuberant sex in a matter of minutes). O'Bannion regales Niles with Marxist revolutionary jargon, and while he drones on the screen images cut to Vixen and Tom passionately having sex. A number of issues are raised by this scene. First is the inherent and inseparable linkage of sex and politics, where the most intimate moments of the human body are infused with political struggle: sex as an exercise of power, "a football scrimmage." Secondly, and similarly, the shots of bodies engaged in sex set to Marxist rhetoric certainly recalls, if not actually parodies, the seminal work of Jean-Luc Godard from the same period, which expressed a similar interest in the relationship of the explicitly sexual and the explicitly political. Third, one is struck by the sheer incongruity and inconsequential oration of O'Bannion as he discusses politics while low-angle shots of Vixen having an orgasm fill the screen. Again, one might argue the Marxist polemic is simply included to give the scene a satirical sense of being "socially-conscious." Finally, one could suggest that there is a theme of "seduction" being set up, with Vixen seducing Tom sexually and O'Bannion trying to"seduce" Niles politically.

Niles initially turns down O'Bannion's attempts to get him to join his cause, but as they are about to leave Vixen hurdles one last racial slur by calling Niles "Rufus," much to the embarrassment of Tom and the disgust of O'Bannion. Motivated by his personal and sexual animosity towards Vixen rather than any sort of class-consciousness, Niles decides to join them on the plane. This, of course, infuriates Vixen and magnifies the tensions already apparent on the ill-fated flight. The cramped confines of the small plane only serve to exacerbate racial, sexual, and political tensions. For those viewers who managed to stay until the end of the film, they are treated to a short political debate. As noted previously, Ebert suggested the debate was quite possibly tacked on to provide the film with needed "socially-redeeming" subject matter, and it became well-known to film goers that once the characters got on the plane the sex scenes were over. However, the nature of the debate does give Meyer a chance to satirically criticize draft-dodgers (Niles), communists (O'Bannion), and racists (Vixen). Shortly after take-off, O'Bannion pulls a gun and announces his plans to hijack the plane to Cuba. Vixen, of course, takes her anger out on Niles rather than O'Bannion, who slaps her at one point in response to her derogatory, racist remarks. Tom is once again at his dead-pan best; he pleads for calm "and Niles – quit punching her out!" As the flight proceeds, Vixen continues to criticize Niles and then O'Bannion for their political stances, probably voicing Meyer's own opinions on the issues, and soon cracks in their alliance are revealed. Again, Niles has once again become a pawn in the white man's war, but instead of the war in Vietnam or the battlefield of the bedroom, he is now enlisted as a "token" in the revolutionary class struggle. When O'Bannion is unable to answer the growing criticisms, in true Stalinist fashion he waves a gun and tells everyone to shut up. Still pressed by Niles, O'Bannion pauses in frustration (and great dramatic tension) before spitting the almost predictable racial epithet "nigger,"something even beyond Vixen's overt racism. A fight breaks out and

CHAPTER FOUR ◊ SWINGING SIXTIES

O'Bannion is rendered unconscious. However, Niles now has the gun and orders the plane back to Canada. "Once a Mau-Mau, always a Mau-Mau!" Vixen snarls at him. Niles relents and allows the plane to land on American soil, deciding that as bad as things are, in comparison to O'Bannion, Vixen is the lesser of two evils. Tom and Niles exchange goodbyes, and Vixen even attempts an apology, but cannot form the words. "It's OK... *Vix*," Niles smiles, and in a hilariously contrived way, Vixen, the sex-crazed white girl, and Niles, the angry black man, reach an accord. Niles makes his escape, presumably back to Canada, while O'Bannion is handed over to the authorities (while Meyer can respect a draft-dodger with strong convictions, he cannot tolerate a hypocritical communist).

While Vixen and Tom recuperate from the ordeal, they are informed that they have potential new clients, an unsuspecting tourist couple on vacation (the husband being Russ Meyer in a brief cameo). The film ends with a close-up of Vixen as she inquisitively cocks her head and almost innocently smiles. Her expression regarding what will be another sexual conquest is not one of sadism or maliciousness, but one of unbridled curiosity. The close-up freeze-frames and "THE END?" appears on screen, posing a question, rather than a finish. One possible answer is that while Vixen may be a predator, she is hardly immoral.

CHERRY, HARRY, AND RAQUEL (1969)

Art(-Film) Imitates Life

Amid the social disorder of the late 1960s, Russ Meyer made what is probably his most surreal and inventive film, the suitably chaotic *Cherry, Harry, and Raquel*. Its disconnected, experimental film style clearly situates the film in the late 1960s, although Meyer claimed the original source for *CHR*'s inspiration was not the European avant-garde but the action films of Don Siegel, specifically *Coogan's Bluff* (1968), which *CHR* parodies in several plot points.[135] Nonetheless, between the film's violent action, surreal imagery, radical editing, and disjointed narrative, it is quite possible to describe *CHR* as a cross between Siegel and Pasolini. With its mixture of mock-documentary, crime melodrama, and extended surreal sequences and sex scenes, *CHR* almost calls to mind a *Dragnet* episode if Jack Webb had actually dropped LSD-25 and kicked the doors of perception wide open to his sexually-repressed visions. Meyer noted, "The picture is the most successful I've had on cable television – or hotel vision – because you never have to come in at the beginning. It doesn't matter. It could be a loop."[136]

However, the avant-garde aesthetics of the film were as much due to internal production problems as to artistic vision; the working conditions lead to the sudden departure of actress Linda Ashton, who played Cherry:

135. See Frasier, 119.

136. As quoted in "Russ Meyer Interviewed by Ed Lowry and Louis Black." Originally published in *Film Comment*, Jul/Aug 1980. Page 3 of 7. Copy available at www.fmcinema.com/russmeyer/rmint.html.

145

"She had a couple of Pomeranians and she would lock them inside [the hotel] all day, and they would just devastate the room. We had a real redneck hotel owner, who was drunk all the time – like Chill Wills, only fatter – and he'd yell about her 'goddamn dogs.' She took such offense – the very idea this man would object to her dogs using the rug. Finally, about two days before we finished, she said, 'I've had it. I'm going home.' It was good. The pictures's better because of her leaving."[137]

Undeterred, Meyer devised a unique strategy. He hired sexploitation legend Uschi Digard to appear as "Soul." Ebert noted:

"[Meyer] hired [Uschi Digard] to symbolize some of the missing scenes. When footage was missing, Meyer simply cut to Uschi doing something that substituted for the lost action or replaced it. He also shot a great many of other brief takes of Uschi (who nowhere appears in the story proper) in order to give the film a consistent texture."[138]

These inserts range from the mundane (Uschi sunbathing) to the risqué (Uschi pouring milk over her breasts) to the positively surreal (Uschi spinning around in a swimming pool with a mammoth saxophone). Given the sparse narrative, "Soul" becomes the central organizing focus of the film, a surreal or even metaphysical figure through which the film's action revolves. This film is not organized not so much by the crime narrative but by what might be termed three separate "acts," or sexual encounters, between the three title characters: Raquel (Larrisa Ely) and Harry (the granite-jawed Charles Napier, who, like Alex Rocco, has enjoyed a successful film and television career); Cherry and Harry; and, finally, Cherry and Raquel. These three acts are as much connected by the reoccurring, metaphorical images of Soul as much as the threadbare plot, where, as in *Pussycat!* and *Finders*, criminal situations are the means by which the characters are thrown into the originary world of violent and sexual impulses. Moreover, unlike previous Meyer films such as *Goodbye!* and *Vixen*, which celebrate the *female* libido and are primarily centered in forests and streams, *CHR* marks a return to the desert, and is very much an essay on *male* libido.

CHR actually has three beginnings (and also appropriately has three endings). The film first begins with a short, visual polemic on free speech and censorship. It is a furious barrage of images culled from *CHR*, many of them featuring Uschi Digard. Over these images a warning is issued to the viewing public about the dangers and potential threats of censorship to their personal rights; it scrolls up the screen in written form accompanied by music that sounds like John Phillip Sousa on crank. While probably included as a personal aside by Meyer for the legal difficulties that occurred with *Vixen*, the images bombard and

[137]. "Russ Meyer Interviewed by Ed Lowry and Louis Black," page 3 of 7. See also Schneider, ed., 45-6 for a similar account of Ashton's departure and *CHR*'s arduous filming conditions.

[138]. "Russ Meyer: King of the Nudies," page 7 of 14.

CHAPTER FOUR ◊ SWINGING SIXTIES

bewilder the viewer, and the written, "socially relevant" message soon becomes a distraction, irrelevant to the underlying sheer visual energy generated by the feverish montages. The film next moves to a "serious" narrated prologue that sets the tone for the film. The quasi-documentary format discusses the issue of drug smuggling through somber narration and corresponding visuals: a stock shot of the U.S. Customs checkpoint building is shown as the narrator discusses drug traffic over the U.S.-Mexican border. However, at other points in the narration the visuals are dominated by Uschi Digard lying on the deck of a yacht, applying suntan lotion on her body. One is lead to the conclusion she is some sort of crime lord moll, but in fact it is "Soul" who is being shown for the first time, the symbolic character who appears throughout the film, here serving as a metaphor for the opulence and decadence of drug trade money. This narrated prologue moves to the credit sequence. Underneath the credits are a series of shots of a blonde woman, soon revealed to be Raquel, and a male, whose identity is not revealed until the end of the film. They drive and carouse through the desert amid its phallic rock formations as the country-rock film theme "Toys of Our Times" is heard on the soundtrack. The credits culminate as the man and the woman begin to make out as a large, phallic rock looms in the background, but is only after the film has run its course does the viewer realize the scene is completely unrelated to the narrative, despite the presence of one of the main characters.

Act I: Raquel and Harry

Following the disjointed beginnings of the film (the free-speech preamble, the prologue, and the credits) the narrative as such finally begins. Harry is a crooked cop with ties to a local criminal, Mr. Franklin (Franklin Bolger), who orders him to come to his place to get instructions for job he wants done. Meanwhile, the misogynistic Mr. Franklin is also "entertaining" Raquel, the blonde woman from the opening credits, who is a local prostitute. When Raquel begins to administer oral sex on Mr. Franklin, Harry makes his untimely arrival, buzzing the door bell and laughing when he hears Mr. Franklin groaning over the intercom. It is another typically Meyer moment where a sexual encounter is underscored by the voyeuristic presence of a male who enjoys the encounter in a sadistic way: Harry's reaction to interrupting Mr. Bolger is cruel satisfaction rather than erotic interest (Meyer once said that Napier was the one actor who captured the "humor/evil" tightrope best out of all his actors). With Meyer's usual lack of subtlety, when Mr. Franklin reaches orgasm, the shot cuts to his hand shaking violently and spilling wine all over the bed sheets. In between reprimanding Raquel over the spilled "wine" that has stained the plush sheets, Mr. Franklin gives Harry the assignment he wants carried out while he is in the hospital for minor surgery: Harry is to murder "the Apache," a local marijuana smuggler

Uschi Digard

whose dealings with Mr. Franklin have gone sour.

Raquel gets dressed and Harry offers her a ride home in his police Jeep. During the ride they pull over to the side of the road and soon engage in sex. However, rather than the nudity and simulated sex of *Vixen*, they remain clothed during their sexual encounter, which is punctuated by an odd, recurring close-up of Raquel's white boot heel. The nudity is instead reserved for the surreal inserts of Harry and Raquel cavorting in the desert on foot and in the Jeep, as well as shots of Raquel striking pin-up poses. Furthermore, the sex scene in the Jeep is not only interrupted by this footage of Raquel (and Harry) naked in the desert, but also inserts of Soul dressed only in cowboy boots and a native American headdress: the headdress is a symbolic reference to the Apache as well, and the strong libidinal bond between him and Harry that underlies the film. In one insert, Soul gyrates on Harry's jeep, the "turned-on" police siren in the foreground positioned to obscure her vagina; in another insert, she is shown in an extreme long shot writhing against one of the many phallic rock formations in the desert. Such images obviously suggest sexual intercourse and orgasm. Remembering that the desert is the site of masculine libido, and thus explaining the myriad phallic rock formations that occupy the desert landscape, the *objective* shots of the sex scene in the Jeep are freely intermingled with Harry's *subjective* thoughts and fantasies of Raquel and him occurring in the desert, while the inserts of Soul metaphorically act out the missing action from the scene. As a coda to this thoroughly disorientating sex scene, there is a wonderful sequence when Harry drops Raquel off at her shack. The shot of fully-dressed Raquel walking away from the camera in the moonlight cuts to a close-up of Harry watching her, and then to a shot of Raquel, naked except for a long red scarf wrapped around her neck which billows around her body, walking away from the camera in the sunlit desert. The objective shot of the camera and the subjective shot from Harry's perspective again become freely intermingled (once again, Pasolini comes to mind).

The plot line revolving around the Apache is reintroduced at this stage when Harry rouses Enrique (Bert Santos), who happens to be sleeping with Raquel, and brings him out to the desert with him to ambush the Apache. The attack on the Apache is a tautly filmed action sequence, comparable to the best work of Siegel or Peckinpah. Yet the depiction of violence in *CHR* is at once *thematically* similar to, but *cinematically* markedly different from Peckinpah. While violence contains an erotic undercurrent in *CHR* (and in all of Meyer's films), violence is sudden and brutal, depicted by fast-motion and rapid-fire editing, providing a kinetic and almost slapstick effect. Conversely, Peckinpah pioneered the use of slow-motion cinemaphotography to capture the aesthetic and erotic fascination of violence in *The Wild Bunch* (1969) and his subsequent films. Nonetheless, Meyer and Peckinpah *both* essay the aesthetic and erotic

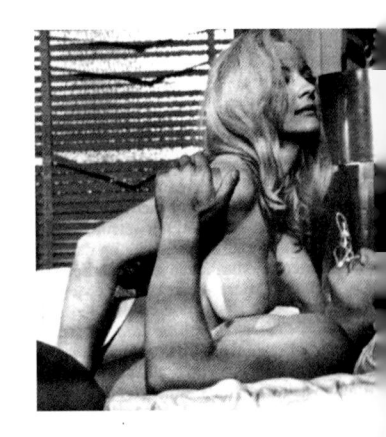

CHAPTER FOUR ◊ SWINGING SIXTIES

nature of violence, despite their vastly different film techniques.
An almost interminable tension is created by recurring long-shots of the Apache's slow moving car as it winds through the desert passes, intercut with close-ups of the tense, sweaty Harry and Enrique. Finally, as the vehicle slowly approaches them, Harry and Enrique suddenly and indiscriminately fire into the car, which rolls off the side of the road and overturns. Following the disabled car, Harry executes a baseball slide next to the overturned vehicle and blasts away into the driver's seat through the car window. However, Harry and Enrique quickly realize they are the ones who have been ambushed: they are pinned down by gunfire next to the empty car. Long shots scan the desert ridge, which may or may not point-of-view shots from Harry and Enrique's perspective: again, the objective and subjective point-of-view is indistinct. No one is seen, but gunfire is heard, rendering the Apache an "invisible" enemy. One is reminded of both Brahmin in *Motorpsycho!*, who is rendered almost "invisible" in the desert landscape in the film's violent conclusion, and even *The Naked West*, and the "painted Redman" who blended into his surroundings "as no human could." Eventually making their way to the desert ridge, Harry and Enrique discover no sign of the Apache save for some blood splattered on the ground. Leaving the Apache for dead, Harry and Enrique return home.

Act II: Cherry and Harry

The second portion of the film revolves around Harry and Cherry, a nurse at a nearby hospital and Harry's girlfriend. After the attempt on the Apache's life, Harry returns to his cabin and Cherry. She is introduced to the narrative by a shot of her sleeping naked on her stomach; however, this shot has been inserted into the film twice before: first, when Mr. Franklin gives Harry the assignment to kill the Apache and briefly asks Harry about "that looker he's shacked up with," the second time when Raquel mentions to Harry (before their sexual encounter) that she would like to meet Cherry sometime – her sexual interest is also apparent. In both these cases, the shot of Cherry is inserted to simply give a literal image to what is being discussed on-screen: when Cherry is mentioned as an object of sexual interest, Cherry is shown naked.
A lengthy sex scene develops between Harry and Cherry, and like the previous sex scene between Harry and Raquel, it is punctuated by long, surreal sequences of the couple in the desert, as well as inserts of Soul. Moreover, Harry provides a voice-over narration recounting his first sexual encounter as a teenager, and it is unclear if the on-screen images, the subjective desert scenes, and nondiagetic inserts refer to his nostalgic memories, a present sexual encounter with Cherry, or a freely intertwined combination of the two. In what is the most fascinating of these desert images, the naked Harry comes across Cherry buried in the desert sand except for her face. Harry begins to dig up the

LIPS HIPS TITS POWER ◊ **THE FILMS OF RUSS MEYER**

sand as if he were sculpting her: her breasts appear first (naturally), then her torso, then her legs. Suddenly, she comes to life, and begins to kiss Harry passionately. It is a fascinating sequence in which "the woman," as a female image-ideal, is a fantasy product of male desire, literally created out of desert

CHAPTER FOUR ◊ SWINGING SIXTIES

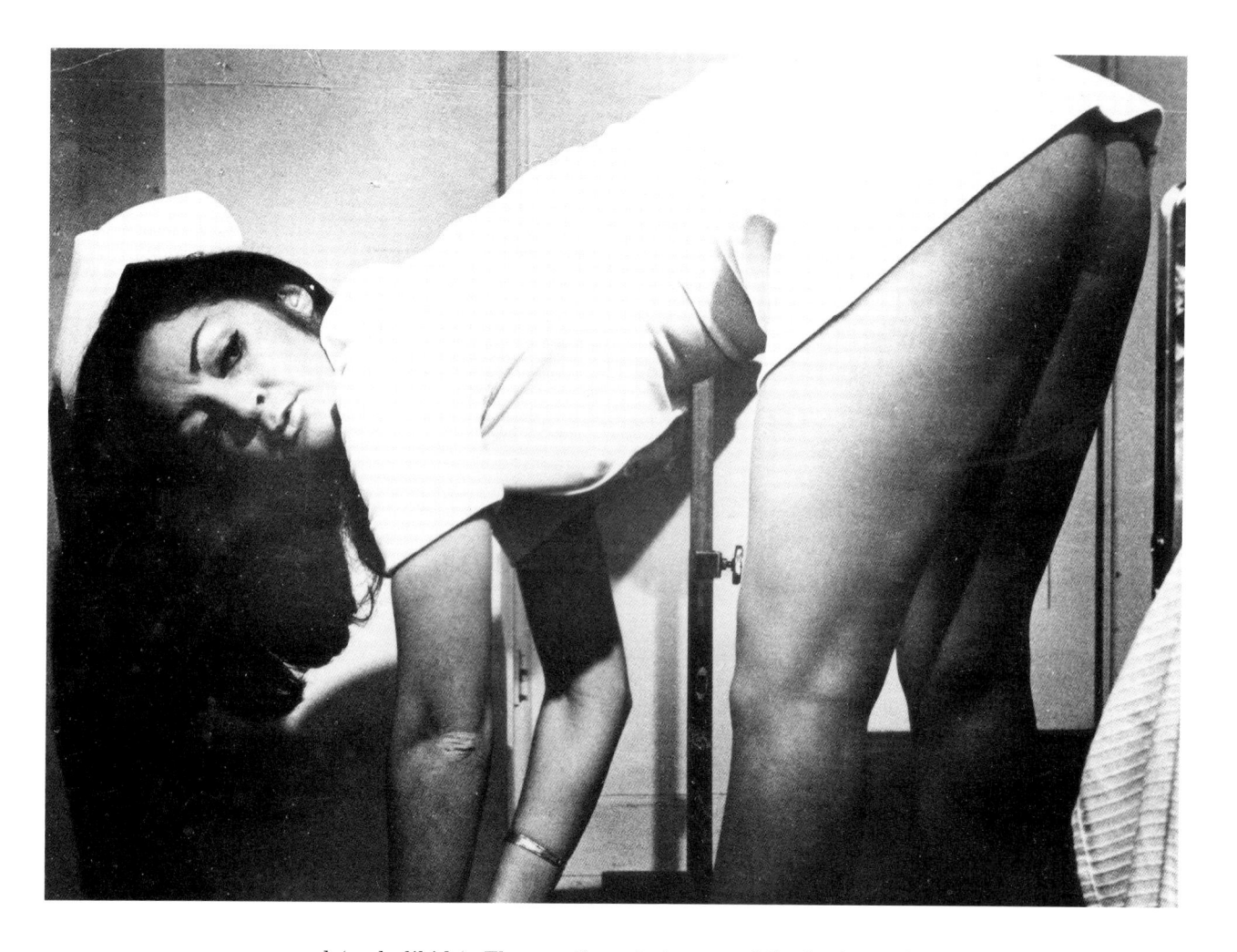

139. See "*Beyond the Valley of the Dolls* and the Exploitation Genre": 21.

sand (male libido). The nondiagetic inserts of *Soul* take on importance as well, their bizarre ambiguity creating as much disorientation as they do associative montage. Craig Fisher quite perceptively pointed out that the inserts of *Soul* actually serve as metaphors for the sex act itself: the insert of Soul eating celery a metaphor for fellatio; the insert of Soul in a vibrating weight reduction machine suggests female orgasm; the insert of Soul waist deep in the water of a swimming pool batting the water with a tennis racket a metaphor for male ejaculation.[139]

As noted, the presence of Soul serves to provide a surreal continuity to the film, and at brief points in this "second act" she actually appears within the film in moments highly reminiscent of Luis Buñuel. In the first scene, Soul, naked except for her Native American headdress and cowboy boots, sits on top of an abandoned car in the desert. Driving past in his Jeep, Harry stops, gets out, tip his hat, and begins to change a flat tire on the car for her. This is intercut with a scene where Cherry is assisting a gynecologist, and the close-up of the doctor's lubricated finger cuts to a close-up of a tire iron being inserted into a jack (the meaning of the montage is obvious). In a second, equally surreal scene, Harry attempts to call Mr. Franklin at the hospital after trying to kill the Apache. The shot of Harry in the phone booth cuts to Soul, naked except for knee-high leather boots, seated at an operator's switchboard in the middle of the desert directing his phone call while speaking in French. In one similar, hilarious insert, Soul is shown leaning against the edge of the swimming pool on the phone while a bare-chested Russ Meyer stands in the pool behind her (!). Such scenes serve to disrupt narrative altogether, moving the film towards pure surrealism.

Act III: Cherry and Raquel

The finale of *CHR* depicts the bloody conclusion of the film with the deaths of the male characters juxtaposed with the final sex scene of the film, a lesbian encounter between Cherry and Raquel. As for the crime narrative, it becomes apparent that the Apache is still alive and now seeking vengeance on the parties involved; however as Fisher noted, "the digressive nature of the sex scenes drains all suspense from the plot."[140] Indeed, between the length of the strange sex scenes and the intermittent appearance of Soul, the narrative becomes all but useless in the film's bombardment of nondiagetic and surreal images.

Following Mr. Franklin's surgery, Raquel arrives at his hospital room to "visit" him. When she rolls the unresponsive Mr. Franklin over, she turns him toward the camera, revealing that his throat has been slit and his chest and the sheets below him are covered in blood. This is quickly followed by the death of Enrique, who has gone to the desert to get some smuggled goods out of an abandoned car. He is unaware that the Apache has stolen Harry's Jeep and has come to kill him. Recalling *Pussycat!*'s race scene, Enrique's car and Harry's Jeep careen through the barren desert, the dueling automobiles becoming an almost living things with palpable sexual energy. Eventually Enrique's car becomes stuck, and rather than attempt to run, Enrique challenges the Jeep with a switchblade (parodying the Old Man's challenge of Varla's car in *Pussycat!*). The gesture is at one masculine, suicidal, comical, and highly theatrical; as a long shot depicts the Jeep slowly circling him, Spanish bull-fighting music is heard on the soundtrack. Similar to the shootout earlier in the film, the tension and anticipation of violence is stretched out to a breaking point, but the actual on-screen violence happens at a breakneck pace, rendering the actual moment of

140. "Beyond the Valley of the Dolls and the Exploitation Genre": 22.

CHAPTER FOUR ◊ SWINGING SIXTIES

violence almost indiscernible. When the Apache finally bears down on Enrique, the split-second editing follows the approaching car and suddenly cuts to Enrique's bloodied body as it is thrown across the desert. There is a close-up of the cracked, parched desert floor with Enrique's twitching hand reaching for the switchblade. Both the hand and the knife are covered in brilliant, bright-red stage blood, ending the scene with a send-up of Greek tragedy.

In the first ending of *CHR*, the viewer is presented with two climaxes: the simultaneous deaths of Harry and the Apache intercut with Cherry and Raquel's lesbian encounter. Raquel has been admitted to the hospital as a result of the shock of finding Mr. Franklin's body, although she is rather calmly filing her fingernails when Cherry enters to check on her condition. Soon the women are smoking pot and dancing with each other, a "dance of life" which contrasts to the previous "dance of death" between the Apache and Enrique and the forthcoming "dance of death" between Harry and the Apache. Soon the women are naked, holding each other in a spinning chair that obscures the viewer's line of sight when the chair's back is to the camera. New inserts are intercut into this scene as well: stunning underwater photography of two naked women swimming together as the sun reflects on the surface of the water in the background (the scene was actually filmed in Meyer's backyard swimming pool). To add a touch of absurd comedy, a sonar ping is heard on the soundtrack. Unlike the previous sex scenes which featured Harry and the images in the desert, the encounter between the two women is fittingly marked by images of water.

Meanwhile, Harry and the Apache consummate their own relationship in a violent shoot-out in the desert outside Harry's cabin that leaves both dead. The Apache is finally seen, although the viewer never sees his face; his back is invariably towards the camera. Possibly one of the most astonishing scenes Meyer ever filmed, the shoot-out is at once chilling, visceral, slapstick, and yes, beautiful. Eroticism and violence, humor and evil, tragedy and farce are all effortlessly intertwined. In what amounts to a male-male dance/duel to the death, Harry and the Apache blast away at each other with revolvers and rifles over, around, and even under the Jeep in a burst of destructive libidinal energy. When the dead Apache falls on Harry's lifeless body, the encounter clearly manifests its homoerotic overtones. In *CHR*, the male order extinguishes itself through violence, and masculine libidinal energy between men can only be expressed through violence, as in all of Meyer's films. It is the female homoerotic order that survives intact, the spinning of the chair suggesting their perpetual, unbridled libidinal energy. In terms of Freud, the *female* homoerotic order is expressed through Eros, and the *male* homoerotic order is expressed through Death.

This is the first of three endings for *CHR*. Following the climax of the film, with the men lying dead on atop the other, a narrated epilogue follows. It is

LIPS HIPS TITS POWER ◊ THE FILMS OF RUSS MEYER

another jarring visual summary of the film, its myriad images accompanied by a dour narrator who sums up the moral lesson of the film, once again managing to sound very important and nonsensical at the same time. The epilogue is pure satire, and one can recall Ebert's recollection that this was the epilogue that Meyer read to him over the phone at six o'clock one morning, a reading punctuated by uncontrolled bursts of laughter. Meyer himself noted, "We also had a great put-on at the end of *Cherry, Harry, and Raquel* about the evils of marijuana. It was so tongue-in-cheek, but people would say 'You're not really serious.' We had this corny Mexican guitar, a torn fence, and a deserted road. What does it mean?"[141] The epilogue is little more than an absurd polemic that not only satirizes itself, but the very strategy used to make the film "socially-redeeming." This cuts to the third ending of the film, and the last shot of the

141. "Russ Meyer Interviewed by Ed Lowry and Louis Black," page 3 of 7.

CHAPTER FOUR ◊ SWINGING SIXTIES

epilogue cuts to a shot of female hands on a typewriter and then to a shot of Raquel sitting behind the typewriter. The whole film has turned out to be a trashy novel Raquel is writing, a tale from the subjective view of the character of Raquel, the writer, filtered through the objective view of the camera. Harry is revealed to be her apparently straight-laced husband, and he asks her brother Tom (Robert Akien, Dave King in *Vixen*) if he reads her "anti-social drivel." Tom, in fact, is the man seen with Raquel in the opening deserts, making out with her amid the phallic rock formations: another moment where the subjective viewpoint of a character and the objective viewpoint of the camera are erased. Moreover, it reveals that the opening credit sequence has actually been an incestuous fantasy of Raquel with her brother (an obvious reference to *Vixen*). The camera freeze-frames on a medium close-up of Raquel as she slyly smiles. The credits begin to roll and the film's theme song "Toys of Our Time" is reprised. To close the film, Soul is shown running naked through the desert. Like *Good Morning... And Goodbye!*, the film ends with the supernatural female essence that has guided the film running freely in the originary world.

CHR is one of Meyer's most fascinating films, by far his most challenging and experimental film with its surreal scenes, ambiguous nondiagetic inserts, free interaction of subjective and objective viewpoints, radically jarring editing, and minimal narrative. *CHR* also begins an analysis of male and female sexual relations that becomes key in Meyer's next film, his *magnum opus*, the legendary *Beyond the Valley of the Dolls*.

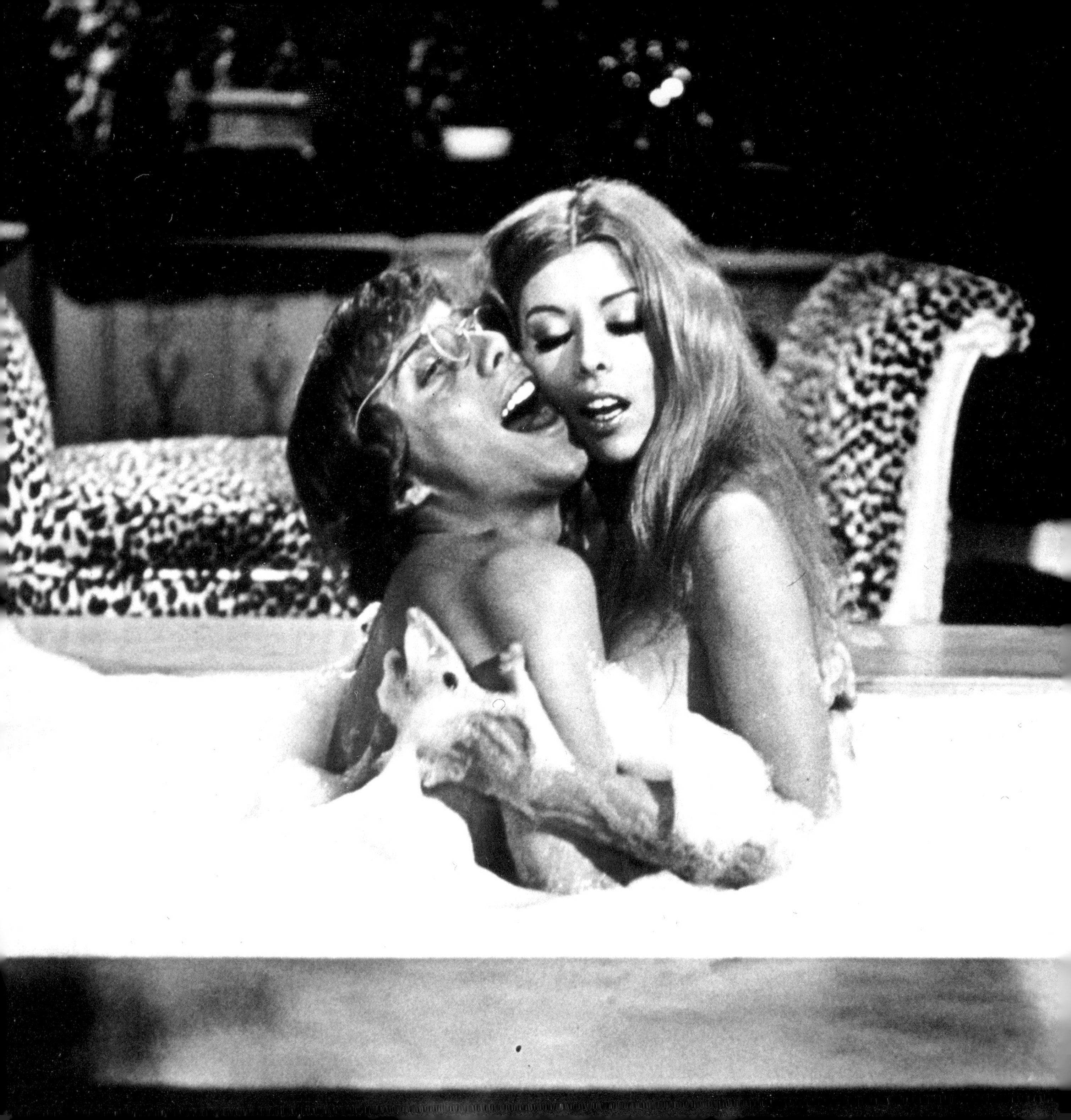

CHAPTER FIVE
"BEYOND THE VALLEY OF THE DOLLS"

This ain't Rock and Roll — This is Genocide!
–David Bowie, *Diamond Dogs*

The Big Time

Impressed by the unprecedented financial success of *Vixen* and Meyer's other films of the period, 20th Century Fox hired him for a multi-picture deal in 1969. The first film for Fox was *Beyond the Valley of the Dolls* (1970), a film Meyer calls his greatest achievement. In addition to his pride in the film, Meyer spoke fondly of his tenure at Fox, especially the behind the scenes perks and creative battles with studio executives. "That represents my having been to the mountain. My career wouldn't have been nearly as exciting if I had not been to a major studio."[142]

Mainstream critics did not share the excitement of Russ Meyer joining forces with Fox. Reviews for *BVD* were, by and large, scathing: the film was savaged for its tawdry tone and absurd histrionics, and some critics went so far as to blast Fox for striking a deal with Meyer for financial rather than artistic considerations. By 1970, Fox was still reeling from *Cleopatra* (1963), the trouble-plagued epic that nearly single-handedly bankrupted the studio, as well other more recent big-budget box-office disappointments such as *Dr. Doolittle* (1967) and *Hello, Dolly!* (1969). Moreover, the disastrous *Myra Breckenridge* was released by Fox the week before *BVD*, and many critics lumped the two films together as proof positive of the artistic and moral decline of Hollywood.[143] Nonetheless, *BVD* did generate some much-needed box-office for Fox, making

142. As quoted in Schnieder, ed., 47.

143. See Fischer: 30-1.

back over six times its production costs, although Mayer claimed later that the film could have made much more money had it been marketed differently.[144] Also, the film did gain some enthusiastic reviews from critics who indeed "got the joke." Most mainstream critics completely missed the fact that *BVD* was as much a *satire* of the turgid Hollywood soap-operas of the time as it *was* a turgid Hollywood soap-opera. The fact that the film was taken seriously at all was cited by film critic Ted Maher as evidence that *BVD* was all the more successful in is satire (Maher interestingly argued that *BVD* was a satire of the Hollywood melodramas about the corrupting influence of show business on young females).[145] This ensuing confusion over whether *BVD* was "serious" or "satire" was very much the intent of Meyer. Screenwriter Roger Ebert noted:

"It was also slightly easier to keep the characters in mind because each one was drawn as a caricature and then typecast. Meyer was able to heighten this effect by directing all the actors in an absolutely straight style. *This was the intention from the outset: to write a parody and direct it deadpan.* If he succeeded, [Meyer] said, there should never be a moment in the film when the actor seems to understand the humor of his dialog or his situation."[146]

Of course, this confusion as to whether or not the film was a "serious" drama or "humorous" satire was an often confounding situation the *audience* had to deal with as well. As will be discussed, at several points Meyer felt it necessary to camouflage the satire and/or otherwise keep the audience absolutely bewildered as to what was going on in the film in order to preserve the "thin edge" between the serious and the satirical.

In short, *BVD* is the tale of the rise and fall of an all-female rock band consisting of guitarist and lead singer Kelly McNamara (Dolly Read), bass guitarist Casey Anderson (Cynthia Myers), and drummer Petronella "Pet" Danforth (Marcia McBroom). None of the three principal female leads were Hollywood "stars" and were inexperienced actresses. Dolly Read and Cynthia Myers were best known for being *Playboy* playmates, and Marcia McBroom was a model before appearing in *BVD*. But like any good soap opera, there is also a vast array of supporting characters and complex subplots in *BVD*. Ebert noted, "Meyer's personal opinion was that *BVD* was really about Harris, the bedraggled manager who passes through impotence and paralysis and lives again to walk through the valley of the dolls. I was never really sure whether the movie had a focus on a single character; in writing it, it felt more like a juggling act."[147] My own reading of *BVD* will emphasize the trajectory of Kelly McNamara from teen rock-queen to Hollywood whore to domesticated girlfriend, and, moreover, my own view of the film is to read Harris Allsworth (David Gurien) not as the hero, as Meyer did, but as a *villain* in *BVD*.

144. See "Russ Meyer Interviewed by Ed Lowry and Louis Black," page 3-4 of 7.

145. See Frasier, 138; pgs. 133-41 are an indispensable catalog and synopsis of the critical response to *BVD*.

146. "Russ Meyer: King of the Nudies," page 12 of 14. Emphasis mine.

147. "Russ Meyer: King of the Nudies," page 12 of 14.

CHAPTER FIVE ◊ "BEYOND THE VALLEY OF THE DOLLS"

"Not a Sequel...There Has Never Been Anything Like It!"

Following the success of *Valley of the Dolls* (1967), Jacqueline Susann, author of *Valley of the Dolls*, was hired by Fox to write a sequel *Beyond the Valley of the Dolls*, which was to be produced by her husband Irv Mansfield. After several potential screen treatments were rejected by Fox, Mansfield was fired and Susann's entire project scrapped save for the title. When signed by Fox, the studio approached Meyer to do a possible *Beyond the Valley of the Dolls*, with creative control given to Meyer provided the film was in some way a sequel. However, an acrimonious legal battle ensued between Fox and Susann, who unsuccessfully tried to block *BVD* on the grounds it would damage her "literary reputation."[148] Because of the legal action, any characters and references to the original *Valley of the Dolls* ultimately had to be eliminated. Ebert recounted:

"We did screen Mark Robson's film version of *Valley of the Dolls*... and this gave us the notion of doing *BVD* as a parody. We would take the basic situation (three young and talented girls come to Hollywood, find love and success, and then are brought low by booze, drugs and pride), and attempted to exaggerate it wildly... I originally saw the film as a total parody. Meyer, with his characteristic unwillingness to stop at the merely total, saw it as a total parody and a total sex-and-violence trip. At one point we described our project to Fox executive David Brown as 'the first-exploitation-horror-camp-musical,' and that wasn't far off."[149]

Indeed, the "exploitation" nature of the film can be seen in its tawdry tone and sensational situations, as well as its use of the murder of actress Sharon Tate, who, ironically, starred in the original *Valley of the Dolls*. The "horror" aspect can be seen in the film's grisly conclusion (again, inspired by the Tate murder) and its climatic revealing of "the monster": in this case, the murderous rock producer who happens to be a woman disguised as a male homosexual. The "camp" quality is evident in the film's willful use of cliché and bad taste, not to mention Meyer's amazing and garish use of Technicolor as a sort of Pop Art nightmare. But perhaps most important is how *BVD* parodies the musical, not only in its self-referential use of musical numbers to comment on the action, but in the way *BVD* satirizes the ideological mission of the musical. In his book *The American Film Musical*, Rick Altman observed that the musical's ideological vision was the construction of a stable social order through the establishment of the heterosexual couple.[150] In *BVD*, this establishment of heterosexual order is taken to a hilarious, brutal, and absurd lengths by the film's quadruple murder of the lesbians, male prostitute, and homosexual butler as well as the death of the female transvestite which is followed by a triple wedding which closes the film.

---

148. The legal battle between Susann and Fox did not reach a settlement until the fall of 1975, when a jury awarded the estate of Ms. Susann two million dollars for alleged damages to her career and reputation (the award was posthumous; Susann died of cancer in 1974). The parties subsequently agreed to a 1.5 million dollar settlement. See Frasier, 123-33.

149. "Russ Meyer: King of the Nudies," page 10 of 14.

150. See *The American Film Musical* (Bloomington: University of Indiana Press, 1987). My analysis of *BVD* owes greatly to Altman's work on the musical.

BVD begins with the 20th Century Fox logo and fanfare, important to note in that the studio's musical theme is later incorporated into *BVD* in a moment of absolute black comedy. There is a fade-in to an establishing shot of a mansion. A disclaimer appears over the establishing shot:

The film you are about to see is not a sequel to Valley of the Dolls – *it is wholly original and bears no relationship to real persons, living or dead. It does like* Valley of the Dolls *deal with the oft time nightmare world of show business but in a different time and context.*

The disclaimer was included because of the on-going legal dispute between Fox and Susann. Yet by its very denial *BVD* invokes an inevitable comparison to *Valley of the Dolls*, and rather than distancing the two films, the disclaimer actually ties them together. As previously noted by Ebert, *BVD* was intended very much as a parody of *Valley of the Dolls*, with its basic premise lifted and taken to ridiculous (or even more ridiculous) extremes. However, *Valley of the Dolls* is not the only source of parody for *BVD*; many classic Hollywood and contemporary films become a source of parody throughout *BVD*. With typical Meyer disregard for narrative, *BVD* begins with the film's violent finale, parodying the master of the Hollywood melodrama Douglas Sirk and his classic film *Written on the Wind* (1956). Both films begin by showing the tragic climax as the opening credits rolls, and then proceed to tell the story of what led up to the tragic ending (or beginning, as the case may be). As the credits are shown, the audience encounters a variety of bizarre and unexplained images: a scantily-clad woman running from the mansion, followed by a portly man in a Nazi uniform, followed by a slender man in Shakespearean theatrical garb. This Shakespearean figure then slaughters the Nazi on the beach of the Pacific Ocean with a giant broadsword as the woman looks on in horror. The scene shifts to the interior of the mansion, where the camera tracks the Shakespearean figure, a close-up fixed on the back of his head. He pulls a pistol from the dresser drawer and proceeds over to a sleeping Erica Gavin, familiar with audiences as the title character in *Vixen*. In one of the more infamous moments in any of Meyer's films, Gavin, still asleep, begins to perform fellatio on the barrel when the Shakespearean figure places the pistol in her mouth. As she opens her eyes and realizes what is happening, there is a close-up of her terror-filled eyes and the sound of her scream.

Gavin's close-up and scream cuts to a close-up of Kelly McNamara screaming into a microphone as her band, The Kelly Affair, perform their anthem "Find It" at a high-school dance. The scream of the murdered woman is connected to Kelly's scream in a song about her "liberation" and self-determination, and throughout *BVD* one underlying theme is the gradual

CHAPTER FIVE ◊ "BEYOND THE VALLEY OF THE DOLLS"

"murder" of Kelly's independence by the men in her life, especially her boyfriend and the band's manager, Harris Allsworth. Indeed, this tension is first revealed when the close-up Kelly cuts to a long shot of the band performing on stage, which cuts to a shot of Harris as he spins a color wheel, which also resembles a wheel of fortune: the male figure "behind the wheel," managing the group's fortunes. At another point in "Find It," Kelly sings the lines:

"Dressed in the color of bright crimson —"
 (Kelly is performing in a red blouse)

"Wearing a long black wedding gown – "
(foreshadowing Kelly's eventual marriage to Harris, the image of a"long black wedding gown" equating marriage to a funeral)

"I've got to find my answers on my own – "
(The montage shows a long shot of the band, then a medium low-angle shot of Kelly, then a close-up of Kelly's face; the word "own" carries over from the close-up of Kelly to a close-up of Harris, not only foreshadowing Kelly's independence and estrangement from Harris, but the word "own" puns Harris and his final "ownership" of Kelly through his failed suicide attempt and their marriage).

Throughout *BVD*, the band's music is used to satirically comment on the action of the film. Sometimes the commentary is quite overt, as when their cliché ode to West Coast peace and love, "Come with the Gentle People," is heard when a brawl breaks out at a party. Other times, the music comments with more textual subtlety, such as with "Find It," or as will be discussed in detail, when the band performs "Sweet Talkin' Candy Man" at a party hosted by record producer Ronnie "Z-Man" Barzell (John LaZar).

Following the gig, the band retires to their van to smoke a joint. Kelly begins to make out with Harris. Pet and Casey leave the two alone, with Pet telling Casey "the principal's gonna hit me with a couple of caps of acid." Casey also uncomfortably remarks that "making it" is all Kelly and Harris seem to do; this foreshadows the revelation that Casey is a lesbian (and she may or may not have a sexual attraction to Kelly). However, Harris and Kelly do not "make it." Instead, they begin to discuss the band's future; Kelly decides the band should head to Los Angeles, where she has a rich aunt, Susan Lake (Phyllis Davis), and Harris tries to talk her out of the move. However, their debate is not played out in a standard shot-and-reverse-shot dialogue between the two, but in rhyming couplets and a rapid-fire montage of images: some stock footage, some footage from the movie, and some footage featuring characters in the movie but not from the narrative as such. For instance, when Harris described Hollywood by spitting the words "perverts – fruits!," this is matched by an insert of a shot from much later in the film when Z-Man plants a kiss on the mouth of Lance Rocke (Michael Blodgett). In another example, when Kelly first mentions "rich Aunt Susan," there is a shot of Phyllis Davis running in a see-through purple nightgown; this shot does not appear in the film except for this montage. When Kelly further discusses "rich Aunt Susan," a hood ornament of a Bentley is shown, and when Harris counters with "bitch aunt Susan" a run-down Volkswagen is shown, using the automobile as a metaphor of financial success and social status (and, later in the film, *sexual* success as well). At another point in the montage, Harris pleads, "We'll get crushed!" and the on-screen image is of a egg being smashed by a shoe. "Not us!" answers Kelly, and the on-screen image cuts to a daisy. The images do not only provide visual metaphors of the argument, but in this case foreshadow the conclusion of the film: Harris, who is "crushed" by the trip to L.A. which culminates in a suicide attempt that leaves him a cripple, and the "Not us!" which refers to the happy ending with the survival of their relationship rather than the envisioned success of the band.[151]

The band begins their cross-country trek to Los Angeles. Meyer quite hilariously records the journey by using the cinematic cliché of superimposing a roadmap of the USA over the entire sequence. Long shots of the band's Volkswagen van driving down winding roads are intercut with various medium shots and close-ups of the band sitting in the van as they gleefully sing "Come With the Gentle People."[152] In contrast, Harris, who is driving and still "behind the wheel" of the band, seems less than enthused about the journey, and at one point sardonically flashes a peace sign while the band excitedly sings. Upon arriving in Los Angeles, Kelly quickly meets up with Aunt Susan in her fashion studio, where exotic models in various states of undress roam about (Haji appears as one of the models). Ebert noted that much of this scene regrettably ended up cut for time reasons, but was intended to parody Michaelangelo Antonioni's *Blow-Up* (1966).[153] Kelly and Susan rekindle their relationship in a tear-filled reunion, much to the concern of Susan's lawyer, Porter Hall (Duncan McLeod), who is convinced that Kelly has come to swindle Aunt Susan, which would severely affect his own devious plans for the Lake fortune. And almost immediately, Kelly and the band get their first break when Susan invites them to a party at the mansion of "the teen tycoon of rock," producer and rock impresario Ronnie "Z-Man" Barzell.

"This is My Happening and It Freaks Me Out!"

The scene at Z-man's party begins with shots of miscellaneous characters delivering one-liners and snappy repartée. "They banned my last film in Cinncinatti!" proclaims adult film-star Ashley St. Ives (Edy Williams) in one shot, a not-so veiled reference to Meyer's obscenity battle with the Ohio courts

[151]. See Fischer: 27-8.

[152]. The source of parody for "Come With the Gentle People" may have been Scott McKenzie's idealistic hit song about the West Coast hippie movement "(If You're Going to) San Francisco," which contains the line, "You're gonna meet some gentle people there."

[153]. See "Russ Meyer: King of the Nudies," page 11 of 14.

CHAPTER FIVE ◊ "BEYOND THE VALLEY OF THE DOLLS"

over *Vixen*. Other partygoers include Princess Livingston from *Mudhoney* in a pink wig and mod clothes chatting with actor Lance Rocke, a gay couple commenting on penis size, and various others exchanging *double entendres*, insults, and puffs of marijuana.

When Kelly arrives at the party, Z-Man is instantly taken with her; he

163

introduces himself by telling her, "So, OK – I'll say it – haven't I seen you somewhere before?" At this point in the film the viewer assumes that Z-Man is, in fact, a man, and that he may have a romantic interest in Kelly. He quickly escorts her around the party and points out the major supporting characters in his campy, Shakespeare-meets-Oscar Wilde delivery. Throughout this scene, Z-Man functions very much like an on-screen narrator, serving to not only introduce but also comment on the complex web of characters to both Kelly and the film audience as well. First he introduces Ashley St, Ives, "famous indeed" for her adult films. He then points out Roxanne (Erica Gavin), with veiled commentary about her being a lesbian. Following Roxanne, Lance Rock is introduced as "Greek god and part time actor." Emerson Thorne (Harrison Page from *Vixen*) is next to be introduced, the friendly waiter and aspiring law student; Z-man whispers to Kelly that inside him "is the unholy seed of... *a lawyer.*" Finally Otto, the bartender and Z-Man's butler, is introduced, and Z-Man both balefully and absurdly ponders if he could be "another face of Martin Bormann?"

Following these introductions, Z-Man escorts Kelly through a tour of his mansion where they almost inevitably encounter people having sex. In one room they see a couple in the bed: "Pray, let them joust in peace!" whispers Z-Man to Kelly as he closes the door. In another room, Z-Man and Kelly interrupt the gay couple having oral sex. As they leave the bedroom, one bitches to Kelly, "What is this – a studio tour?" His comment is a self-reference about the film itself, with Kelly indeed getting "a studio tour" of the film's set. Finally, Z-Man leads Kelly through his master bedroom and into the master bath. Of course, there is a naked couple having sex in the bathtub, but Kelly is far more impressed by the plethora of plants in the bathroom. She exclaims, "I've heard a tree grows in Brooklyn but never ferns in the biffy." In an ominous shot of Z-Man feeling one of the plants, he tells her they serve as a reminder that "Los Angeles is a jungle." This abruptly cuts to a shot of the party, the word "jungle" carried over to describe the party, a social and sexual "jungle" of bodies and animal passions that make up the film's surreal version of decadent Los Angeles.

Harris, Casey, and Pet soon arrive at the party and begin to circulate; their entry quickly begins to set up the romantic parings and tensions that develop throughout the film. Harris, while looking for Kelly, meets Ashley St. Ives; she makes her sexual interest in Harris clear and in a classic line tells him, "You're a groovy boy – I'd like to strap you on sometime." Similarly, Casey encounters Roxanne, who expresses an interest in designing some clothes for her; these two will also become romantically involved. Pet and Emerson also meet at the party, and for them it is love at first sight; their relationship problems will figure into the film as well. It is here that "the juggling act" between the characters is especially obvious, with the film trying to introduce

CHAPTER FIVE ◊ "BEYOND THE VALLEY OF THE DOLLS"

and condense as many subplots as possible into a limited time frame.

Eventually, Harris becomes more and more uncomfortable with the party scene, manifest in one tracking shot where he aimlessly walks through the dancing party guests looking for Kelly, as if he were "lost in the jungle" of bodies. Finally, he encounters Kelly with Z-Man. She introduces Harris as "my – uh,… manager," careful to avoid mentioning Harris is also her boyfriend. The novice Harris is no match for the seasoned rock producer Z-Man, who sardonically informs him that the name "The Kelly Affair" is "awfully 1950s… you might as well just call them The Haircuts." Offended by Z-Man and the party scene as a whole, Harris curtly informs Kelly that they are leaving, but Z-Man executes his first *coup* in what will soon be his complete takeover of the band's fortunes: he invites the girls to perform a song in front of the party guests.

With an introduction by Z-Man, the band launches into the song, "Sweet Talkin' Candy Man." Not only does the song lyrically comment on the narrative action in the film, but its deft editing and staging serves to set up vital subplots and disguised meanings in the film. In the first verse, Kelly sings about leaving home and meeting up with a man; while she sings the first verse, ending with the line "I thought I could land a sweet talkin' candy man," there is a shot of Z-Man, then a shot of Harris, and a shot of Z-Man looking at Harris in a sinister manner, serving to comment on the ensuing battle for Kelly's future between Z-Man and Harris, and which one will be her "sweet talkin' candy man." As Kelly sings the second verse, she begins to weave her way through the crowd, singing to the various supporting cast members. When she reaches the end of the second verse and sings the words "sweet talkin' candy man," she is facing Lance Rocke, who blows kisses at her. This foreshadows Kelly's romantic involvement with Lance and his manipulation of Kelly later in the film. The most striking moment of the song occurs when Kelly begins the third verse. She walks determinedly towards Harris and, facing him, belts out the first line, "He played around and brought me down and finally threw me out." There is a shot of Harris intercut with Kelly singing the line to him; he is staring back at her with an almost sadistic smirk. Again, as with "Find It," the underlying tension between Harris and Kelly is played out through the song lyrics and sharp editing as much as narrative. As the lyrics indicate, Kelly is used by a man who "played around" (a reference to Harris's fling with Ashley), "brought me down" (referencing her remorse after Harris's suicide attempt), "and finally threw me out"(referencing Harris's final "victory" over Kelly by "throwing her out" of the band and ending her musical career and life in the L.A. fast-lane in favor of caring for him). Turning her back on Harris, which is a visual metaphor for Kelly "turning her back" on Harris later in the film in favor of fame and selfish ambition, she sings the second line of the third verse, "I got burned but I learned what life was all about." This line comments on the "lesson in life" that Kelly ultimately learns by

165

the end of the film: the (cliché) message that love is more important than fame and money. As Kelly finishes the song, she ends the third verse by singing "sweet talkin' candy man" while she is face-to-face with Z-Man, signifying his impending and complete takeover of the band. Indeed, after the song ends, the thrilled Z-Man steps up to the stage to proclaim that they will storm the country "like Carrie Nation – nay, nay – they *are* The Carrie Nations!" This marks another victory for Z-Man over Harris: he has renamed the band in his own image.

"In the Long Run"

The next shot of the film are the words "The Carrie Nations" in black on an orange background which fill the screen; the camera pulls back to reveal it is the new name of the band written on Pet's bass drum. In the first of two similarly constructed sequences (the second being for the song "Look on Up at the Bottom"), the band performs the song "In the Long Run," a syrupy ballad about trust and dependability in a relationship which satirically mirrors the growing estrangement between Kelly and Harris as well as the growing hold Z-Man has over the band. Ebert recounted that these

"transitional montages, intended to symbolize Z-Man's growing influence with the rock trio and Harris's personal disintegration, were conceived as a kind of throwback to Forties and Fifties musical biographies. We didn't use Variety headlines only because we had already used a series of roadside signs superimposed on a map to indicate a journey [the trip to L.A. sequence]; we wanted our visual fun to be as eclectic as possible."[154]

154. "Russ Meyer: King of the Nudies," page 11 of 14. Parenthesis mine.

The song begins with a shot of the full band, then a close-up of Harris is superimposed on the left side of the frame. This is the only time Harris is seen until the song reaches its conclusion. A spinning tape reel is superimposed in the center of the frame through much on the song, obviously indicating that the band is being recorded, as well as suggesting yet another "wheel," specifically the "wheels" of the Culture Industry being set in motion. As the song continues, close-ups of Z-Man are superimposed over the band on the right side of the screen and shown with some degree of frequency. They begin to dominate the screen, suggesting his growing control over the band as he "oversees" the group as well as literally pushing Harris "out of the picture." As the song concludes, the scene shifts from the recording studio to a posh night club where The Carrie Nations are performing in evening gowns to a well-dressed, appreciative audience of friends and fans, except for the alienated Harris, who sulks in the backstage wings wearing his plain jacket and jeans.

After the gig, there is another party at Z-Man's mansion. Harris refuses

CHAPTER FIVE ◊ "BEYOND THE VALLEY OF THE DOLLS"

to go, and has a tense dressing-room encounter with Kelly, played out with overwrought music in the background. He pathetically asks Kelly, "Where do I fit in?" and bitterly complains that he's been reduced to the status of "a god damn groupie" (a position in the rock world almost exclusively reserved for women, and his reduced status in the band becomes one of many blows to Harris's masculinity in *BVD*). A wonderful shot from this sequence shows Kelly sitting in front of her dressing room mirror with Harris standing behind her, suggesting both she has "turned her back" on Harris and that she is more concerned with her "reflection" in the mirror and her growing obsession with a narcissistic self-image. Kelly and Lance Rocke decide to attend the party together, leaving Harris alone. He soon learns that he "fits in" with Ashley St. Ives, "the high priestess of

LIPS HIPS TITS POWER ◊ THE FILMS OF RUSS MEYER

carnality." She offers the dejected Harris a ride home in her Rolls-Royce, and finally succeeds in seducing the timid Harris. As Harris climbs into the back seat with her, "In the Long Run," bursts onto the soundtrack, a satirical commentary on the "infidelity" occurring between Harris and Ashley as well as Lance and Kelly – there is an insert of Lance and Kelly dancing at the party that is intercut as Harris joins Ashley in the backseat. "It's my first time in a Rolls," he sheepishly tells Ashley (and perhaps it is his "first time" anywhere). "There's nothing like a Rolls," she coos, and as she repeats the line the shot cuts to an

CHAPTER FIVE ◊ "BEYOND THE VALLEY OF THE DOLLS"

insert of Lance and Kelly having sex on a bedframe. The line "There's nothing like a Rolls," also suggests that Lance himself is a "Rolls" in the bedroom compared to Harris (a Volkswagen, perhaps). The shot of Lance and Kelly on the mattress springs cuts to a non-diagetic insert of a close-up of a Rolls-Royce hood ornament, a shot that serves to literalize the connection between a Rolls-Royce and Lance Rocke as "sex-machines." As Harris begins to have sex with Ashley, she begins to moan, "There's nothing like a Rolls – not even a Bentley! A Bentley!" Here Meyer inserts tilted close-ups of hood ornaments and logos of a Bentley automobile to literally match Ashley's mention of the car. Finally she orgasmically squeals, "A ROLLS!" and the shot cuts to a close-up of Kelly kissing Lance, once again connecting the Rolls-Royce to both great sex and the figure of Lance Rocke. In other Meyer films such as *Pussycat!*, *Finders*, or *CHR*, the automobile is equated with the destructive power of sex, whereas in *BVD* the automobile is a symbol of "making it," both sexually and financially.

Now together with Kelly, Lance quickly sets his sights on Susan Lake's money. The conniving, manipulative, and egotistical Lance easily talks Kelly into staking her claim for half the Lake fortune, and the scene appropriately shifts to Susan and Porter in her office. Porter continues to denigrate Kelly as a "tramp" and a swindler, and when Kelly arrives at the office he offers more unflattering comments directly to Kelly, calling her "a hippie… with the morals of an alley cat." "I doubt if you'd even recognize a hippie," Kelly hilariously responds, "*I'm a capitalist, baby!*" The confrontation between Porter and Kelly degenerates into name-calling as the horrified Susan begs for some calm. As a close-up of Kelly fills the screen, Porter describes her with "the innocent face… the sweet virgin-whore." It is a moment of self-referential commentary on Kelly's character, the close-up literalizing her "innocent face" while offering an unflattering description on her personality, which is growing more ruthless and manipulative under Lance Rocke's tutelage. Indeed, when Kelly turns to Susan and pleads her case in a teary-eyed, close-up of "her innocent face," she delivers a pathos-fueled plea about her mother deserving the money she never got, accompanied by satirically dramatic violins on the soundtrack: Kelly very much (over)plays the "sweet virgin-whore" that Porter has just described to the audience.

The scene abruptly shifts to Emerson and Pet having a picnic in a field where she is questioning Emerson on important court rulings in order to help him prepare for his bar exams. However, Emerson's mind is on other matters:

Emerson: Enough! Tomorrow I'll study. Tomorrow and tomorrow and tomorrow.
Pet: You sound like Z-Man.
Emerson: And Z-Man sounds like Will Shakespeare. And right now I feel like making love.

Unlike other "bookworms" in Meyer films (Jim in *Lorna*, Lamar in *Ultravixens*), Emerson knows when it's time to put aside the studies and engage in more important activities (sex). The shot cuts to wonderfully cliché scenes of Pet and Emerson playing and running hand in hand in a flowery field in slow motion. Eventually, they end up at a stable and have sex in the hayloft (or, "a roll in the hay"). Meyer defuses any eroticism by showing their faces in focus, but intercuts shots of their bodies in the hay out-of-focus, making their two bodies indistinguishable (one might also suggest that the out-of-focus technique also makes "two become one," creating a sense of intimate passion and sexual ecstasy). Also, whereas Kelly and Lance's sexual activities are confined to the bedroom, a zone which Lance has complete control over Kelly, Emerson and Pet have sex in the outdoors (as do Roxanne and Casey in their initial lesbian encounter). As in many Meyer films, the bedroom in *BVD* is a site of manipulation and domination of one sex by the other, whereas the outdoors is a place where sexual encounters can reach their fullest potential.

The scene shifts back to Kelly and Lance in bed. Porter calls in a desperate attempt to sooth the rift between Kelly and him, although his motives prove to be far less noble than an apology. Lance proceeds to orchestrate a plot to have Kelly meet up with and seduce Porter. She follows Lance's instructions to the letter, repeating everything he tells Kelly to say to Porter. After the arrangements are made, Kelly and Lance discuss their relationship:

Kelly: Why do I do everything you tell me to?
Lance: I don't know... why do you?
Kelly: I can't help myself – you've made me into a whore.
Lance: And you dig it, you little freak.

The line "you've made me into a whore" is lifted directly from *Good Morning... and Goodbye!*, when Angel tells her lover Stone the exact same thing. It also suggests that it is men who turn women into "whores": that women are not simply "whores" by choice or design, but rather products of male domination and fantasy. This scene also reinforces the pattern in *BVD* where sex that occurs in the bedroom is inevitably "corrupted," and it is only in the sex scenes that occur in the *outdoors* where sex is not in some way tainted by ambition, power, or money. Indeed, a huge publicity photo of The Carrie Nations hangs over Kelly's bed, suggesting her all-consuming obsession with fame and her narcissistic "self-image." She has not only been turned into a "whore" in bed, but a "whore" to Hollywood ambition and a "whore" to the Culture Industry that manufactures and disposes of rock stars. She is "a capitalist, baby" – a "sweet-virgin whore" to capitalism.

The shot of Lance and Kelly in bed cuts to a a close-up of two hands

CHAPTER FIVE ◊ "BEYOND THE VALLEY OF THE DOLLS"

touching across a table; it is revealed that the hands belong to Kelly and Porter, and the montage links Lance and Porter, *both* of whom are manipulating Kelly for her money. The apparently contrite Porter blames their rift on "the generation gap," and recounts a story about him and his father's rough relationship: "I came home in a pinch back suit and he thought I went the way of Oscar Wilde." The line also serves to comment on Porter's own sexual orientation, and the probability he is a closeted homosexual. However, Porter's reasons for meeting with Kelly soon take a more sinister turn: he offers her $50,000 in return for dropping all future claims for the Lake money. Insulted, Kelly shoves him into a table, causing him to spill his drink on his suit. After a momentary pause, Kelly puts the next phase of Lance's plan into effect; she apologizes and tells Porter things might be better discussed at her place. Of course, Kelly's seduction of Porter is played out for laughs rather than drama. Back at her apartment, Kelly offers Porter some grass, which he puffs on like pipe tobacco; Kelly has to instruct the insufferably "square" Porter on the proper method of smoking marijuana. She then utters the woefully cliché line about "slipping into something more comfortable," and Porter watches through the doorway of her closet as she strips and puts on a pink negligée, although more time is spent on Porter's stunned reactions rather than Kelly's "strip tease." Kelly then puts on a record, and "Sweet Talkin' Candy Man," is once more heard on the soundtrack to comment satirically on the action in the film. Gender roles are reversed; the seducer, the "sweet talkin' candy man," is now Kelly, who dominates and manipulates Porter in the bedroom much in the same way Lance does her. In this case, the (biological) woman assumes the (cultural) male role of the seducer, again marking the bedroom as a sight of "male" domination. She removes the negligée and crawls into bed, imploring Porter to "lose your laundry." While Kelly waits impatiently in bed, Porter carefully folds his clothes as he disrobes in an almost effeminate manner, and finally he tentatively joins Kelly, still wearing his underwear and sleeveless t-shirt, which exposes his less-than-virile physique. As Kelly takes his underwear off under the sheets, there is a close-up of a highly agitated Porter. "Ah... Miss McNamara..." he finally stutters, unable to finish his sentence. Kelly smiles and tells him, "it's our little secret." It is obvious that Porter is unable to perform sexually with Kelly.

"Look on Up at the Bottom"

The scene cuts to another party, where Z-Man proudly announces the release of the first album by The Carrie Nations; when he says "Carrie Nations" there are three quick inserts from shots that appear elsewhere in the film: the shot of Kelly and Lance having sex on the bedframe, a close-up of Casey having an orgasm during her second sex scene with Roxanne, and a shot of Pet and Emerson from their encounter in the stable. While the band's *musical*

LIPS HIPS TITS POWER ◊ THE FILMS OF RUSS MEYER

accomplishments are being celebrated at the party, the montage serves as a brief aside that it is the individual band member's *sexual* activities that is the concern of the film. Once again, "In the Long Run," can be heard on the soundtrack, satirically commenting on the fermenting sexual tensions and relationship problems that come to a head at the party.

At this party, two more important characters also enter the film. First is Baxter Wolfe (Charles Napier), Susan Lake's former love interest. In a humorously cliché-filled scene derived from soap-opera staging and theatrics, Baxter and Susan step outside for a discussion, which is done almost entirely in shot/reverse-shot close-ups of the characters as they talk and soon rekindle their love affair with a passionate kiss. The other character to enter the film is Randy Black (James Inglehart), a muscular black man who arrives at the party barechested except for a towel wrapped around his neck like a boxer; indeed, Randy Black just happens to be the heavyweight boxing champion of the world (also, like "Lance Rocke," the *double entendre* of his name should be obvious). He meets

CHAPTER FIVE ◊ "BEYOND THE VALLEY OF THE DOLLS"

Pet and the two are immediately attracted to each other, and after the party deteriorates into a drunken brawl and failed pick-up attempts, Randy Black consoles Pet in a bizarre monologue that mixes existential philosophy with strained boxing metaphors. Despite his incoherency, he somehow succeeds in impressing Pet, and ultimately spends the night with her.

During the course of the party, Harris, high on pills and booze, goes outside with Ashley where she unsuccessfully tries to have sex on the beach with him. As she stands over Harris, who is lying on his back, his point-of-view shots become patented Meyer extreme low-angle shots of an imposing, formidable woman. Exasperated, Ashley finally belittles Harris's sexual performance and suggests that maybe he should find a "nice, tender boy." She leaves Harris (and the film) with a sardonic salute and quickly meets another young male who will presumably be the next of a continuing series of sexual conquests. Harris drunkenly makes his way back into the party where he explodes in rage seeing Kelly and Lance kissing. A fight erupts between Harris and Lance as "Come With the Gentle People" is hilariously and mockingly heard on the soundtrack. Randy Black acts a cross between referee and boxing corner man, shouting instructions and encouragement to the two battling parties, briefly assuming the role of on-screen commentator for the audience as well. Lance proceeds to thrash Harris, who stumbles out of the party beaten, bloodied, and embarrassed.

The party also becomes Porter Hall's downfall as well. In one hilarious moment, Haji, dressed in a metal headdress and black body paint, walks through the party, prompting Porter to sarcastically exclaim to Z-Man, "Now you're inviting motorcycles to your parties – what's next, truck drivers and longshoreman?" Pet replies, "You mean, *really* rough trade?" It is yet another comment on Porter's closeted homosexuality, and while Porter is oblivious to what Pet has implied, she and Z-Man laugh knowingly. When Kelly attempts to flee from the chaos of the party, she is rudely stopped by Porter, who, in a very ill-timed moment, asks he what she has decided about his $50,000 offer. Kelly responds by taking the legal document and slapping him in the face with it. She throws the paper on the floor and contemptuously spits, "Take your $50,000 – *lover!*" To make matters worse for Porter, Baxter picks up the agreement he drafted, reads it, and shows it to Susan, who disgustedly tells Porter, "I never want to see you again." When Baxter attempts to explain, the square-jawed Baxter tells him he better leave, and the cowered Porter is dismissed as Susan's lawyer and exiled from the film as violins sardonically flood the soundtrack.

After the fight, Lance is alone, sulking at the bar. "We could have used you on the Russian Front," smiles Otto, suggesting not only his Nazism but his own sexual attraction to the blonde, blue-eyed Lance, the Aryan male personified. Lance is soon the object of another homosexual advance, this time by Z-Man himself. While bemoaning the fact that Lance isn't a "switch-hitter," Z-Man nonetheless propositions him. Lance responds by punching him in the jaw. As Lance storms out of the party, the prone Z-Man muses, "This really isn't your night, *pussycat*," although it is unclear whether he is referring to Lance or himself.

The scene shifts to Casey's apartment. Uncomfortable with the band's meteoric rise and alienated by the L.A. scene, Casey is coping with the pressures of the band's whirlwind success with isolation and a growing reliance on booze and pills. After being humiliated at the party, Harris comes over to her place for

CHAPTER FIVE ◊ "BEYOND THE VALLEY OF THE DOLLS"

consolation, and in a hilarious conversation, Harris explains his problems to Casey:

Casey: Do you want a downer?
Harris: Casey –
Casey: I'm here.
Harris: Ashley called me a fag.
Casey: Oh, Harris, that's a lot of crap.
Harris: I don't know!

Unsure of his masculinity after losing the band to Z-Man, Kelly to Lance, Ashley's insults ("she called me a lousy lay") and his pummeling by Lance, Harris asks Casey if he can sleep with her. Casey, who has also been drinking and popping barbiturates, agrees: "I've got all the room in the world," she sighs.

  The next morning proves disastrous for both Pet and Casey. Not surprisingly, their respective sexual encounters, which end in ruin, take place in the bedroom. Pet has slept with Randy Black, and Emerson unknowingly walks in the apartment the next morning, catching the two in bed. "You said you were going to study!" Pet pathetically exclaims. Dejected, Emerson walks out of the apartment and Pet angrily orders Randy out. As the shirtless Randy hops into his convertible, Emerson stands in the path of his car. "You're in my way – *again*!" snarls Randy, referring to Emerson being in the way of both his car and his relationship with Pet. Blasting his car horn and ordering Emerson to "move his ass," Randy grows more and more agitated until he finally hits Emerson with the car. As Emerson desperately hangs onto the hood, Randy drives the car in circles around the apartment courtyard, his animal and sexual rage released through the erotic release of assaulting Emerson with the car. Finally he stops and throws Emerson into the courtyard flower bed before speeding off. Sobbing, Pet runs outside to console the battered Emerson, crying apologetically and holding him in the flowers, sardonically recalling their romantic afternoon in the field.

  Meanwhile, Casey comes out of her blackout in the morning only to realize that she had sex with Harris. "You bastard!" she spits, "You're just like the rest!" She vehemently orders Harris out of her bed and her apartment before she staggers into the bathroom, perhaps to be ill. This scene soon cuts to almost industrial-stock footage of black globs of plastic being pressed into records as a funky guitar-riff that begins the song "Look on Up at the Bottom" starts on the soundtrack For several consecutive shots, a hand throws lumps of black plastic onto a record pressing machine. Recalling the sex between Harris and Casey that leads to her unwanted pregnancy preceding this scene, and foreshadowing the "black sperm of vengeance" that Z-Man announces his party guests will "drink"

175

in the concluding massacre of *BVD*, these black globs can be said to represent male reproductive fluid, or "black sperm." Record production and sexual reproduction are equated. Sex is not only productive, suggested by the black plastic "sperm" giving birth to consumer products (records), serving to further equate sex and capitalism (as the montages of sex scenes and expensive cars also suggest), but sex in the form of "black semen" has a destructive quality: not only the "black sperm of vengeance" that Z-Man will force his guests to metaphorically drink by murdering them, but the devastating effect impregnation has on Casey. Indeed, the "black sperm of vengeance" that leads to Casey's pregnancy and unwanted abortion "comes" from Harris, who has slept with Casey as an act of "vengeance" against Kelly as well as a need to prove his masculinity.

The record-pressing montage segues to the band performing the soul-music inspired "Look on Up at the Bottom." The sequence is constructed in the same fashion as "In the Long Run," with the band shown performing the song as various shots of Harris and Z-Man are again superimposed over them. When Kelly sings the line "Now you're actin' immature," a shot of a glowering Harris rubbing his hands together nervously is superimposed on the right side of the screen (Z-Man, in contrast, is periodically superimposed on the left side of the screen ecstatically clapping along to the music). Close-ups of the sullen Harris continue to be superimposed on the right side of the frame while the band sings the chorus "You're going down, so far down, when you turn around – Look on up at the bottom, look on down at your luck." This foreshadows Harris's descent into despair and alienation, the "descent" of "going down, so far down" literalized when he attempts suicide by jumping from the catwalk of a TV studio while The Carrie Nations are performing "Find It" on a talk show. To further suggest Harris's estrangement, there is a close up of Kelly singing the following lines:

You warm your hands in empty pockets
Where's the good life that you knew
You took a back seat, now don't knock it
When no one remembers you

The lyrics seem to comment directly on Harris's fall from the band's manager to non-entity; the loss of his status as Kelly's manager and boyfriend and the loss of "the good life that he knew"; the take over of the band by Z-Man, who Harris took "a back seat" to; and ultimately that "no one remembers" him, suggested by his very absence from the shot itself. Indeed, here Meyer employs a fascinating visual strategy. The obvious technique would be to have Harris superimposed over Kelly while she pointedly sings about him. However, while Kelly faces towards the right side of the frame, the filmic space occupied by Harris, he is not

CHAPTER FIVE ◊ "BEYOND THE VALLEY OF THE DOLLS"

there: he has literally "disappeared," suggesting his complete disconnection from the band. Harris is not shown until the closing moments of the song, while the band repeats the refrain "Look on up at the bottom – look on down at your luck." A shot of Harris aimlessly walking the streets is superimposed over the band, and the shot of the band fades-out as Harris stands in front of a record store. Covers of The Carrie Nations's new album, also ironically titled *Look on Up at the Bottom*, are being displayed in the record store window. As Harris turns away in disgust, he runs into a sidewalk newspaper box, and, in a fit of rage, hurdles the newspaper box through the record store window.

The song abruptly stops and the shot of the shattering window cuts to a TV camera facing directly at the audience, a moment of self-reference that overtly announces to the viewer that what they are watching is a movie. The Carrie Nations have been booked to appear on a live talk-show by Z-Man to perform "Look on Up at the Bottom." However, Pet suggests to Kelly that they perform "Find It" as "a thank you to someone" (Harris): Meyer even inserts the shot of Harris spinning the wheel and the close-up of Harris when "Find It" is first performed at the high school dance as the band discusses performing the song. The band decides to play "Find It" on the talk-show instead, and as they start the camera tracks upward from the band performing the song on a sound stage to the catwalk above them; the camera then zooms upward to reveal Harris standing amid the lighting rigs of the studio. As Ebert recounted:

"The movie had to be outrageous: a total put-on, and *still* work as a melodrama. Individual scenes were conceived on two levels, usually: at the dramatic level, and then at the level of whatever inside joke was being conveyed. Sometimes this dualism worked quite effectively... as when (a) Harris is discovered on the catwalk of a TV studio, prepared to commit suicide on live time, and (b) the camera movement quotes Welles' famous opera-house shot in *Citizen Kane*."[155]

155. "Russ Meyer: King of the Nudies," page 11 of 14.

What is *BVD*'s most dramatic and tragic scene is also rendered the most absurd and comical. The distraught Harris throws himself to the ground, landing in front of the band, his suicide attempt juxtaposed by the hilarious and incongruous insertion of a sound effect of a plane crashing. As the motionless Harris lies bleeding on the stage in front of the band, the horrified onlookers gather around him and the talk-show host frantically orders the cameras to keep filming (another moment of self-reference in the film, especially since Russ Meyer himself plays a cameraman).

The scene immediately cuts to the hospital, and is played out as pure soap-opera, even down to the cliché organ music that accompanies the scene. There is also a uproarious confrontation between Kelly and Casey:

Kelly: It wasn't enough to mess up my own life, I had to screw up Harris's...
Susan: Sometimes you learn too late... [she pauses as she takes Baxter's hand which extends into the right, lower corner of the frame] ...how much people mean.
Kelly: I don't give a *damn*! It's still my fault.
Casey: Don't blame yourself, Kelly. What happened to Harris happened for reasons... you don't know anything about.
Kelly: What the *hell* do you know about it?
Casey: I'm going to have his baby!

Following this exchange, "Dr. Scholl" enters to inform the characters of Harris' condition (the name "Dr. Scholl" is taken from an American brand of foot care products). As the campy, soap-opera organ music swells and the piano tinkles in the background, Dr. Scholl announces that Harris has been paralyzed in the fall, but in his hilariously deadpan delivery he informs them that "with the proper rehabilitation, it is possible that the patient can adjust to a useful, and yes, a rewarding life as a paraplegic."

The scene shifts to the morning after Harris's suicide attempt, where Casey has come to Roxanne's studio to discuss her situation. Learning that Casey is pregnant, Roxanne turns her back to Casey and faces the camera; her expression is one of obvious displeasure. Roxanne suggests an abortion, but Casey is reluctant (one has to recall that *BVD* was done in 1970, before American women had any sort of legal reproductive rights). Once again, the scene is played out in soap-operatic clichés, strained (and intentionally ridiculous) dialogue, and generic organ music.

Roxanne: Then you're going to have the baby?
Casey: I have to... after what happened last night this could be the only child Harris could ever conceive.
Roxanne: And you feel loyalty to a man who *raped* you in a state of unconsciousness?
Casey: It's crazy – but in a funny way I do.
Roxanne: The child of a man you never loved conceived in a moment you don't even remember –
Casey: Oh, that's easy to say!

The scene cuts to Casey at a doctor's office accompanied by Roxanne; she has decided to have the abortion at Roxanne's urging. He is greeted by an impatient nurse and "Dr. Downs," who will be performing the abortion ("Downs" obviously punning her addiction to "downers" as well). Casey looks around the room nervously and finally puts her hands on her head and emits a horrifying scream. In a montage of utter black comedy, the medium close-up of Casey screaming

CHAPTER FIVE ◊ "BEYOND THE VALLEY OF THE DOLLS"

cuts to a shot of pancake batter being poured into a skillet; Casey's abortion is metaphorically and quite crudely depicted by what appears to be runny pancake batter hitting a frying pan (even more tastelessly, one might suggest the liquid could be "scrambled eggs"). The scene is Emerson and Pet happily eating breakfast, when a knock on the door interrupts their morning together. Emerson, beaming with pride, tells Pet he has ordered roses celebrating the one-week anniversary of their engagement. However, it is Randy Black at the door, returned after a one-month stay in jail for his assault on Emerson. Randy invites himself in for breakfast, and needless to say, the visit soon turns ugly. Emerson is once again beaten by the volatile Randy until he is finally forced out by Pet, who threatens Randy with a kitchen knife. He departs with another ridiculous mixture of philosophy and boxing metaphors, telling Pet it won't work out between them unless he has "a good cut-man" and that he's "throwing in the towel." However, as he opens the door the delivery-man with the flowers stands in the doorway, and Randy sprinkles the red roses over Emerson, once again suggesting the strong libidinal ties between the two males in the romantic triangle.

    Maintaining the frenetic, soap-operatic chaos, the scene cuts back to Casey and Roxanne, now relaxing in a field after the traumatic visit to the abortionist. Casey confesses to Roxanne how much she means to her, and Roxanne responds by feeling her stomach, breast, and then kissing her. What is notable about this scene is that it is a love scene that is seemingly *not* played for laughs, which actually lends further irony to the film: the love scene that is the most poignant is the one between the lesbian couple. Indeed, this is contrasted with the pure hilarity of the next scene, a chess game and strained conversation between the heterosexual leads, Harris and Kelly. Ebert recounted "[the hospital] scene was written and scored as soap-opera, as was the chess game scene with Kelly and Harris."[156] The shot of Casey and Roxanne kissing cuts to a shot of a chess piece being moved across a board, signifying the game of "human chess" that goes on between the various characters of *BVD*. Harris resigns, telling Kelly absolutely straight-faced, "There's no way I can move." He turns his wheelchair around and looks out the window; Kelly comes up behind him and puts her hands on his shoulders and asks Harris "Is the stiffness gone?" "Pretty much so," replies Harris; of course, the line about his "stiffness being gone" is a hilarious *double entendre* about his loss of sexual function and impotence as a result of his fall. Kelly leans down to talk to Harris, and the remainder of the scene is shot exclusively in close-ups between the misty-eyed Kelly talking to Harris, who listens to her, similarly on the verge of tears. As well as the histrionic acting and the stereotypical film techniques, the music is once again campy, soap-operatic organ music. As she stares lovingly at Harris, the deadpan Kelly delivers the "moral message" of the film:

156. "Russ Meyer: King of the Nudies," page 11 of 14.

"I don't have anything to do that's more important than this, Harris, dig? You're racing through life full steam ahead and not giving a damn, then something happens that makes you stop short and you realize people are what count. *You're important to me, Harris.*"

Three Weddings and Four Funerals

The climax of *BVD* begins when Z-Man invites Lance Rocke, Casey, and Roxanne over to his mansion for a party. Otto, Z-Man's butler, wearing a Nazi WWII outfit, passes out costumes for the guests to wear. Z-Man dispatches him with a campy cross between a Hitler salute and a wave, and in a tasteless joke appropriate to *BVD*, reminds him to "make sure you turn off the ovens." Each guest is given a costume to wear and the identity of a superhero to assume. Lance Rocke is forced to don a skimpy pair of leopard skin briefs and takes on the role of "Jungle Lad," recalling the line about L.A. being "a jungle" and satirically references Lance's role as a cheap gigolo in this sexual "jungle." Casey and Roxanne wear Batman and Robin outfits; the hilarity of the lesbian couple playing Batman and Robin is also a parodic reference to Dr. Fredric Wertham's 1954 anti-comic book polemic *Seduction of the Innocent*, which argued Batman and Robin were an archetypal homosexual couple. Z-Man dons his Shakespearean outfit replete with crown and cape and tells his guests, nay *insists*, that he is "Superwoman," an identity that takes on monumental importance in the conclusion of the film.

The party guests begin to get stoned, which is depicted on-screen in a fast-paced montage of close-ups of each character getting progressively higher as they are highlighted with red and green lighting. Dukes's "The Sorcerer's Apprentice" accompanies them on the soundtrack, and Meyer edits the sequence so that the rhythm of the shots corresponds to the swirling rhythms of Dukes' piece. Again, the sequence serves as a point of satire as well, referencing Walt Disney's *Fantasia*, a film rumored to have drug references as well as being highly popular for younger people watch while high on drugs during the peak of the Psychedelic Revolution.

The respective couples (Roxanne and Casey, Lance and Z-Man) retire to the bedroom. Casey and Roxanne have sex, and again, the lesbian love scene is played out as deadpan as possible, including a schmaltzy love song accompaniment by The Sandpipers, an easy-listening vocal group popular at the time. It resembles any number of Hollywood love scenes of the era (for instance, the one between Lyon and Anne in the original *Valley of the Dolls*), with the obvious exception that the scene is between being two women. The scene effectively satirizes the Hollywood conventions of the time by depicting a lesbian encounter absolutely "straight," utilizing the exact same techniques as a

CHAPTER FIVE ◊ "BEYOND THE VALLEY OF THE DOLLS"

heterosexual love scene would be played out. Unfortunately for Casey and Roxanne, their encounter takes place in one of Z-Man's bedrooms, a site coded in *BVD* as a point where sex is inevitably tainted by power, domination, and dire consequences. They become victims of not only Z-Man's psychotic megalomania, but the ideological drive of the musical to create heterosexual order, a mission ultimately carried out by Z-man/Superwoman him/herself. As the closing narration ponderously states, "Theirs was not an evil relationship, but evil did come because of it."

The scene shifts to Z-Man and Lance in bed, with Lance repeatedly rejecting Z-Man's sexual overtures. In one hilarious moment, as Z-Man reaches under the covers to feel up Lance, "Stranger in Paradise" is heard on the soundtrack. He also plants a kiss on Lance's mouth (a shot used in the "debate" montage early in the film), only to be rejected by Lance. Spurned one too many time by Lance, the enraged Z-Man announces "I vow it – *you will drink the black sperm of my vengeance*!" The scene cuts to Lance hog-tied on the floor of Z-Man's bedroom, and Z-Man boasts, "The king of the jungle comes under the imperious reign of she who is unconquerable – *Superwoman!*"

This is further manifest in the climatic moment of *BVD* when Z-Man opens his robe and reveals that he has breasts, which Meyer once again depicts through an extreme low-angle shot, a common technique Meyer uses to photograph *women* in his film to accentuate their "power" over men. The unveiling of Z-Man as a woman was not a deliberate plan but rather a impromptu moment of inspiration. Ebert noted:

"Z-Man began his career as a boy, and it only occurred to us to make him a secret transvestite as we were writing the orgy scene. We had done the lesbian encounter between the two girls, and symmetry seemed to dictate a homosexual encounter between Z-Man and the movie's other heavy, Lance Rocke. Meyer was of the opinion that the American mass audience was not ready for an erotic homosexual encounter played straight, and we had already written the Z-Man/Lance bedroom scene as it now exists when it occurred to us, off-hand actually, to reveal Z-Man as a character who had been female the whole time. This kind of triple-twist (girl plays male homosexual) would have the audiences coming out of the theater, Meyer said, 'totally confused.' He greeted this possibility... with an immensely satisfied chortle."[157]

157. "Russ Meyer: King of the Nudies," page 11 of 14.

Within a heterosexual, phallocentric social order, Z-Man/Superwoman can be seen as such an order's greatest threat: a figure that eliminates sexual distinction, a woman that is not only a man, but a woman who also wields the (phallic) power of a man. In the context of the Hollywood musical's ideology, Z-Man/Superwoman represents a dangerous challenge to the formation of phallocentric, heterosexual order; the "unconquerable" Superwoman (the female)

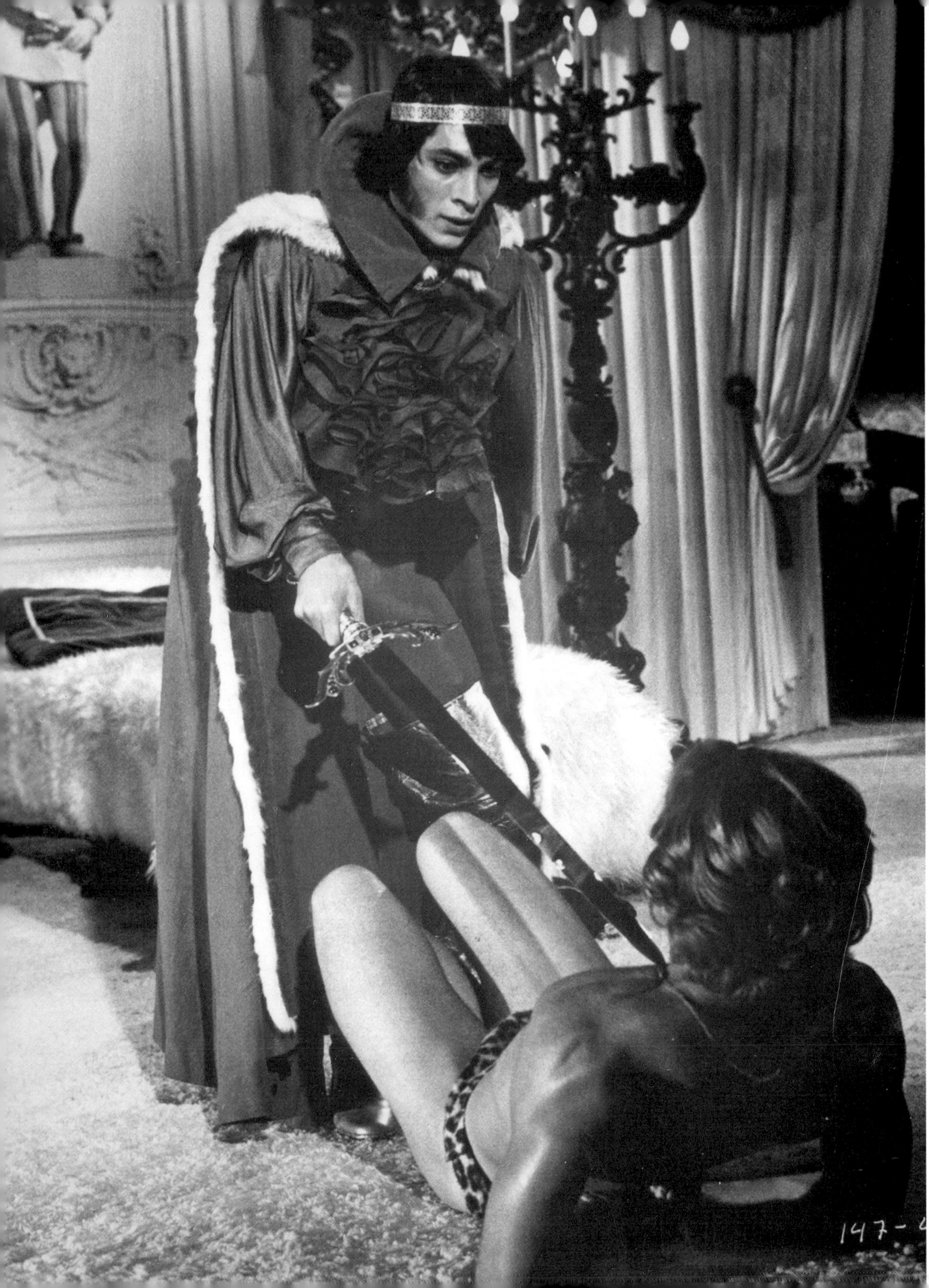

CHAPTER FIVE ◊ "BEYOND THE VALLEY OF THE DOLLS"

has subdued the "king of the jungle" (the male). Becoming a threat to the "stability" of the sexual order the musical seeks to establish, Z-Man/Superwoman is suddenly and necessarily recast as the villain.

Lance is utterly repelled by learning that Z-Man has breasts, and that he is "a broad – and a god damn ugly broad at that!" Z-Man/Superwoman responds by severing Lance's head with his/her phallic broadsword, and in a truly inspired bit of filmmaking, the 20th Century Fox fanfare is heard as Z-Man/Superwoman decapitates Lances. It is a moment of pure incongruity, and has an almost Brechtian effect on the scene, turning it from horrifying and brutal to humorous and bizarre. It also offers a rather sardonic commentary on the Hollywood apparatus that uses actors like cattle, depicting the slaughter of a young actor, whose beheading is accompanied by the musical staple of one of Hollywood's greatest studios. Casey witnesses the murder, and there is a close-up of her terror-stricken face. The shot cuts to the long shot of the mansion, the same establishing shot as in the beginning of the film. The viewer now realizes that what was shown in the beginning of *BVD* was actually the climax of the film shown in an edited form over the opening credits.

Otto, the Nazi butler, has the unfortunate luck to stumble onto the murder scene, and he is the next to be murdered by Z-Man/Superwoman, who chases him onto the shores of the Pacific Ocean to the strains of Wagner's "Ride of the Valkyries" before brutally impaling him with the broadsword, a scene shown in an abbreviated form in the opening of the film. Z-Man/Superwoman leaves him on the shore, his body pinned into the sand by the broadsword plunged through his body as the waves pummel him. Fittingly, he is murdered at a spot by a figure with a dual-gender where male and female libido conjoins: sand and water. Z-Man/Superwoman then returns to the mansion, and the viewer can easily remember this sequence from the opening credits: the camera following behind Z-Man/Superwoman getting a gun and joining Roxanne in the bedroom. Once again, the viewer witnesses the grotesque scene in which Roxanne seemingly performs fellatio on the gun barrel before she realizes she has a pistol in her mouth. Obviously, one is struck by the apparent misogyny of the scene, but in the logic of the film's satire the viewer is witness to the film's drive to expel sexual "abnormality" in order to ruthlessly establish the heterosexual order consistent with the Hollywood musical. The scene is especially disturbing in that the lesbian Roxanne is summarily "punished" in a highly "phallic" form of death, the handgun that serves as a substitute penis, made all the more "phallic" by the obvious connotation of Roxanne performing fellatio on the gun. Z-Man/Superwoman pulls the trigger, releasing a discharge both violent and sexual: ejaculation, "the black sperm of vengeance," is equated to the "hot lead" of a bullet.

Desperately, Casey calls her band mates for help; seeing the phone is being used, Z-Man/Superwoman gets on one of the other lines. As Casey attempts to describe the situation to Kelly, Harris grabs the phone. As Casey tries to explain her emergency, Z-Man/Superwoman chillingly tells Harris there is no need for "the police" because he/she is "the greatest law enforcer of them all!" Once again the issue of the Law in a phallocentric order, a law defined by the presence of the Phallus as a signifier of power, is brought into question. Z-Man/Superwoman constitutes a threat to the sexual order by his/her position as both a (biological) woman and a (cultural) man. He/she has attained the status of the enforcer of the phallocentric Law, by not only his/her status as a powerful "man" in show business, but also a "superwoman," a woman who exercises phallic power: the possessor of the phallic instruments (the broadsword, the gun) and the dispenser of "the black sperm of vengeance." Z-Man/Superwoman, much like Varla in *Pussycat!*, is a sexual "aberration" that must be eliminated to bring heterosexual order to fruition. As noted, Z-Man/Superwoman becomes the unlikely enforcer of "the law" of the musical itself: the law of heterosexual order.

As Harris hangs up the phone, he barks with resolute determination, "Casey's in trouble! Let's go!" The four are shown dashing out onto the street in a high-angle shot, with Emerson frantically (and hilariously) pushing Harris's wheelchair. They pile into a station wagon, the standard "family-car" of the 1970s, which is incongruent with the decadent Hollywood splendor of much of the film, which serves to suggest that the couples are becoming "squares" themselves, adapting to sexual and social normalcy demanded by the musical. The scene cuts back to Casey cowering from Z-Man/Superwoman behind the bar in the recreation room, as he/she pursues her. The approaching figure of Z-Man/Superwoman is announced by his angular shadow on the wall, holding the pistol; the shot parodies both Expressionism and *film noir*. When Casey attempts to flee, she is shot dead, the bullet striking her between the eyes. The shot cuts to Casey laying dead on the floor, blood covering her face and body: another figure of sexual abnormality "punished" by the film. Just as Casey is murdered, the station wagon speeds into the driveway of the mansion. They all bolt out of the car, leaving the paralyzed Harris sitting in the car pleading for assistance. Harris's paralysis and his ineffectiveness, with typical Meyer dark humor, becomes a running source of comedy during the climax of the film. Emerson is the first to reach Z-Man/Superwoman, and they begin to wrestle for the gun. Kelly and Pet soon join in the fray. The struggle for the gun is hilariously intercut with shots of Harris desperately struggling to get his wheelchair out of the car and into operating condition. Indeed, just as Harris is able to get into his wheelchair and propel himself towards the front door, the melée spills out of the entrance and onto the sidewalk, knocking the wheelchair over on its side. Harris is once again helpless as the bodies tumble, and he responds by covering his head to avoid any blows, utterly ineffectual in the battle

CHAPTER FIVE ◊ "BEYOND THE VALLEY OF THE DOLLS"

with Z-Man/Superwoman. Indeed, it is Emerson who ultimately succeeds in wresting the gun into Z-man/Superwoman's torso where it suddenly discharges. Z-man/Superwoman goes limp on the sidewalk, his/her breasts covered in blood. Not only has heterosexual order won out with the elimination of the man/woman figure who briefly assumed control of "the Law," but there is an unexpected and utterly absurd turn of events. After Pet sobs that Casey is dead, Kelly bursts into tears. Meanwhile, the prone Harris miraculously begins to move one of his feet. Harris, who has been rendered powerless through the course of the film by Z-Man, even left "impotent," is now able to begin to once again exercise his masculine power with the elimination of his male/female rival. With the death of Z-Man, Harris can now start becoming "a man" again. He jubilantly exclaims "Kelly, I can move my legs!" Kelly's tears of grief instantly turn into tears of joy.

"BVD": Sermon or Satire?

The scene shifts to Kelly and Harris walking in the field, and a narrator begins to summarize the moral message of the film in the classic Meyer style of narration that sounds deeply profound but says very little:

The act of death has caused another life to be reborn. Together we share the wonder of human existence, and let there be no doubt that we are brothers. There can be no beginning or ending that does not in some way touch another, for our actions affect the lives and destinies of the many.

One irony present is that while the heterosexual couple Kelly and Harris are shown, the narrator insists that "there is no doubt we are brothers"; this implies that the relationship between Kelly and Harris is one of "brotherly love" rather than "romantic love," and that indeed there is (still) no sexual relationship between them. The narrator then begins to list each character and provide an analysis of the character flaws and what led to their downfall or what moral lesson they learned. As each character is described, there is a montage of shots of that character culled from the film:

Z-Man – he forgot that life is lived on many levels, and by choosing to live on only one, lost touch of reality. Ashley – men were toys for her amusement, her total disregard for their feelings made love a stranger to her. Lance Rocke – he never gave of himself; those who only take must be prepared to pay the highest price of all. Porter Hall used his profession to mask selfish interests, to betray the trust that should have been sacred. Susan Lake – perhaps too pure; excessive goodness can often blind us to the human failings of those less perfect. Emerson found that something as precious as love brings with it a demand for greater understanding. Casey and Roxanne – light and shadow; theirs was not an evil relationship, but evil did come because of it. Otto – an end to Martin Bormann? Harris – he forgot yesterday is only for remembering; those who choose to live there lose sight of today. Pet's mistake, a fleeting thing born of emotion, yet it almost ruined the lives of two others. Randy's body, a cage for an animal; it lifted him to the top of his profession, but in the end the beast almost killed him. And Kelly, her selfish involvement, so eager to turn her back on friendship; the road back is painful – by her pain she will never again forget.

The scene dissolves back to Kelly and Harris, wobbling in his crutches, walking through the field and reaching a stream. Kelly steps over it, and, with Kelly's encouragement and helping hand, Harris is able to cross the stream as well; he is greeted by Kelly's applause as he joins her on the other side of the stream. While the scene functions as a hilarious parody of the Hollywood love story ending, the inspiration for the scene was actually an Easter Seals commercial (a charity for people with disabilities). Ebert recounted, "There was talk of having [Harris] fall into the water, but Meyer felt this would sabotage the emotional uplift of the scene and its function as visual satire."[158] The narrator concludes while this scene is shown:

You must each decide what your life will be. You must know a hand extended to your fellow man is a gesture of love: love that asks nothing, expects nothing, it is simply there. And if love is in you, then gentle will be all your steps as you walk beyond this valley.

Again the scene is utterly ironic. When Kelly extends her hand to Harris to help him across the stream, it is a "hand extended to your fellow man," again suggesting the love between Kelly and Harris is not erotic or romantic, but rather "brotherly" and Platonic love between her and her "fellow man." Moreover, The Sandpipers' song played during Casey and Roxanne's lesbian encounter is reprised; in the context of the film, this song has in fact been coded as a homosexual love song.

This cuts to the final scene in the film: the triple wedding between Kelly and Harris; Pet and Emerson; and Susan and Baxter. The film has violently purged the sexual "villains" in the film (above all the man/woman who violates gender classification). However, there is one exception left, the closeted homosexual Porter Hall, who shows up in a disheveled state and attempts to watch the wedding ceremony through the window from outside. The Justice of the Peace, who is officiating the triple wedding, momentarily interrupts the ceremony to close the blinds over the window frame. Porter is literally "shut out" from any participation in the ritual establishment of heterosexual order. The film ends in a freeze-frame of the newly-married couples standing side-by-side as

158. "Russ Meyer: King of the Nudies," page 10 of 14.

CHAPTER FIVE ◊ "BEYOND THE VALLEY OF THE DOLLS"

the Justice of the Peace begins the wedding ceremony which is quickly drowned out by a bizarre swing version of "Here Comes the Bride." Interestingly, Kelly is the only bride who wears white, suggesting she is still pure or "virginal" in her unconsummated sexual relationship with Harris. However, having been turned into the acquiescent, domesticated, wife, she may as well be wearing the "long, black wedding gown."

In his book *Cult Movies*, Danny Peary launched a vitriolic attack on not only Russ Meyer's filmmaking abilities, but also for being determinately unclear on whether *BVD* is a satire on Hollywood morality, or actually an example of Hollywood morality.[159] Perhaps Peary was unwilling or unable to comprehend the "thin edge" that *BVD* walks between seriousness and satire, and needed his satire dished out on a sliver platter *à la* Mel Brooks. I would also disagree with David Frasier, who has written highly insightful work on Meyer, when he suggests:

"a rigid code of sexuality exists in the Meyer universe, and that code is to be strictly observed if it is to function properly. 'Normal' heterosexual sex is the primary component of that universe. It guarantee the harmony. In film after film any character who disrupts this harmony by breaking this moral code is punished. Lorna, the adulteress, and Varla, the loveless lesbian, are both punished by their deviance from the moral norm."[160]

I absolutely concur that many of Meyer's films end with the establishment of a heterosexual order (*Goodbye!*, *Supervixens*, *Ultravixens*), and there often seems to exist a narrative punishment of characters who stray from the sexual norm (excepting, of course, *Vixen*, where adultery, lesbian sex, and incest are not punished but celebrated). However, my own view of the films Frasier cites is to read them as *dark satires* on heterosexual order. *Lorna* ends with sexual stability established through the elimination of "the woman" in a perverse, male homeosocial order; *Pussycat!* ends with the death of Varla – the toughest man and the sexiest woman in the film – leaving the utterly banal heterosexual couple of Kirk and Linda to survive. Similarly, as a satire on the Hollywood musical, *BVD* almost necessarily satirizes the ideological mission of the film musical that Altman discusses: the stabilization of social order through the unification of the heterosexual couple. Indeed, *BVD* explodes this mission by summarily eliminating and punishing the sexual "deviants" (homosexuals, lesbians, transvestites) in a quadruple murder and hilariously establishing the heterosexual couple in a moment of darkly comic overkill with the closing triple wedding. As perplexing as any other Meyer film, it is at once a "serious" Hollywood melodrama-musical and an absolute mockery of the generic conventions and ideological mission of the Hollywood musical-melodrama. It represents Meyer's finest hour both *in* Hollywood and *on* Hollywood.

---

159. See *Cult Movies* (New York: Delacourte, 1981).

160. *Russ Meyer – The Life and Films*, 22.

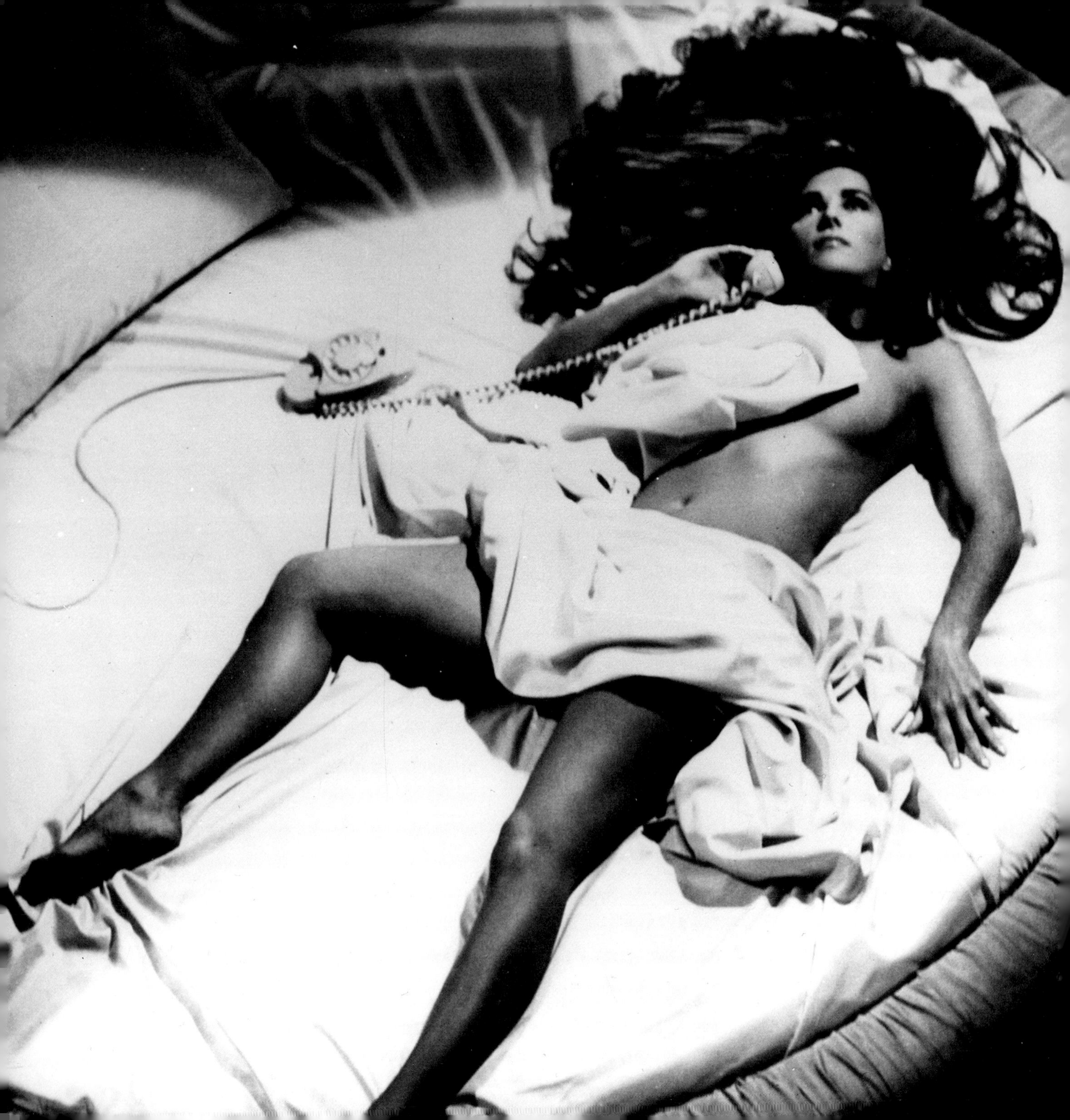

CHAPTER SIX
THE DEATH OF SEXPLOITATION

The ideal of Brando, the Academy Award winner, in there putting butter up some broad's ass and jumping her and you see his ass twittering as he's on top of her, it's hard to compete with that.[161]
–Russ Meyer

161. As quoted in Turan and Zito, 35.

162. *The Seven Minutes* is the only Meyer film I have been unable to see; it is not in print either in VHS or DVD format. My accounts are admittedly second-hand, and I owe greatly to Ebert, Fischer, and Frasier in their account of the film.

163. See Fischer: 31. Indeed, other Fox projects envisioned for Meyer included an Edward Albee play (*Everything in the Garden*) and a Peter George novel (*The Final Steal*).

164. See Frasier, 141.

Opposite: *The Seven Minutes*

Between "BVD" and "Supervixens"

The early 1970s did not go well for Russ Meyer. Following the achievement of *BVD*, Meyer soon tackled his next project, a film adaptation of Irving Wallace's novel *The Seven Minutes*. The title refers to a fictitious banned book which describes the thoughts of a woman during seven minutes of sexual intercourse; the book then becomes the center of a heated controversy when a young man commits a rape after reading the book. Much of film depicts courtroom arguments over censorship and free speech and other contemporary issues Meyer was well-acquainted with. However, *The Seven Minutes* was critically maligned, performed dismally at the box-office, and left all the principals creatively frustrated.[162] Fox hoped *The Seven Minutes* would be the film that established Russ Meyer as a "respectable" filmmaker; obviously, the financial and critical failure of the film derailed this strategy.[163] Irving Wallace subsequently blasted Meyer for the way the film turned out, citing his heavy-handed direction, his overuse of camp, and Meyer's decision not to stray too far afield from the book, which resulted in long-winded dialogue in place of action.[164] Meyer also was quite direct in analyzing the film's failure.

LIPS HIPS TITS POWER ◊ THE FILMS OF RUSS MEYER

"I made the mistake of acquiring a big fat head while I was [at Fox]. I was flush with victory from *Vixen, Cherry, Harry, and Raquel*, and *BVD*. They told me, 'You must do *The Seven Minutes*. You are the spokesperson against the forces of censorship.' And Irving Wallace sits there with this profound look. They gave me $2.7 million for the film, but no tits and ass. The first night in every theater was packed. And the next night three people. Why? The audience knows. I had another property I should have done instead. But [Fox executive David] Brown gave me the blue smoke up my ass."[165]

The failure of *The Seven Minutes*, coupled with corporate turmoil at Fox, ended Meyer's association with Fox after only two films. Returning to independent productions, his first effort was *Blacksnake!* (1973), a colonial-slavery epic set in the British West Indies ca. 1850 (the film was done entirely on location in Barbados). Designed to cash in on current "blaxploitation" trends, the film backfired. One can only imagine that the sight of slender plantation mistress

165. "Russ Meyer Interviewed by Ed Lowry and Louis Black," page 5 of 7. See also Fischer: 31-2.

CHAPTER SIX ◊ THE DEATH OF SEXPLOITATION

Lady Susan Walker (Anouska Hemple) routinely whipping her "damn niggers" did not sit well with black audiences expecting supercool pimps and drug dealers; conversely, the overall lack of nudity and the brutal slave revolt ending in the context of 1970s Black Power militancy did not appeal to a "raincoat" crowd expecting standard soft-core roughie fare where the woman was usually on the receiving end of the whip.[166] Meyer observed, "We thought we were making a picture that the blacks would really love. Now if we had made the film about four years before it might have been a blockbuster. But we ended up with a film both blacks and whites hated. The only place it did good business was Little Rock"[167] Meyer also blamed the casting of primarily British actors, especially Ms. Hemple: not that her acting was inadequate, but that her breasts were small.[168] "It had a skinny leading lady and she was British. All the actors were British. It was a costume movie. Like everything you could possibly do wrong, I did."[169] Nonetheless, *Blacksnake!* does have its moments. Violence is taken to new graphic yet comic extremes, utilizing jump-cuts and fast-motion, and the effect makes it difficult for the viewer to tell what even happened. *Blacksnake!* also offers a typically hilarious epilogue, with half-naked interracial couples running in slow motion through plantation fields while the serious narrator intones about racial harmony. But the major problem with *Blacksnake!* is not the film itself, but that its logical comparisons, plantation-film genre staples such as *Mandingo* (1975) and *Drum* (1976) are little more than glorified sexploitation films masquerading as self-important, serious Hollywood historical epics, as stereotypical racist and sexist as any other sexploitation film. Moreover, the films offer more unintentional humor than any satire could. Meyer himself labeled *Blacksnake!* "a weak *Mandingo*."[170]

With two successive box-office failures, things proceeded to get worse for Meyer. Between 1972 and 1973, Meyer planned on making a sequel to the legendary *Vixen* titled *Foxy!* (later briefly retitled *Viva Foxy!*), starring then-wife Edy Williams. Extensive promotional groundwork was done for *Foxy!*, including a March 1973 *Playboy* pictorial "All About Edy" and a trailer added to the end of *Blacksnake!* which showed Edy Williams water-skiing in the nude. However, the film was never completed. In the summer of 1973, Meyer cancelled the project in the wake of the U.S. Supreme Court's "community standards" ruling, which meant that local municipalities could determine their own respective standards of what constituted obscene material. Fearing the ruling meant that the possible showing of an "obscene" film would be subject to the whims and decisions of virtually every censor board in any market it played in, Meyer decided not to risk his and his investors' $400,000 on what "might end up the most expensive home movie ever made."[171] The decision to cancel *Foxy!* exacerbated Meyer's already tumultuous relationship with Edy Williams, and a very acrimonious divorce soon followed. Meyer would not return until 1975, with *Supervixens*.

166. See also Vale and Juno, eds., 86.

167. "Russ Meyer Interviewed by Ed Lowry and Louis Black," page 5 of 7.

168. See Frasier, 150.

169. "Russ Meyer Interviewed by Ed Lowry and Louis Black," page 5 of 7.

170. "Russ Meyer Interviewed by ed Lowry and Louis Black," page 5 of 7.

171. As quoted in Turan and Zito, 34.

Porno Chic

In 1972, Linda Lovelace took sexploitation and, with apologies to the reader, gave it its knockout "blow." *Deep Throat* made hardcore pornography as American as baseball and apple pie. The first hardcore film to break into the mainstream, *Deep Throat* showed in graphic detail everything that sexploitation only could or would imply. The unprecedented success of *Deep Throat* paved the way for other hardcore films, and soon after *Deep Throat*, *Behind the Green Door* made Marylin Chambers an adult film icon. The American sex-industry was quickly and permanently changed, and an era of "porno chic" was ushered in. Watching hardcore became synonymous to being sexually "hip." The grindhouse was no longer the domain of lonely guys in raincoats, but curious couples as well as celeberties who bragged about seeing *Deep Throat* on *The Tonight Show*. By the early 1970s, *Playboy* reversed its long-standing policy against showing pubic hair, a decision owing to the growing competition from hardcore and magazines such as *Penthouse* and *Hustler*: the former infused its spread-eagle nudes with jet-set decadence, the latter presented professional and amateur "beavers" with crude, white-trash glee.

As hardcore quickly emerged as the dominant mode of the sex film, the old guard of sexploitation responded in different ways. Some of sexploitation's leading practitioners left the business altogether, such as H.G. Lewis and David Friedman. As Faris and Muller observed, Friedman's distaste for hardcore was not moral, but that "it violated every principle of good showmanship."[172] Friedman himself bluntly stated, "The old con game was working just fine... until a few assholes decided to go hardcore and show the last act right up front."[173] Others, notably sexploitation *auteur* Radley Metzger went the hardcore route: he directed *The Opening of Misty Beethoven* (1976) and subsequent hardcore films under the pseudonym Henry Paris.

The creators of some of the roughest of the roughies, Michael and Roberta Findlay, gained some undeserved notoriety in cinematic history, when, in 1971, they traveled to Argentina to make a film about a murderous hippie-cult, obviously inspired by the Manson Family phenomenon, entitled *Slaughter*. The Findlays, not the most adept filmmakers to begin with, had a non-existent budget and used non-professional actors and crews. Deemed unreleasable upon completion, *Slaughter* sat on the shelf for some four years before producer Allan Shackelford bought the film, deleted the original credits, and added an ending which purportedly showed an actual on-screen murder. Shakelford released the film as *Snuff* (1975), in order to capitalize on rumors of alleged south of the border "snuff films." Film goers and protesters alike, some apparently too dumb to even assume that the "murder" might be faked, bought into Shakelford's scheme and turned *Snuff* into a publicity-soaked leviathan, perhaps proving that "the old con game" still had some life after all. Michael Findlay continued in the

Deep Throat

Behind The Green Door

172. Grindhouse, 136.

173. As quoted in Muller and Faris, 136.

CHAPTER SIX ◊ THE DEATH OF SEXPLOITATION

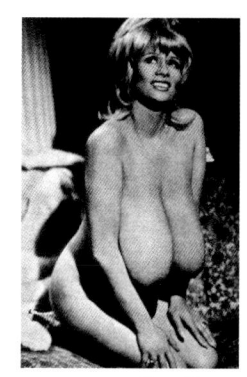

vein of *Slaughter* and moved into low-budget horror films, such as *Shriek of the Mutilated* (1974), before his own untimely and macabre death in 1977 (Findlay was waiting for a helicopter on the roof of the Pam Am Building when it crashed: the rotor decapitated him). Roberta Findlay eventually moved into hardcore, her best-known film being *Glitter* (1983), which starred future porn-industry casualty Shauna Grant.

Fittingly, sexploitation's two most unique talents maintained their singular vision for as long as possible. Doris Wishman expressed little interest in standard hardcore, and instead made two of the most wonderfully idiosyncratic sex films ever made: *Deadly Weapons* (1973) and *Double Agent 73* (1974). Both films starred legendary stripper Chesty Morgan and her 73" bustline as a secret agent who dispatches evil-doers by smothering them with her breasts. All of Wishman's trademark, unorthodox editing and framing is featured as well, with the camera seemingly determined to focus on any object except the person actually speaking (a strategy to avoid post-production dubbing costs). Likewise, Russ Meyer refused to do hardcore, not for any moral outrage but because of hardcore's relentless humorlessness: his reaction to *Deep Throat* was to describe Linda Lovelace as "a piston engine... and I just don't see the humor in a guy being sucked off."[174]

Chesty Morgan

174. As quoted in Turan and Zito, 34.

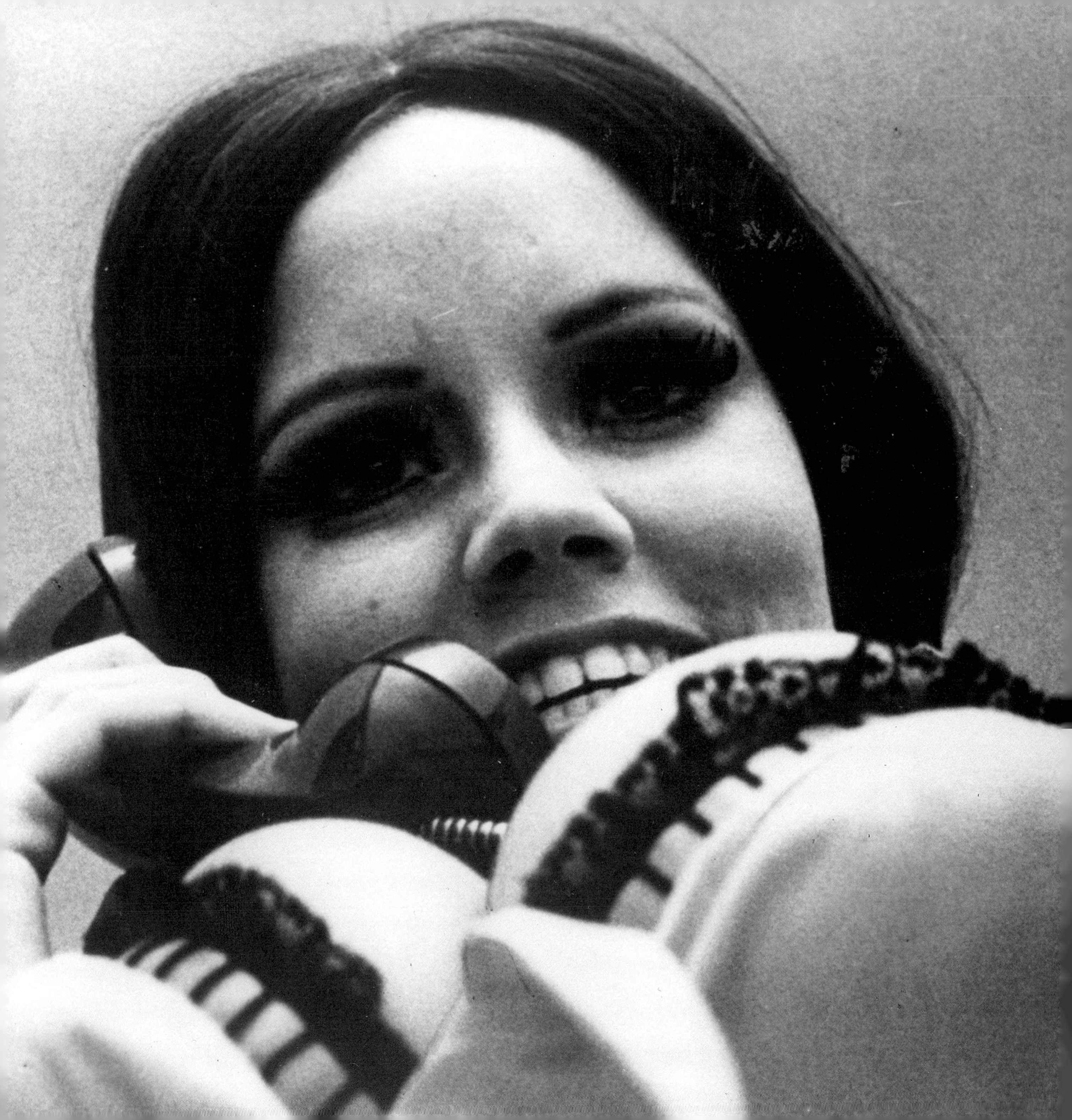

CHAPTER SEVEN
SURREAL SEVENTIES

What I do best is parody.[175]
–Russ Meyer

175. As quoted in "All About Edy," *Playboy* (March 1973).

The Birth of the "Bustoon"

In his final three films, *Supervixens* (1975), *Up!* (1976) and *Beneath the Valley of the Ultravixens* (1979), Russ Meyer did not simply return to his old formula for success, he took every bit of it and exploded it. The breasts became even bigger, the men even more buffoonish, the (simultaneous) sex and violence even more graphic and cartoonish, the plots even more ridiculous and surreal, the editing and shot composition even more unorthodox, and the humor even more parodic and self-referential. Indeed, Meyer's favorite object of parody became his *own* films; *Supervixens* is made up almost entirely of references to previous films. His films became, as Meyer repeatedly insisted, "cartoons." Granted, cartoons done on an X-rated scale. This final series of films are by far the most graphic in their depiction of sex and violence. Full frontal nudity (both male and female) became standard, and lengthy scenes of simulated sex also became commonplace. The violence, especially the rape scenes, became even more brutal, but was treated with slapstick comedy and cartoon frenzy in a move designed by Meyer to exaggerate the violence so much the critics and audience would have no choice but to see it as "jokey" (this move was, for the most part, unsuccessful). The humor became more overt and crude, yet often the funniest moments were the most subtle. It was the birth of what Meyer once called the "bustoon": a bizarre, cartoon world of well-endowed superwomen and burly men engaged in surreal and slapstick acts of sex and violence.

195

The three 1970s films were also defined by a growing fascination with Nazism. In *Supervixens* and *Beneath the Valley of the Ultravixens*, Henry Rowland, who also portrayed the Nazi butler Otto in *BVD*, plays "Martin Bormann." In *Up!*, Edward Schaaf portrays a sado-masochistic homosexual named Adolph Schwartz, who is obviously a Hitler caricature. The fascination with Nazism in the later Mayer films produced a certain degree of controversy. Some argued that, given the episodic melodrama and celebration of virile masculinity, the Nazi references seems to be an indication of Meyer's own fascist tendencies. Others, notably David Frasier, argued these scenes were not merely offensive for their own sake, but Meyer's own satirical commentary of Nazism, a target of some obvious political contempt for a World War II veteran. My own impression is that the satire of Nazism may not have been so much the vision of Meyer but Roger Ebert. In all of the films prior to *BVD*, any reference to Nazism is non-existent. It is *BVD* and after, films scripted or co-scripted by Ebert, that the presence of Nazism becomes more pronounced, and, as Frasier has rightly suggested, Nazis are included as to be objects of derision, such as in the films of Mel Brooks.[176] Nonetheless, in these final films, sexual repression and perversion became equated with authoritarian politics. Frasier observed, "In the late sixties and early seventies Meyer had told several interviewers that he seldom included 'perversion' in his films be cause he considered it to be 'un-American'."[177] I would contend that there is more to these films than simply making fun of the sexual habits of Nazis. Meyer seems to be taking the traditional stance that sexual repression and perversion are prerequisites to authoritarianism, an idea best propagated in Wilhelm Reich's *The Mass Psychology of Fascism*, which argued that the organization and maintenance of authoritarian regimes must necessarily include the repression and control of the peoples's sexual instincts and behavior: Foucault's "Repressive Hypothesis" *par excellence*. For Reich, Fascism was not only a mass political movement, but an authoritarian attitude that permeated all aspects of the libido and libidinal energy: love, sex, work, family, and life. While Meyer could ultimately be accused of making a rather reactionary statement by which All-American heterosexual fucking is set against "un-American" and "unnatural" forms of sexual expression (notably male homosexuality), I would argue that such an equation is not as simple as it appears in the final three films, which complexly address issues of the "fascism of everyday life" through issues of social and sexual practices.

176. One of the films Ebert spoke of in comparison to *BVD* was Brooks' *The Producers*. See "Russ Meyer: King of the Nudies," page 12 of 14.

177. *Russ Meyer – The Life and Films*, 20.

SUPERVIXENS (1975)

A Return to Form

Supervixens proved to be Russ Meyer's comeback. A huge commercial success, topping even *Vixen*'s phenomenal box-office, the film also polarized a majority of critics who found the film offensive and incomprehensible and a smaller number who enthusiastically appreciated the satire. In that most of *Supervixens*' humor is self-referential, some familiarity with Meyer's previous films is almost a necessity to fully appreciate the film. In one scene, Harry Sledge (Charles Napier) calls the operator; he is answered by a nude woman in the middle of the desert running an phone operator's switchboard. The scene seems to be included for no other reason except simply as a brief in-joke and self-reference to the scenes of Soul as a phone operator in *CHR*. Similarly, Russ Meyer appears in a cameo as a hotel manager, and there is a wonderful shot of Meyer in the doorway with a sign reading "MANAGER" posted next to the door. It is simply included as another self-referential moment in the film: indeed, Meyer is the film's "manager."

Supervixens also generated a large amount of controversy for its violence, particularly the infamous "bathtub murder" and the "dynamite-between-the-legs" finale. Meyer felt that the overdone violence would clue the audience and critics that the film's violence was designed to have a comic-book effect: a cartoon done with actors. Nonetheless, despite the slapstick effects, Meyer's relentless editing and the graphic detail makes *Supervixens*' violence some of the most harrowing ever committed to the big screen. It is the thin edge of "evil and humor" that is tested throughout *Supervixens*. Meyer recounted, "Even with *Supervixens*, people kept asking 'Why did you have to have the bathtub murder,' when really the success of the film *was* the bathtub murder, since there was so little sex in the picture."[178] Also distinguishing *Supervixens* was the casting of Shari Eubanks in two roles. She first appears as the über-bitch SuperAngel, who is killed early in the film, and then as loving and warm-hearted SuperVixen, a reincarnation (but complete opposite) of SuperAngel. Meyer was originally intent in casting six big-breasted women as a sort of publicity gimmick, yet only could find five women well-endowed enough to meet his requirements. Production was even nearly suspended until Ebert suggested the idea of bringing Eubanks back into the picture in a dual-role.[179] Having Eubanks in two roles benefits the film in two ways. On one hand, her appearance in the beginning and end of the film brings the almost dispensable narrative to a sort of circular closure, bracketing the meandering middle of the film with the conflicts and tensions of the "love triangle" between Harry Sledge, Clint Ramsey (Charles Pitts), and SuperAngel/SuperVixen. Indeed, the middle portion of *Supervixens* is a collection of episodes revolving around the various encounters between Clint and the "supervixens." These encounters do not further the plot, but are included primarily as comical references to, and parodies of, previous Meyer films. The dual-role also allows more screen time for the charismatic Eubanks, who executes one of the finest performances in a Meyer film as the acid-tongued SuperAngel and her antithesis, the loving SuperVixen.

178. "Russ Meyer interviewed by Ed Lowry and Louis Black," page 5 of 7.

179. See Frasier, 18.

Sex Über Alles

Supervixens begins with scratchy German marching music over a shot of the desert as a tow-truck pulls a Volkswagen into an isolated gas station. The driver of the tow-truck is also the owner, Martin Bormann (Henry Rowland), an intentional reference to the WWII Nazi war criminal. Clint Ramsey works diligently at the gas station, "Martin Bormann's Super Service," where the day to day workings of the gas station as a staple of the American economic system is equated to the ruthless efficiency of the Final Solution. Clint immediately encounters the first supervixen, SuperLorna (Christy Hartburg), an obvious parody of *Lorna*. When Clint offers to check her oil, he holds the dipstick like a erect penis (one of a multitude of phallic symbols which appear throughout *Supervixens*), and recommends "10-40." "That sounds like a good number!" SuperLorna obliviously purrs as she gets out of her car to use the gas station's bathroom. Meanwhile, Clint's obnoxious wife SuperAngel, an obvious reference to Angel in *Goodbye!*, calls Clint and demands he come home and keep her company with an afternoon of sex. The scene crosscuts between SuperAngel talking on the phone in the nude, striking pin-up poses; a beleaguered Clint trying to do his job; and SuperLorna standing in the doorway of the restroom suggestively dancing in white hot pants and a red shirt tied at the midriff. SuperAngel is infuriated when she overhears SuperLorna, and is convinced Clint is having sex with her. This sexual tension is exacerbated during the next phone call SuperAngel makes to the gas station, which SuperLorna answers (in a prototypical Meyer shot, she picks up the phone in an extreme low-angle shot so her breasts nearly fill the screen). SuperAngel asks if she's "the bitch my husband's been screwing," and SuperLorna casually answers, "I can't wait to strap on your groovy old man" (a line directly lifted from *BVD*). SuperLorna then abruptly drops the phone, leaving SuperAngel "hanging" on the line. Incensed, SuperAngel calls back and finally reaches Martin, telling him that Clint better get home before she "burns down this fuckin' lean-to!" Martin delivers the message to Clint: "The *führer* has given you an ultimatum: get your ass home *mach schnell* – or you won't have a home."

Exasperated, Clint reluctantly leaves work and goes home, where he promptly delivers an angry diatribe to SuperAngel about how he has had it with her behavior, her control, her embarrassing him at work, and the other domineering things she is doing to destroy their relationship: in short, her *fascist* behavior. The camera cuts back between an enraged Clint pacing the bedroom and a negligée-clad SuperAngel sitting on the bed, reacting with doe-eyed innocence. SuperAngel tries to calm Clint down by seducing him, and they ultimately do end up having sex as a form of "peace treaty." Yet instead of concentrating on their bodies, the camera focuses on SuperAngel's distracted facial expressions and close-ups of her hand as she absent-mindedly fondles the

CHAPTER SEVEN ◊ **SURREAL SEVENTIES**

phallic knobs on the bed frame. When Clint climaxes, there is a close-up of SuperAngel's hand rubbing part of the bedframe that resembles a down turned, flaccid penis. She asks him if he enjoyed it, then angrily interjects if he enjoyed it more with her than with the woman he "screwed in his truck" (presumably referring to SuperLorna). Sex itself becomes a political act, a form of manipulation and domination. Thoroughly irate by SuperAngel's deception,

199

Clint is shown from behind with a huge (rubber) penis hanging between his legs (a filmic technique that Meyer repeatedly uses in these later films); he quickly and angrily stuffs it back in his pants. Their heated argument ensues once again, and quickly spills out from the bedroom to the front lawn. As Clint gets in his pick-up truck and tries to leave, the profanity-spewing SuperAngel throws a concrete block through his windshield and then attacks the hood of the truck with an axe. They begin to wrestle on the front lawn and Clint drags SuperAngel into the house. Witnessing the battle, their white-trash neighbor Rufus (F. Rufus Owens) frantically calls the police.

Harry Sledge arrives in full police regalia: uniform, motorcycle helmet, and mirrored sunglasses. He breaks up the domestic dispute by knocking Clint unconscious. While SuperAngel is taken to the hospital, Harry remains with Clint, and the most important aspect of the scene is the camera's fetishization of Harry's police nightstick, which Harry throws in a chair. The camera periodically returns to the nightstick laying in the chair to emphasizes its phallic nature. This is further manifest when Harry sits in the chair and fondles the nightstick just out of frame, but the viewer is nonetheless able to tell that he rubs it across his knees and at one point stands it erect between his legs and taps it on the chair: two gestures suggesting his masturbating with the "nightstick." After telling Clint he's going to let him go back to work and cool off rather than take him to jail, Harry places the nightstick under Clint's chin and lifts his head, a sadistic gesture in which Harry exercises both his masculinity and his legal authority: the nightstick becomes a phallic symbol, a symbol of the law, and a symbol of masculinity (this relationship is the central issue in the subsequent *Up!* as well).

The scene cuts to SuperAngel at the hospital, where a "Dr. Scholl" is crudely examining SuperAngel by feeling up her breasts. Arriving at the hospital to question her, Harry sits down and removes his sunglasses; the viewer is struck by the amount of eye-liner Harry is wearing, rivaling that of SuperAngel. Whereas with Clint the encounter is centered around Harry waving and fondling his phallic nightstick as well as his swaggering macho demeanor, with SuperAngel Harry is *feminatized*: his phallic nightstick is conspicuously missing and replaced by made-up eyes. This "emasculation" of Harry in SuperAngel's presence will foreshadow the dynamics of their sexual encounter as well, in which Harry is unable to have sex with SuperAngel, or rather, is "unable to be a man."

The Bathtub Murder

Later in the day, when Clint returns home from the gas station, SuperAngel refuses to let him into the house. Dejected, Clint proceeds to "Haji's Bar" to drown his sorrows, where SuperHaji (played, of course, by Haji) tends bar

CHAPTER SEVEN ◊ SURREAL SEVENTIES

dressed only in flowers that strategically cover her nipples and pubic region (referencing her role as the Catalyst in *Goodbye!*). Meanwhile, the viewer learns that SuperAngel has not allowed Clint into his home because she is now "entertaining" Harry, who voyeuristically watches her dance from the sofa while he puffs on his cigar. "I like a good cigar, too," SuperAngel tells him, "but at least I take it out of my mouth once in a while." The line, directed at Harry's compulsive sucking on phallic cigars, is a veiled commentary on Harry's own latent homosexuality masquerading as a tough-guy veneer. Indeed, Harry quickly proves not to be "the man" that he presents himself to be in the bedroom, and when SuperAngel attempts to perform fellatio on him, he snarls, "Knock that queer shit off!" When it is apparent Harry can not get it up with SuperAngel, she hilariously grabs his obviously fake, limp penis, well over a foot long, and contemptuously shakes it before throwing it back on the bed. Enraged that Harry can't perform sexually ("with my beautiful body, you got a lot of nerve, buster!"), SuperAngel orders him out. When Harry informs her he will be back tomorrow, presumably to do what he couldn't do today, SuperAngel bluntly retorts that there *won't be* a tomorrow, and she launches into another profanity-laced tirade about Harry's sexual inadequacies. Suddenly, Harry punches her in the stomach and chillingly tells her in a low-angle close-up, "That's what you get for bein' *sassy*!" Throughout this sequence, and *Supervixens* as a whole, violence and black comedy are inseparable, and in one of the more macabre moments of the scene, Harry changes radio stations from the go-go music favored by SuperAngel to some corny, shit-kicking country music, which is completely at odds with the frightening on-screen violence.

Terrified, SuperAngel locks herself in the bathroom as Harry pursues her. Initially, he tries to talk her out of the bathroom, but quickly decides to simply break down the door instead. However, he proves unable to budge the door, which becomes an unlikely source of comedy in the film, and SuperAngel's terror-filled screams soon turn into acerbic sarcasm. With the film making another rapid shift between horror and comedy, she again mocks Harry for his many inabilities, and to further point out his sexual and masculine incompetence, she asks if that is why he "carries that big nightstick," again making clear the relationship of the male penis, the male phallus of the Law, and the phallic nightstick which is Harry's way of proving his "masculinity" which he sorely lacks in the bedroom. Infuriated, Harry retrieves a butcher knife from the kitchen, and he attempts to pry the door open to no avail, resulting in further taunting from SuperAngel. He explodes with anger, hacking at the door with the butcher knife while screaming profanities and vowing he is "gonna cut you up like a hog!" Yet by now SuperAngel is almost oblivious to Harry's rage: she turns on the radio, begins to runs a bath, and nonchalantly dances around the bathroom as Harry continues his frenzied assault on the bathroom door.

Eventually, the knife itself becomes lodged in the door, further enraging (and embarrassing) Harry. In frustration, he braces himself against the wall and pushes at the door with both legs. Suddenly, the door, with the knife still imbedded in it, caves in – it lands on top of SuperAngel, impaling her. Harry crashes into the room, stumbles over the door, further crushing SuperAngel, and caroms into the bathtub. Escalating the assault, Harry drags SuperAngel out from under the door and into the bathtub, where he repeatedly stomps on her and even jumps on her with both feet, a highly disturbing scene captured by low-angle shots of Harry intercut with close-ups of the now-crimson bath water. However, Harry has yet to finish his assault, and he grabs the small radio off the bathroom shelf as the (unbelievably) still-living SuperAngel pulls herself to a seated position in the bathtub. In a shot directly quoted from *Motorpsycho!*, the bloodied SuperAngel is shown in the background sitting in the tub in a state of shock, framed between Harry's spread legs, her head beneath his crotch, his back to the camera. As in *Motorpsycho!*, the shot heightens the unnerving quality of the sexual assault by the proximity of Harry's crotch to SuperAngel's bloody face. Indeed, "SuperAngel" can be said to be a reference not only to the bitchy Angel of *Goodbye!*, but the sexual assault victim Angel from *Motorpsycho!*. The electrical cord of the radio hanging between his legs (recalling his large, flaccid penis in the bedroom), Harry drops the radio into the bathtub, electrocuting SuperAngel, the visible current rising around her body. This cuts to a low-angle close-up of the sinister, grinning Harry as the electric current fills the air, parodying the famous moment in *Frankenstein* when Doctor Frankenstein screams "It's alive! It's alive!" Indeed, it is the murder of SuperAngel, climaxed in a burst of electric energy, which has "brought life" into Harry's dead dick.

Clint Ramsey's Odyssey

Following SuperAngel's murder, Harry frames Clint for the crime and he is forced to flee on a cross-country trek. This middle section of the film is purely episodic, with encounters which do not provide any narrative drive or continuity, but exist simply to parody previous Meyer characters and films. After Clint has gone on the run, he is hitch-hiking and is first picked up by Cal McKinney (John LaZar) and his girlfriend SuperCherry (Sharon Kelly). Cal McKinny is an obvious parody of Calif McKinney from *Mudhoney*, and SuperCherry a reference to Cherry from *CHR*. The sinister Cal drives while SuperCherry attempts to seduce Clint, who refuses to respond to SuperCherry's amorous advances and finally asks to be let out of the car. Cal pulls the car over, but promptly gets into a fistfight with Clint, highly insulted that Clint didn't find his girlfriend attractive enough to have sex with her. SuperCherry leans against the car, watching the fight with vicarious glee and sexual arousal, but also intervenes when Clint gets the upper hand on Cal by kicking Clint in the crotch. With Clint

CHAPTER SEVEN ◊ **SURREAL SEVENTIES**

vanquished (by his girlfriend), Cal rests against his car when he is suddenly bitten by a rattlesnake. In a direct parody of the rattlesnake scene in *Motorpsycho!*, Cal orders SuperCherry to "suck out the poison," and he forces her head down to suck the poison out of the bite in his leg. Sickened, SuperCherry spits out a large and grotesque mixture of saliva and poison while Cal yells at her, "You don't even give good head!" As in *Motorpsycho!*, the metaphor of forced fellatio taking place in the scene is obvious. Also managing to have most of her clothes torn off while she struggles with the delirious Cal, SuperCherry finally gets him into the car and they speed away, leaving Clint unconscious on the side of the road.

As Cal's car drives off in one direction, a white station wagon approaches from the other, a parody of *Motorpsycho!*'s frequent filmic technique of characters and cars intersecting within the same shot. The station wagon is driven by Lute (Stuart Lancaster), parodying his role as Lute Wade from *Mudhoney*. He brings Clint to his farm and introduces him to his much-younger, European "mail-order bride" SuperSoul (Uschi Digard, referencing her previous appearance in *CHR*). Clint spends the night on the farm, and uncomfortably listens to Lute and SuperSoul have sex in the bedroom next door. Soon there is a knock on his door: it is SuperSoul, stark naked, and she pounces on Clint. Petrified with the possibility of Lute catching them, Clint succeeds in fending off her advances and throws her out of his room.

Clint is hired to help with the daily jobs on Lute's farm. However, the Lute of *Supervixens* is hardly the ailing, honorable Lute of *Mudhoney*; in *Supervixens*, Lute is an insatiable, horny old man who does not shirk his farming responsibilities due to failing physical health but rather constant sexual preoccupation. A series of shots show Clint diligently doing the farm work while Lute and Supersoul are in the background having sex; there are also montages of Clint pounding fenceposts or performing other chores intercut with Lute and SuperSoul engaged in sexual activity. In one hilarious shot, SuperSoul runs naked holding two phallic ears of corn high in the air while Lute runs naked across the screen in the opposite direction holding a chicken over his genitals, as if he were copulating with the farm animal.

However, SuperSoul still has unrequited sexual designs on Clint, and one morning Clint is asked by Lute to bale some hay in the barn where SuperSoul is milking a cow (a close-up of her hand squeezing the udder for milk bears more than a passing resemblance to an ejaculating penis). SuperSoul follows Clint up to the hayloft and once again attacks him in a seduction attempt. Clint tries to resist, fearful that Lute will catch them. To magnify Clint's fears as he struggles with SuperSoul, Lute can be seen out of the hayloft window in the background using a mammoth drill to dig holes in the ground for fenceposts; the sexual connotation of the drill digging and twisting into the

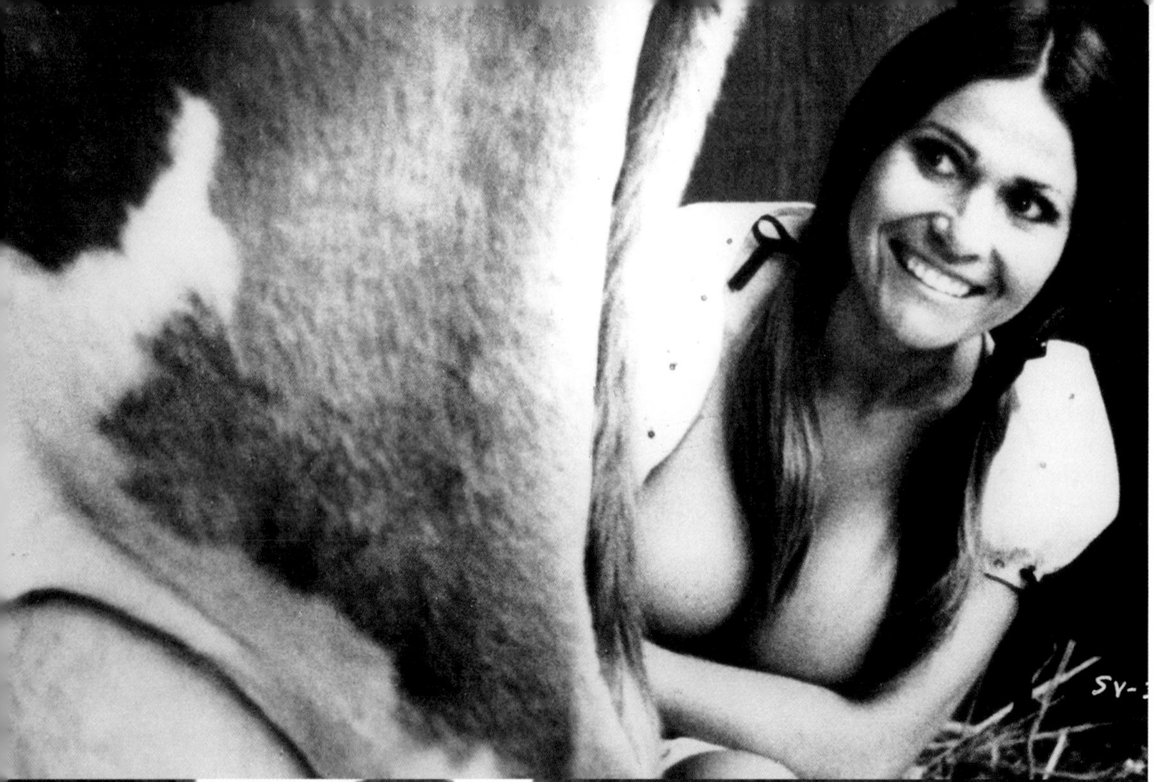

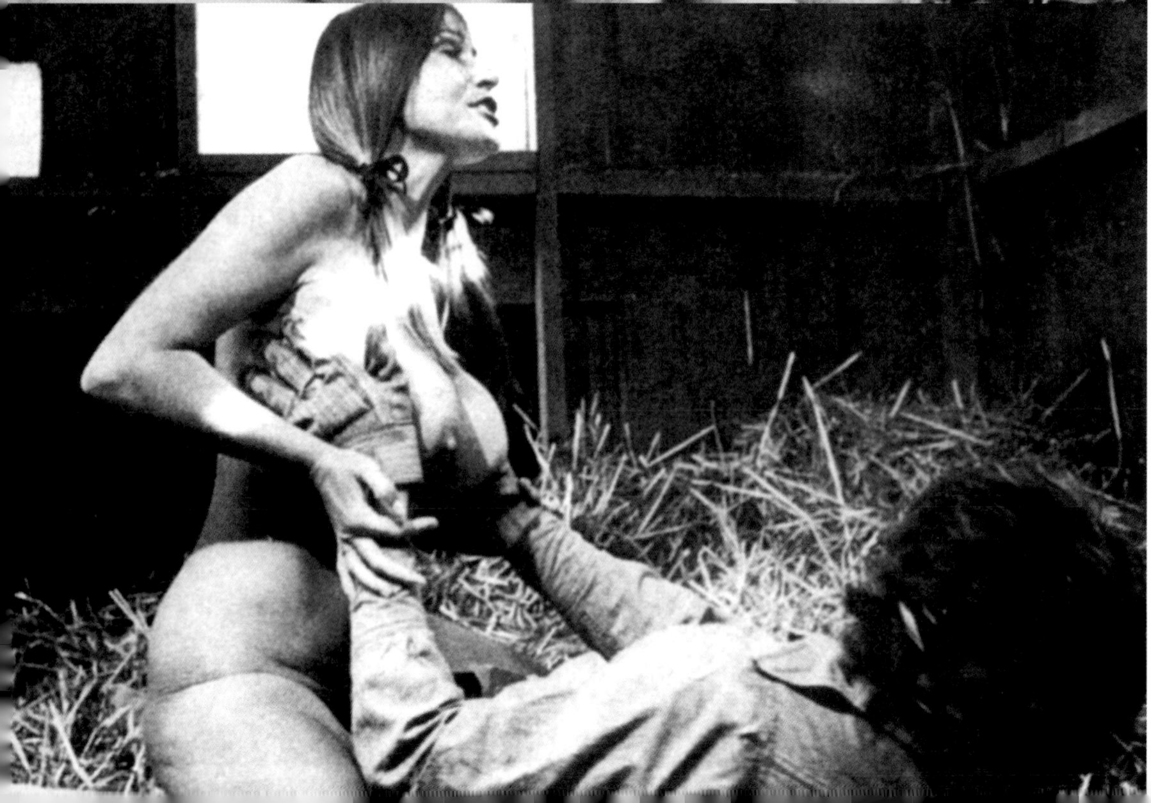

CHAPTER SEVEN ◊ SURREAL SEVENTIES

ground is an obvious counterpoint to the action in the hayloft. Despite Clint's best efforts to fend off SuperSoul, Lute does indeed finally catch them; he brandishes a pitchfork at Clint and vows "You'll not live to fuck another man's wife." However, with swashbuckling verve, Clint manages to escape by diving out the window and climbing down a rope. As he flees the farm, Lute pursues him, hurdling the pitchfork like a javelin and shouting epithets such as "desecrator of connubial bliss!" With Clint now banished, Lute returns to SuperSoul, promptly slugs her in the jaw, and orders her to "wrestle up some grub." The shot cuts to SuperSoul laying in the hay giving Lute the Nazi party s*ieg heil* salute and answering, "*Jawohl, mein herr!*" (one might also consider the outstretched arm of the Hitler salute is a gesture of phallic power signifying an erect penis). Once again, marriage is depicted as a fascist relationship; however, the last laugh is ultimately on Lute: while climbing down from the hayloft he falls, fittingly skewering himself in the ass with the pitchfork.

Clint's next encounter with a supervixen takes place at an isolated desert motel. The owner has a deaf-mute, black daughter named SuperEula (Deborah McGuire), obviously parodying Eula from *Mudhoney*. However, being deaf does not stop her from incessantly dancing to the ragtime music on the soundtrack, which abruptly shuts off when her and her father argue in sign language, suggesting the soundtrack music is itself a product of SuperEula's imagination. She is warned by her father to avoid Clint and stay out of trouble while he goes to the Rotary Club. Of course, SuperEula disobeys her father the moment he leaves. Communicating with Clint by writing on a notepad, she "talks" (or more correctly, "writes") Clint into going for a ride in her dune buggy. The scene abruptly cuts to the desert where Clint recklessly drives the dune buggy and SuperEula sits behind him topless. Here the sources of parody are the desert sex scenes in *CHR*, as well as the strange introductory shots of *Finders Keepers, Lovers Weepers*. At one point in their adventure, SuperEula takes a large red towel and goes off in the desert; when Clint sees her she is laying on her stomach naked on the towel, a virtual quote of a shot of Raquel laying naked in the desert on her long, red scarf in *CHR*. Unfortunately for Clint, SuperEula's father, accompanied by the local sheriff, has tracked them down and once again Clint is pursued by an irate male. After a protracted car chase in the desert between Clint and SuperEula's father, Clint has the fortune to meet up with a passing motorist who agrees to give Clint a ride.

Kissing SuperEula goodbye, he escapes; SuperEula waves goodbye and then holds her fist in the air in a Black Power salute. After they drive off, the film takes a brief, utterly surreal turn when a muscular, black strongman replete in a leopard-skin outfit and weightlifting gear appears out of nowhere, and he and SuperEula have sex in the middle of the desert highway. While SuperEula gyrates on top of him, the weightlifter concentrates on lifting weights. As he

LIPS HIPS TITS POWER ◊ THE FILMS OF RUSS MEYER

begins to struggle with the twin effort of pumping iron and having sex, SuperEula offers "encouragement" by telling him to "Keep it up... keep it up, god damnit!" Certainly, one source of parody is the hilarious failed seduction scene between Billie and the Vegetable in *Pussycat!*, yet another more subtle point of parody is the end of *Mudhoney*, where the deaf-mute Eula enters the realm of language with a horrifying scream. Here SuperEula enters the realm of language through the cathartic power of sex with a muscle-bound male (it is also possible to conclude that this sequence between SuperEula and the strongman is a *subjective* fantasy of SuperEula's filtered into the story rather than an actual narrative event).

206

CHAPTER SEVEN ◊ SURREAL SEVENTIES

Returning to Clint, the passing motorist turns out to be none other than Garth Pillsbury, who played Tom Palmer in *Vixen,* and Pillsbury reprises his role as Tom for *Supervixens.* In a clear reference to *Vixen,* he invites Clint to his fishing lodge: "My wife and I would love to have you." This line is matched by an insert of Tom in bed with Ann-Marie wildly bouncing on top of him. In what is a not-so-subtle reference to Erica Gavin, who at the time *Supervixens* was made criticized Meyer in a number of interviews for both his filmmaking abilities and his views of women, at the end of the film Ann-Marie is billed as "Tom's other wife."[180]

SuperVixen Cometh

Declining Tom's offer, Clint continues his lonely walk down the desert highway, when there is a burst of smoke in the desert mountains behind him. As a trumpet fanfare is comically heard on the soundtrack, the camera shows SuperAngel on a desert hilltop, naked and covered in blood as fire roars around her. The shot cuts to a close-up of SuperAngel smiling, blood trickling down the side of her face, flames superimposed over her. Parodying the mythological Phoenix, SuperAngel has been reincarnated into SuperVixen, and as the final burst of smoke comes from the desert hills, Clint arrives at "Supervixen's Oasis," another gas station in the middle of the desert. It is also fittingly called an "oasis" in that it is a point connected to *female* libidinal energy, a "watering-hole" in the desert (site of male libido). Moreover, unlike "Martin Bormann's Super Service," which is a magnet for fascist behavior, "SuperVixen's Oasis" proves to be a heterosexual utopia, free from the sadism and domination that has marked Clint's previous relationships. In keeping with the "cluckoid" tendencies of Meyer's males, Clint naturally fails to recognize that the owner of the gas station, SuperVixen, is identical to his deceased wife, but nonetheless politely offers to help her out with the busy flow of customers. However, for SuperVixen, the encounter with Clint is love at first sight: she adoringly watches him pump gas and change oil as swelling violins are comically heard on the soundtrack. Clint soon departs, but SuperVixen chases him down the highway and convinces him to take a job at the gas station. This quickly cuts to a montage of Clint and SuperVixen frolicking through meadows and deserts as easy-listening jazz is heard on the soundtrack. They wind up cavorting naked in a mountain stream, another point where rugged earth and water conjoin. As they embrace in the waist-deep water, the shot cuts to a low-angle, long shot of SuperAngel orgasmically writhing as she is precariously balanced on a desert hilltop.

However, Clint and SuperVixen's happiness in both love and work is short lived with the return of Harry Sledge, who one day arrives at the gas station. As the men strike up conversation, Harry asks where the "shithouse" is, and Clint asks Harry if he "wants some company," which Harry agrees to "as long

[180]. One interview in particular was done in 1975 for the film journal *The Velvet Light Trap*; the interviewer was Danny Peary, who subsequently featured her in his book *Cult Film Stars, op. cit.* I world also contend that Peary's highly negative assessment of *BVD* that appeared in *Cult Movies* reflected many of the prejudices expressed by Gavin.

as you ain't no queer." Yet the homoerotic bond between Harry and Clint is suggested by both Harry's macho, woman-hating, homophobic swagger and Clint's outfit of shorts, sleeveless shirt and tennis shoes which would not be out of place a gay porno film. They enter the bathroom together, a white building with "MEN" written on the wall in red letters, designating the building is not only as a restroom but an exclusive, homeosocial space for men only. Harry and Clint exit simultaneously, both zipping up in unison, further implying that a homosexual liaison could have taken place. Harry sets up a "date" with Clint to bring him and SuperVixen out that evening and go fishing with Clint the next morning. However, as he drives off, Harry looks back angrily (and, perhaps, jealously) as SuperVixen and Clint playfully cavort in the gas station parking lot. Moreover, the shot of Harry's menacing glare is interrupted by an insert of a naked SuperAngel, washing the blood off her body in the stream where SuperVixen and Clint had sex, an eerie juxtaposition that recalls the murder of SuperAngel and the returning presence of "the woman" interfering in Harry's relationship with Clint. To recall Eve Sedgwick's work, *Supervixens* offers an excellent example of the homoerotic politics of "the romantic triangle," where the relationship between the two men is ultimately as important as the relationship between the man and the woman. In *Supervixens*, the primary "romantic" relationship is between Clint and Harry, with Harry bent on eliminating any woman that comes between them and a male, homeosocial order. Indeed, in the film's violent finale in the desert, Harry throws a knife into Clint's thigh as he charges up a hill to save SuperVixen, and an odd version of "Here Comes the Bride" played on the organ can be heard on the soundtrack. This brief musical fragments serves to underscore the homoerotic nature of the male-male libidinal relationship that can only be expressed through he-man aggression in Meyer's films: music associated with a romantic moment of union is set to images of masculine confrontation and violence.

That evening, Harry, Clint, and SuperVixen all go out for drinks and dancing, and as SuperVixen and Clint fondle each other on the dance floor, Harry watches them with a mixture of disgust and contempt. At Clint's urging, the reluctant SuperVixen asks Harry to dance; he declines and tells her that a cigar is his only "vice." SuperVixen repeats the line "I like a good cigar too, but at least I take it out of my mouth once in a while," used previously in the film by SuperAngel: again, the line is a veiled reference to Harry's latent homosexuality. The role of the cigar as a phallic symbol and a substitute penis for Harry to have sex with is manifest in the next scene. After the respective parties turn in for the evening, a sequence of shots of Clint and SuperVixen having sex are intercut with Harry smoking his cigar. One close-up shows the cigar sliding in and out of Harry's mouth as if he were performing fellatio on it (an act, of course, designated by Harry as "queer shit"). The montage ends with Harry maniacally

CHAPTER SEVEN ◊ **SURREAL SEVENTIES**

laughing, setting the stage for the unveiling of his plot against Clint and SuperVixen.

The apocalyptic climax of *Motorpsycho!* is recalled and parodied in *Supervixen*'s conclusion: the hero and villain locked in a duel to the death in the originary world of the desert. Moreover, the film sets up a hilarious mockery of the classic melodrama climax of the hero saving the "damsel-in-distress" from the villain. Harry kidnaps SuperVixen and then calls Clint on the CB radio and informs him that he is going to do the same thing to her that he did to SuperAngel (only then does Clint finally make the connection between his dead wife and SuperVixen). Clint desperately drives out to the desert where Harry has taken SuperVixen, and suddenly he sees SuperVixen tied up on a desert ridge next to Harry, who has inexplicably changed from his blue denim outfit he wore when he kidnapped SuperVixen to a khaki safari outfit and a black beret, as if he has dressed especially for their violent rendezvous. He begins to throw sticks of dynamite at Clint, who runs through the desert dodging explosions. SuperVixen, by now tied to the ground spread-eagled (adding yet another dimension to the sexually-charged violence of the film), desperately attempts to save Clint's life by "sweet talking" Harry, telling him what a big man he is and how tough he is. While SuperVixen does this, she is shown on a brass bedframe which appears out of nowhere in a feathered boa, then a negligée, and finally naked as she bounces on the bed springs. Again, the subjective perspective of a character freely interacts with the narrative, but it is unclear whether these images are of Harry's perception of the "sexy" SuperVixen or SuperVixen's own thoughts of what constitutes "sexy" to a man. I would tend to suggest the latter, in that while Supervixen attempts to "seduce" Harry and flatter him about his manliness, Harry likewise brags abut his physique but exhibits no sexual interest in SuperVixen. His erotic energy is concentrated elsewhere: Clint.

With his dynamite supply exhausted, Harry saves the last stick with its extended fuse for SuperVixen: he shoves it in the ground between her legs, next to her vagina, and tells her it's "a long fuse with a big bang." The "long fuse" can be referenced to Harry's long, limp penis as well as the electrical cord of the radio that dangled between his legs when he electrocuted SuperVixen in the bathtub. The "big bang" is obviously a reference to both sexual intercourse and the impending explosion which ends in death (as in *Motorpsycho!*, a stick of dynamite becomes a blatant phallic symbol). Clint manfully attempts to save SuperVixen as Harry shoots him and stabs him. Despite his wounds, Clint valiantly succeeds in grabbing the fuse and pulls the dynamite out of the ground, away from between SuperVixen's spread legs. Infuriated, Harry knocks Clint unconscious and drags him over to SuperVixen. He tears SuperVixen's clothes off and throws Clint on top of her so they are in the missionary position. Harry then takes the dynamite and he shoves it between Clint's clenched thighs, and it appears as through the dynamite has been inserted up Clint's anus. The homoerotic nature of Harry and Clint's relationship is again clearly manifest. Nonetheless, Harry's plan is foiled when the fuse of the dynamite burns up and there is no explosion. The "big bang" does not happen, mocking Harry's impotence and inability to perform sexually: like his penis, the dynamite is a "dud." Harry takes his impotent "stick of dynamite" and walks away, setting it on the ground while he packs up his gear. However, in a moment of poetic justice, the dynamite suddenly sparks, and the ensuing explosion blows Harry to pieces.

Meyer closes the film by making two explicit references to comics and cartoons, as if to explicitly announce to the viewer that the film has all along simply been a cartoon (or "bustoon"). "Leapin' lizards!" exclaims SuperVixen after the explosion kills Harry, directly borrowing Little Orphan Annie's catch phrase. The shot then cuts to the low-angle, long shot of SuperAngel naked on the desert peak. "That's all, folks!" she announces, quoting the end motto of Warner Brothers cartoons. However, a small subtitle that says "...except" flashes across the screen: Clint and SuperVixen are shown running naked through the desert, presumably to live, love, and work in a fascism-free world. As they run free through the desert, one last metaphor of copulation can be seen: a tire hangs over the phallic branch of a cactus, unifying images of "gas station" and "desert" into a utopian, heterosexual order.

UP! (1976)

The Case of the Missing Penis

Given the controversy generated by *Supervixens* and its violence, Meyer assumed that if he made the sex and violence even more outlandish that critics and audiences would have no choice but to see it as a "put-on." "I always felt that they would take it in the manner that I presented it. That if a man got a double-bitted axe buried in his chest, he could still wrench it out, run 100 yards and kill a giant with a chainsaw. But they just took it very seriously."[181] *Up!* succeeds in being perhaps Meyer's most offensive film, and among the film's "highlights" are an extended beginning which features Adolph Schwartz, an Adolph Hitler caricature, who is the center of an S&M orgy that culminates in him being buggered by a man dressed as a pilgrim; the murder of said Hitler caricature by an assailant who puts a piranha in his bathtub which devours his penis; and a repulsive gang rape of the two main female characters by drunken lumberjacks in a bar.

Up! begins with the line "Once Upon a Time..." written on the screen, obviously evoking the fairy-tale beginning, and, in fact, *Up!* is "the tale of two 'fairies'" – the homosexual Nazi Adolph Schwartz and the naked wood-nymph

181. "Russ Meyer Interviewed by Ed Lowry and Louis Black," page 6 of 7.

CHAPTER SEVEN ◊ **SURREAL SEVENTIES**

narrator, the Greek Chorus (Kitten Natividad). "Ladies and Gentlemen, I give you... the body," she says, her narration coinciding with a medium shot of her body, followed by quick, consecutive close-ups of her nipple and then her vagina. Naked throughout the film, she cavorts in the woods, sits on logs, and perches in trees as she delivers her absurd, puzzling narration "in a prose style that sounds like Shakespeare on LSD."[182] She speaks directly to the audience throughout the film rather than interacting with any of the characters, and frequently her almost incomprehensible narration is accompanied by blazing montages that both flash back and flash forward to other parts of the film. These narrated moments are themselves intermittently edited into the film, and what is especially hilarious about the narration is the great lengths the film goes to in order to explain a mystery narrative that makes absolutely no sense to begin with. Indeed, much of the film is simply a series of episodic events, most of which are lengthy sex scenes among the various characters, which are loosely connected by the preposterous murder mystery.

182. Frasier, 22. Due to Natividad's Spanish accent, another actress was used to dub the voice of "the Greek Chorus" with a very stagy English accent.

The introduction of the Greek Chorus cuts to the aforementioned orgy with Hitler caricature Adolf Schwartz. Two women spank him: one is black ("The Ethiopian Chef") and the other Asian ("Limehouse").[183] It is a parodic moment where "race-mixing" is introduced to the sexually and racially pure world of Nazism. Following the spankings, a man dressed as a pilgrim (a symbol of Puritanism and its underlying sexual repression) whips him on his buttocks, all to Schwartz's delight. Schwartz then offers the man in the pilgrim outfit payment to bugger him, and features what becomes a standard Meyer shot in his later films: as the man prepares to have sex with Schwartz, he is shown with his buttocks facing the camera, a large (rubber) penis hanging between his legs. For good measure, a close-up of lubricant being poured on a long, plastic penis is thrown in as well. The pilgrim proceeds to have anal sex with Adolph Schwartz and secures his payment by pulling a wad of cash out of Schwartz's wallet.

183. "Limehouse" is referenced from Thomas Burke's *Limehouse Nights* (1917), a collection of short stories set in London's "Chinatown" district, Limehouse. One of the stories, the rather racist "The Chink and the Child," served as the basis for D.W. Griffith's film *Broken Blossoms* (1919).

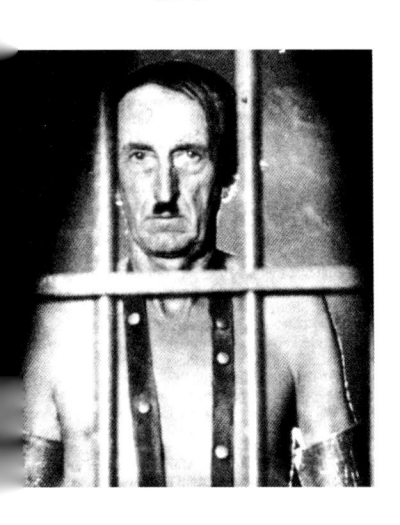

The scene then cuts to Schwartz happily goose-stepping around his house, putting on a record, and then relaxing in his bathtub as he mock-conducts the German marching music. However, a mysterious figure clad in a black leather outfit sneaks into the bathroom carrying a piranha in a fishbowl, and empties the contents into Schwartz's bathtub. The piranha promptly eats Schwartz's penis in a torrent of red, bubbling bath water (quite possibly a parody of *Supervixens* controversial bathtub murder, with a man on the receiving end of the sexually-fused violence). "Murder most foul!" exclaims the Greek Chorus, and a montage of shots from the film accompany her convoluted explanations of events. As noted, these blazing rapid-fire "narration montages" do little to help the viewer, and actually further confuse the situation. Indeed, in one of the montages, there is a close-up of a woman in a bondage mask sticking her tongue out at the audience, seemingly as a sign of good-natured contempt for the viewer

211

Russ Meyer's
Up!

Russ Meyer's
Up!

Russ Meyer's
Up!

Russ Meyer's
Up!

Russ Meyer's
Up!

Russ Meyer's
Up!

Russ Meyer's
Up!

CHAPTER SEVEN ◊ SURREAL SEVENTIES

attempting to make any sense of the film.

After Schwartz's murder, Margo Winchester (Raven de la Croix) enters the film. She is walking down a deserted, backwoods road when a local fellow offers her a ride in his pick-up truck. She grudgingly accepts; of course, within moments the driver of the pick-up pulls over to a secluded spot where Margo is dragged out of the car, stripped, beaten unconscious, and raped on the shore of a river. However, when Margo regains consciousness, she responds with decisive vengeance: she drags her rapist into the ankle-deep water and kills him with a series of martial arts blows. In a wonderful editing move, Meyer inserts an extreme long-shot of the two in the middle of their battle, rendering them nearly invisible in the river. The shot both disorientates the viewer, disrupting the continuity in the fight sequence, and also parodies the cinematic strategy of using long shots to convey the "epic" nature of the battle. The self-reference point is Varla's murder of Tommy in *Pussycat!,* and one also sees that while masculine violence again takes place on dry land (the rape), female revenge now takes place in the water (Margo's killing of her attacker). Water is no longer only the site of female sexual desire (as in *Pussycat!* and many other Meyer films) but, for the first time in a Meyer film, a site of merciless female *violence*. However, the local deputy Homer Johnson (Monty Bane) witnesses the event, and informs Margo he is bound by his duty to arrest her for murder. Then, in a lengthy digression, he proceeds to describe his own (subjective) version of events, which the camera depicts on-screen. In his version, Margo's assailant is not killed by her, but falls from a cliff while chasing her. The lengthy, subjective account parodies Kurosawa's celebrated *Rashomon*, in which different versions of a rape a shown onscreen based on each character's perspective (the attacker, the victim, the witness). Moreover, with the male figure of the law attaining an authoritative presence, *Up!* begins to tackle what will be its primary question by the conclusion of the film: the establishment and enforcement of a phallocentric law thrown into chaos by Schwartz's "castration." Of course, the appreciative Margo "rewards" Homer's benevolence, and a long sequence of them having sex in various positions follows. Throughout this sex scene, Meyer uses a combination of quick jump-cuts, extreme long-shots, and shots of the couple's shadows having sex to diffuse any possible "erotic" qualities that might build. Their encounter culminates in a lavish bedroom where Margo is leaning against the bed frame sitting on Homer's face. She breaks his glasses with the pressure from her thighs. Looking down, she mutters, "Hmm... don't know my own strength," in her best Mae West impersonation. This serves as a hilarious commentary about the woman, the one without a penis, who doesn't "know her own strength" against the male figure who embodies "the law" itself, and this important in-joke reaches its delayed punch line at the end of the film.

Meanwhile, Paul (Robert McLane), previously seen as the man dressed

213

as a pilgrim who had sex with Adolph Schwartz in the beginning of the film, and his wife, Sweet Li'l Alice (Janet Wood), who has been having her own extramarital affair with a lesbian truck driver, are opening their new bar and restaurant. A group of lumberjacks, led by the behemoth Rafe (Bob Schott) enter the bar and proceed to get as drunk as humanly (or inhumanly) possible. "More beer!" is Rafe's mantra, shouted at the top of his lungs. Margo, dressed in a black evening gown that gives new meaning to "plunging neckline," has been hired as the bar's dancer, and she begins a burlesque routine on the bar. The drunken rednecks, seeing an attractive woman dancing, take this for a sign that she obviously wants to be gang-raped, and they throw her onto one of the bar-room tables. The mammoth Rafe begins to rape Margo (Russ Meyer appears briefly as one on the lumberjacks shouting encouragement, although in the credits he is billed as "Hitchcock," a clear aside to that director's famous cameos). When Sweet Li'l Alice tries to prevent the attack, she is stripped and assaulted as well. In what is perhaps the most repugnant shot ever in a Russ Meyer film, Rafe is shown during the sexual assaults with his back to the camera: his enormous, blood-covered (rubber) penis dangles between his legs. Deputy Homer Johnson arrives and attempts to intervene, only to have Rafe bury an axe into his chest. Holding Margo and Sweet Li'l Alice under each arm, Rafe then runs into the woods (a parody of the classic horror films such as *Frankenstein* and *The Mummy*, in which the monster kidnaps the female lead and carries her away). Having lost the battle but not the war, the scene cuts back to Homer as he manfully pulls the ax out of his chest, grabs a chainsaw, and follows Rafe into the woods. In a grisly yet homoerotic moment, Homer saves the day and the damsels-in-distress by shoving the chainsaw deep into Rafe's gut (perhaps a parody of *The Texas Chainsaw Massacre*). The two violently quiver as blood sprays in all directions like ejaculated semen (blood and semen *both* being "erotic fluids"), and, clenched tightly together, they tumble over a cliff to their deaths. Horrified, Margo and Alice embrace, but their shock quickly turns into sexual curiosity about each other. The end of *CHR* is recalled, where man-to-man sexual energy can only be expressed in homoerotic violence and self-destruction, while woman-to-woman sexual energy can be expressed through sex. Indeed, there is a sense that with the men dead, the women seem to simply decide, "Who needs 'em?" This initial homoerotic attraction between Margo and Alice is also carried over to the conclusion of the film.

Following the violent spectacle at the bar and in the woods, Margo is taking a shower when the same leather-clad assailant of Schwartz enters the bathroom. The scene is shot as a obvious parody of Hitchcock's shower scene in *Psycho*, even quoting specific shots (such as the silhouette of the assailant behind the shower curtain). However, Margo is able to elude the attack and escapes by running naked into the woods. The assailant pursues her, and then stops to

CHAPTER SEVEN ◊ **SURREAL SEVENTIES**

undress while attempting to explain his/her side of events in a vain attempt to give the film some coherency. In a completely nonsensical turn of events, when the leather is stripped off the murderer is revealed to be Sweet Li'l Alice, who is actually Schwartz's daughter, Eva Braun Jr. (?!). The women, both naked, begin a martial arts duel to the death in the woods while each spout *non-sequiturs* at each other about the situation. Suddenly, they come to a mutual conclusion, and decide to have sex rather than kill one another (a proposition unthinkable between two men in Russ Meyer's film world). Their initial attraction, suggested when they embraced each other after the deaths of Homer and Rafe, is now made clear. Arm in arm, they make their way to a bedframe in the middle of the woods with Sweet Li'l Alice/Eva Braun Jr. carrying a violin case. Opening it, she pulls out a huge, rubber dildo, and the two prepare to consummate their relationship. Suddenly, a stark naked Paul comes from out of nowhere and shoots the dildo out of Alice's hand with a WWII German Luger, preventing the women from possessing the penis which Alice/Eva removed through "castrating" Schwartz. Paul mourns Schwartz, bitterly complaining that no one understood him and how he did so much for world; it also implies that Paul's homosexual liaison with Adolph may have been more than simply for the money. While Paul attempts to establish an order of sexually "pure" male superiority through brandishing his phallic handgun, Margo is able to grab the dildo and, using it like a police baton, knocks the pistol out of Paul's hand. She establishes order by waving the rubber penis and commanding Paul and Alice/Eva not to move, as if she were a police officer. Indeed, this is the punch line of the film: Margo has been an undercover cop the whole time, and the film, which begins with "the law" thrown into disarray by Schwartz's "castration," ends with the phallocentric Law intact, abeit in a perverse form. The Phallus, represented by a big, rubber dildo, is now literally in the hands of a policewoman who "doesn't know her own strength." In the case of *Up!*, the heterosexual couple cannot be formed because the married couple, Paul and Alice/Eva, are both primarily attracted to members of the same sex. While the phallus as a symbol of "The Law" is reestablished, it is now *the woman* who possesses the Phallus. Never so overtly has the ideal Russ Meyer woman been depicted. Margo is indeed "a man with big tits," a busty, naked woman who literally wields the symbol of masculine power and authority: a big penis. Perhaps *Up!* can ultimately only be summarized by paraphrasing Joesph Goebbels: "When I hear the word 'culture,' I reach for my big, rubber cock."

WHO KILLED "WHO KILLED BAMBI"?

The Best Laid Plans...

Russ Meyer's brief involvement in the abortive Sex Pistols movie project, *Who*

Killed Bambi? rates as one of the most potentially interesting moments in the history of Western culture. Sex Pistols manager Malcolm McLaren and the band were huge fans of *Beyond the Valley of the Dolls*, a film which certainly reflected two of punk's favorite modes of discourse: shock value and sarcasm. Instead of simply modeling a film on *BVD* and other rock films, McLaren approached Meyer in the fall of 1977 about doing a film with the Sex Pistols. Meyer not only agreed to do the film, but coaxed Roger Ebert into providing a screenplay.

Accounts vary about what went wrong, but all concur that the possibility of a creative collaboration faded fairly quickly. McLaren later blamed the failure on Meyer's basic inability to do anything other than a soft-core porn film. Julian Temple, who later directed the abomination *The Great Rock and Roll Swindle*, blamed the collapse on an alleged incident on the third day of filming: he claimed Russ Meyer shot a deer point-blank in the head on the set, causing a horrified cameraman to quit and production to grind to a halt (Meyer later sued Temple for his statements and Temple subsequently apologized in *Screen International*).[184] Additional rumors implied there was intense animosity between Meyer and the Sex Pistols, especially Johnny Rotten, making any working relationship all but impossible.

Meyer himself has presented a different side of the story. He blamed the project's failure on a financially ill-prepared McLaren: "We cast the picture. We literally built every set on stages, shot three days, and then McLaren blew the whistle. He realized, I would guess, that the picture couldn't be made."[185] As for his relationship with the Sex Pistols, Meyer has for the most part spoken positively of them.

"I did a lot of rehearsing with them. Two of them were very intelligent, level-headed guys – Jones and Cook. Rotten and poor Vicious, whose no longer with us, were absolutely nuts. Both of them had an intense hatred for McLaren... Rotten definitely had a charisma. Vicious, reputedly and in the script, was fucking his mother. Marianne Faithfull was cast for the part. Vicious embraced the sex scenes with his mother but he objected to us showing them shooting up."[186]

Of course, the Sex Pistols themselves collapsed in a flurry of animosity in 1978, and Temple's telling of the saga would focus on McLaren as the Svengali *cum* P.T. Barnum of punk, with Johnny Rotten, the *enfant terrible* of rock, all but written out of Sex Pistols history. In any event, *Who Killed Bambi?* remains one of the great "might-have-been" moments in both rock music and cinema. One can only imagine the possibilities of a Meyer-directed parody of *A Hard Day's Night* with the Sex Pistols substituting for the Fab Four. Perhaps in a perfect world...

184. My account of the *Who Killed Bambi?* debacle owes greatly to Frasier; see 196-7.

185. "Russ Meyer Interviewed by Ed Lowry and Louis Black," page 2 of 7.

186. "Russ Meyer Interviewed by Ed Lowry and Louis Black," page 1 of 7.

CHAPTER SEVEN ◊ **SURREAL SEVENTIES**

BENEATH THE VALLEY OF THE ULTRAVIXENS (1979)

Last Tango in Small Town, U.S.A.

Beneath the Valley of the Ultravixens is Meyer's final film, and in some ways perhaps accomplishes what may have been his goal all along: to do an X-rated version of *Li'l Abner*. Set in "Rio Dio, Texas," *BVU* is a marked contrast from *Supervixens* and *Up!*. The graphic violence of the previous two films is almost non-existent, except for the occasional punch in the jaw. However, the episodic string of sex scenes remain, infused with a raunchy, burlesque, and somewhat outdated sense of humor more reminiscent of the nudie-cuties of the 1950s than the sex-satires of the late 1960s and 1970s.

Like *Up!*, *BVU* features an on-screen narrator who acts as an intermediary between the film and viewer. In *BVU*, he is "the Man from Small Town, USA," hilariously portrayed by Stuart Lancaster. While the primary source of parody is Thornton Wilder's *Our Town*, Meyer explained, he is "the grand old shit-kicker of them all, and he observes, comments, explains."[187] In his opening narration, the Man from Small Town, USA proceeds to introduce the viewer to the various characters in the film: "average people" (which is matched by an insert of Martin Bormann and Eufaula Roop in a coffin having sex); "friendly people getting to know one another" (which is matched by an insert of Lavonia and Mr. Peterbilt having sex); and people "pulling together" (which is matched by an insert of Lamar forcing Lavonia to have anal sex). Continuing this pattern throughout the film, the Man from Small Town, USA freely bounces from offering homespun wisdom, industrial film hyperbole about the greatness of the American economic system, Brechtian commentary about the film itself, and smutty observations about living and loving in Small Town, USA.

Another target of satire in *BVU* is Southern Evangelism, which first became a source of satire in *Lorna* and *Mudhoney*. At the time *BVU* was made, right-wing Christian groups spearheaded by the likes of Jerry Falwell's "Moral Majority" were making inroads into American politics by decrying the "indecency" in contemporary American life and culture (of which Russ Meyer would be a prime example). *BVU* responds by featuring a radio evangelist Eufaula Roop (Ann-Marie), a buxom blonde for whom "rapture" and "orgasm" are one and the same. Indeed, the opening scene of *BVU* is the ubiquitous Martin Bormann (Henry Rowland) and Eufaula having sex in a coffin as they sing "Gimmie that Ol' Time Religion," a satirical commentary on the sexual proclivities of the "moral majority." Just as "the Man from Small Town, USA" appears throughout the film to provide wry commentary and observations, Eufaula Roop can be seen and heard from time to time throughout the film

187. "Russ Meyer Interviewed by Ed Lowry and Louis Black," page 7 of 7.

Russ Meyer's
Beneath the valley of the ultraVIXENS

STARRING
Francesca *Kitten* Natividad

delivering radio sermons that seem more directed at the groin than the soul. To further sexualize the sermons, Meyer intermittently inserts extreme low-angle tilted shots of radio towers that stand in the air with as much robust, phallic imagery as the desert rock formations in *CHR* and *Supervixens*.

    Much of the story of *BVU*, as minimal as it is, centers around the sexual problems of Lamar Shedd (Ken Kerr): Lamar can only perform by having anal sex, and the film's plot revolves around Lamar's and others attempts to get him "straightened out," not only in the sense of getting an erection, but getting him to be able to perform "normal, straight" sex: the film's focus on the anal sex issue also seems to parody Bertolucci's controversial *Last Tango in Paris* from 1972. Lamar lives with Lavonia (Kitten Natividad), who lives in a state of perpetual sexual arousal ("Never a headache," as the Man from Small Town, USA describes her). Their first scene together is yet another parody of the bedroom scene from *Lorna*. The naked Lavonia is (always) in the mood for sex, but Lamar is too busy working on his correspondence school homework to be interrupted. Lavonia decides to entice Lamar and begins masturbating with a vibrator. The buzzing of the vibrator and Lavonia's moaning proves to be too much for Lamar as he vainly tries to concentrate on his homework, and he finally storms in the bedroom, but not to pleasure Lavonia. He grabs the vibrator and throws it against the wall, smashing it to pieces, and resumes his homework. Undaunted, Lavonia crawls under the table and begins to perform fellatio on Lamar, who can finally no longer resist temptation. However, Lamar insists on anal sex, much to Lavonia's displeasure ("I *hate* it!" Lavonia blurts as Lamar begins to have anal intercourse with her). He single-mindedly bends her over the table and buggers her. Following Lamar's eye-rolling, comic climax, Lavonia delivers a vengeful, swift kick to Lamar's crotch and seeks sexual satisfaction with local garbage man Mr. Peterbilt (Patrick Wright), his name a reference to the American semi-truck manufacturer and a *double-entendre* on his sexual equipment. Following her torrid encounter with Peterbilt, the sexually-satisfied Lavonia returns home and patches up her marital woes with Lamar by gently attending to his injured penis with a towel and cold water.

    The next morning Lamar goes to his job at the local junkyard; Lavonia spends the morning deflowering the local virgin Rhett (Steve Tracy) in a nearby river. Meanwhile, Lamar's boss, the voluptuous Junkyard Sal (June Mack) has a sexual interest in Lamar, and he is ordered to stay after work to do some "overtime" in her office, which, needless to say, means sex. In one of his more inspired observations, the Man from Small Town, USA notes, "It's all well and good for Lamar to fuck his way through correspondence school as long as he doesn't forget he's a rear-window man." Two white-trash locals, Beau Badger (Don Scarborough) and Tyrone (Aram Katcher), who bear more than a passing similarity to Luther and Jonah from *Lorna*, also work in the junkyard and peep

LIPS HIPS TITS POWER ◊ **THE FILMS OF RUSS MEYER**

through the office window to watch Lamar and Sal "work overtime." Lamar is still only interested in anal sex, and Sal reluctantly agrees. He is on the verge of coming when Tyrone, again recalling Jonah in the opening rape scene in *Lorna*, climaxes in his pants while watching them; he spits his cigarette through the air and hits Lamar in the anus. Enraged, Lamar chases after the two miscreants and dispatches each one with a single, mighty blow of his fist. In one of the running jokes throughout *BVU*, the male characters cartoonishly bleed the color of their personality: Beau, the "envious son-of-a bitch," bleeds green, and Tyrone, "the yellow-bellied bastard," bleeds yellow after they are each trashed by Lamar. Earlier in the film, Zebulon (DeForest Covan), the elderly black man who also works at the junkyard, bleeds white when he is punched in the mouth by Beau, in that he has "a lot of white man in 'im." Exasperated by the whole ordeal, Sal fires Beau and Tyrone for being a couple of "god damn *pre*-verts" and tells Lamar he too is out of a job until, in what becomes the moral message of *BVU*, he can "look a good fuck square in the eye."

CHAPTER SEVEN ◊ SURREAL SEVENTIES

Meanwhile, Lavonia is sold some "Frederick's of Wisconsin" clothes by traveling lingerie salesman Semper Fidelis (Michael Finn), who, of course, she finds time to have sex with as well. In one of the more bizarre moments of *BVU*, Semper Fidelis and Lavonia speak in rhyming couplets, creating a trajectory between the bawdy Restoration Comedy of late-17th century Europe and the American sexploitation circuit, perhaps making Russ Meyer "the Molière of the drive-in." With encouragement from Semper Fidelis, Lavonia embarks on a new, part-time career as "Lola Lagusta," the "numero uno" stripper at a local bar. Coming off his disastrous day at work, Lamar stops at the strip club and sits down at the front of the stage, completely oblivious to the fact that Lola is actually Lavonia. Lola/Lavonia drugs Lamar's beer and brings him to the club's upstairs bedroom where she attempts to "cure" Lamar of his anal sex affliction. The Man from Small Town, USA is there to offer colorful (and off-color) commentary on the scene as well; he even bores a peep hole through the wall with a large drill so as to witness matters firsthand. Recalling the close-up of the peeping eye in *Mr. Teas*, there is a close-up of Lancaster's bulging eye as it looks through the peephole, which also recalls Sal's line about "looking a good fuck square in the eye": the act of seeing, fucking, and "being straight with someone" by looking them in the eye are all inherently linked. Even the act of drilling the peephole is sexualized with the Man from Small Town, USA thrusting and twisting the hand drill through the wall (which certainly recalls Lancaster as Lute drilling the fencepost holes while SuperSoul seduces Clint in *Supervixens*). Lavonia succeeds in getting Lamar to have "straight" sex, but the cure is only partially successful as Lamar was drugged and unconscious throughout the session. As the Man from Small Town, USA observes, "– *and this is important* – Lamar was able to fuck straight... but still has yet to look a good fuck straight in the eye."

Lavonia arrives home from the strip club before Lamar and proceeds to have yet another sexual liaison, this time with the aforementioned Mr. Peterbilt. Their frequent sexual couplings maintain a precarious balance between soft-core pornography and Loony Tunes animation: their naked bodies cartoonishly collide and bounce on the bedframe while the camera records the action in jump-cuts from across, above, and below the bed. When Lamar arrives home, he discovers the "Spanish Made Simple" book and other clues that reveal that "Lola" was actually Lavonia. He barges in to the bedroom and insists Lavonia "say somethin' in Mexican," angered by the fact he was deceived at the strip club and yet, being the typical Meyer "cluckoid," is completely unaware that she is having sex with another man in front of his own eyes (one could say that at this point Lamar is still incapable of "seeing a good fuck"). They continue to argue, while, in a classic Meyer shot, Peterbilt ignores both of them and flexes his bicep, nonchalantly admiring his own masculine physique while Lavonia gyrates on top

221

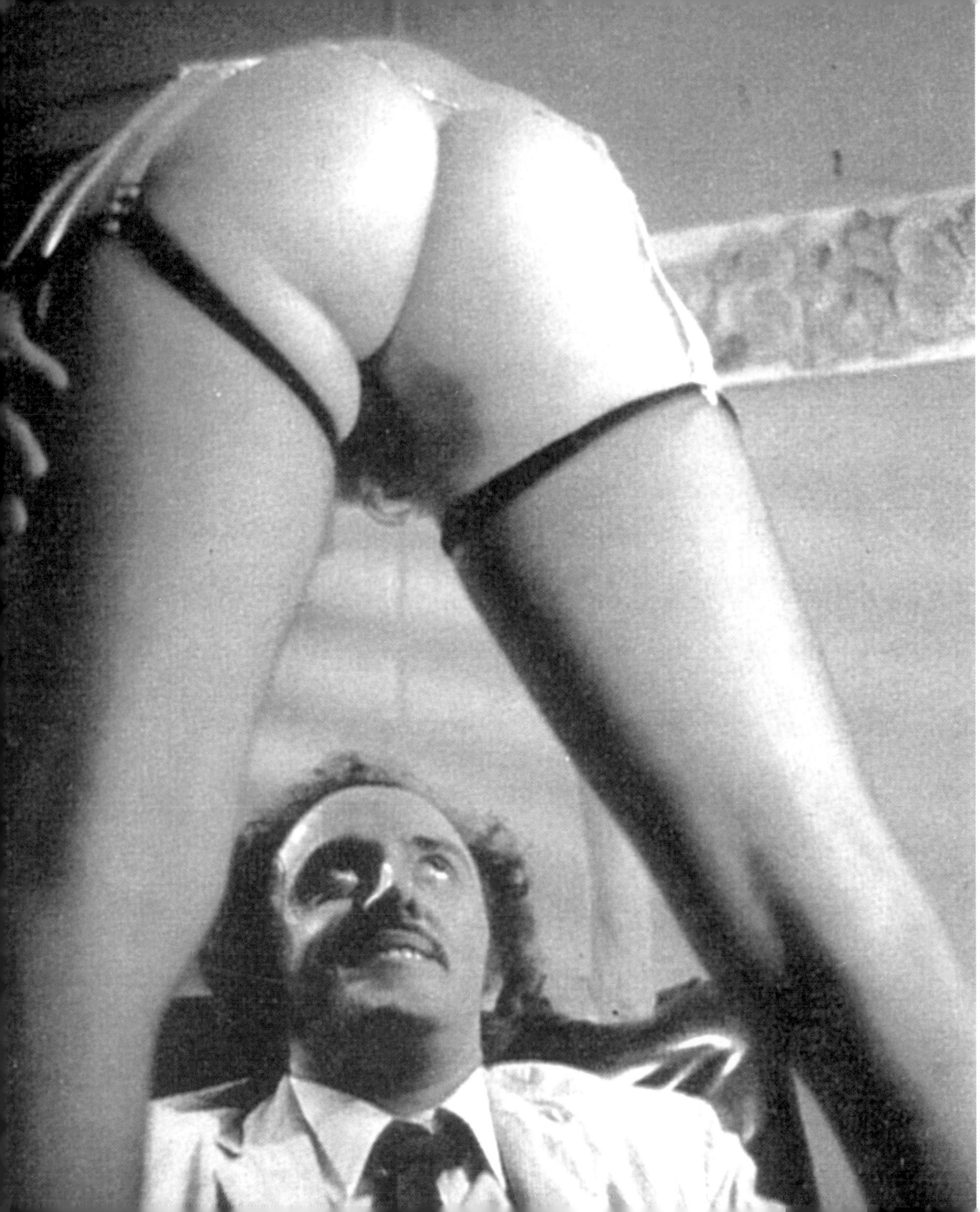

CHAPTER SEVEN ◊ SURREAL SEVENTIES

of him. "Who the fuck is that?!" Lamar suddenly exclaims, finally noticing that there is a naked man underneath his wife. He attempts to throw Mr. Peterbilt out of the bedroom but is instead quickly put in a headlock and subdued. However, Lavonia saves Lamar by grabbing a lamp and burning Peterbilt's scrotum with the light bulb. Brandishing the phallic lamp, she chases Peterbilt out of the house. Beaten and unconscious, Lamar lays in the corner of the bedroom, a trail of blue blood running down his chin. It is not specified why Lamar bleeds blue, unlike the other male characters, but a possible interpretation is that Lamar is "blue" over his marital and sexual problems.

Deciding he and Lavonia need marriage counseling, Lamar goes to Asa Lavender (Robert Pearson), the local dentist and marriage counselor for help in "saving their relationship." "Save their relationship?! Maybe a means to an end!" the Man from Small Town, USA comments, reiterating the Russ Meyer creed that good sex builds good relationships rather than the other way around. While Lavonia endures a sadistic round of Lavender's "limp-wristed dentistry" (as the publicity synopsis for *BVU* describes Lavender's methods), Lamar is seduced by Nurse Flovilla Thatch (Sharon Hill). Once again Lamar can only perform anally, and as he buggers Nurse Thatch he ponders aloud, "Why can't a woman be more like a man?" Indeed, Asa Lavender's solution for Lamar's problem is to introduce him to the world of homosexuality. However, fending off Lavender's advances, Lamar locks himself in the closet. Of course, being "in the closet" is a visual pun on Lamar's proclivity for anal sex and his own possible latent homosexuality (also clearly manifest in his wondering "why a woman can't be more like a man?"). Lavender tries a variety of methods to get Lamar "out of the closet," including cajoling, threats, and finally using a variety of tools on the door (a crowbar, a hammer, a shotgun, and eventually a chainsaw); in this scene one can also see a parody of Harry Sledge's attempts to break down the bathroom door in *Supervixens*. Oblivious to the situation between Lamar and Lavender, Lavonia and Nurse Fovilla Thatch have a lesbian encounter in the dentist chair, again enforcing the sexual "code" in Russ Meyer's films that two women having sex is highly acceptable, but two men can only express libidinal energy towards each other through violence. Indeed, when the door is chainsawed open and Lamar finally emerges from the closet, he punches Lavender square in the jaw, causing him to bleed pink, the all too "obvious" color choice for the effeminate, mincing Lavender.

With growing desperation, Lamar informs Lavonia that he is seeking one last cure, and if it fails then he will end their relationship. He drives to the radio station where he exposes himself to Eufaula Roop through the control booth; the camera provides an extreme close-up of the tip of Lamar's half-erect penis, which uncannily resembles an eye. Eufaula is both stunned and aroused, scattering tapes about the booth and apologizing to her listeners that her show is being temporarily halted "due to technical difficulties beyond our desires – ah – control." Lamar informs her he wants to be "saved," and Eufaula "slips into something more devout" and leads Lamar to the Studio A "Tub of Joy," where she conducts a live, on-the-air baptism, which, of course, turns into a live, on-the-air sexual encounter in the bathtub. Consistent with the symbolism of Russ Meyer's films, Lamar is finally cured of his "abnormal" sexual affliction by his immersion into water while he gets a frenetic fucking: a sexual baptism in the healing waters of female libido.

Meanwhile, Lavonia has hurried home where she has yet another sexual tryst with Mr. Peterbilt, who has apparently forgiven her for searing his scrotum. The encounter between Eufaula and Lamar is intercut with the encounter between Lavonia and Peterbilt, who listen to the on-air "service" while they again have slapstick sex. Once cured by Eufaula, Lamar begins a triumphant march home while Lavonia and Peterbilt continue their sexual romp. Suddenly, their encounter is cut short when Lamar's arms emerge in the film frame, pulling Peterbilt out of bed by his shoulders and throwing him into the corner of the bedroom in a heap. Lamar eagerly strips and joins Lavonia in bed. However, he turns her over on her stomach and is about to penetrate her anally, much to Lavonia's disappointment. "Excuse me, Lavonia," Lamar apologizes, and turns her over onto her back and begins to have vaginal sex with her in the missionary position: finally, by being in a sexual position where he not only fucks "normally" but can see the woman's face, Lamar succeeds in "looking a good fuck straight in the eye." The now-expendable Mr. Peterbilt vainly tries to "reassume his position" with Lavonia, but is dispatched by a single punch from Lamar, who does not miss a stoke with Lavonia as he vanquishes his male competition. Normal red blood seeps from Peterbilt's mouth, and as Meyer noted, "The only man that bleeds red is Peterbilt, he's our redneck – the only straight screw in the show. I mean among the men. The women are all very straight."[188]

With marital order and sexual normalcy restored between Lamar and Lavonia, *BVU* does not so much end but veers off into a number of strange directions and tangents. Junkyard Sal, Peterbilt, Beau and Tyrone are all summarily killed when they are crushed in Peterbilt's garbage truck by Zebulon, who achieves the American Dream of owning his own junkyard. Eufaula performs another on-the-air "baptism" with the young Rhett: "Teenagers need succorin', too!" she exclaims directly to the camera. Following his "baptism," Rhett runs off to have sex with his own mother, SuperSoul (a cameo by Uschi Digard). The Man from Small Town USA, who has been providing the epilogue up to this point, catches them and informs Rhett, who turns out to be his son, to "move over," and he takes over having sex with SuperSoul (which raises the possibility that the Man from Small, Town, USA may have been Lute from *Supervixens* all along). The Oedipal relationship of father-mother-son is turned

188. "Russ Meyer Interviewed by Ed Lowry and Louis Black," page 7 of 7.

CHAPTER SEVEN ◊ SURREAL SEVENTIES

from traumatic psychodrama into cartoonish farce.

With the Man from Small Town, USA now occupied with other matters, the narrated epilogue of the film is taken over by Russ Meyer himself, who appears onscreen carrying his camera and provides the summation of the film as he walks through the desert and inquires "Where the hell is the crew?" (in yet another of *BVU*'s many in-jokes, Meyer's voice is actually that of John Furlong doing an impersonation of Meyer). A montage of each character mentioned accompanies Meyer's nonsensical summation. Finally, Martin Bormann returns to the desert in full World War Two uniform and his coffin, as if to "retire" in the desert, a fitting conclusion in that *BVU* would prove to be Meyer's final outing as a filmmaker as well. The film closes with Bormann laying in his coffin with an unspecified female; it is precariously balanced on a desert hilltop as it rocks back and forth to the motion of sex. Yet, to further confuse matters, *BVU* ends with the promise of a sequel about the further adventures of Lavonia entitled *The Jaws of Vixen* ("...she'll never let go!"), a film which, of course, was never made. In this way, Meyer completes his film career with neither a bang or a whimper, but rather a wink and tongue firmly in cheek.

CONCLUSION

In his overview of Meyer's work, close friend Roger Ebert suggested that *Vixen* is the "quintessential" Russ Meyer film, although *Mudhoney* and *BVD* are his "best" films.[189] My own assessment would be to place *Faster, Pussycat! Kill! Kill!* as the "quintessential" Russ Meyer film while considering *Lorna*, *CHR*, and *BVD* his "best" films. However, the main purpose of this project has been to analyze each of Russ Meyer's films in order to find common thematic and stylistic trends in his films. That I consider Russ Meyer an important filmmaker is a given; at the risk of hyperbole, I would also contend that Russ Meyer, for better or worse, is one of the most important commentators, and even theorists, of sexual politics in the 20th century: America's answer to the Marquis de Sade.

Meyer's film world is one that eliminates dichotomies and boundaries. The lines between sex and violence, humor and evil, tragedy and farce, high art and low culture are all erased in a surreal assemblage that is both hilariously satirical and unnervingly brutal. Ultimately the dichotomy that is most problematically questioned is that of "male" and "female" itself. Russ Meyer constructs a world where "buxotic" women are often more "masculine" than the men, and cloddish men are more "feminine" than the women. Russ Meyer's films are a celebration of virile, he-man "masculinity" and a dismissal of demure, passive "femininity," although in countless films the relationship between "biological" gender and "cultural" gender is continually skewed and satirized.

Several new Russ Meyer movies have been announced at various times, but none has ever materialised; titles include *Blitzen, Vixen, And Harry, Mondo Topless II,* and *The Breast Of Russ Meyer*. In 2001, video footage shot by Meyer surfaced of the surgically-enhanced porn star Pandora Peaks.

189. "Russ Meyer: King of the Nudies," page 8 of 14.

LIPS HIPS TITS POWER ◊ THE FILMS OF RUSS MEYER

Russ Meyer's ideal film world is indeed one of "men with big tits," a nexus where Amazonian über-women wield phallic power. In Meyer's film world of "big bosoms and square jaws," it is clear that women possess the "big bosoms." It is less clear whether men or women possess the "square jaws."

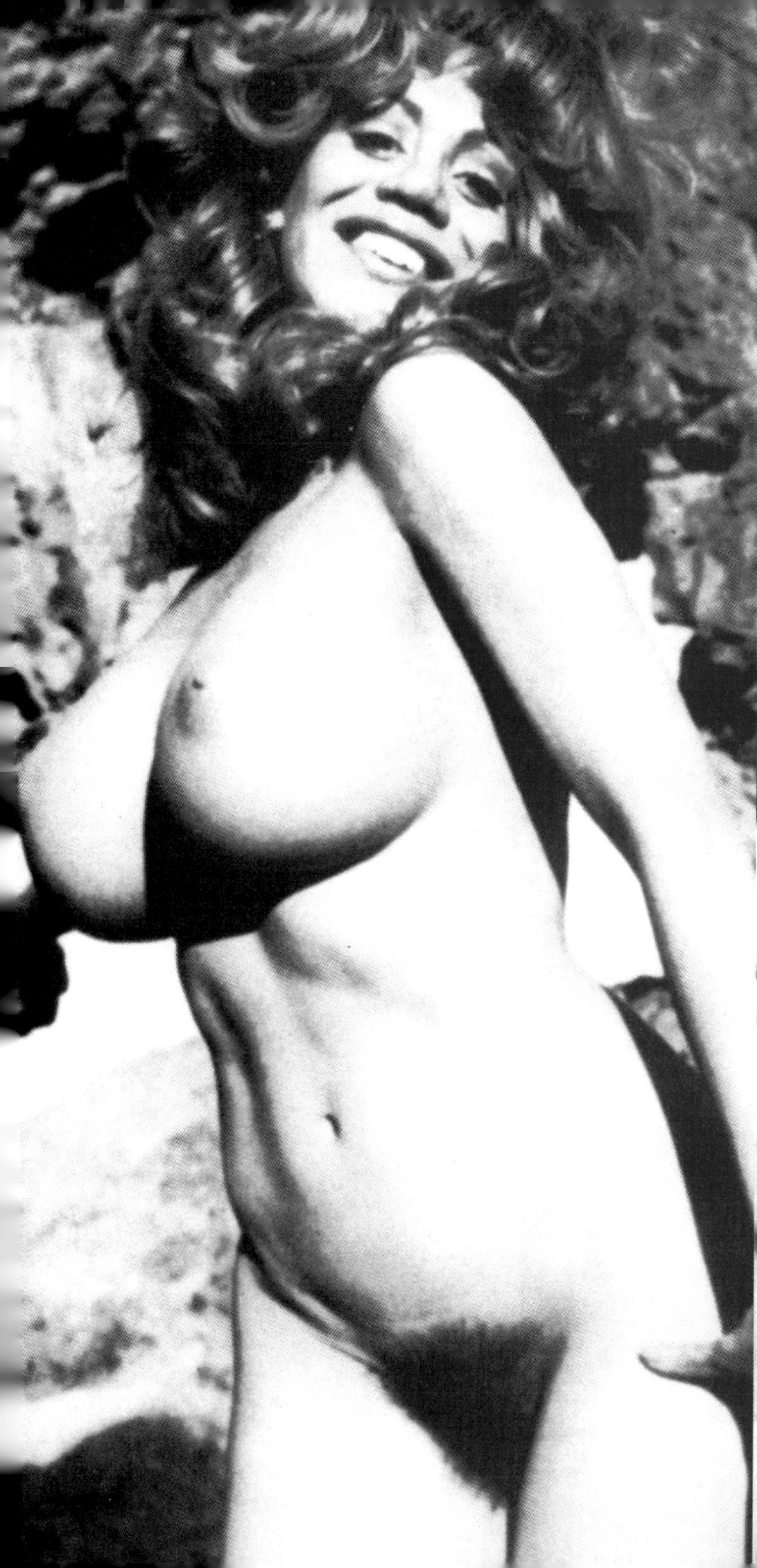
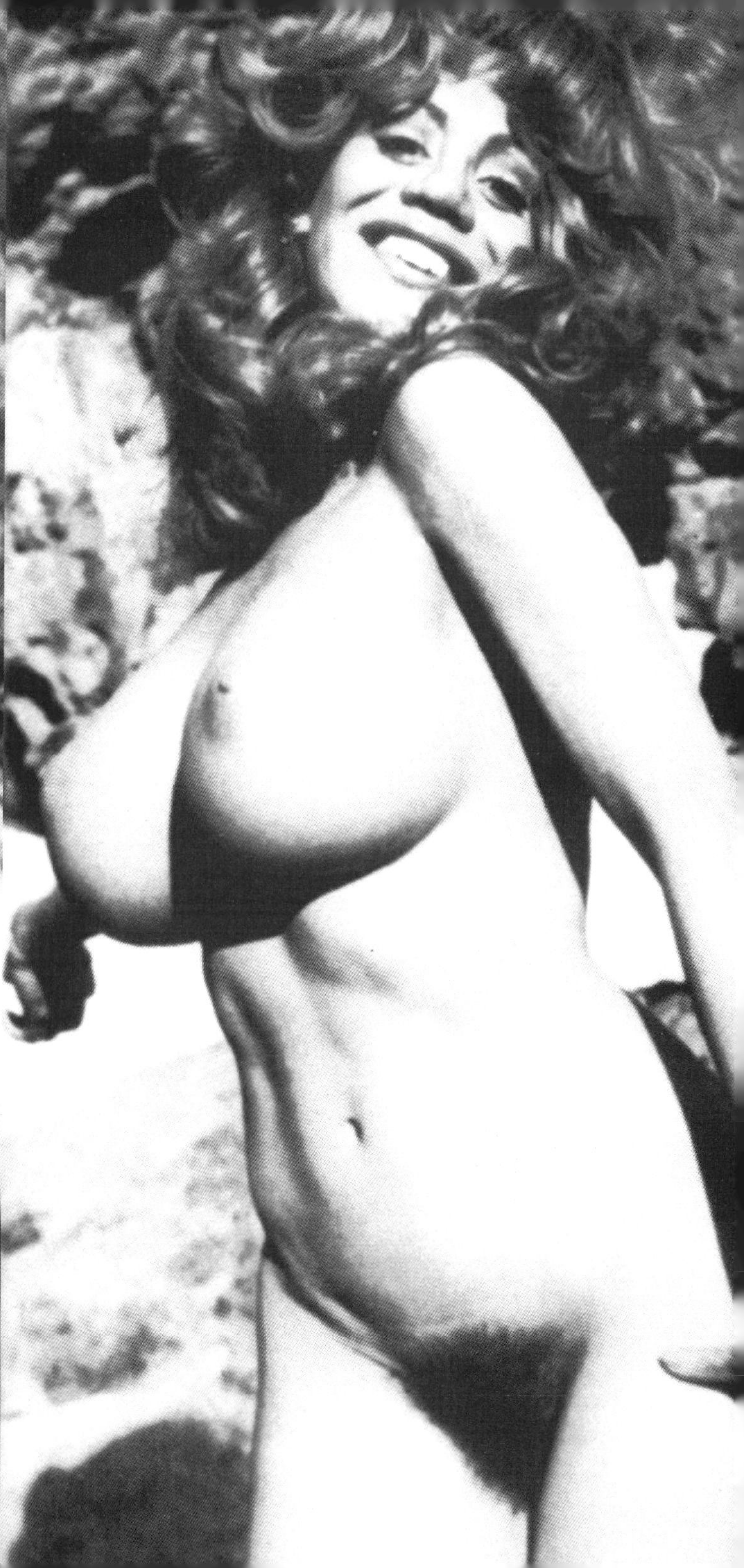

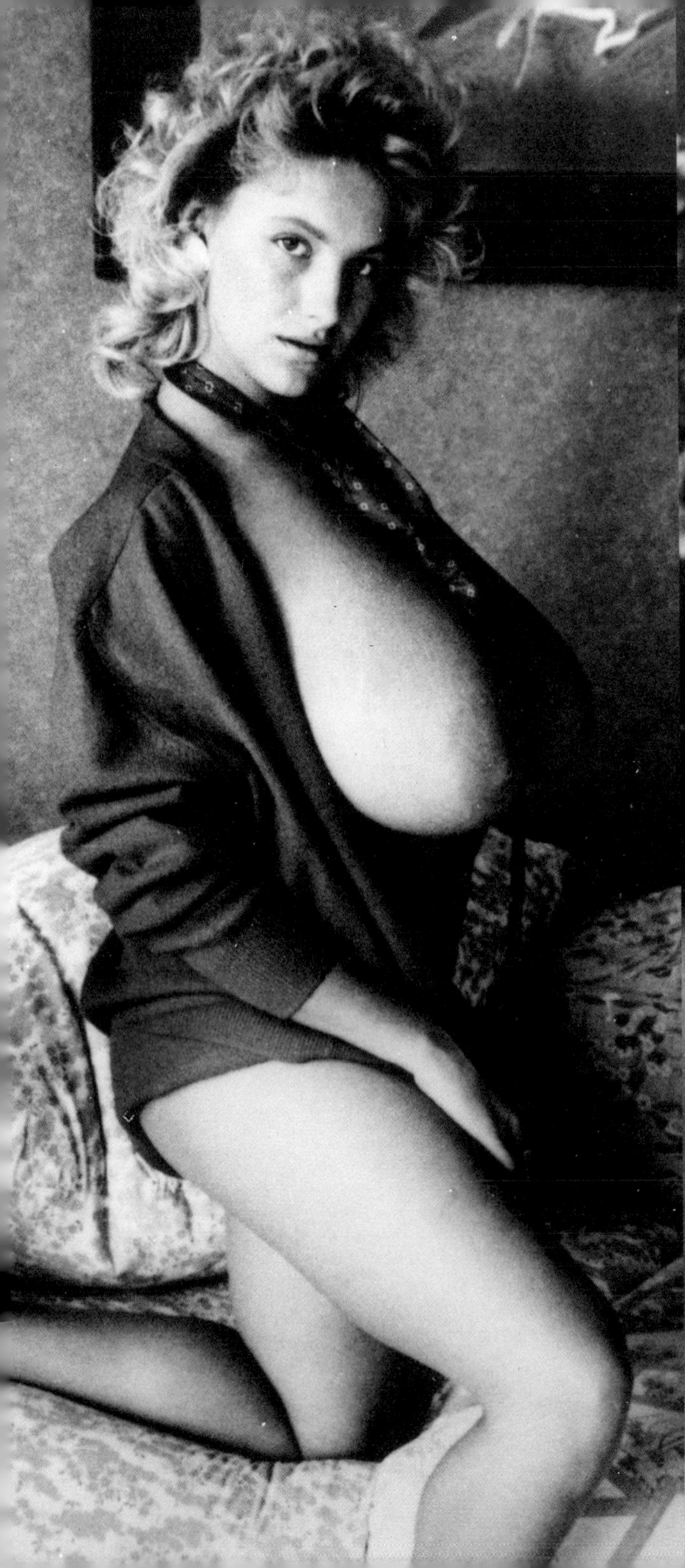
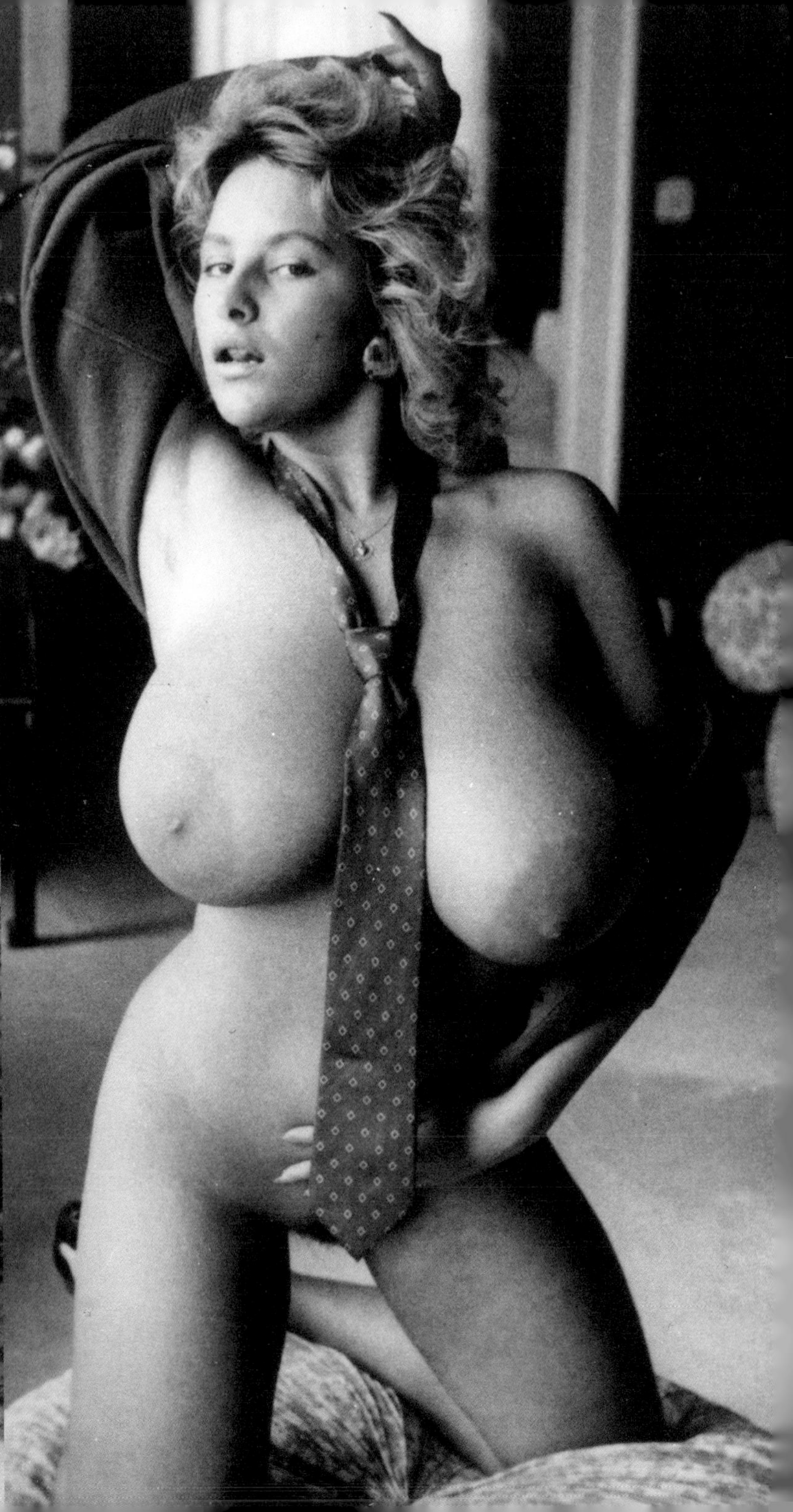

RUSS MEYER FILMOGRAPHY

THE FRENCH PEEP SHOW (1950)

THE IMMORAL MR. TEAS (1959)

THIS IS MY BODY (1959)

EVE AND THE HANDYMAN (1960)

NAKED CAMERA (1960)

EROTICA (1961)

WILD GALS OF THE NAKED WEST (1962)

EUROPE IN THE RAW (1963)

HEAVENLY BODIES (1963)

SKYSCRAPERS AND BRASSIERES (1963)

FANNY HILL (1964)

LORNA (1964)

MUDHONEY (1964)

MOTORPSYCHO! (1965)

FASTER PUSSYCAT! KILL! KILL! (1966)

MONDO TOPLESS (1966)

GOOD MORNING AND GOODBYE (1967)

COMMON LAW CABIN (1967)

FINDERS KEEPERS, LOVERS WEEPERS (1968)

VIXEN (1968)

CHERRY, HARRY AND RAQUEL (1969)

BEYOND THE VALLEY OF THE DOLLS (1970)

THE SEVEN MINUTES (1971)

BLACKSNAKE! (1972)

SUPERVIXENS (1975)

UP! (1976)

BENEATH THE VALLEY OF THE ULTRA-VIXENS (1979)

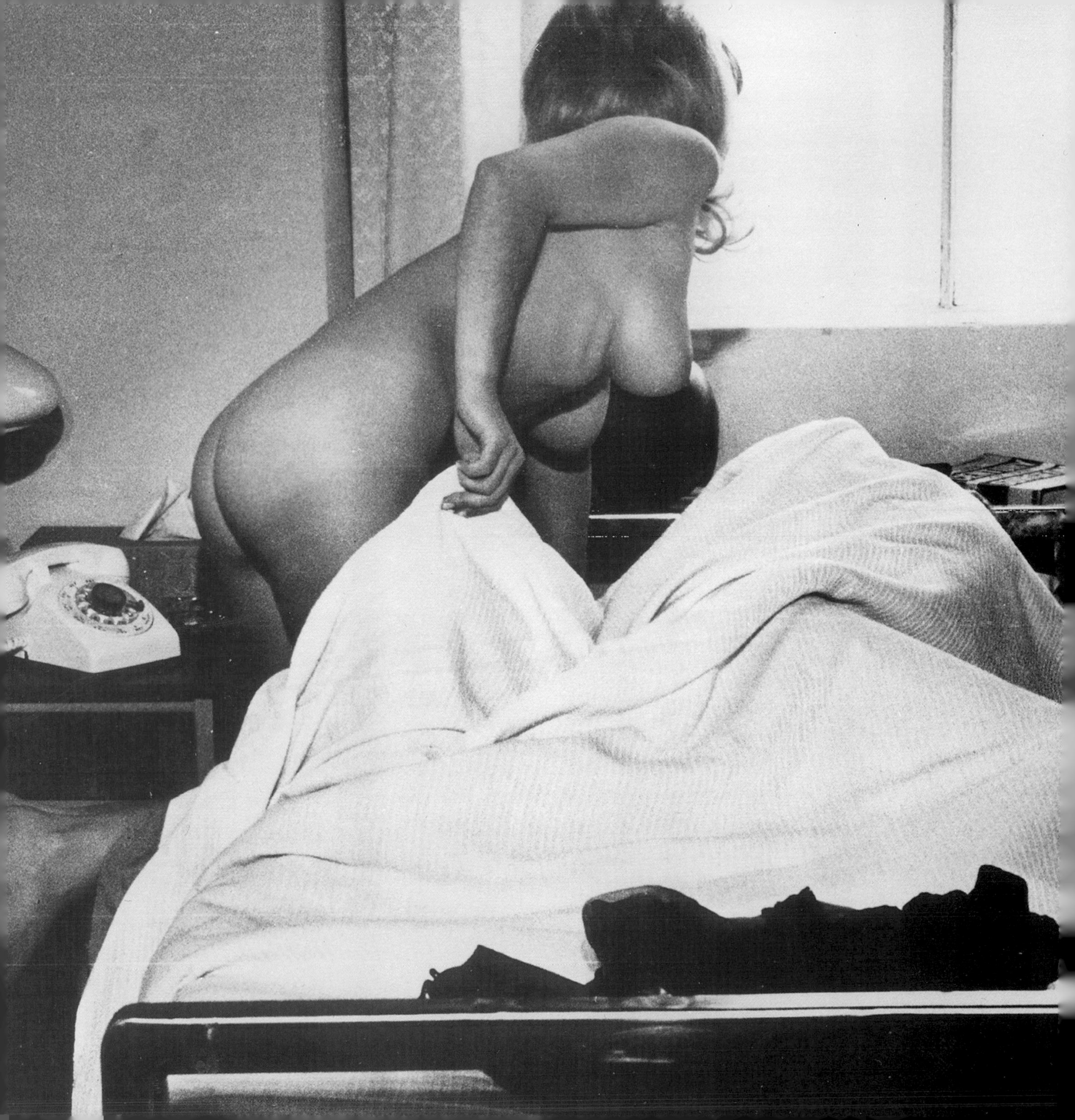

INDEX OF FILMS

Films in bold indicate a Russ Meyer film; page numbers in italic indicate an illustration.

Astro-Zombies 81
Behind The Green Door 192, *192*
Beneath The Valley Of The Ultravixens 11, 12, 14, 170, 187, 195, 196, 217-225, *217*, *218*, *220*, *222*
Beyond The Valley Of The Dolls 9, 14, 17, 104, 141, 155, *156*, 157-187, *163*, *167*, *168*, *172*, *173*, *182*, 190, 196, 198, 216, 225
Blacksnake! *190*, 190-191
Blood Feast *41*, 41
Blow-Up 162
Born Losers 69
Cherry, Harry And Raquel 11, 12, 14, 15, 17, 107, 108, 141, 145-155, *148*, *150*, *151*, *154*, 190, 202, 203, 205, 214, 219, 225
Citizen Kane 176
Color Me Blood Red 41
Common-Law Cabin 14, 30, 107, 112-119, *114*, *117*, 119, 121, 123
Coogan's Bluff 145
Curse Of Her Flesh, The 40
Deadly Weapons 193
Death Wish 70, 75, 76
Deep Throat 192, *192*, 193
Defilers, The 11, 41
Doll Squad, The 81
Double Agent 73 193
Drum 191
Easy Rider 69
Ecco 109
Erotica 21, *36*, *37*
Europe In The Raw *18*, 21, 21, 111
Eve And The Handyman 17, 25-30, *28*, 43, 59, 127
Fanny Hill *105*, 105
Fantasia 180
Faster, Pussycat! Kill! Kill! *1*, 4, 8, 10, 12, 13, 14, 15, 30, *38*, 43, 68, 81-105, *82-83*, *85*, *87*, *88*, 92, 93, 94, 96, 98, *100*, *103*, 107, 112, 115, 118, 119, 121, 129, 131, 146, 152, 169, 184, 206, 213, 225
Finders Keepers, Lovers Weepers 17, 107, 108, 118, 127-131, *128*, *130*, 146, 169, 205
Fingered 41
Frankenstein 202, 214
Freaks 89
French Peep Show, The 21, *21*
Friday 13th 41
Glitter 193
Good Morning... And Goodbye! 14, 15, 30, 107, 119-127, *120*, *124*, *126*, 129, 133, 146, 155, 170, 187, 198, 201, 202
Heavenly Bodies 21, *21*
Hell's Angels On Wheels 69
I Spit On Your Grave 42
Immoral Mr. Teas, The 12, 19, 20, 21-24, *22*, *23*, 25, 30, 34, 39, 40, 64, 70, 83, 139, 221
Killers, The 128
Kiss Of Her Flesh, The 40
Last House On The Left 42
Last Tango In Paris 219
Lorna 11, 12, 13, 14, 17, 40, 43-58, *44*, *47*, *48*, *52*, *56*, *58*, 59, 62, 63, 66, 68, 72, 92, 102, 112, 113, 119, 121, 122, 123, 124, 125, 129, 135, 170, 198, 217, 219, 220, 225
Mandingo 161
Mondo Balordo 110
Mondo Cane 108, 111
Mondo Topless 30, 107, 108-112, *109*, *110*,
Motorpsycho! 13, 14, 68-80, *71*, *73*, *74*, *76*, *77*, *78*, 81, 82, 83, 92, 95, 102, 104, 105, 121, 139, 149, 202-203, 209
Ms. 45 42
Mudhoney 12, 13, 14, 43, 59-68, *61*, *63*, *64*, *65*, 68, 70, 81, 82, 86, 89, 92, 163, 202, 205, 206, 217, 225

231

LIPS HIPS TITS POWER ◊ THE CINEMA OF RUSS MEYER

Myra Breckenridge	157
Naked Camera	21
Olga's Girls	*41*, 41
Olga's House Of Shame	40
Opening Of Misty Beethoven	192
Orgy Of The Dead	*111*, 111
Outlaw, The	101
Promises! Promises!	*39*, 39
Psycho	214
Rashomon	213
Sadist, The	*70*, 70
Satan's Sadists	69
Seven Minutes, The	*188*, 189-190
Sexy Proibitissimo	111
Shriek Of The Mutilated	192
Slumber Party Massacre	42
Snuff	192
Straw Dogs	70, 75

Supervixens 12, 14, 187, 191, *194*, 195, 196-210, *199*, *204*, *206*, 217, 219, 221, 223, 224

2000 Maniacs	11, 41
Take Me Naked	12
Taste Of Honey, A Swallow Brine!, A	41
Texas Chainsaw Massacre, The	214
This Is My Body	21
Touch Of Her Flesh, The	40

Up! 11, 195, 196, 200, 210-215, *211*, *212*, *213*, 217

Valley Of The Dolls	159, 160, 180

Vixen 7, 12, 14, 15, *106*, 107, 130, 131-145, *135*, *137*, *138*, *140*, *142*, 146, 157, 160, 163, 164, 187, 190, 191, 197, 207, 225

Weird World Of LSD, The	111
Who Killed Bambi?	215-216
Wild Angels, The	69
Wild Bunch, The	148

Wild Gals Of The Naked West, The 11, 13, 30-35, *31*, *34*, 149

Wild One, The	68, 69, 72
Wolf Man, The	104, 118
Written On The Wind	160

232

www.creationbooks.com